AUG

14. NOV

19. JUN

09 OCT 24.

CRW

Please return/renew this item by the last date shown on this label, or on your self-service receipt.

To renew this item, visit **www.librarieswest.org.uk**, use the LibrariesWest app, or contact your library.

Your borrower number and PIN are required.

Libraries**West**

FIRE AND FLEET AND
CANDLELIGHT

CAROLINE NEWARK

Matador
Unit E2 Airfield Business Park,
Harrison Road, Market Harborough,
Leicestershire. LE16 7UL
Tel: 0116 2792299
Email: books@troubador.co.uk
Web: www.troubador.co.uk/matador
Twitter: @matadorbooks

ISBN 978 1803132 181

British Library Cataloguing in Publication Data.
A catalogue record for this book is available from the British Library.

Printed and bound in the UK by TJ Books, Padstow, Cornwall
Typeset in 11pt Minion Pro by Troubador Publishing Ltd, Leicester, UK

Matador is an imprint of Troubador Publishing Ltd

For Kathryn Warner
historian, writer and friend

THE LYKE-WAKE DIRGE

14TH CENTURY FUNERAL CHANT

This ae neet, this ae neet,
Every neet and all,
Fire an' fleet* an' candleleet,
And Christ receive thy saul.

If thou from here our wake has passed,
Every neet and all,
To Whinny Moor thou comes at last,
And Christ receive thy saul.

And if ever thou gavest hosen or shoen,
Every neet and all,
Then sit ye down and put them on,
And Christ receive thy saul.

But if hosen or shoen thou ne'er gavest nane,
Every neet and all,
The whinny will prick thee to thy bare bane,
And Christ receive thy saul.

From Whinny Moor when thou may'st pass,
Every neet and all,
To Brig o' Dread thou comest at last,
And Christ receive thy saul.

From Brig o' Dread when thou may'st pass,
Every neet and all,
To Purgatory thou comest at last,
And Christ receive thy saul.

And if ever thou gavest meat or drink,
Every neet and all,
The fire will never make thee shrink,
And Christ receive thy saul.

But if meat nor drink thou ne'er gav'st nane,
Every neet and all,
The fire will burn thee to thy bare bane,
And Christ receive thy saul.

This ae neet, this ae neet,
Every neet and all,
Fire an' fleet an' candleleet,
And Christ receive thy saul.

* from the old English word *flett* meaning dwelling

THE FAMILY TREE

(SO FAR)

Edward the First, King of England, married Marguerite of France, and had by her issue Edmund of Woodstock.

♥

Edmund of Woodstock, Earl of Kent, married Margaret, daughter of Lord John Wake, and had by her issue Joan of Kent.

♥

Joan of Kent in her own right Countess of Kent, married Sir Thomas Holand, to whom she bore issue Thomas Holand.

♥

Thomas Holand married Alys, daughter of Richard Fitzalan, Earl of Arundel, by Eleanor of Lancaster, and had by her issue, Eleanor Holand.

♥

Eleanor Holand married Thomas Montagu, Earl of Salisbury, to whom she bore issue Alice Montagu

♥

Alice Montagu, in her own right Countess of Salisbury, married Sir Richard Nevill, Knight of the Most Noble Order of the Garter, younger son of Ralph, First Earl of Westmorland by Lady Joan Beaufort, the daughter of John of Gaunt, to whom she bore issue among others, Kathryn Nevill.

LIST OF MAIN CHARACTERS

THE NEVILLS

Kathryn Nevill	a low-ranking Nevill daughter
Her father	Richard Nevill, Earl of Salisbury
Her mother	Alice, Countess of Salisbury
Her brothers	Richard, Earl of Warwick
	Thomas (Tom)
	John
	George, a cleric
Her sisters	Joan, Countess of Arundel
	Alice, Lady Fitzhugh
	Alianore
	Margaret
Her sisters-in-law	Anne, Countess of Warwick
	Maud, Lady Willoughby
Her uncle	Lord Fauconberg

THE ROYAL FAMILY

The king	Henry VI
The queen	Margaret of Anjou

THE PERCYS

Henry Percy	Earl of Northumberland
His sons	Lord Egremont, Ralph and Dickon

THE CROMWELLS

Lord Cromwell	sometime Treasurer of England
His wife	Lady Cromwell
His sister	Lady Stanhope, Maud's mother

THE YORKS

The duke	Richard, Duke of York
His duchess	Cecily Nevill
Their sons	Edward, Earl of March
	Edmund
Their daughter	Anne (Nan)

THE BONVILLES

Lord Bonville	Lord of Chewton Mendip
His second wife	Lady Bonville née Courtenay
His son	William Bonville
His daughter-in-law	Dame Elizabeth
His grandson	William (Will)

THE DYNHAMS

Lady Dynham	Jane, Lady Dynham
Her eldest son	John
Her daughters	Margery, Edith, Lizzie, Joan and Kitty

OTHERS

Edmund Beaufort	Duke of Somerset
Harry Holland	Duke of Exeter
Thomas Courtenay	Earl of Devon
His eldest son	Sir Thomas Courtenay
Nicholas Radford	a Devonshire lawyer
William Hastings	a friend of Edward, Earl of March

Prologue

YORK 1453

Ralph Percy toyed with his knife, idly cutting a mutton pasty into smaller and smaller pieces.

'How many?' he said, still contemplating his food.

'A thousand. And if you don't want that, I'll have it,' replied Egremont, reaching across the table.

Without warning, a flick of Ralph's wrist and a blade sank deep into the wood next to Egremont's outstretched hand.

'You're a fool, Ralph. You nearly had his fingers off,' said the man with the flat, cold eyes seated at the end of the table.

'I'll thank you to mind your own business, Dickon,' growled Egremont, kicking his youngest brother viciously on the shin.

The three brothers had been drinking steadily in the back regions of The Lamb since early evening and didn't much care who overheard what they said. Besides, this was a Percy drinking hole, somewhere they and their supporters met and exchanged nuggets of information, unlikely to be frequented by their enemies. As sons of the earl of Northumberland they were well known to the denizens of York. Those not of their persuasion or possessed of a peaceable nature, kept well out of their way. It was said trouble followed the Percy brothers like flies in the wake of a dung cart and there were few who enjoyed an encounter with a pile of stinking shit.

Lord Egremont raised his head and yelled, 'Hey Landlord! This wine tastes like cat's piss. Bring us something better.'

The man came running. 'I've a little Rhenish, my lord,' he grovelled. 'Laid by for men like yourselves.'

'Well, get it then!' Egremont picked up his cup and emptied the dregs onto the floor. 'Where's your daughter this evening?'

'Gone to her sister's, my lord,' lied the landlord, congratulating himself for his quick thinking in sending the girl upstairs.

He backed away through the crowd, half-listening to the buzz of conversation – the iniquitous price paid for wool, down a shilling, barely worth a man's effort in taking the fleece; amongst the old soldiers, despair at the English army's latest defeat in France.

'They were seen yesterday, travelling south,' said Egremont to his brothers.

'You're sure they'll come back this way?'

'It's a wedding party. Tom Nevill's found himself a bride.'

'Some two-penny whore,' Dickon sniggered.

'Lord Cromwell's niece.'

Ralph whistled under his breath. 'Rich pickings! If she's Cromwell's niece that means…' He was quicker to understand the implications of this particular match than Dickon who seldom bothered his head with such things.

'Exactly!' said Egremont. 'Which is why we take them

on their way back from the nuptials. Surprise them when they least expect it.'

'How many have they got?' asked their younger brother, rubbing his thumb up and down the side of his knife, a sure sign of nervous excitement. Dickon liked nothing better than a chance of violence at the expense of his Nevill cousins.

'Three hundred. Maybe four. That's why we need as many men as we can raise.'

Overwhelming force coupled with good intelligence won battles as the Percy brothers knew only too well. Their incursions into Nevill territory the last few years, marked as they'd been by an orgy of bloodshed, burnings and rape, had given them plenty of practice.

'Who's in the party?'

'Old man Salisbury and two of his sons.'

'Warwick?'

'No such luck. But there's the women.'

'Women?'

'The countess and a couple of daughters.'

'Married?'

'No, the younger ones.' He laughed. 'So there's a treat for you brothers – two ripe little virgins.'

'What's the plan?'

'We kill Salisbury and his sons, take the women. But leave the countess alone. She's of no use to us. And whatever else, don't forget – the bride is mine.'

1

TATTERSHALL 1453

My sister Alice prodded me in the chest with her forefinger.

'You be careful!' she said. 'Remember, they're wolves! Fiends! They hide beneath their silks and satins like proper lords but given half a chance they'll tear a man apart.'

'We're only going into Lincolnshire,' I protested.

'Far enough,' she said darkly, jerking my belt tight with unnecessary force. 'Men from across the Trent are not to be trusted. And the women are worse. Serpents! Snarl you up in their shiny coils, they will.'

'But Alice, our father chose Maud Willoughby for Tom, himself.'

She clasped my face in her hands and looked me straight in the eye. 'You listen to me, young Kat. Lady Maud may be a widow but Ralph Willoughby was sixty years and more on their wedding day, and her sitting in her bridal chair sewing his shroud.'

'You mean she killed him?'

'You may well gasp.' Alice put her lips together into a thin hard line. 'I shall say nothing and you'd better say nothing either. Now, let me look at you.'

That had been a week ago. But Alice was right – Lincolnshire *was* far enough. I was hot and tired, the horses were sweating as much as the men and it was miles to go before we would reach our destination. I scuffed my feet in the dirt at the side of the causeway wondering how safe we were. The flat lands east of the Trent did not appear to be overrun by men in silks and satins or by women with serpentine coils, but you could never tell. People hid in the most unlikely of places.

We had stopped in the middle of nowhere for a reason known only to my father. I'd left my mother and Alianore discussing wedding clothes and gone looking for Tom. I tried to appear humble and contrite which Alice said was always wise when dealing with my brothers as they liked biddable women.

'Please, Tom.'

My brother's face looked down from his great height. 'Why should I?'

'Because Alianore's being horrible to me.'

'Is that not what older sister's do?'

'Alice says she should set an example. So, will you, Tom? Please!'

His horse shifted uneasily and I stepped back, not liking the look of those massive hooves so close to my toes. The rest of the procession had remounted and were only waiting for my father's word to continue our orderly progress towards Tattershall. Lances were raised, banners unfurled and horses brought into line. Last minute stragglers scrambled into position, shouting for servants and thrusting half-drunk cups of ale at anyone to hand. A carter climbed onto his seat, cursing a man for making use of his wheel. The man made a rude gesture and quickly laced up his breeches.

It was all I could do not to hop up and down. If Tom didn't hurry I would be left behind. I could only see bits of him because shafts of sunlight were glancing off the silver buttons on his doublet and blinding my eyes.

'Very well.' A great gauntleted hand stretched down and with one heave he had me up in the saddle. I wriggled a little to get myself comfortable and leaned back against his chest. Something hard and unyielding was pressing on my spine.

'Why are you wearing your breastplate?'

'In case there's danger.'

The hairs on the nape of my neck began prickling the way they did when our father was angry and started shouting.

'Have you a battle-axe slung from your saddle?'

'I have not.'

'What if the Percys should come?'

Tom laughed. 'There's not a single Percy in the whole of Lincolnshire.'

'Swear?'

'I swear.'

'So why are you wearing your breastplate?'

He put his mouth close to my ear. 'Because a man should always be prepared for danger.'

'Even on his wedding day?'

'Especially on his wedding day. What if my bride were of a mind to attack me?'

I gave a nervous giggle recalling what Alice had said about the widowed Lady Willoughby.

'I don't think Lady Maud will do that. Have you seen her yet? Is she beautiful?'

There was a small pause while Tom considered the question.

'Uncle Fauconberg says she is.'

Uncle Fauconberg was our father's brother and our favourite uncle. Alice said he flirted unmercifully and no woman was safe from his advances. But Alianore and I didn't think he advanced much on his wife as Alice said she was a woman of monstrous stupidity and quite unable to control her servants.

This was the first family wedding I could remember. Alice's had been a long time ago when I was only a child and children, as I had told my sister Margaret, do not attend weddings. Margaret must remain in the care of her governess at Middleham doing her lessons, while I would accompany our mother and Alianore to Tattershall.

Tattershall was Lord Cromwell's castle and since the beginning of May Tom had been contracted to marry Lord Cromwell's niece. The family had spent three whole months preparing for this expedition. Alianore and I acquired lengths of silk and pieces of ribbon and under Alice's watchful eye had industriously contrived our wardrobes. I'd wanted pearl buttons but there were none to be had and Alianore meanly wouldn't part with any of hers.

'You do love her, Tom, don't you?'

'I love her Uncle Cromwell's money.'

This wasn't the answer I wanted. Alianore and I were reading *The Adventures of Bevis of Hampton* and I couldn't imagine two people marrying without love. Josiane and Bevis were devoted to each other and their lives had not been easy. Nobody had presented *them* with a carefully worded contract agreeing their marriage and laying out terms. Treachery had forced them apart yet neither a

4

poisonous dragon nor assaults on Josiane's chastity by King Yvor could prevent them from marrying. Money had not been mentioned, not even once.

'Is Lady Maud to inherit?' I asked curiously.

'Yes. Lord Cromwell has no children so Lady Maud and her sister will get everything.'

'Everything?'

'The lot.'

'I wish I was an heiress,' I sighed.

'If you were an heiress, Kat, our father would marry you to a greedy young lordling who wanted your money and cared nothing for your comfort.'

I gazed with interest at the flat land on either side of the causeway. No lordlings, greedy or otherwise; no trees or bushes or hills; indeed nowhere for a Percy to hide. A spire poked up from amid the acres of marshy flatness but it was a great distance away. We'd passed only two villages since leaving the London road and they'd been shabby affairs: stubby little churches with a few hovels huddled on raised bits of land like islands. People stared as we'd ridden by but they hadn't cheered, not like they did when we rode out to Ravensworth to visit Alice. Perhaps as well as being untrustworthy, Lincolnshire men didn't care for strangers.

'What's that?' I said pointing to a flash of silver in amongst the vastness of green and grey and yellow.

'Water.'

'Are there sea monsters? Alice says sea monsters can swim up rivers. She says it's good to live at Middleham because no sea monster could make it that far.'

Tom laughed. 'It's not a river, it's a drainage ditch and will you stop worrying, Katkin. We are well protected.'

Indeed we were. In that golden dawn when we'd left Middleham, I'd looked back and seen an enormous snaking procession of armed men following our party; close on four hundred our mother had said.

'Why has father brought so many men?'

'To show Lord Cromwell how powerful we Nevills are.'

'We are powerful, aren't we?' I said contentedly, thinking of our father's castles, his nine deer parks, his banners, his many titles, the offices given to him by the king, the solid walls of Middleham and the huge number of men who'd come willingly in answer to a call from the mighty earl of Salisbury.

'The most powerful lords of the North,' agreed Tom.

The gates of Tattershall opened and our procession, led by my father on his favourite black stallion, passed through into Lord Cromwell's domain. I was unsure what to expect but in an instant the massive stone walls and sturdy gatehouse of my imagination vanished and in their place stood a magical castle lit by the afternoon sun and glowing like a flame. What took my breath away and caused me to utter a gasp of surprise was a huge tower which soared up into the sky. Pierced by elegant windows and banded by cream-coloured stones, each of the rosy-red walls resembled a perfect illumination from a book. And as if it could not have been any more perfect than it already was, crowning the top were four small turrets.

'Close your mouth,' hissed Alianore. 'You look like a fish. Do you want Lady Cromwell to put you on her table?'

Lord Cromwell was waiting on the steps to greet us and close behind him were two women. One must surely be Lady Cromwell. I hoped the other was not Tom's bride because she was small and stooped and had wrinkles.

There were formal introductions and shoulder-clutching embraces by the men and graceful curtseys and inclines of heads on the part of the women. Smiles were exchanged. A swift summing-up of the Cromwell ladies' attire assured us we would not be outdone in the all-important matter of fashion. Honour was satisfied by my mother's new apricot-coloured hennin with its floating veil while Lady Cromwell, who stood a full step higher, wore her hair confined in a filigree net topped by an elaborately pleated roll of green and yellow silk. Her houppelande might sit high at the neck and be gathered tightly at her wrists as last year's fashion dictated but my mother's showed a daring amount of her kirtle and, even more audacious, a glimpse of her embroidered chemise. Alice had said she doubted Lady Cromwell would be privy to the *robes déguisée* of the ladies in Burgundy in the way that our mother was, and she'd been proved right.

The other woman, the one with wrinkles, wore a dark blue houppelande which must have been sewn in the time of old King Edward it was so unfashionable, and a plain green chaperon, not particularly wide and lacking an elegant feather.

Occasional bursts of booming laughter erupted from Lord Cromwell which bore no relevance to any joke as far as I could tell although my father was smiling. Tom, as the bridegroom-to-be, was subjected to a litany of questions while my other brother, John, was treated like a long-lost companion-in-arms from some bloody bygone battle.

Nobody bothered with Alianore and me where we stood several paces behind my mother.

'Can you see Lady Maud?' I whispered.

'Lord Cromwell has kept her well hidden,' she whispered back.

'Why? Is she deformed?'

At this, Alianore collapsed into giggles which caused one of our mother's women to turn and subject us both to a furious frown.

I fidgeted, wriggling my toes, wanting to be rid of my riding boots which pinched. I was also hungry. It was an age since our last meal and that had been exceedingly meagre, only bread and cheese and small ale. At last, with a cursory wave of a hand and orders to the surrounding ranks of men, Lord and Lady Cromwell escorted my parents up the steps and into the castle. Alianore and I fell into line as we had been taught, with me, as usual, bringing up the rear. Since Alianore's return from our aunt's household, my whole existence consisted of trailing round in her wake like a forgotten piece of baggage. She said it was good training for me because our father was bound to find her a duke to marry so I would always be her inferior.

We were taken to one of the sumptuous guest apartments to remove our boots and refresh ourselves with warm water scented with rose petals. Once our faces were washed and our dusty garments removed we joined Lady Cromwell in her beautifully appointed chamber. There, amidst cushions and tapestries and tables laid out with books, my mother and Lady Cromwell exchanged confidences.

'Such terrible news from France!'

'What will Lady Talbot do?'

'Is it true the queen is at last with child?'

Occasional words floated our way – 'Cut down in his prime.' – 'What of the daughters?' – 'Fifty marks they say.' – 'It will be October, for sure.' But Alianore and I were not included in the conversation.

Maud, dowager Lady Willoughby, niece of Lord Cromwell, was not what I had expected. She sat with her head lowered in a suitably demure way, her dark lashes brushing her cheeks and her mouth trembling slightly as if meeting her prospective mother-in-law was an honour almost more than she could bear. I'd imagined her dressed in velvet silk with an elegant headdress. Instead she was wearing fine grey wool and a plain cap covered by a white linen veil. I was horribly disappointed.

'How old do you think she is?' whispered Alianore.

'Very,' I replied.

'Her skin is quite smooth.'

'Paste,' I said knowledgeably.

I wondered at what hour the Cromwells took their supper and pushed my foot along the floor to see how even the oak boards were.

All of a sudden Lady Maud's carefully lowered lashes snapped up and I was treated to a stare from a pair of bright dark eyes. I stared back and she curved her lips into a small secretive smile which brought dimples to her cheeks.

I was wrong. She wasn't old. Not much older than Alice. She wasn't beautiful but I thought Tom might like her. She had a sharp nose and a chin which was definitely pointed but her eyes and eyebrows were set wide apart and

9

Alice would most certainly approve of her brow. I thought she plucked her hairline but it was difficult to tell when it was mostly hidden beneath her cap.

Sitting quietly at Lady Maud's side was a fair-haired young woman I took to be her sister. She said nothing but from the way she occasionally laid her hand on Lady Maud's arm I decided she was a stalwart friend, someone to turn to in time of trouble. Not that trouble would follow Lady Maud once she was married to Tom. Her life would be like Alice's: serene, domestic and blessed with a nursery of plump little children.

At an invisible sign from Lady Cromwell, a servant stepped forward to announce supper. The ladies rose as one and I hastily scrambled to my feet. Lady Maud rearranged her skirts so that they fell in neat folds and, clasping her sleeves, allowed her sister to help her from her chair. It was the kind of movement you'd expect from a young woman with a dagger secreted somewhere about her person. Undoubtedly Tom was wise to have come armed.

Next morning Alianore and I stood with our parents in Lord Cromwell's chapel and watched our brother marry Maud, Lady Willoughby. Uncle Fauconberg arrived in time for the nuptial mass which was a surprise as I hadn't known he was coming. Our mother had said he was serving the king since his return from France and could hardly desert his royal duties simply to see his nephew wed so Tom's marriage must be of great importance to risk the king's displeasure. But, as Alice once said, our uncle always favoured our father's sons having none of his own.

Afterwards, when prayers were finished and the married couple had been liberally showered with flowers and silver pennies, we sat down in Lord Cromwell's great hall to enjoy the wedding feast. I thought the room showed a sense of grandeur so often missing from other people's houses no matter how hard they tried. My mother said Lady Maud's uncle had grown rich in the king's service and his device of a tasselled purse was testament to his success as England's treasurer. The Cromwell arms were everywhere: chiselled into the surrounds of huge stone hearths, carved deep into panels on dark oak doors, stitched on the borders of each piece of elegant napery on display and painted in shining gold on the glass in every window.

Tom and his bride had special gilded chairs set in the middle of the dais while Lord Cromwell and our father were banished to the side as if they were of lesser importance which, of course, for one day, they were.

Despite Lady Maud's efforts to engage Tom in conversation, I noticed he was gazing with more interest at Lord Cromwell's display of silverware. The pieces were laid out on the sideboards for his guests to admire which they did with varying degrees of delight and envy.

'Why is Tom not paying attention to Lady Maud?' I whispered to Alianore. 'She is his wife. Surely he should favour her?'

Alianore rolled her eyes. 'Because it's not her he's marrying, stupid, it's her money. That's all that matters to our brother.'

Alianore and I sat at one of the ladies' tables with a group of women who were cooing over the bride and her handsome new husband. We were quizzed as to our parents and the households in which we'd been educated and asked what we thought of Lord Cromwell's new castle. The woman next to Alianore told a rude joke which made everyone laugh while the faded dowager on my right, who was vaguely related to Lady Cromwell, kept asking were my sister and I betrothed.

'Not yet, madam,' I replied politely.

'Best be quick,' she said seriously. 'So many dead in the French wars. Fine young men like the one Lord Cromwell has netted for Maud are a rarity.'

'He is my brother and I love him dearly.'

She looked startled. 'Your brother! Does that sort of thing go on in Yorkshire these days? And you so young!' She lowered her voice to a whisper. 'Oh my dear, does your mother not protect you?'

I had no idea what she was talking about and merely murmured that my mother had a great many daughters in her care of which I was the least.

She grasped my hands in her bony ones. 'It is a sin, y'know. Has he not told you?'

Before I could reply, a tall thin man who had been sitting at one of the lower tables, stood up. In his hand was a long length of parchment.

The woman next to Alianore clapped her hands and exclaimed. 'Richard Roos! What a treat.'

'Who is Richard Roos?' I whispered to Alianore.

'You've not heard of him?' said the faded dowager. 'But no, of course not . Yorkshire.'

'Richard Roos is an incomparable writer of verses,' explained the other woman. 'Lady Maud has a connection, I believe.'

12

The fortunate Richard Roos with his connection cast a look around the hall until everyone fell silent. It was an exceedingly long verse with tedious allusions to people I didn't know but it was strong in its praise of Lady Maud, likening her wit and her eloquence to a person called Mercury. It wasn't amusing like Master Chaucer's verses which were sometimes read aloud at home, but by the end the faded old dowager was almost weeping in appreciation.

'Beautiful,' she murmured. 'Quite beautiful.'

Once the verse readings and the speech by Lord Cromwell to his guests were finished, we had games. And then dancing which lasted for hours. It wasn't long before the women became as boisterous as the men and when someone clumsily spilled a cup of best Bordeaux down the front of my gown I remembered Alice's warning about coils.

A servant came running with a large napkin which he proffered but it was too late, the damage had been done.

'I shall have to change,' I grumbled to Alianore. 'Look, it's soaked!'

'Shall I come?' she offered with one eye fixed on a pretty young man with flaxen hair who was staring at her.

'Oh don't bother. I shall manage myself,' I said. I was a kind sister and hoped I'd remember my good deed when I next made a confession of my sins.

My mother's maid had been having a nap in the corner of our room but she leapt up and helped me remove the gown, muttering all the while about the need to make haste before the stain set fast and the gown was ruined. She laced me into my yellow silk kirtle and fetched the pale blue gown with the narrow fur trim on the hem. After a quick glance in my mother's looking glass I left her fussing away about the carelessness of young girls and how they never thought of the consequences.

I ran back across the little bridge which connected our quarters to the main buildings and hurried past the entrance to the stairway which led into the tower. I don't know what made me stop. Perhaps it was curiosity. Lord Cromwell and my father had disappeared up the curved stone steps yesterday evening but I didn't know where they'd gone. It was well known that great lords kept young women in chains in the topmost tower rooms of their castles and Alianore and I had read how King Yfor threatened Josiane with imprisonment if she wouldn't give in to his demands. I'd studied Lord Cromwell and he didn't seem a cruel man, and my father favoured him, but, as Alice said, you never could tell with men.

I placed one foot tentatively on the bottom stair and then hastily removed it. My heart was thudding and my mouth was dry. I knew what I was doing was forbidden but after a swift look behind me, I climbed a little higher. I clutched the rail and peered upwards. There was a flicker of light up above but I couldn't see beyond the three steps which curved round the inner wall of the stairway. I listened. No sound except for some distant singing. Quiet as a mouse, I crept up another step.

'Are you exploring?'

The voice came from below me. I turned in panic and nearly fell.

It was Lady Maud and she was smiling at me.

I opened my mouth but couldn't speak.

'It's Kathryn, isn't it?'

I nodded, unsure if I should curtsey or not now that Lady Maud was part of our family.

She climbed up until she stood only one step below me.

'When my sister and I came here as little girls we loved exploring the stairway. We had nothing like it at my mother's house in Tuxford, and thought it immensely exciting. Would you like to go to the top?'

'Yes, please.' The words came out as a squeak.

Lady Maud laughed. 'Don't be frightened. I don't bite.'

It wasn't the biting I was worried about but the dagger. Perhaps, being her wedding day, she had left it behind in one of her chests. Certainly she was much prettier than yesterday but Alianore said that was what marriage did and marrying Tom would surely please any woman.

At last I remembered my manners. 'Thank you.'

'You go first and I'll catch you if you should happen to fall.'

Up we went, round and up and round and up, until my head felt quite dizzy.

Suddenly from somewhere above my head came the sound of heavy footsteps, and then a huge dark shadow. I gasped and stopped.

'What is it?' called Lady Maud.

'Who's there?' A man's voice echoed off the stone walls.

A pair of strong brown legs and a deep blue brocade doublet appeared filling the stairway. It was Uncle Fauconberg. But he wasn't looking at me, he was looking over my shoulder at Lady Maud. He smiled and Uncle Fauconberg had a particularly engaging smile. Alice said his mouth was made that way but what he had to smile about she didn't know what with a fool for a wife, no heir and four daughters at home.

Uncle Fauconberg's voice was larger than himself as he was quite a small man and today he sounded pleased.

'Lady Maud! On the stairs and without your new husband.'

'I have protection, my lord, in case you should think otherwise.'

My uncle dropped his gaze to me.

'Aha! A minder! Young Kathryn, can it really be you? You were a babe in arms last time I saw you.'

I giggled. 'It was only three months ago, my lord uncle. You visited us at Middleham on your way north.'

He scratched his chin and peered at me more closely, a feat of some difficulty as his boots were level with my waist. 'I could have sworn... Has your mother been overfeeding you? Is that it? Remind me how old you are.'

'Almost twelve, my lord uncle.'

'Ah, now I understand. All those years I spent in France and think what I have missed. You have grown from a small creeping weed into a tender blossom.'

I wasn't sure I wanted to be a creeping weed or a tender blossom but was saved the problem of answering as Uncle Fauconberg's gaze slid back to Lady Maud. 'And you, my lady? Have the gods been kind to you in my absence? Did you think of me in my exile?'

I twisted round to see what Lady Maud thought of my uncle. She wasn't smiling.

'I have not thought of you once, my lord. Why would I?'

My uncle crinkled up his eyes and twitched his mouth as if he wanted to laugh. 'Remembering old times perhaps?'

'I didn't know you knew my uncle,' I said to Lady Maud.

'We had a acquaintance.' Her voice was chilly and not inviting of any more questions.

'A pleasant acquaintance,' remarked my uncle.

'For some perhaps.'

With an exaggerated flourish he placed his right hand flat on the front of his doublet. 'My heart was engaged so I remember those days with great fondness.'

'Your heart was fickle,' replied Lady Maud sharply.

Uncle Fauconberg raised his eyebrows. 'Fickle? Ah, you mean the lovely Barbalina! She was but a passing fancy, my lady, nothing of any importance. Whereas you…'

'Whereas I discovered my own strength.'

'Matchless,' he murmured.

'On the contrary. I have made two excellent matches since I last saw you, Lord Fauconberg.'

'Ah yes. Old Willoughby. A sound marriage but a man of declining years.'

'A good husband and a loyal one. He never strayed.'

My uncle grinned. 'Of course he didn't. I doubt he'd have reached the gate in those embroidered slippers of his.'

'I was content.'

'And is contentment what we seek in marriage? Is it enough for a man or for a woman? And now, there is my nephew. You have yet to discover what you've wed this time, Lady Maud. He's a mettlesome young man. You'll need your wits about you.'

17

'Tom will make Lady Maud a fine husband,' I said leaping to my brother's defence. I wasn't sure what their conversation meant but it sounded as if Uncle Fauconberg didn't think highly of Tom whereas I knew he was a wonderful brother and would make a wonderful husband.

Uncle Fauconberg laughed. 'Indeed he will. And now young Kathryn, let me escort you two enchanting young ladies up to the top of this tower for there is nowhere else to go and I fear for your safety in such a high and dangerous place.'

I could almost feel Lady Maud's reluctance as we made our slow way up the rest of the stairway. When we reached the top and walked out into the sunlight, she stood as far away from my uncle as was possible. The guards on duty gave us no more than a cursory glance before returning to their endless searching for signs of danger beyond the walls of Lord Cromwell's castle.

'Don't you like him?' I whispered.

Maud shrugged. 'I like him well enough. He can be amusing but I think him untrustworthy in the way of most men.'

Lincolnshire men, I thought, remembering Alice's warnings. Did my father trust Lord Cromwell? Perhaps mistrust of Lady Maud's uncle and not fear of the Percys was the reason for our four hundred armed men. And if, as Alice said, the women were as bad as the men, perhaps Tom should not place his trust in Lady Maud.

Two days later my mother announced that it was time to make our farewells to the Cromwell ladies and prepare for the long journey home. Lady Maud's mother wept copious tears and kept mopping her eyes as if we were pirates about to carry her daughter off and make her scrub floors in some distant castle on the other side of the sea. The sister said little, merely hugged Lady Maud close as if unwilling to part with her and then buried her face in her hands. There were sobs and whispered promises of visits as we edged closer to the moment of departure. At the last, Lady Maud kissed them both fondly and thanked her Aunt Cromwell for her manifold kindnesses this past year and promised to remember both her and her uncle in her prayers.

When I had peeped out of the window early that morning I had seen the Cromwell servants out in the dewy fields with their baskets and wondered what they were doing. Now I knew. The bridal wagon carrying Maud's chest was smothered from front to back with a froth of wild roses and lady's bedstraw. The other wagons had garlands of trefoil and fat white daisies attached to their sides and were decorated with red and white streamers. Behind Tom's chestnut courser was a smart white palfrey whose silver mane and tail were plaited with pale blue ribbons. The harness was studded with tiny bells and the lady's saddle decorated with intricate carvings. This, Alianore said, was a bridal morning gift to Lady Maud from her new husband.

Tom was dressed in his best blue velvet with red hose and shiny new riding boots and a sprig of rosemary in his hat. He had taken Lady Maud up in the saddle in front of him to show her uncle that he would be a good and caring husband. One of his hands was clasped round her waist, his fingers splayed across the front of her yellow gown. He grinned at John making a covert gesture with his other hand. John grinned back. Tom looked greatly pleased with himself while Lady Maud was pale and perfectly composed. Everyone was cheering as the Nevill groom handed Tom his reins.

It was time to go.

'Is he about to ravish her?' I asked Alianore as we sat waiting to move off.

She rolled her eyes heavenwards. 'On horseback? You are such a fool Kathryn Nevill. I am ashamed to have you as a sister.'

'Well I don't know what married couples do.'

'And you never will because no man will marry you if you say such stupid things.'

The minstrels we had brought from Middleham capered in front of our procession, their trumpets and whistles and tabors announcing to anyone who cared to listen that the bride and groom were coming. As we followed my father's banner out through the gates I cast a final longing look at the flame-coloured castle and the tower which reached up to the sky. Perhaps one day I might marry a wealthy man, one who was trustworthy, and I would ask him to build me a castle just like this, only bigger. And taller. And closer to Middleham.

2

HEWORTH MOOR 1453

The journey home was tediously slow. At every house where we stopped for the night we sat down to a supper served in silver dishes with the finest wines poured into silver goblets and more food than we could possibly eat. There were musical interludes for the newly married couple and verses in praise of Nevill men both living and dead. Indeed, our father's friends were so lavish with their hospitality that each morning the sun was high in the sky before we were safely on our way. Twice, fresh flowers were required to replace those which had withered through lack of care, though nothing was done about the ribbons and streamers which, by the time we reached York, were in tatters, fit only for tying round parcels of cloth.

We entered York through the great Micklegate Bar with its sharp-toothed portcullis, making our way along the bridge across the river. It was comforting to see the familiar rugged mass of Clifford's Tower perched high above the castle but if I was a new visitor I would be surprised I had to pass the town's disgusting privies in order to enjoy the gardens and orchards of St Mary's Abbey. Despite the stench, which our mother said was pernicious, I loved every bit of York: the bustle, the noise, the pedlars with their trays of knives and medallions, and the guild apprentices in their smart new tunics hurrying down Petergate. Best of all was the tiny goldsmith's shop off Pavement where our mother went to buy her trinkets. Sadly on that Thursday our father was in too much of a hurry to reach Sheriff Hutton before nightfall so there was no time to make any purchases. My mother said Alice would be waiting for us and might be anxious if we did not arrive.

We quit the city to the accompanying sound of the Minster's bells and our procession became part of a great throng. Ahead of us men were hurrying past Monks Bridge on their way to the market at Heworth Green, some with packs, some pushing carts, others herding animals or carrying baskets of produce. The noise and the dust and the foul smells were horrible and I hoped Lady Maud would not think Yorkshire was always like this.

Eventually we left behind the market crowds and the water mills of York and began the long slow climb up towards the moor. I breathed in the sweet scent of gorse and heather and thought how wonderful Yorkshire was; so much more welcoming than Lincolnshire with its flat grey fields, reed-filled ditches and silent, disapproving people.

As we climbed higher a gentle breeze blew off the moor, stirring the grass at our feet and cooling our faces. Our snaking procession followed the drovers' track between verges of short springy turf and occasional clumps of bright yellow gorse To one side the ground sloped steeply down to a tumbling beck and on the other, stretched out in grassy strays where the people of York grazed their cattle. There were numerous gullies where gnarled old oaks and twisted holly trees grew barely higher than the top of a man's head but there'd be no proper woodland until we reached the far side of the moor.

Maud rode up beside me and our escort dropped back to give us some privacy. The flowers she'd pinned to her riding cloak that morning had become windblown and bedraggled but the bells on her harness jingled as merrily as ever.

'I have been deserted by my husband,' she laughed. 'Already he prefers the company of his brother. I think this does not bode well for my marriage.'

'But he is a good husband, isn't he?' I badly wanted Maud to be pleased with my brother and couldn't bear to think he had fallen short of her expectations.

Maud gave me a sideways look. 'He is very energetic.'

I was unsure what she meant and didn't like to ask. Despite her insistence that I should call her Maud, I was still somewhat shy in her company, not quite at ease the way I was with my sisters.

'Shall we ride down to the beck?' she suggested.

'No,' I said quickly. 'We must keep to the path. There are holes and loose stones on the banks. The horses might stumble.'

'You are a very obedient girl,' she said with a sparkle in her eye. 'Do you always do what you're told?'

'Yes, you see I don't like to be beaten and somehow my misdeeds are always discovered.'

Maud laughed. 'You must learn to be discreet, then nobody will know what you do.'

She lifted her face to the sky. A moment later she turned. 'Can you hear that?'

All I could hear was the slight murmur of the breeze, the cry of a curlew and the distant barking of a dog. And of course the relentless rumbling sound of wagons, men and horses at our back.

'There! Listen!'

Maud was alert. But I could still hear nothing unusual.

It happened so quickly I had no time to think. One moment we were picking our way peacefully along the track, the next, hundreds of shrieking, screaming men waving pitchforks and staves were running towards us across the moor. Men with scythes appeared from behind a brake of gorse as a line of horsemen galloped into view. With one horrified look I saw a sword raised, a battle-axe swung high and a hail of arrows fly through the air. Above the din was my father's voice calling for his sons and the bellowed orders of the captains. Our escort whirled and tried to encircle us but Maud shouted 'Ride!' and without thinking twice I put my heels to my horse and followed her as she careered off the track and down the bank.

Behind us I heard screams and shouts as metal clashed against metal and wood collided with wood but the wind quickly blew the sounds away. We cantered fast along the narrow track beside the beck skirting some tangled hawthorn bushes and leaping over several muddy ditches. I had never ridden so hard in my life and needed all my skill to keep my mount steady. Once, Maud looked back to make sure I was with her but mostly she lay low across her horse's neck concentrating on the way ahead. Her chaperon had come loose and her hair streamed out behind her like a veil. The pretty windblown flowers had been lost in our precipitous descent as had the red ribbons I'd woven into my hair.

We rounded a high grassy bank strewn with boulders and then another, plunging us further and further into a narrow ravine only to find our way blocked by a fall of rock and scree. On the far side of the beck was a sheer grey cliff.

Maud swore.

She jumped off. 'Quick! We must lead the horses over the rocks.'

I slid off my saddle making sure I held tight to the reins but before I could take a single step, two men on horseback appeared at the top of the bank. One was a small rough-looking man wearing a padded jerkin and a battered old sallet, the other was a knight in half armour with a bascinet covering his face. He wasn't one of our ours. My belly clenched as I recognised the arms on his jupon – a *lion rampant azure*. He was a Percy!

'Get behind me!' ordered Maud. 'Say nothing!'

I didn't need telling twice and slipped into her shadow wishing she was broader, anything to offer more protection. She had no need to warn me to keep silent as I couldn't have said a word even if I'd wanted to. My mouth was dry and my tongue stuck fast to the back of my throat.

The knight removed his helmet giving us a sight of his dark short-cropped hair. He was a middle-aged man with a ruddy face. 'I do believe it's the bride,' he said, looking at Maud as if he wanted to eat her for dinner. 'When I saw you disappear over the ridge, lady, I thought I might find you here. A little lesson for you for next time you decide to run – I know the terrain better than you.'

'What d'ye want me to do with her, m'lord?' said his companion.

'Nothing yet. We'll see how compliant she is. Now lady, are you going to come quietly or do I have to get rough?'

Maud said nothing.

The knight smiled unpleasantly. 'Your bridegroom won't come to your rescue, y'know. My men will have hacked him to pieces by now. There is no-one to protect you but me. So you'd best do as I say.'

Wordlessly, he handed his helmet to his companion and dismounted. With studied slowness he removed his gauntlets. He glanced behind him and then began climbing down over the rocks with a surprising agility until he stood blocking our retreat. His brow was covered in sweat and his face marked with dirt. It was not a kind face. He had a cruel mouth and his eyes were menacing.

Maud still said nothing. Her arms were hanging loosely at her sides, her hands balled into tight fists.

He took a step closer and I felt myself shrink.

'There's no point in screaming y'know, in case you were thinking of calling for help. There's no-one to hear you 'cept for Tam and he's not going to lift a finger, are you Tam?

The small man grinned. 'Not unless ye want me to apply a bit of pressure like, m'lord?'

The knight smiled. 'All in good time, Tam. Let's see how obliging she is.'

He scrutinised Maud, slowly running his gaze over her body from top to toe, noting every rip and tangle, every inch of flesh inadvertently revealed and every piece of clothing left in disarray. I saw the tip of his tongue wet his lips as if he wanted to deal with her right there in the ravine where we stood. At last he nodded his head.

'Right, lady, what we're going to do is this. You're going to come with me and in case you should get any foolish idea about running away I'm going to bind your wrists. So let's have your hands.'

Maud put her arms out slowly, first one and then the other. Her eyes never left the knight's face.

'Throw me a rope,' he called to his companion and as the coil came snaking through the air, he momentarily looked away. Quick as a flash, Maud's arm went up and then down as she slashed at her enemy.

'You bitch!' he screamed as blood began pouring from a wound on his hand.

Maud stood there grasping a small evil-looking bade.

'Touch me and I'll have your balls off,' she hissed.

'By God, lady, you'll regret that. I'd not intended violence to your person but now I think it will give me the greatest of pleasure. I shall enjoy making you beg for mercy. And if you try to defy me I shall hurt you all the more. When I've finished, no other man will want you which is just as well as I intend to keep you for myself. I've always fancied a wife with a bit of spirit.'

'I'd not take you if you were the last man left alive,' hissed Maud.

'No? We'll see about that.'

'Enemy coming!' came a shout from the man at the top of the bank. 'A dozen or more. Ye'd best get outta there quick, m'lord.'

The knight cursed under his breath.

'It seems we are not to continue our acquaintance today, lady. But I'll be back for you, make no mistake. And when I do I'll have that little Nevill fledgling behind you as well.'

With that he climbed back up over the rocks nursing his hand as best he could. At the top the other man helped him onto his horse and handed him his helmet and gloves. Their horses whirled round and in a moment they were gone.

I felt my legs giving way, I sank to the ground and burst into tears.

'Stop that!' ordered Maud. 'You must not weep.'

'But he said he'd come back.' I sobbed.

'I know. But he won't come now and you must never let anyone see you're afraid. You must appear to be brave even if your legs are trembling and you're sick with fright.'

She bent down and put an arm round my shoulders. 'You're not a child any more, Kathryn, you're a young woman. You must learn to act like one.'

The next moment my father's men were scrambling down the bank calling for us to stay where we were and not to move.

I was in disgrace. By the time we reached Sheriff Hutton, news of the attack had already spread and I had begun to appreciate the depth of my foolishness. In truth it would have been hard not to.

'How could you have been so stupid?' hissed Alice. 'You know the rules perfectly well, don't you? Don't you?'

Having hit me twice, once on either side of my head, she now had me pinned hard against the wall and was interrogating me like a prisoner.

'Keep close, don't leave the line, obey the captain of your escort,' I muttered.

'And did you do any of those thing? No you didn't.' Another blow, this time to my right ear. 'By the blessed womb of St Anne you are the most disobedient girl I have ever had the misfortune to have as a sister. And don't start whining to me that your backside hurts, you fully deserved what you got. If I'd had the ordering you'd have got ten switches not six. And I'd have used a thicker rod.'

From the moment I'd been hauled up the precipitous grassy slope and set back on my feet I knew I'd be punished. I'd been shouted at by my father and suffered the ultimate humiliation of a beating administered by my mother in front of my sisters and the women of my mother's household. First there had been Tom, his face white with anger, shouting at me, calling me a stupid child, a useless, witless idiot; and shouting at Maud, using words I'd not care to repeat. I had stood gazing intently at my boots, with a furious tirade going on above my head. Maud had said nothing, just let Tom rage at her. I thought he might hit her but he didn't. I thought he might hit *me* but he didn't. He said I'd be dealt with later which was far worse.

My horse was led slowly back along the lower path of the ravine by one of my father's grooms while I was hoisted unceremoniously up behind one of Tom's men and returned to my mother. She'd been standing, surrounded by her women with Alianore at her side, looking none the worse for the attack. She'd taken one look at my scratched hands, my mud-spattered clothing and my tangled hair and slapped me hard across my face. There were no words but her eyes said it all – I was foolish, thoughtless, ignorant and disobedient. I was not worthy in any way to be called a Nevill daughter. I had disgraced not only myself but her as well. I had placed others in danger by my actions and would pay a heavy price for what I'd done. She noted the torn hem of my gown, the tattered lining of my cloak, the snags where buttons and ribbons had been ripped from my sleeves, and my hair which was snarled and tumbling over my eyes. With her back rigid with displeasure she had turned and walked away, leaving me in tears amongst the debris of the attack.

None of the wedding party had been hurt. Only Maud and I had been at risk and that was entirely because of our own stupidity. If we'd stayed with our escort instead of riding off down the bank we would have been perfectly safe. The attackers had been no match for our well-armed and properly trained men and despite the ferocity of the assault we'd sustained no casualties. It had been a raid by the Percys together with a band of ruffians from the alleyways of York, that much was clear. Less obvious was why.

'They wanted to kill our father,' said Alianore.

'They wanted me,' said Maud quietly. She'd said almost nothing since we'd returned to Sheriff Hutton and I'd begun to think she too had been beaten.

'Why should anyone want *you*?' snapped Alice.

'Indeed,' said Alianore, determined to make the most of her position as the obedient daughter. 'I can see no reason at all. I doubt they knew who you were.'

'It's because she's an heiress,' I muttered, remembering what Tom had said on our way to Tattershall. 'The Percy lords want her uncle's money.'

'You are such a child,' retorted Alianore. 'Heiresses don't carry sack-loads of coins on their person.'

'You can be certain I have no sack-loads of coins,' Maud smiled ruefully. 'For if I did they would now belong to your brother. But my Uncle Cromwell has three handsome

Yorkshire manors and they are far more valuable than sack-loads of coins.'

'And you think to inherit these?' said Alice, her voice still icy with contempt for this interloper in our midst who had caused her mother and father so much distress.

'Yes. My husband says they will do very nicely when joined with those your father has already settled on us.'

'I don't understand,' frowned Alianore, who, for all her pretensions, was really rather stupid.

'It's quite simple,' said Maud gently in the way one would to a child. 'A long time ago The Yorkshire manors belonged to the Percy family. They were taken by the king's grandfather and given to my uncle.'

'And the Percy lords want them back.' I said.

'I believe so.'

It was as if the horror of what might have happened suddenly dawned on Alice. 'They would have killed my brother and taken you and then…'

'Yes.'

'Then they would have killed you.' said Alianore, her eyes wide.

I suddenly felt much older than my sister. 'The Percy lord wasn't going to kill her, stupid. He was going to ravish her. And with Tom dead she'd be dishonoured and forced to marry him. Then he'd be the one to get her uncle's manors.'

Alice's head turned. 'Kathryn Nevill! Where did you learn about such things?'

'But it's true, isn't it?'

'Yes,' said Maud sadly. 'It's true.'

3

MIDDDLEHAM 1453

As soon as we returned to Middleham my father called a meeting of his council. We were not told the reason but obviously it had to do with the attack on Heworth Moor and what should be done to punish the Percys. The first person to arrive was Lord Fitzhugh, Alice's husband, who had come straight from Ravensworth. He was quickly followed by Sir Christopher Conyers, our steward at Middleham, and his son, both loyal retainers of my father. They smiled when they saw me watching them from the shadow of an archway and gave me a little bow which made me blush with pleasure. Sir James Pickering and Sir Robert Ogle were the last to arrive. I recognised them but they didn't notice me and I doubt they'd have smiled and bowed even if they had. They were my father's comrades-in-arms of many years and had always been his faithful supporters. I hoped Uncle Fauconberg might come but my mother said he had gone to Westminster on the king's business.

For two days private discussions took place behind closed doors and all Alianore and I could hear were some raised voices as the servants carried large green enamelled wine ewers in and out of the room at regular intervals.

'Thirsty work!' smirked Alianore.

Tom came out and cuffed us half-heartedly for listening at doors and sent us back to our mother's room.

After that we were set to sewing shirts, a job which I hated but which Alice said would keep us out of mischief.

At last my mother informed us that a decision had been taken. Letters were to be dispatched to all Nevill retainers in Yorkshire and Westmorland telling them that no-one was to exact retribution against the Percy family for the attack on Heworth Moor except under the express orders of the earl of Salisbury himself. The last thing my father wanted was a disorderly descent into lawlessness.

'There has been sufficient violence,' he announced to a gathering of the whole household that evening. 'If the Percy family and their followers choose to act like barbarians it does not necessarily mean that we should do likewise. If there are to be reprisals they will be carefully planned and will be at my behest. No-one is to act on his own in any way without my permission. The king desires an end to violence and if we are not provoked further we shall obey his wishes.'

What my father didn't say was that both he and my brothers had received letters from the king's council ordering them to cease and desist from riotous assemblies and other gatherings of their supporters. There had also been a threatening letter reminding my father of his privileged position which in no wise permitted him to take the king's law into his own hands. If he had a complaint against another lord, it was not for him to settle the matter himself by a display of arms; rather it should be put in writing and placed before the council.

'If the king will not enforce the law what do the council expect your father to do?' complained my mother to Alice. 'Do they think he should stand idly by while the earl of Northumberland's sons kill our men and abduct your father's womenfolk. Your sisters and I were exposed to real danger on Heworth Moor and that was a disgrace.'

'Lord Fitzhugh says the Percy brothers pillaged the church at Garston last week,' remarked Alice.

'Holy Mary!' said my mother, absentmindedly crossing herself. 'Was it bad?'

'The Staincliffe bailiff was dragged away and no-one knows what has happened to him. The vicar begged the men to leave but they pushed him aside. Lord Fitzhugh says they were jumping on the altar and shouting obscenities.'

'Unchristian behaviour,' said my mother. 'Unfortunately what your sister did by chasing after Lady Maud on the moor has merely made matters worse. It seems they were both threatened by one of the Percy brothers and your father cannot ignore that insult.'

I slipped out of the room and went to find Maud. She was sitting in the garden reading. When she saw me she lowered the book into her lap.

'May I ask you a question?' I said.

'Of course you may.'

'Was what we did on Hewoth Moor so very wrong?'

Maud considered for a moment and then said, 'For you, if your mother says it was wrong then you must believe that it was.'

I pushed a pebble with the toe of my shoe and blinked away a tear.

'We might have been killed.'

Maud laid her book aside and patted the bench.

'Come, sit beside me. You're very pale. You're not still afraid, are you?'

'A little,' I admitted.

'Don't be,' she said. 'Remember what I told you.'

I did remember but found it difficult to pretend I was not afraid when I was.

'Have you never been frightened?' I asked.

'Oh yes. There was one time when I was very frightened.'

When I continued to sniffle she said, 'Listen, Kathryn. A priest will tell you what is forbidden but that is not always helpful when you're facing danger. Shall I tell you what happened to me? Then you can decide what you would have done in my place.'

I nodded. 'Yes please.'

'You know my first husband was an old man.'

I nodded, recalling what Alice had told me about Lord Willoughby – sixty years or more on his wedding day, she'd said.

'He was like a grandfather to you.'

Maud gave me a crooked smile. 'I doubt many men imagine themselves a grandfather when they take a young bride. He married me because he wanted a son.'

I knew about the making sons but couldn't imagine Maud in bed with a man old enough to be her grandfather.

'Did you mind?'

'Mind what?'

'Him being old and wrinkled.'

Maud gave a delicious giggle. 'No. I thought I knew about men but my wedding night with my first husband was not quite how I imagined it would be.'

'Did he find you pleasing?'

The matter of pleasing a husband was a continuing

worry for Alianore who had spent time in our Aunt Stafford's house learning how to be a good wife and could talk of little else.

Maud laughed. 'Oh yes, he found me very pleasing. But, sadly his pleasure was of little use. I didn't give him the son he desired.'

'Why not?' I thought of the regular arrival of little Fitzhughs in the Ravensworth nursery and doubted Maud's marriage to Lord Willoughby was any less worthy in the eyes of God than Alice's to Lord Fitzhugh. Yet Maud's marriage had been childless.

'When you're older you'll understand. My first husband was near seventy when he died and a grandfather cannot always, shall we say, rise to the challenge.'

I had known neither of my grandfathers. They were heroes of our nursery stories when Alianore and I were little: my mother's father, the great English war commander Thomas Montagu who'd fought in the French wars for the fifth Henry and been present at the battle of Agincourt; and my father's father, Ralph Nevill, who'd kept the northern border safe and the Percy lords in check and helped put the fourth Henry on the throne. Both my grandfathers had risen to the challenges they'd faced. Perhaps, despite the kind things Maud said about Lord Willoughby, he wasn't a true hero.

'Were you sad when he died?' I asked curiously.

'Yes, he was a kind husband and believed he had left me well provided for. Do you understand?'

I nodded. I knew a little about dowers and jointures and how men made provision for their wives in case they should die, which they often inconveniently did, according to Alice.

'It wasn't his fault,' continued Maud. 'The manor of Eresby, where we'd been living, was to be mine. It was written into my marriage contract and I loved the house dearly. However, my stepdaughter's husband wanted it for himself.'

'But it was yours.'

Maud sighed. 'Yes, it was, However I should have realised the possibility of danger. My stepdaughter disapproved of her father's marriage to me. She'd grown up expecting to inherit everything and swore I'd fooled an old man whose wits were wandering. With her father dead she knew I'd get a third of his wealth so she encouraged her husband in his thievery.'

'He wanted to steal your house?'

'Worse. He sent armed men to turn me out. I was a grieving widow, quite alone with only a small household and very little protection. Suddenly there were men at my gate with cudgels and axes, threatening to burn the house to the ground if I didn't leave.'

'Were you scared?'

Maud nodded. 'Very. I thought they meant to kill me.'

'What did you do?'

'I sent one of the stable lads with a message to my uncle. It was nearly dark but it was only a few miles to his castle so it didn't take the boy long. I just prayed my uncle was at home.'

'Was he?'

'Yes. And he sent men to bring me to Tatterhall. But I lost Eresby. Perhaps if I'd stayed I might have kept my house. You must understand, I hadn't expected to have to fight for what was lawfully mine and there was no time to make plans; I had to decide in an instant. '

'Like when we were on Heworth Moor.'

'Yes.'

I wondered what would have happened if I'd let Maud ride off alone and not followed her down the slope to the beck, if I'd stayed obediently with my mother and our escort.

'Everybody says we were foolish, that we made a wrong choice. Was it wrong?'

She laughed. 'For you, yes. Your mother has the ordering of you and you should have obeyed her instructions and not followed me. But one day when you're older you'll no longer be in your mother's care and then you'll have to make your own decisions.'

'But I'll be married and my husband will have the ordering of me. I shall have to do what he says.'

Maud smiled. 'Husbands are not always to hand. Sometimes a wife has to think for herself.'

Thinking for myself was a tempting proposition. I wouldn't have to listen to Alice and do what she said. I rather liked the idea.

'Did your first husband leave you anything else?' I asked. 'Proper things like silver dishes or dogs?'

'Yes,' said Maud. 'He did. A basin and ewer of silver and a red bed of tapestry and a green one of worsted.'

'And his embroidered slippers?' I said slyly, remembering what Uncle Fauconberg had said.

'No,' Maud laughed. 'Those went to his chaplain.'

A month later when the fields by the river were bare of crops and the autumn mists had begun creeping over the fells and into the dales, my father called a family conference.

We were to go to his room off the great hall where he met with his tenants and conducted his private business. It was the first time Alianore and I had been allowed into our father's room and we were suitably nervous, clutching hands like two small children.

The walls of the room were covered in painted cloth and there were several intriguing-looking coffers and a long low iron-bound chest. My father sat in his high-backed chair at the end of a long table with my mother beside him. Uncle Fauconberg and our Uncle Robert, the bishop of Ely, sat on chairs down one side of the table while the rest of us stood – apart from Alice who had been given a stool as a gesture of kindness to her condition. Lord Fitzhugh was behind her, hovering like an over-eager nursemaid. Alianore and I stood near the door hoping nobody would expect either of us to speak. There was also a strange young man I didn't recognise. He was leaning on my father's chair.

I nudged Alianore. 'Who's that?' I whispered.

She looked at me as if I was a halfwit. 'Richard, you fool. Our brother.'

Of course it was. Richard Nevill, earl of Warwick, the eldest of my parents' four sons. He was thirteen years my senior and I'd not seen him since I was a little girl. No wonder I didn't recognise him. I smiled, hoping he would notice me but he was too busy whispering in our father's ear.

Our father looked round the room, nodding his head with satisfaction.

'It is a long time since we've had such a fine gathering of Nevills. Welcome to you all especially our two youngest members – my dearest daughter, Alianore, who may not be with us for much longer, and Kathryn. Welcome also to my son Tom's wife, Maud. She has had a somewhat brutal introduction to our life in Yorkshire. I wish it had been otherwise but part of the reason we are here today is to settle matters concerning our continuing difficulties with the Percy family.'

Maud looked remarkably cool, unlike Alianore who had blushed to the roots of her hair when father had drawn attention to her presence.

'But first, some news. I have received a communication today informing me that Queen Margaret has given birth to a son. The child was born at Westminster Palace just over a week ago and will be called Henry.'

My mother smiled. This was surely good news but father didn't look at ease. He picked up the letter, started at it for a moment and then put it down again.

He turned to Uncle Fauconberg. 'I suppose if nothing else this will end speculation about the relationship between our king and his queen.'

John grinned. 'You think so?'

Richard regarded his younger brother. 'I should be careful what you say, John. We may be a long way from court here in Yorkshire but certain of our enemies have an extremely long reach.'

'That is enough.' My father rapped the table. 'Your mother and your sisters are present. I do not wish to hear a discussion about this. Whatever gossip you may have heard, keep to yourselves. Understand?'

My brothers nodded their heads while Lord Fitzhugh rested his hand firmly on Alice's shoulder as if for reassurance.

'I shall tell the household the good news at dinner and we shall drink to the health of the little prince.'

'A bit of a kick in the necessaries for Aunt Cecily's husband,' remarked Tom.

'The duke of York has no expectations,' said my father sharply.

'You cannot say that, father. It's common knowledge he considers himself a better candidate for the throne than the king.'

'Watch your tongue,' said Uncle Fauconberg, folding his arms and glaring at my brother. 'We have an anointed king and wish for no other. Your Aunt Cecily's husband knows that and is a loyal subject.'

Tom shrugged. 'If you say so, uncle.'

'And mind your manners. Remember who you're speaking to.'

Tom flushed a dull red. 'I beg your forgiveness,' he mumbled, clearly resenting the rebuke in front of his wife.

Uncle Fauconberg's eyes flickered towards Maud but her expression didn't change.

'This matter would not arise if the king ruled with a stronger hand,' said my father. 'But he does not. He is a man who desires peace and harmony but does little to enforce the law. So we must try to quell this feuding ourselves. I have summoned you today to inform you that I have asked for a meeting with the earl of Northumberland.'

I gasped. Henry Percy, Earl of Northumberland was our enemy.

I saw John slide his hand to where his sword would be if he was wearing one.

'Henry Percy?'

'Yes, John. The same Henry Percy whose sons have been running riot across Yorkshire these past two years, raiding my manors and attacking my family. The same Henry Percy whose tenants you and Tom threatened to hang and whose properties your men have been burning at will. A quarrel involving my sons is not what I need right now. I have to go south and I cannot leave while you and the young Percys are at each other's throats.'

'So we are to make a truce.'

'We are. Tomorrow you and your brothers will accompany me to Topcliffe. Archbishop Booth will be with us to help conduct negotiations. We shall demand Northumberland hands over his sons into my custody so that they can be escorted to London, to appear before the royal council. Once that is done your brother Richard and I will ride south.'

As soon as my father had concluded his speech-making, Alianore and I trooped dutifully back to our mother's rooms.

'Is the little prince going to die?' I asked Alice.

For daring to ask the question I received a sharp slap on my face.

'For the love of Our Lady! Why say something so dangerous and so stupid? The child is perfectly healthy. Don't ill-wish him.'

'I wasn't,' I protested, rubbing my cheek. 'Is it the queen?'

I'd never seen Margaret of Anjou but Maud had once served in her household in the years before she married Lord Willoughby.

'I was a very lowly person,' she had explained. 'I doubt the queen knew my name.'

Her description was of a passionate dark-haired beauty who revelled in her position as queen. She was immensely proud and looked with disdain down her long Angevin nose at those who displeased her. I wondered if by touching such a woman Maud had been cloaked in the grandeur of majesty in the same way gold dust left a slight sheen on the tips of one's fingers.

Alice tutted. 'There is nothing wrong with the queen. She is resting like any other woman in her condition. When you birth a child of your own you will understand.'

I understood nothing. I wanted to know why our father was hurrying south if the baby was healthy and the queen was not sick. Why was there such urgency?

'Kathryn Nevill, you listen to me. Your father is an important man and leaving us at this time is nothing unusual.'

'Do you truly think so?' Maud's voice came from the other side of the room where she was sorting her silks into pleasing rows of different colours. 'Would you not expect him to remain here?'

Alice sniffed. 'Why?'

'The Percy brothers are still at large.'

'Not for long.'

'You think their father will give them up?'

'I think the archbishop will broker a deal.'

Maud abandoned her silks and joined us in the window embrasure where we were busy with our sewing.

'The archbishop will fail. A truce perhaps but not one involving Northumberland's sons. They will remain free to do further damage to your father's properties.'

Alice set her mouth in a thin hard line which showed how cross she was. Alianore and I had long ago developed a care for our bodily wellbeing and rarely countered her opinions because our sister had a heavy hand.

'There is a pressing reason for your father's journey south,' Maud continued.

'Are you going to enlighten us?' said Alice in the sort of voice she used when addressing her servants at Ravensworth.

'If you like. Your father is going south because the king is sick.'

'How do you know that?'

'My husband had it from his father. I'm surprised Lord Fitzhugh has not informed you, Lady Alice.'

A red stain rose from Alice's neckline along her throat and into her cheeks.

'Lord Fitzhugh tells me what he considers I need to know, not every piece of tittle-tattle which comes his way.'

'Oh it's not tittle-tattle, it's perfectly true. The king has been sick for some months and his doctors cannot say what is wrong with him.'

'Won't say, more like,' sniffed Alice.

'The king will recover, won't he?' I asked anxiously. 'He won't die?'

'Don't be stupid,' said Alianore. 'King's don't die from a cold in the head.'

Maud patted my hand. 'No-one has suggested the king's life is in danger.'

Alice returned her attention to her sewing. 'You see! I said there was no particular reason.'

Maud smiled. 'Your father sees reason enough.'

'And what is that?' said Alice, thrusting her needle into one of Lord Fitzhugh's shirts and looking as if she'd like to jab it hard into Maud's arm.

'The question of who rules the kingdom.'

'The king does,' said Alice as if talking to a foolish five-year-old who had not been attending to her lessons.

'Ah, but if the king is sick and the queen is confined to her rooms, who rules then?'

There was silence. The flush in Alice's cheeks vanished.

'Not Lord Somerset, surely?' she said.

'For certain it will be the queen's very good friend, Edmund Beaufort, Duke of Somerset.'

I knew a little of the duke of Somerset. He was kin to my Nevill grandmother and neither of my parents could say his name without seemingly wanting to spit. My mother said he was a menace, a highly dangerous man who should have been dismissed from the king's side years ago. My father believed him a disastrous military commander and mistrusted him utterly.

'The thought of Edmund Beaufort, Duke of Somerset, getting his hands on the reins of power has caused your father to ride south. With the king sick, the royal council might easily let Somerset take control and your father is afraid of what he'd do. So is your brother, Lord Warwick. They are hurrying to Westminster to ensure such a thing will not happen.'

Maud had told me a little of how things were beyond the walls of Middleham, of the jostling for favours which swirled about the king; how the wolves in their silks and satins fought for the fattest and juiciest of royal bones. The duke of Somerset, she said, had jostled more adroitly than most and been heavily rewarded by the king.

'It was Somerset who lost us the king's lands in France,' said Maud, returning to her silks, 'but he has the trust and admiration of the queen and she controls the king. Now that she has given the king a son, he will reward her with whatever she asks for.'

'Once he is recovered,' said Alianore.

'Once he is recovered,' agreed Maud. 'Meanwhile the duke of Somerset will do whatever he likes and the queen will not stop him.'

Queen Margaret must be one of those women Alice talked about, women who snarled you up in their shiny coils. Perhaps this new prince was not like other babies, all pink and white and dimpled; perhaps he was covered in silvery scales and that was why our father was so afraid. When I mentioned this to Alianore she looked at me as if I was stupid and tapped the side of her head.

Three days later the invitation arrived.

'It doesn't mention us,' whispered Alianore.

'No, it doesn't,' I agreed.

'Hush,' whispered Maud, putting her finger to her lips.

My mother held the precious invitation in her hand, smiling as she peered at it for the fourth time. It had been expected but its actual arrival sent shivers of excitement through my mother's rooms. Her women sat with their backs a little straighter, their smiles a little brighter and their voices murmuring a little more sweetly. Their manners were impeccable and everyone sat like little dolls with their gowns spread evenly over their knees. Nobody wanted to be left behind.

The Nevills were to attend the ceremony at Westminster to celebrate the queen's return from childbirth and naturally my mother could not take the whole of her very large household. Everyone was hoping they would be one of those making the journey to London.

She looked up and smiled at Alianore and me.

'Your sister Joan will be there.'

Everyone said Joan was the prettiest of my mother's daughters. She had silvery fair hair and was married to the earl of Arundel. Her husband's castles were a great distance from Middleham, further than Lincolnshire, further even than London, and he never brought her to visit. Alice said he was careful of his wife and kept her close for his own pleasure and delight and why would he want to visit a disagreeable young girl like me who had no idea how to behave.

'Your father's sisters will be in attendance.'

I wrinkled my nose. 'Will Aunt Cecily be there?'

My mother noted my expression and frowned. 'Of course. Your Aunt Cecily is the duchess of York and her husband is an important man.'

Alice had once explained to me how the duke of York could trace his royal descent from two of old King Edward's sons and considered himself the king's rightful heir. I'd only seen him once when he and Aunt Cecily paid a visit to Middleham. I remembered him as a cross, dark-haired man, luxuriously dressed in a pale blue doublet, embroidered with tiny silver birds and liberally trimmed with fur. Alice said he was a man with a grudge because the king had treated him badly but she didn't say why that should be.

'I believe all duchesses have been invited,' continued my mother.

'Even Cousin Nan?' said Alianore with a slight sneer.

Aunt Cecily's husband had arranged a very prestigious marriage for their eldest daughter and when Nan was only eight years old she had married her father's ward, the young duke of Exeter. Upon hearing the news, Alianore had stamped her feet with rage and thrown her sewing onto the floor.

My mother sighed. 'I know Nan is the same age as you, Alianore, and I know you are jealous of her good fortune, but marriage to Harry Holland has made her a duchess so naturally she will be there.'

'It's not fair,' muttered Alianore. 'Why does she get to go and not us?'

'Did you say something of importance, my daughter?' our mother enquired.

Alianore flushed. 'No, Lady Mother. I was hoping... I was wondering if...'

'You were wondering if you might come to London, is that it?'

Alianore nodded. 'Yes.'

'And what about you, Kathryn? Do you also wish to come to London?'

I looked up at my mother and smiled as sweetly as I could manage. 'If it pleases you, Lady Mother.'

My mother turned to Maud. 'What do you think, daughter-in-law? Shall we burden ourselves with these two unworthy creatures?'

Maud put her head on one side as if considering the question carefully. I held my breath. Surely she would want me to come. I was her friend.

'I was fourteen when my uncle sent me to the duchess of Gloucester's household, my lady. It proved an excellent education. I can think of no better introduction to the world of the royal court than a ceremony like this one. Your daughters can only benefit from the experience.'

I gave a contented sigh.

'Very well. You may come,' said our mother. 'But pay heed. If I hear reports of foolish behaviour you will be sent straight back to Alice at Ravensworth. Is that understood?'

'Yes, Lady Mother,' we chorused.

'Will Aunt Stafford be there,' enquired Alianore, breathless with excitement.

'Yes. And you will meet the duchess of Suffolk who was once my stepmother and is now my dearest friend.'

'Will Uncle Fauconberg's wife come with us?' I asked, hoping the answer would be no. I thought her a stupid woman with little to say, given to outbursts of foolish giggling.

My mother smiled sadly. 'Being away from home distresses her. She will remain at Skelton. But Richard's wife, Anne, will be there.'

4

LONDON 1453

We left Middleham in a cold grey dawn with layers of gauzy mist hiding the fells and spilling down into Coverdale. Beads of moisture soaked my cloak as our men circled the courtyard, impatiently waiting for the last of the women to be ready. My horse fidgeted, sidling up against Alianore's. She glared at me so I drew my hood a little further over my head, hoping Maud and Tom would hurry and conclude their leave-taking. He had already kissed her twice.

The coffers containing our precious jewels and furs were safely stowed in the wagons and we had armed men stationed on both sides to provide protection. After our experience on Heworth Moor in August my mother was taking no chances. Everyone knew that a party of women was vulnerable to attack and despite our father's truce with the earl of Northumberland we had no idea where the Percy brothers were hiding. My father had left three hundred men to escort us to London but I feared it wasn't enough. I would have liked a thousand at the very least.

It is hard to describe London to someone who has never been there but once we passed through Bishopsgate on that raw November afternoon three weeks after leaving Middleham, my first impression was of a seething mass of people and animals. On either side were houses, some as high as three storeys, crowding out the sky, a continual blur of black and white and grey. There were ale houses on every corner and churches on every street, A wagon, laden with sacks, trundled past us, followed by a dozen packhorses, a man driving a flock of sheep and a goose girl trying to negotiate her charges through the crowds. Coming towards us were a group of men following a priest and behind them a little procession of filthy urchins yelling obscenities and throwing stones. A woman rushed out of a house, grabbed one boy and beat him soundly about the head with a pan.

The noise was tremendous, a huge cacophony of sound: shopkeepers shouting at the tops of their voices, women screaming for their children, men bellowing for their servants and from every corner of the city, the sound of bells. Above the rooftops hovered a pall of thick grey smoke and the ground beneath our horses' hooves was a churned-up mess of mud and dung and filth. The stench was worse than the privies by Micklegate Bar.

We passed down a street lined with shops which Maud said was called Cheape. Here there were men and women dressed in rich velvet robes, their hoods lined with expensive fur, and others wearing nothing but a few tattered rags. We were headed for our father's inn, The Erber. which our mother said was by the river. I could already smell that indefinable mixture of fish and mud and sea air which I now recognise as so much a part of London.

The Erber was nearly as large as Middleham but spread out and mainly painted black and white. It was like a little town complete in itself with everything my father needed within its walls. He had been in residence for more than a week so the servants were ready for us and it was with great relief that Alianore and I allowed our maid to remove our travelling clothes. At our mother's insistence, Maud ordered the floor to be spread with sheets ready for our bath.

Two hefty men brought in a great wooden tub and set it down where Maud directed. They were followed by a procession of serving men carrying buckets of hot water which they poured into the tub. When it was half full the men left and one of my mother's women sprinkled dried rose petals into the steaming water which gave the room a heady scent reminiscent of summer. Maud ordered first Alianore and then me into the tub and watched while one of the maids scrubbed us until every bit of dirt and grime acquired on our journey had been banished. She then ordered more water and oversaw the washing of our hair. By now my skin was a bright rosy pink and my hair was so clean it squeaked.

Once we were wrapped in our drying sheets, Maud inspected our feet, checked our ears for wax and our hair for lice. She examined us for flea bites and traces of dirt under our fingernails and then permitted us to dress. I was used to Alice's ministrations, which were even more searching, and made no complaint but Alianore grumbled. For five years she'd been living with our Aunt Stafford in her husband's castles at Stafford and Maxstoke. Our father had summoned her home to find her a husband and she swore it must be a duke because nothing less would do now that she had tasted luxurious ducal living.

'Nobody fussed so in Aunt Stafford's household,' she announced grandly.

'That I do not believe,' said Maud, as our maid combed out Alianore's long fair hair. 'The duchess is known for her immaculate appearance. You won't find her with dirty fingernails.'

'At least she doesn't order your mouth washed out with soap and give you nothing but bread and water like Lady Talbot does,' I said, remembering the terrifying few months I had spent in the countess of Shrewsbury's household before Alice rescued me and had me brought back to Ravensworth.

'If you blaspheme it is what you can expect,' said Maud firmly. 'I'm sure Lady Alice does the same.'

'She slaps me,' I giggled. 'And tells me I am a disgrace to our family.'

When the day came for the queen's special ceremony, The Erber was in a flurry of excitement. Even Alianore, who professed to be above such things, kept dashing to the window to see what might be happening outside. My mother's rooms were full of women fetching last-minute requests for jewel boxes, and maids rummaging for lost stockings which they swore they'd packed before we left Yorkshire. The littlest maid was in tears because she'd accidently tipped my mother's box of powders onto the floor making a terrible mess.

We dressed in our finest clothes, the rich velvets and brocades we'd brought with us from Middleham. I pulled on a pair of new stockings made from fine pale-coloured wool which made me feel very grown up although Alianore said I still looked like a child straight from the nursery. I ignored her and tied my best pale blue ribbons round the top of the stockings to prevent them slipping down my legs. The cobbler at Middleham had made me a pair of soft leather shoes especially for the occasion. They had red laces with tiny gold tassels on the ends and I kept drawing up the hem of my gown to look at them which Maud said was not a good idea. She said young ladies should keep their feet covered in case they were accused of displaying their ankles to the gaze of young men.

'Why would anyone want to look at my ankles?' I whispered to Alianore.

She shrugged. 'Men are like that. They always want to see the bits of us we keep hidden.'

I didn't understand why but thought it better not to ask.

Once I was dressed Maud allowed me a little rosewater to dab on my neck and my wrists and helped our maid fix my hair. Alianore wanted a chaperon but our mother had ordered that our hair should be left unbound so Alianore had to make do with a narrow chaplet woven with green and yellow ribbons.

'Warm cloaks,' advised Maud. 'It will be cold on the river.'

That first slow journey in the great Nevill barge, with its intricate gilding and our Nevill arms proudly displayed on the prow, was one of the greatest of thrills of my life. My parents sat on large blue velvet cushions beneath the gold-fringed canopy while Maud, Alianore and I sat below them on smaller blue cushions. There were six oarsmen dressed in our father's livery, dipping their oars in and out of the water to the rhythmic banging of a drum. Crouched in the bottom of the barge and probably invisible to the thousands of people watching from the shore were half a dozen Nevill servants chosen for their strength and their dependability. My mother's maid sat behind my parents on a little seat where she couldn't be seen by anyone.

The river was full of boats: little wherries darting to and fro like buzzing insects, bigger ones bobbing about in mid-current and long sleek barges like ours making their way to Westminster. Some boats had square sails but most were pulled through the water by men using oars or poles or a flat sort of paddle. Maud said that further along the river, beyond the king's palace, was a horse ferry which, because the animals were heavy and prone to take fright at strangers with ropes and staves, had to be pulled across the river by chains.

Earlier a fretting mist had obscured the buildings on the shore but suddenly, as if by magic, the wisps of mist disappeared and a pale yellow sun winked merrily, reflected from the windows of a huge palace. The palace walls were lapped by the dark waters of the river and the towers rearing up into the morning sky were higher than any I'd seen before, even higher than Lord Cromwell's tower at Tattershall.

'Is that the royal palace?' I whispered to Maud above the creak and splash of the oars.

'No, that's Castle Baynard. It used to belong to the king's uncle, the duke of Gloucester, but he died and now I believe it is the town house of the duke of York.

'Alice says the duke of York is almost as royal as the king himself.'

Maud leaned over and murmured, 'That is a dangerous thing for Lady Alice to say. I should not repeat it if I were you and certainly not in the king's palace.'

The king's palace at Westminster was magnificent, five times as large as Middleham and with many more towers. We entered through an archway of cream-coloured stone into a series of courtyards, each one grander than the one before. A chapel as tall as the Minster in York stood to one side and beyond that a flight of shallow stone steps led up to an even more magnificent archway. Double doors, flanked by rows of guards bearing gleaming halberds, stood wide open ready to receive us because we were honoured guests.

Inside, the rooms were vast and the colours a blur of crimson and gold and blue and green. No panel had been left uncarved and not an inch of bare wall could be seen. Everything was gilded or painted or hung with cloth. I'd never seen so much glitter before in my life.

'The king must be very rich,' I whispered to Alianore.

'Of course he is, he's the king.'

We followed our parents through a maze of rooms, deeper and deeper into the palace, so deep I wondered how we'd find our way out. In every chamber servants dressed in royal livery lined the walls and guarded doorways while men and women in robes of lustrous velvet and figured damask swept by, each garment trimmed with fur and sewn with magnificent of jewels.

'It's like a moving tapestry,' I whispered.

'Look!' hissed Alianore. 'There's Aunt Cecily and Cousin Nan.'

'Where?' I said, standing on tiptoe. But my view was blocked by a pair of young men in doublets so short I thought they'd forgotten to put on their clothes.

I nudged Alianore.

'It's the fashion,' she said. 'Think nothing of it.'

'Shall we see the king?' I whispered.

'Not today. Mother says he's still sick.'

'But we shall see the queen, shan't we?' I thought it sensible to be sure in case I had misunderstood.

Alianore sighed. 'Naturally we shall see the queen. This is her *elevée*. They'd hardly pop someone else into her bed.' Then she giggled. 'What a surprise if they had. Suppose it was Aunt Cecily.'

I stared at a group of men and then wished I hadn't. They were large and impossibly grand, their robes lined and trimmed with copious amounts of rich fur, not just on the sleeves but sweeping the floor and up the front. The expression on their faces was one of disdain for each other. Then I remembered Alice's warnings. These weren't men, they were wolves, and not prowling the council chamber ready to tear each other apart, but here in the royal ante-chambers. Their hands were hidden in their sleeves, sheathing their claws in velvet, but one or two had their lips parted in superficial snarls, exposing a few of their sharp white teeth.

'Which one is Edmund Beaufort?' I whispered, shivering at the thought of our father's worst enemy, a man even more dangerous than the Percys.

Alianore, being braver than me, asked the woman on her other side.

'Oh hush,' she said. Then leaning close she whispered, 'They have him in the Tower. He'll not be peacocking around here for a while.'

Maud had told me about the Tower. Part-royal palace, part-fortress, part-prison, it stood further down the river beyond the bridge and past Billingsgate at the eastern edge of the city walls. Men who had broken the king's laws were sent to the Tower while the king's council decided how they should be punished.

'Usually the king forgives them for that is his nature,' Maud had explained. 'But the queen, if she dislikes them, would rather have their eyes put out and their tongues slit.'

Alianore and I were not permitted into the great bedchamber for the special ceremony as only those, like my mother or our Aunt Cecily who had received a royal invitation, could pass through. From our vantage point in the outer room we watched as two of the duchesses drew back the royal bed curtains and allowed us our first sight of the queen. She was dressed in scarlet and sable and smaller than I had expected, but beautiful in a dark sort of way with delicate features and a small red mouth. My Aunt Cecily's husband and another man, a duke whose name I didn't know, extended their hands and helped her climb out of bed. She managed it very elegantly and didn't once show her ankles or any other parts of herself which ought to remain hidden from the eyes of the dukes.

Once her feet were set on the floor and she was steady she lifted her chin and straightened her back as if she'd been lying in the bed all morning, longing to get up.

'She's forgotten the baby,' I whispered.

'Shh!' said several voices.

One of the duchesses put a lighted candelabra into the queen's hand. Then, taking very small steps, the queen led everyone out of the bedchamber. The men and women in the outer chamber drew aside like the waters of the Red Sea parting for Moses. I peeped back into the empty chamber to see if someone had remembered to fetch the baby prince but no-one was there and there was no sign of a cradle. I hoped he wasn't lying forgotten amongst the queen's bedclothes.

After that, everyone rushed outside to grab a good position for watching the next part of the queen's progress.

'Look at the quantity of fur!' whispered Alianore as we watched the procession pass from the palace to the abbey. Behind Queen Margaret, now dressed in magnificent robes of tawny cloth-of-gold, lined with hundreds of sable backs, came our Aunt Cecily bearing the prince's chrisom gown. Following her was a long line of dukes and duchesses, earls and countesses and lords and ladies, all ranked correctly in order of precedence. Our father was there with our brother Richard, and further back, Uncle Fauconberg. Amongst the women I caught sight of Maud and Lady Cromwell and near the head of the procession, our cousin, Nan. Somewhere too was Richard's wife but I didn't know what she looked like. She was a great heiress and had brought Richard his earldom in what Alice had said was an amazing stroke of luck and surely well-deserved.

Alianore pointed out our sister Joan, distant and beautiful, probably the most beautiful of all the women. I had been forewarned that the Percy ladies would be present – my father's sister, the countess of Northumberland, and her daughter Lady Grey – but there were so many women I couldn't name that I almost forgot they were the enemy. There were choirs of boys singing anthems in praise of the queen and little girls in white, dancing. In some ways it was more like a wedding than a solemn ceremony for the return of a queen from the dangerous world of childbirth.

'Who is the young man walking with our Aunt Cecily's husband, the one who's scowling?' I asked Alianore.

'Duke of Exeter,' said the woman behind me. 'You keep well clear of him, sweetheart. Harry Holland's a bad apple.'

'Aye,' said her friend. 'A wicked temper and no respecter of the king's law.'

'Should the council not send him to the Tower?' I asked, which made the women snigger into their hands.

I thought I caught a glimpse of the Percy lord who'd attacked us last summer but the man vanished into the abbey and was gone and I might have been mistaken.

'Where is the baby prince?' I asked. 'Have they forgotten to bring him?'

'Windsor,' said Alianore shortly.

'Where's that? Did we pass it on our way?'

'Alianore felt the need to explain to the ladies behind us that I was young and had never been away from my governess's skirts before, which was a lie.

'Poor lamb,' murmured one of them and I wasn't sure if she meant me or the little prince.

At last the celebration of the special mass inside the abbey was over and the queen and her procession snaked back to Westminster Hall. There would be a feast but only for the queen which seemed rather unfair as I was certain the other ladies must also be hungry. Our mother said they would kneel in silence while the queen ate. Later there would be dancing but Alianore and I had not been invited to watch so were taken back to The Erber by two of our father's men, much to our annoyance.

There was no need to despair as next day we discovered other delights.

The invitations sent out by Aunt Cecily were more like royal commands. From the words used to the beauty of the parchment on which they were written, they could have come from the hands of the king's secretary, himself. There was to be a feast at the York family's London residence to celebrate the appointment of the duke of York as King's Lieutenant. This was an office we had never heard of and sounded remarkably grand to Alianore and me but as I told Alianore, Aunt Cecily's husband was almost as grand as the king and almost as royal.

There were hushed conversations between my parents and between my mother and Richard's wife, and between my mother and her one-time stepmother the dowager duchess of Suffolk. Apparently it was the duke of Norfolk who had persuaded the council to imprison the duke of Somerset in the Tower and now Aunt Cecily's husband wanted to be named Protector and Defender of England, a title even grander than that of King's Lieutenant. Maud said the duke of York not only coveted such a title but considered it appropriate for the man who would carry the burden of ruling the country until the king recovered

'He is taking a very long time to recover,' I remarked. 'If I were him I would change my physician.'

There was an awkward silence in the room and Maud busied herself with her embroidery.

'What have I said?' I asked.

The others all looked at my mother. She laid aside her sewing and, in a voice that was less measured than usual, said, 'I suppose you should be told because soon there will be no hiding the truth from anyone.'

'What truth?' said Alianore, forgetting she was not supposed to put herself forward.

My mother gave a great sigh and leaned back in her chair. She looked at each of us in turn.

'The king's illness is like no ordinary illness. In my lifetime I have not heard of anyone struck down in such a way. It seems he has been deprived of his senses. Men who have been to Windsor to see him say he doesn't speak and he doesn't use his limbs. His arms lie uselessly at his side and he does nothing. His servants have to support him because he is unable to stir himself.'

'Is it an enchantment?' said Alianore.

'Certainly not!' said my mother.

'It sounds like one,' muttered Alianore.

'I will not have a daughter of mine talk of witchcraft in that way, Alianore. Do you hear me?'

Alianore lowered her head and mumbled, 'Yes, Lady Mother.'

I gave a secret little smile. For as long as I could remember Alianore had been the favoured one and it was a sweet moment to hear her receive the sharp edge of our mother's tongue.

'Will he die?' I asked politely.

My mother shook her head. 'Let us pray he recovers and soon. But nobody knows what is amiss nor when he will recover his wits. This is a malady unknown to any physician.'

'What if he doesn't get better?' said Alianore, busily calculating what advantage there might be to her in this new situation.

'That will be for the council to decide.'

'Will our uncle of York become king?' I asked, thinking that would surely be the best solution. I was certain Aunt Cecily would like to be queen.

'Don't be a fool,' hissed Alianore. 'How can the duke of York be made king if the king is still alive? Besides, there is the little prince. If the council want another king they will choose him.'

We turned to look at our mother.

'Are we safe?' I asked.

She smiled. 'Yes Kathryn, of course you are safe. We are all safe. Your father and your brothers will protect us.'

But at the back of my mind was an image of the Percy lord with blood dripping from his hand, swearing he'd come back one day and take me away.

The York feast took place two days later. I was seated beside my cousin Nan who was the eldest of my Aunt Cecily's seven children. There were three girls but I liked Nan best because although she was of an age with Alianore, she preferred me. Languishing near the tail end of my family I was used to being overlooked so it was gratifying to be Nan's favourite cousin. We met rarely but when we did she would tell me her secrets, the ones she told nobody else, and I would share with her things I didn't even tell Alianore.

'I saw your husband at the abbey,' I confided. 'He was walking with your father and someone pointed him out. Do you like him?'

She turned her face away and, to my surprise, when after a moment she looked back, there were tears in her eyes.

'What's the matter?' I asked, laying my hand on hers in a cousinly way.

'My mother says I must go and live with him,' she whispered. 'She says he is impatient to make me his wife. But Kat, I don't want to. I know it is my duty but he's horrible. He's cruel. He says he'll beat me when he gets me to himself. My mother doesn't know what he's like and the things he does, but I know.'

'What does he do?' I asked, curious to discover what a man might do to his betrothed.

Nan's mouth trembled. 'He hurts me. He twists my arm until I want to scream and then digs his fingernails into the flesh at the base of my thumb under the pretext of wanting to hold my hand. I've seen him whip his servant and once, when he knew I was looking, he strangled a dog with his bare hands. He says he'll do the same to me if I don't do as I'm told.'

'Whatever he does you will have to accept it,' I said, recalling Alice's lectures on the duties of a young woman to her husband. 'You are his wife. Perhaps he will improve. Alice says young men mellow when they enjoy regular marital intimacy.'

Nan shuddered. 'I cannot bear the thought of him touching me.'

'A man is required to honour his wife.'

'You don't know what a man does to his wife,' said Nan, looking as if she might start weeping in earnest.

'Yes, I do. Alianore told me. She says young men think of little else. They want to do it all the time, even in the mornings.'

'What are you two whispering about?' said Alianore.

'Nothing that concerns you,' I retorted.

64

'Everything concerns me,' said Alianore loftily. 'Has Edward spoken with you? He was looking for you earlier.'

Edward was the eldest of Aunt Cecily's four sons and exactly the same age as me. When we were little and the York family came to Middleham we would play together. Now he spent his days with my brother, Richard, the magnificent earl of Warwick, learning how to be a man. He was tall and lanky with long legs, golden hair and a pleasing face. I liked him.

'Here he comes with his shadow,' said Alianore.

The shadow was Edward's brother, Edmund, a year younger and always one pace behind: a little slower to reach the oak tree down by the river, unable to climb as high as Edward who could easily reach the topmost branches, not as quick with a joke or a witty reply, but warm-hearted and kind and if I hadn't preferred Edward I would have liked Edmund best. As it was I barely noticed him.

'Our lady mother has sent us to pay our respects,' grinned Edward. 'So here we are being respectful.'

'How pleasant,' said Alianore who wasn't sure she liked Edward and even if she did, wasn't prepared to let him know.

He turned to me and examined me carefully from the top of my head down to my slippers. 'You've grown, Kat.'

'So have you,' I replied, feeling a little flutter in my belly and thinking how good-looking he had become.

'Of course I have. Soon I shall be as tall as our father.

'But not as tall as our brother, Richard,' said Alianore.

Edward laughed. 'There's plenty of time and Lord Warwick reckons I'll outstrip him if I grow at this pace. He stands me up against the wall with a measuring rod each month to see how tall I am. Has your father found you a husband yet, Ali?'

'What is it to you?' said Alianore.

'Perhaps Edward wants you for himself,' smirked Edmund.

Edward aimed a playful kick at his brother. 'I'll take Kat for preference.'

My stomach gave a little lurch and I found I was blushing.

'What do you say to that, Kat?' said Edmund. 'Kissing cousins?'

'She's not permitted to marry until I do. I'm older so I go first,' pronounced Alianore.

Edward gave Alianore a wicked smile. 'Your father was sniffing round the stables this morning. Our horse master lost his wife last month and hopes to marry again. What d'you say, Ali? Will he do for you?'

Alianore turned her back.

'I pity the girl who marries you, Edward,' she said over her shoulder.

'Oh but Ali, I am my father's heir. One day I shall be duke of York. Men are queuing up to offer me their daughters. Didn't you know? But I don't intend to marry a green girl like you who knows nothing. I shall marry a woman of experience.'

The warm feeling in my stomach dissipated and I laughed with the others to hide my confusion.

At that moment the conversation in the hall ceased and everyone scrambled off the benches and stood up as the duke and my Aunt Cecily took their place on the dais under the silken canopy. Like Uncle Fauconberg, the duke was not the tallest of men but what he lacked in inches he more than made up for in grandeur. He carried himself like a great prince and wore rich robes, lined with fur and decorated with golden motifs of birds and butterflies. Embroidered onto the canopy were his impressive arms: part royal, part House of Castile and Léon, part Mortimer and de Burgh and part Holand, a blazing statement of his noble ancestry stitched in crimson and blue and gold and green.

The canopy stood on a raised part of the dais so that the duke and my Aunt Cecily were sitting higher than my parents and my brother Richard and his wife. I was about to open my mouth to say something when Nan shook her head and placed her finger to her lips. Not a sound was heard as the serving boys began their procession up the hall with the dishes. They knelt in front of the duke who helped himself to a little of whatever he wanted and then indicated that they should serve the rest of those on the dais. Some dishes he sent down the hall to certain favoured guests and I watched in dismay as my favourite flampets passed me by and were set in front of an elderly man with a forked beard. Eventually a couple of dishes were placed on our table and we were permitted to eat. But there was no conversation, only hushed requests to pass this dish or that dish or the whisper of someone requiring the salt. The duke dined in the way the queen had dined on the day of her *elevée*, the way royalty always dined – in silence.

'He would be a good match for you,' remarked Maud as we prepared for bed that night.

'Who?' I said, pushing my hair under my cap and fumbling with the ribbons under my chin.

'Young Edward.'

Alianore choked on a snort. 'Aunt Cecily would sooner walk through fire than allow her precious firstborn son to wed the younger daughter of an earl. Edward is to have a princess at the very least, preferably a queen. And I doubt you will ever be a queen, Katkin.'

Maud smiled. 'Young men sometimes surprise their families. You'd be amazed to know how many marriages are love matches, the man choosing a wife for himself.'

Alianore aimed a gentle punch to my shoulder. 'I cannot see Edward loving you enough to defy his mother. And would you really want Aunt Cecily for your mother-in-law?'

So saying, she went skipping gaily across the floor to look over her slippers singing a song about the joys of springtime which the minstrels had played at Castle Baynard.

I thought of the faded dowager at Tattershall telling me to hurry before all the young men were netted, and the words Edward had said at the feast about the wife he wanted for himself.

'I doubt anyone will want me,' I said miserably. 'Alianore will come first and Alice says there are precious few good men left. She is married to a lord and our sister Joan to an earl but Alice fears our father will be unable to purchase anyone of note for us.'

Maud came and sat beside me. 'She was teasing you. Besides, if your father cannot find you a husband you can always go hunting for one yourself.'

We remained at The Erber for the Christmas festivities, dining twice more with our York cousins and having a difficult visit from my father's sister, the Percy duchess of Northumberland and her daughter Lady Grey. However pleasant they were it was impossible to forget the bad feeling between our father and the countess's husband and how her sons had attacked us on Heworth Moor.

Uncle Fauconberg visited and, despite my mother's disapproval, spent most of the time in her rooms talking to Maud. Once Lady Cromwell came to pay her respects to my mother and to see her husband's niece.

'You are grown uncommonly pretty, young Kathryn,' she said to me.

'Oh please, Lady Cromwell, do not encourage her,' said Alianore. 'She is only just out of the schoolroom and we do not want her to become too pleased with herself.'

Lady Cromwell patted my knee. 'Your sister is right. It does not do to be proud of your looks. Like all good things, they fade with time. Look at me! I was a beauty once but alas no more.'

Lady Cromwell did indeed look grey and faded and not very well though I doubted I would look as old and wrinkled as she did even if I lived to be a hundred.

Our most frequent visitors that festive season were our brother, Richard, and his wife. Countess Anne spent a great deal of time on her knees and was one of those good women who puts everyone else to shame with her piety. She gave tentative smiles in reply to questions but seldom ventured opinions of her own. Perhaps she was wondering when she might oblige my brother in the matter of an heir. The only child in the Warwick nursery was little Isobel and that was not much good to a man who wanted sons. I knew my brother wanted sons because he'd told my father so. Alice said ambitious men always wanted sons. In the meantime, until the Warwick sons came along, my brother would have to make do with Edward.

By January rumours were flying around the city that the king had failed to recognise his own child. Alianore said all babies looked alike so perhaps the king had looked and thought the baby was some other man's son, not his. When I ventured this opinion to my mother she told me I must never say such a thing again and if I did I would be beaten.

'Do you think Lord Fitzhugh will recognise Alice's baby?' I asked Alianore.

'She'll be walled up if he suspects it's not his.'

'Perhaps the king will have the queen walled up.'

Alianore gave me a sharp pinch. 'And you'll find yourself behind the walls of a convent if you go on saying things like that.'

Next day there was news that the herald of the imprisoned duke of Somerset had snapped up all the available lodgings near the Tower. Having secured places for his lord's friends he was now busy insinuating spies into every man's household. According to my mother, a spy could be anyone; it could be a man in your kitchen, a visiting friar eating at your table or the boy who brought up your logs – absolutely anyone. And everything we said would be remembered and reported to the duke in his room in the Tower so we must be very careful. The duke of Somerset would hear about every word we said so I reminded Alianore to watch her tongue but she said it was mine that needed watching.

When two days later Aunt Cecily paid us a visit she brought her own important insights into what was really going on.

'Of course the queen wants the regency for herself,' she announced.

She was perched on one of our mother's chairs, displaying herself like a royal personage and fixing me with her beady little eyes as if she suspected I had designs on her son.

'I doubt the council will allow that,' said my mother who had known Aunt Cecily since she was a little girl and consequently was not the least bit frightened of her. 'A woman ruling for her absent husband may be acceptable in Anjou but it is not the custom in England.'

Aunt Cecily sniffed. 'She is said to be drawing up a list of her demands. She wishes to be given authority to choose the great officers of state: the chancellor, the treasurer, the privy seal. My husband's friends are already arming their retainers because, God knows, if she has her way she'll have Somerset out of the Tower.'

I moved my cushion closer to my mother's feet, feeling the need for the protection of her skirts.

'We must pray she does not succeed,' my mother said smoothly.

'You realise that if Somerset goes free he will have my husband filleted. His very life could be forfeit.'

'Cecily, the council will not allow Somerset's release. It is less than a month since he was committed to the Tower and they'll keep him there until the king recovers from his sickness. He has to answer for his crimes.'

'What if the king's sickness continues?'

My mother shook her head. 'He must surely recover soon. It goes against the laws of nature for a sickness to last so long.'

'And while the king is lost in a fog of his own making, the country goes to rack and ruin. The wool-price has collapsed again, coin is in short supply and everywhere, farmland is lying idle. It is no wonder the people of Kent rioted.'

'That was three years ago, Cecily. And it did your husband no favours when the commons named him as the man they wanted for their king.'

'My husband has sworn an oath of loyalty to Henry. What more can he do?'

'Be more humble,' said my mother tartly.

Aunt Cecily laughed. 'The duke of York is in no wise a humble man. He is proud and I am proud to be his duchess.'

Aunt Cecily might have been inflamed with pride but my mother was no fool.

'Counsel your husband to be patient, Cecily. Too much impatience will likely be injurious to any hope he has of regaining royal favour.'

'When the king recovers.'

'As you say – when the king recovers.'

'In the meantime the country falls apart. Look at your sons! Taking the law into their own hands because the king would not rule and the queen saw no need. And your poor daughters! Attacked on Heworth Moor and left for dead.'

'Nobody was left for dead,' said my mother. 'My daughters were unharmed, merely shaken.'

But Aunt Cecily was not to be deterred. 'I tell you, the earl of Devon and Lord Bonville were near to killing each

72

other before my husband stepped in to restore order. The West Country was in flames, bands of armed men laying waste to their neighbours' lands and good men being attacked in their houses. Yet the duke got no thanks for his actions. Instead the king paraded around our castle at Ludlow demonstrating how little he thought of his cousin of York.'

'He is the king, Cecily. He may parade where he likes. There are a great many who believe he should show himself more, not hide in his palaces listening to his queen.'

Aunt Cecily dabbed her eyes. 'I wish the council would see sense and let my husband rule.'

'Be assured the council knows of only two suitable candidates: your husband and the duke of Exeter. I doubt they'll let Harry Holland anywhere near the reins of power.'

'I curse the day we married our Nan to that scoundrel,' spat Aunt Cecily.

My mother sighed. 'You chose him for his royal kinship, Cecily. Remember?'

'Indeed, but I believed he would improve with age. Unfortunately he is as unpleasant and grasping now as he ever was.'

'Nevertheless, if the council see sense, all will be well.'

My mother patted Aunt Cecily's arm and said what a lovely young woman her daughter had become.

But Aunt Cecily was not to be diverted. 'What if the king should not recover? What if he were to die? What then?'

A sliver of silence slid between them as the question of "Who next?" raised its ugly head again. Alice had once said it would be a choice between the duke of Exeter, the duke of York, or – God forbid! – the duke of Somerset. But that was before the queen gave birth to the baby prince.

'Cecily, the king has twice refused to make your husband his heir and now he has a son of his own.'

'The men would not accept a two-month old babe.'

'If you mean what I think you mean, I do not wish to hear,' said my mother sharply.

Aunt Cecily's voice was low so that not even one of the duke of Somerset's spies could have heard what she was saying. 'My husband has no designs on the throne but you know as well as I do that he has more right to it than Henry.'

My mother glanced into the shadows to see if anyone was there but there was only me, sitting quietly at her feet pretending to be deaf. 'That is dangerous talk, Cecily.'

'Not as dangerous as allowing Somerset out of the Tower. He'll not forgive those who put him there and your husband's life will be forfeit as well as my husband's.'

'If you talk like this it will be your life forfeit as well.'

My aunt shrugged. 'Your Montagu grandfather lost his head defending England's rightful king. It was King Richard's throne and Henry of Lancaster stole it.'

I stuffed my hand in my mouth to prevent me from gasping. Aunt Cecily must have forgotten I was there or she would never have said such a thing.

'Cecily, It was a long time ago. No-one remembers those days any more. The king's grandfather was the rightful king. God's blessing was given on the battlefield at Shrewsbury.'

'He had no right to the crown. His reign was cursed from the beginning as was the reign of his son. They died diseased, marked, and abandoned by God. The Lancastrian claim to England's throne was based on a falsehood and what greater proof do we need than this latest sign of God's displeasure? A man who cannot even recognise his own son; a man struck dumb like one of the beasts in the field, who voids himself where he sits, unable to move his limbs.'

Aunt Cecily's face had become flushed and she was quivering with anger

'That is enough, Cecily,' said my mother firmly. 'You are talking treason and I shall not listen. Tell your husband to cool his temper. I understand his grievances. Dear God, have not all of us been ignored while the riches of the kingdom were poured into the hands of Edmund Beaufort and his friends, but this is not the way forward.'

I knew about the royal connections of Aunt Cecily's husband. Edward had once boasted of his father's importance and Alice had gone to great lengths to explain why the duke of York called himself the king's cousin.

The king was descended, through his father and grandfather, from old King Edward's third son, while the duke was descended from the fourth son. But the grandmother of the duke's mother had been the only child of King Edward's *second* son.

'Of course there will be many who say a man cannot claim the throne through his mother,' Alice had said. 'But our father's title of earl of Salisbury came from our mother's father so why should a man's right to the throne be different?'

Alianore and I knew the names of all our forebears and at night in bed we would whisper them to each other.

And to make the whispering more exciting we would be sure to mention our royal connections.

'Our Nevill grandmother was a daughter of old King Edward's third son,' Alianore would say proudly.

'And our mother's Holand grandfather was the princess's son.'

As always at the mention of the princess we gave a little sigh. The princess was a figure of such mystery it was hard to know what was true about her life and what was myth. Fabulously beautiful, she had married the prince who had captured the king of France in battle, but before that she had been married to another man, one who was the love of her life – or so Alice said. Perhaps there were other marriages but nobody knew for certain. Some said three and some said as many as five.'

'Five husbands!' Alianore would murmur, her eyes gleaming in the shadows across the pillow. 'Think of the jewels and the furs they'd give you.'

'Who would you have? If you could choose, which of course you can't, but if you could.'

Alianore never hesitated. 'I'd have a duke, if one was free. If not I'd take his heir.'

'Well you can't have Edward because I've chosen him so you'll have to choose someone else,' I said firmly.

And so we would carry on until sleep slowed our whisperings and gradually closed our eyes. But all night long the beautiful princess and her five husbands danced merrily through my dreams and on waking I would whisper to myself, 'Edward is the love of my life.'

5

TUXFORD 1454

The two Nevill servants spent a great deal of time securing the larger of Maud's chests with ropes and then carrying it down the stairs. At every doorway they put down their load and stood scratching their heads, wondering how to manoeuvre such an unwieldy object through the narrow gap. I followed them into the courtyard saw them heave the chest onto the tailboard of one of the wagons. It was heavy work but the older one said it kept him warm as it was mortal cold.

'Where are they going?' I asked, curious because no-one had mentioned leaving.

'Middleham,' he said shortly. 'Seems the Lady Maud is anxious to rejoin her husband. Sir Thomas will be that pleased.'

'About time,' said his friend, rubbing his hands together and stamping his feet on the ground. 'No good comes of keeping man and wife apart.'

'Am I going?'

'Don't know, m'lady. Best ask the countess. No-one said nothing 'bout your chest.'

I ran back up the stairs to my mother's rooms and almost fell over Uncle Fauconberg who was loitering in the doorway. I bobbed a curtsey and gave him a huge smile.

'My favourite niece!' he said. 'Would that they were all as pretty as you, my little Yorkshire rose.'

I giggled and then remembered Maud's advice on the correct way to receive a compliment and gave a vague little smile and thanked him for his kind words.

Up went an eyebrow. 'Lessons in flirtation, already, young Kathryn?'

I blushed. 'I have to find a husband, my lord uncle. My sisters say I must acquire the necessary skills.'

'Of course you must. Oh how I wish I was twenty years younger and not your kinsman!'

That made me blush even more which made Uncle Fauconberg laugh.

'Come with me,' he said, tucking my hand into the crook of his arm. 'I seek the whereabouts of the lovely Lady Maud and I choose you as my harbinger. How say you if I pay my respects to your lady mother while you prepare Lady Maud for my arrival? Can you do that?'

I nodded. 'May I tell her the purpose of your visit?'

He touched the side of his nose and grinned. 'Let it be a surprise.'

Maud was sitting in a window embrasure, reading. She looked up at my approach and smiled.

'I am to tell you my uncle is coming to see you,' I said.

Maud leaned forward and glanced up the room to where my mother was talking to Uncle Fauconberg. 'What does he want?'

'He said it was a surprise.'

Maud closed the book and placed it firmly in her lap.

'Shall I leave you alone?'

'Certainly not. A meeting with Lord Fauconberg requires a shield.'

I grinned. 'He likes you.'

'I know he does but I am a married woman and the games Lord Fauconberg wishes to play no longer interest me.'

'What games?'

'You'll see.'

I watched my uncle walk across the room to where Maud sat. He looked enquiringly at me and gave an almost imperceptible jerk of his head.

'He is telling you to go,' murmured Maud, 'but I need you to stay.'

'Lady Maud has requested a companion,' I said to my uncle by way of explanation.

'Has she?' he said sliding onto the seat next to Maud.

'She has,' replied Maud. 'I would have her armed if I could.'

'Cruel words from one so fair.'

'Wise words from one who has learned from her experiences.'

'And what is it that you have learned, my lady?'

'That some men are not to be trusted.'

My uncle laughed. 'You were not so averse to men when I first knew you, my lady. Where did you acquire those darts you now aim with such accuracy at my lonely self?'

'Lonely!' said Maud. 'That is not what I hear.'

'All else is distraction, a vain attempt to forget the sorrow that eats away at my heart and destroys my sleep.'

My head was turning from one to the other trying to follow their conversation. It was an odd sort of exchange and I was uncertain what it meant.

Maud eyed my uncle carefully. 'My lord, if you have something to say I will listen but I would urge you to be brief.'

Uncle Fauconberg leaned over and told me to cover my ears. 'I do not want your lady mother to chase me from her rooms for corrupting her daughter.'

'But if I do that, my lord uncle, she will know you are saying words that you should not.'

He stroked his beard. 'True, So how do I go on?'

'I think you must tell Lady Maud why you have come.'

'But every time I see her my thoughts scatter to the winds and I am left a poor dumb creature.'

'That cannot be, my lord uncle, or you would be unable to speak at all.'

He laughed and turned to Maud. 'You have taught her well, my lady.'

Maud shrugged. 'She needs to learn. And now my lord. Why *are* you here?'

He sighed. 'I hear you leave tomorrow.'

'I do, I wish to return to my husband.'

'A fortunate man,' murmured my uncle.

'A worthy man.'

'Does he treat you well?'

'He is energetic,' I said, wanting to make sure that Uncle Fauconberg understood how good a husband Tom was. 'Lady Maud said so.'

For a moment neither of them spoke and then Uncle Fauconberg began to laugh. He seized my hands and kissed me on both cheeks. 'Stay just as you are, my little rose. Promise me you will not change.'

'Did I say something wrong?'

'No,' said Maud, gently. 'Not at all.'

My uncle wiped his eyes and pulled his face into a

semblance of seriousness. 'I am sorry you are leaving, my lady but not for the reason you might think.'

'Indeed.'

'It has come to my ears that the duke of Exeter is making plans. You know Harry Holland?'

'I have heard of his grace.'

'And what have you heard?'

'That he is an unpleasant individual.'

'And a dangerous one. Unpredictable and violent. He is angry the council have not considered him for the role of protector and swears they have taken against him. He tells anyone who will listen that he has more right than his father-in-law.'

'Does he?' I asked.

My uncle shrugged. 'Perhaps, but he is not suitable. They will choose the duke of York.'

'And what will Lord Exeter do?' said Maud.

'There are rumours, but that is all they are. I have no proof.'

'Rumours of what?'

'A rebellion.'

'Mother of God!' Maud's hand flew to her mouth.

'If you must return to Yorkshire I would beg you to take the greatest of care on the road. I have told my brother but he thinks I exaggerate. Maybe I do, but I am uneasy. In the king's service I hear things my brother does not and there is a great deal of unrest, not just at Westminster but out in the country. It needs only one man to strike a spark for there to be a conflagration.'

That evening my mother said Alianore and I must leave London immediately as the city was no longer safe. Soon men would return for the parliament at Westminster and every lord would bring with him scores if not hundreds of armed men. There was bound to be trouble. She had arranged for Alianore to return to Maxstoke with Aunt Stafford whilst I was to accompany Maud to Middleham and from thence I would go to Ravensworth, to my sister Alice. My mother would travel with my father and our brother, Richard to Caversham.

The days are short in January and our party travelled slowly as the going was hard. The road was rutted and in places frozen into great ridges. My horse was unhappy with the uneven surface and it was only by following Maud's steady mount that I managed to keep mine moving. When a wheel slid into a hole causing our wagon to tip over with a great crash, the old mare shied in fright and nearly unseated me. After that Maud ordered one of the men to ride beside me.

At the priory where we stopped that first night the lay brother who opened the gate smiled with pleasure at the sight of two well-born ladies and their entourage. He showed us to a little white-washed cell where Maud and I were to sleep. At supper the monks fed us a delicate fish I didn't recognise, some pottage, a salty cheese from Essex and huge chunks of bread. We washed our meal down with ale brewed by one of the monks who was said to have some skill in the matter. In the morning, well-rested and well-fed, I was almost sorry to leave.

The next day we made better progress. There were not many travellers but those we met would stop and ask had we heard aught of the king.

'Word is he's took fearful sick,' said an elderly merchant. 'They say the queen has fled to France.'

'Aye,' said his companion. 'Duke of York's planning his coronation.'

'Nay,' said the first one. 'It be Somerset and he'll slit the throats of any that oppose him.'

The further we journeyed from London the wilder the stories became: the king was dead; the queen had held the hand of the duke of Somerset and promised she would marry him; the baby prince was no more, dropped into the river in a sack.

'Don't believe a word,' Maud said as we prepared for bed in a wayside priory near the little town of Grantham. 'They're only tales told to frighten children and simple folk. Tomorrow we cross the Trent at Newark. I've sent word ahead to my mother that we shall stop at Tuxford. She will be delighted to see you again.'

'Will your sister be there?' I enquired, thinking I would like to see more of Maud's fair-haired sister.

'No, she is visiting my Aunt Cromwell who is sick. My mother is alone and will value our company all the more. She dislikes the long empty months of winter.'

Next afternoon we rode through the village of Tuxford with our escort riding at our back. Tuxford was only a small place with a dozen houses clustered round a crossroads, a church, an alehouse and a slow-running stream.

'My mother does very well here,' said Maud. 'The villagers have a weekly market and once a year there is a fair. It is a good place. We moved here after my father died and my mother has no desire to go elsewhere. She says she may be a Cromwell by birth but is a Stanhope by marriage and by inclination.'

The manor house where the dowager Lady Stanhope lived was set a little way back from the road behind a high wall. It was a low building, grey and unprepossessing with a small tower at one end and few windows. The single-storey gatehouse had two creaking wooden doors and beyond was a tiny courtyard.

'Where will the men sleep?' I said looking around at the meagre number of stables and two other outbuildings.

'They'll manage,' said Maud. 'If there's not enough space in the guardhouse there's always room in the village. The ale house has a large barn and is very accommodating; they're well used to passing travellers.'

We dismounted and waited while a couple of stable lads led our horses away. I looked round the courtyard and wondered how odd it must be to live in a place which was so small.

Maud frowned. 'My mother has company. Look! Strange horses, good quality ones. Surely not my Uncle Cromwell.'

An elderly man hobbled down the steps. He was Lady Stanhope's steward and Maud greeted him like a long-lost friend.

'Who's here?' she said.

'Fine folk,' he grinned. 'A duke and a lord. Come to take a cup of wine with the mistress, or so they say.'

'But?'

'They arrived separately. My belief is they be up to some mischief, so you be careful, m'lady. I don't trust neither of them.'

'And you would know, wouldn't you, Matthew?'

The old man smiled, showing a mouth lacking most of its teeth. 'Served your father. Seen many a piece of scum in my time. He was no saint, your father, God bless him, but you know that. His friends were the same. Bad lot, most of them. I learned to smell 'em out.'

'And these two don't smell right?'

'No more they do, m'lady.'

'I see my prayers to St Apollonia on your behalf have done no good.'

The old man chuckled. 'Came into this world toothless, reckon I'll leave it same way.'

Maud laughed. 'If you lead we'd better go and see who these lordly folk are.'

We followed the old man's unsteady progress across the hall, a candlestick clutched in his wavering hand. He climbed the stone stairs to the family's private quarters accompanied by much coughing and wheezing. At the top he opened the door and peered in. The room was poorly lit with only a single branch of candles on a table near the door but the fire gave out a pleasing glow which went some way to dispel the shadows.

There were two men in the room and no sign of Lady Stanhope. One man had his back to us, the other I recognised immediately as Cousin Nan's husband, Harry Holland, duke of Exeter. The duke was dressed in a rich green doublet with a swathe of glossy dark fur round his shoulders. He was not handsome but a well setup young man with a clear skin and for a moment I almost envied Cousin Nan. Then I noticed his weak mouth and his mean expression. He scowled at the interruption but when he noticed Maud and me standing in the doorway his eyes gleamed.

He beckoned us forward with an imperious wave of his hand and said loudly to his companion, 'I see we're being supplied with company for the night and not your usual north country sluts. Which one's to your taste, Egremont?'

His friend turned round and my heart dropped like a stone into my belly.

It was the Percy lord from Heworth Moor!

Into that well of horror came the sound of a woman's footsteps, the curtain at the far end of the solar was drawn back and Lady Stanhope came hurrying across the floor. I grasped at something I knew how to do and dropped a curtsey deeper than was strictly necessary but one which hid my face from the Percy lord.

Maud's mother clasped her daughter in her arms. 'My dear, what a pleasure! The roads so bad, I wasn't sure you'd make it tonight. And little Kathryn! Grown up and prettier than ever. Welcome child, welcome to Tuxford. We're not grand like Tattershall but our welcome is as warm.' She smiled confidingly. 'My brother boasts many smart rooms but I prefer the quiet of my own hearth. Now, before I forget my manners completely, come and meet my other guests.'

She linked arms with us both and drew us forward.

'His grace, the duke of Exeter.'

Nan's husband watched carefully as we curtsied low enough for his rank. He gave a small nod of approval.

'My daughter Maud, Lady Willoughby, now Lady Nevill and her sister-in-law Kathryn, the earl of Salisbury's daughter.'

The duke gave a bark of laughter and turned to the figure of a woman sitting silently in the shadows. She'd been so still I'd not noticed her before.

'Up, madam! Get yourself over here before I'm forced to remind you of your duty.'

The woman crept forward, keeping her head lowered and her hands crossed over her chest as if hugging a shawl for warmth.

The duke put out his hand and gripped her arm, squeezing it tightly. With his other hand he grasped her chin and jerked her head up so that I could see her face.

I gave a gasp. It was Cousin Nan!

'Come madam. Greet your cousin. Tell her how content you are in your new estate.'

Nan mumbled a greeting.

'Louder!' hissed the duke.

She looked at me out of a pair of eyes brimming with tears and stammered, 'Greetings, C-Cousin Kathryn.'

Her husband gave her arm a vicious twist. 'You're not finished, madam.'

'Greetings, Lady Maud.'

Maud's face was impassive but her hands gripped the folds of her cloak as if she longed to strike the duke. A woman was helpless in a situation like this and these men would not have come alone. Somewhere, perhaps in the outbuildings or in a barn in the village there'd be Percy henchmen and servants of the duke of Exeter. They'd be fingering their weapons and sharpening their knives just as the men from the alleyways of York had done on Heworth Moor.

Maud said calmly, 'How thoughtful of your grace and your good lady to visit my mother.'

Harry Holland laughed. 'Sheets are damp, wine's cat's piss, but the prospects are brighter now we have company.' He turned to me. 'You fledged yet?'

I was so nervous I had no idea what he meant.

'My sister-in-law is a little young for your attentions, your grace,' said Maud firmly.

Nan's husband wiped his hand across his mouth and leered at me. 'No such thing as too young. You fourteen?'

'No, your grace'

'My wife here's fourteen. Should have been mine at twelve. Her father kept her from me. Said she was too young, not ready for marriage. But I'll show him who's master now.'

The duke was drunk. The wine might be sour and the candles only recently lit but he'd taken more than enough to fill his belly. His speech was slurred and with a shiver I remembered Nan's words – "he's cruel and says he'll beat me." From the look of her she'd suffered more than one beating at her husband's hands.

'You wed?'

'N-no, your grace,' I stammered.

'Pretty little thing. If I'd not been forced to wed my dear wife here, I could have had you. Your father would've welcomed the connection. What d'you say to that?'

He took a step closer and I thought for a terrible moment he would take hold of me. Lady Stanhope's home no longer seemed safe but a place of great danger where anything could happen. There was no man in the house to whom the duke was answerable and no-one, other than the Percy lord at his elbow, to stop him. There were laws and codes of good behaviour but I doubted Harry Holland took notice of them. He walked in a darker world, one devoid of any rules but his own, a world where no woman was safe.

'And this is Lord Egremont,' said Lady Stanhope as I dropped a shallow curtsey. 'I believe he is known to your husband, daughter?'

Maud returned the Percy lord's bold stare without blinking.

'I believe he is, my lady, though what my husband thinks of Lord Egremont I couldn't say or leastways not in your presence.'

Lord Egremont turned his gaze on me. I remembered what Maud had told me and raised my chin, trying not to look as if my legs were trembling beneath my gown.

'And this is Lady Maud's sister-in-law, Kathryn, daughter of the earl of Salisbury.'

The cruel mouth relaxed into a smile and he nodded to me. 'We meet once more, little lady.'

'You know Lord Egremont?' Lady Stanhope seemed startled.

'A brief acquaintance, my lady. I'd not thought to repeat it,' I muttered.

'And yet here we are again.' Lord Egremont smiled at my discomfort in the way he'd done that day on the moor.

'Where are you bound, my lord?' I said as calmly as I could manage even though my tongue felt rooted to the top of my mouth. 'I doubt you plan to winter in Tuxford?'

He gave a roar of laughter. 'That depends. If you are here, my young friend, perhaps I will avail myself of Lady Stanhope's continued hospitality. As to where I'm bound?' He leaned forward until I could feel the heat of his wine-sodden breath on my face. 'That depends on who wants to know.'

Nan's husband glared at his companion. 'Have a care, Egremont. Women can't keep their mouths shut. They babble like whores on a quarter day.'

Lady Stanhope looked fondly at Maud.

'Matthew has ordered your old room made ready for tonight, daughter. You'll be comfortable there, the two of you. The servants will have brought in your boxes and sent up the hot water. Go and change out of those dusty clothes and by the time you're back there'll be a bite to eat. Just a little cold meat and some bread. And some pears. Nothing to lie heavy on the stomach.'

Maud led me out of the door, through an archway, down two steps and then up a dozen more into a little room tucked under the rafters which she'd once shared with her sister. There was a smell of musty thatch and occasional rustlings above my head which I feared might be mice. The room was big enough for a bed, a small chest and a single stool and not much more.

Our maid, who had been hiding in the kitchen, poured water into a bowl out of one of Lady Stanhope's heavy enamelled ewers. The water had probably been hot when it left the kitchen but by the time the man who'd carried the ewer had crossed the hall, dallied for a while gossiping with our maid and then climbed the stairs and set the ewer down on the chest, the contents were cold. With much shivering and grimacing we rubbed our faces and made ourselves as presentable as we could in the confined space. Once we were dressed in clean gowns and had exchanged our riding boots for our slippers, we went slowly back to the solar.

'Don't leave me alone,' I pleaded.

Maud shook her head. 'I shan't do that. But the sooner we eat, the sooner we can escape. I don't care for either of those men. I'd like to be out of here by daybreak no matter that it will distress my mother.'

A couple of elderly servants, older even than the steward, Matthew, had laid a cloth on the table and were putting out knives and plates and goblets. Lady Stanhope bade us take our places while her chaplain, a white-haired man with a stooped back, shuffled to the table, mumbled some Latin words and then fell on the food as if he'd been fasting for a week.

The meal was interminable and at every mouthful I felt the eyes of one or other of the men watching me. Lord Egremont's manners were acceptable but the duke behaved like a kitchen knave, grabbing the best bits of capon in the way of a small child and dipping his food in the salt. Alice would have slapped me if I'd behaved in such a way.

Throughout the meal the dowager Lady Stanhope gossiped. 'We heard the king was dead,' she said confidentially before munching her way through a mouthful of cold meat, then continued. 'A man passing through the village said all London was afire with the news.' She smiled at the duke of Exeter. 'But his grace here says the king merely sleeps.'

'Ha!' said Harry Holland, his elbow on the table and his knife held aloft. 'Sleeping. Dead to the world like an old man in his cups and doubtless my father-in-law's fingers somewhere in the contriving of it.'

'There's those say it is the French queen's doing,' said Lady Stanhope.

'I do not think that can be so,' said Maud.

'You think a woman incapable of such a deed?' enquired Lord Egremont silkily.

'I think a woman who has just given birth to a prince is not likely to harm the child's father. Her position depends on the king. Without him she is weak.'

'All women are weak,' laughed Harry Holland. 'It is the curse of their sex. Men are strong and wield power; women are feeble and must serve men. It is the position designed for them by God. And by man.'

The elderly chaplain mumbled something in Latin, dabbing his mouth with a napkin to cover a surreptitious belch.

'What did you say, old man?' said the duke.

'*Absentem laedit cum ebrio qui litigat*,' repeated the chaplain.

The duke looked blank. He was clearly not conversant in the language of the church.

'He does not wish to quarrel with you, your grace, as he fears you have drunk too much,' said Maud, half-smiling.

Lord Egremont laughed and slapped his hand on the table. 'Well said, old man!'

'Old fool!' muttered the duke.

'A merchant bound for Leicester swore the duke of York had killed the duke of Somerset and thrown his body into the Thames,' prattled on Lady Stanhope.

'He would if he could,' said Lord Egremont. 'Somerset's days will be short if the council name York as protector.'

'York's days are numbered already.' Harry Holland glared at Nan. 'Before the summer's out I'll have his head on a spike on Micklegate.'

A dog lying under the table yelped as Lord Egremont aimed a kick at his friend.

'I see it's not just whores who blab,' he hissed.

Throughout all this Nan sat mute, barely touching her food, her head bent and her eyes looking miserably at her plate. This was no life for a wife and I wished Alianore was here to witness how a duchess lived if her husband was a man like Harry Holland.

'Strange bedfellows, the duke of Exeter and Lord Egremont,' remarked Maud later, once we were safely alone. 'I wonder what they're planning.'

'Are they planning something?'

'For sure. Did you not notice how the duke silenced Lord Egremont when he thought he might tell you where they were going? And how Lord Egremont later rebuked the duke.'

'A woman at Westminster called the duke a rotten apple. She said he was no respecter of the king's law.'

'No more he is. A year or two back he seized one of my Uncle Cromwell's properties claiming it as his own.'

'Was it?'

'No, it was my uncle's. However the duke had powerful friends. They were persuaded of the justness of his cause, and not content with accusing my uncle of treason they tried to kill him.'

My mouth dropped open and I gaped at Maud, speechless with surprise.

'They almost succeeded so now my uncle is afraid to go to abroad without a strong guard at his back.'

'You think this is another plot against Lord Cromwell?'

'No, I believe it is something much bigger. Lord Fauconberg warned me about the duke of Exeter.'

I bit my lip. 'My father doubted my uncle's warning but he cannot doubt what we've witnessed here tonight.'

'No he cannot and in the morning I shall send him a letter. However, first we must discover more about what the duke and Lord Egremont are planning.'

'We could ask Cousin Nan.'

Maud looked at me soberly. 'Your cousin is terrified of her husband. She'll tell you nothing.'

'Does he hit her?'

'Worse than that.'

I didn't ask what worse might mean because I was a coward and didn't want to know.

Maud went over to the tiny window and pulled down the shutter. She climbed onto a stool and poked her head through the narrow opening. Cold air from outside streamed into the room.

'What are you doing?' I asked, shivering.

'Making sure things are as I remember.'

'Are they?'

'Yes. My mother will put her guests in the chamber at the back of the hall. There's a window which gives onto the orchard. It is shuttered but the shutters are ill-fitting and if you go close you can hear every word said in the room. My sister and I spied on our father's friends in that way.'

'But what if one of the men were to see us creeping out through the hall?'

'We shan't go through the hall. There's another way. We'll go out through this window and climb down. There's an apple tree grown against the wall.'

I'd not climbed a tree since I was a little girl and was not sure if I could remember how.

'Could we not listen at the door?'

'No, it's twice as thick as any other door in the house. You could scream all night in there and no-one would hear. And what if you were discovered with your ear to the door?'

Maud began squeezing herself through the window. She wriggled and twisted but it was no good. Her shoulders were too wide and the window too narrow,

'You'll get stuck,' I said, pulling on her arm and trying not to think of Nan screaming in fear with no-one coming to her rescue.

'You have to go,' Maud said hauling herself back into the room and jumping down from the stool.

'I can't.'

'You have to. You're smaller than me. Here, give me your hand.'

'What about my skirts?'

'Tuck them into your belt. No wait. I've a better idea.'

She lifted up the lid of the chest which stood in the corner and rummaged around inside.

'Here! This will do. Matthew took it from one of the boys for my sister to wear.'

She held up a shapeless brown tunic made from coarse cloth, the kind of garment a servant might wear. I looked at it in horror.

'Do I have to?'

'Yes. We need more information.'

Deftly Maud removed my belt, bundled me out of my gown and pulled the heavy tunic over my head. I must have looked a fool. She regarded me critically then retied the belt.

'I can't go out like this,' I protested. 'Someone might see me?'

'Nobody will see you. It's winter. No-one's in the orchard and if you keep hard against the wall you'll be almost invisible.'

I hesitated.

'Go on! Get yourself out. Legs first. Feel with your toes for that solid-looking branch just below the window and keep tight hold of the window's edge until you're steady.'

Gingerly I climbed onto the stool and, holding, first the bed rail and then the edge of the window, wriggled myself through the opening on my stomach. I flailed around with my feet allowing myself to slide further and further out until my toes touched something hard and rutted. Whatever it was gave a little with my weight and I guessed this must be the solid-looking branch. With my right hand I groped around for something to hold on to. By now my eyes had become accustomed to the dark and I could just make out the shape of the gnarled old tree leaning against the wall. I was in the middle of a tangle of bare branches and there was one level with my shoulder which looked stout enough. I grasped it and gave a tug, hoping it wouldn't break. With a feeling of impending dread I removed my left hand and let go of the window's edge.

I was stranded in the middle of an ancient tree with only my wits to help me. Maud could do nothing. Sliding one hand and then the other and shifting my feet slowly one at a time, I gradually moved closer and closer to what appeared to be a slightly stouter branch. Part of the tree must have been cut back because glancing into the gloom below my feet there appeared to be a gap with a couple of footholds lower down.

'Don't look down!' instructed Maud's voice above me. 'Just feel with your feet and your hands. It's not far, even if you fall.'

That was not a comforting thought but I did as I was told and bit by bit continued to clamber through the space between the branches until Maud's face was nothing more than a pale shape almost hidden by the criss-crossed limbs of the tree. An owl hooted close by and I almost fell the last few feet. I grasped something rough and scaly which turned out to be part of the trunk. But by then I could see the base of the tree. With a feeling of relief I half-fell, half-tumbled as I slithered onto the ground.

I looked about me. Short-cropped grass stretched out pale and ghostly in the moonlight but, like the dousing of a candle, the sliver of moon soon disappeared and the orchard was plunged into darkness. All I could see now were three tall black trunks and beyond them the wavering line of a wicker fence. Above me were the tangled branches of the apple tree and the candlelit window where Maud would be waiting for my return. To my left was the looming mass of a building, probably part of the courtyard. To my right the wall of the house slid away into a greater darkness. Half-way along were what appeared to be bars of light about four feet off the ground. I guessed this was the shuttered window Maud had spoken of.

Using both hands I inched my way along the wall clutching the rough stones so that I didn't stumble. The grass was crisp with frost but although I could hear the slight crunch of my feet on the ground the noise could not be loud enough for anyone else to hear. The bars of light were dim and as I came nearer the shape became definitely that of a window. I peered out into the darkness of the orchard but nothing moved. I could hear rustlings and slitherings and other little noises which I guessed were the movements of small animals.

At last I was almost beneath the shuttered window. Inside I could hear the murmur of voices. Two men. I moved closer.

'They swore an oath,' I gasped. 'I heard them.'

'Why would they swear an oath?' said Maud, helping me struggle out of the hated tunic.

'They have agreed to support each other.'

'In what?'

I examined my hands which were covered in scratches from my fight with the branches and were beginning to hurt.

'They fear Uncle York will be named protector. If that happens the duke will summon his men from Lancashire and Cheshire and also his tenantry from Bedfordshire. He says he will raise his standard and claim the right to rule England.'

Maud turned very pale. 'Was there more?'

'Yes. Lord Egremont swore him to join with the Percy brothers and their allies to attack the city of York. They intend to kill my father. They will also kill the duke of York and your Uncle Cromwell if they dare to show their faces in Yorkshire.'

Maud was silent. Our maid came with a small bowl of water which she placed on the chest before scuttling out. Maud retrieved a bottle from her box and emptied a few drops of dark brown liquid into the water. Using a strip of cloth, she bathed my bruised knuckles and the palms of my hands removing every trace of dirt and grit and dried blood.

'There!' she said, handing me an old drying sheet. 'Did they say from where they would make their attack?'

I shook my head. 'They mentioned the Percy manor of Spofforth. Do you know it?'

Maud nodded. 'Yes, it's on the road to York.'

'Did I do enough? I was so cold in just that tunic and without a cloak. I didn't dare stay longer. Besides they said they were for bed.'

Maud took me in her arms and hugged me. 'You did well. I am very proud of you. Now say your prayers and get under the covers and go to sleep.'

'What about you?'

'I shall sit up awhile. I have letters to write.'

In the end it all came to nothing. The duke of York was named Lord Protector by the council and his first move was to appoint my father as chancellor. The great seals of England were brought to The Erber and placed in my father's hands and my mother wrote that she wished I had been there to witness the ceremony. The Nevills were now tied securely to the Yorks because political favours like this bound a man more tightly than the ties of kinship or marriage. If my Uncle York's star rose, so did my father's. If he fell . But he wouldn't fall. The duke of York couldn't fall, Of that I was certain.

In the middle of May my mother wrote that Lord Stanley and Lord Bonville had been sent to Lancashire to subdue any rising in Exeter's name while the protector, his chancellor and the earl of Warwick were riding north. There had been attacks on my father's houses in the city of York and my uncle was determined to quell the rebellion in its infancy rather than allow it to flourish and grow. But there was no great uprising of men across the country clamouring for Harry Holland to be given the reins of power, merely a few sporadic outbreaks of violence which were easily put down. Alice said my father wanted the Percys punished, but it was in our Uncle York's interests to make peace between the warring lords of the north.

Sessions were held in Newcastle and York where the commissioners, headed by the protector and the earl of Warwick, heard detailed indictments against the forces of the Percy brothers and their ally, the duke of Exeter. However by the time they had deliberated, the Percy brothers had disappeared, the duke of Exeter had fled and the commissioners were not interested in punishing the followers, They wanted the principals.

'Lord Fitzhugh says Harry Holland is in London,' said Alice. 'Much good it will do him. He had no support in the council or in the country to oppose Uncle York. Those who mistrust Aunt Cecily's husband mistrust Harry Holland even more. It was a poor sort of rebellion fermented by a foolish young hothead who'd have done better to mend his relationship with his father-n-law.'

'I feel sorry for Nan,' I said/

'I doubt he is a good husband but she must make the best of it as we all must. It is the first lesson a girl learns: she marries where her family bids and does not complain.'

'And Alianore?'

Alice smiled and tapped the side of her nose. 'Alianore must wait and see and so must you.'

Harry Holland was found hiding in sanctuary in Westminster Abbey. Uncle York had him forcibly removed and despatched under guard to Pontefract. Alice and I were shocked at the breaking of sanctuary but knew our father, who was constable of Pontefract Castle, would relish the keeping of the rebellious Harry Holland.

The Percy brothers fared no better. On All Hallow's Eve, my brothers, Tom and John, completed the sweep of combined Nevill and York victories by capturing Lord Egremont and Richard Percy at Stamford Bridge. They were brought in chains to Middleham Castle and then sent to York for trial.

'Lord Egremont cannot pay the fine the court levied on him,' said Maud with a grin. 'He and his brother have been sent to London, to Newgate gaol. We are rid of him.'

Our battle against the Percy family was over and we Nevills had finally triumphed. As Tom had said to me on that long ride to Tattershall for his wedding, we truly were kings of the north.

6

CASTLE BAYNARD 1454-5

Our room high in the tower was bright with wedding preparations. Gone were the night demons who lurked in the shadowy corners and gone too were our childhood toys and games, consigned to obscurity in a small chest in a distant store room. The last of my sister's belongings were packed and all that remained were her travelling clothes hanging on the perch by the door and her riding boots placed neatly on the floor. From downstairs we could near roars of laughter from the Stanley contingent who had arrived late yesterday like an invading army eager to carry off their prize.

'Will you miss me?' asked Alianore.

'You know I will,' I said, as I poked the narrow cord through the last of the little eyelets and pulled the lacing tight.

'You can lower your arm.' I stood back and surveyed my handiwork. 'Is it comfortable?'

Alianore looked down at the curved seamless front and wriggled her shoulders. 'I thought I might feel trussed but I don't. Do I look alluring?'

I grinned. 'With breasts like yours you will be the most alluring bride to grace Middleham chapel for many a year.'

I was jealous of my sister's good fortune but tried to be glad for her. It was less than a month since she'd been brought back to Middleham to prepare for her wedding to Lord Stanley's son and heir. The measurements for the bridal clothes were taken and for three weeks the Nevill seamstresses were busy cutting and snipping and stitching to ensure my sister's gowns were ready.

'Thomas Stanley will suit me very well,' said Alianore, examining the sumptuous fur lining of her sleeves and the little ruffle of white silk at the neckline of her blue kirtle.

'It's very daring,' I remarked, surprised our mother had approved.

'It will ensure he notices me.'

'Does he like you?'

Her eyes gleamed. 'Oh yes, he likes me.'

'And you, do you like him?'

'I have the measure of him,' she said, smiling. 'Which is more important than mere liking.'

'Of course,' I said doubtfully. 'But you don't dislike him?'

'Why would I?'

I shrugged. 'I was thinking of Cousin Nan.'

'Of pouf! Cousin Nan doesn't deserve to be a duchess. If I had married Harry Holland...'

'You'd have a bruised mouth and your husband would be lying under guard in Pontefract Castle.'

Alianore twirled round. 'What do you think?'

'You look lovely,' I said, admiring the effect of the blue and gold against my sister's pale skin and fair hair.

'Of course I do. I'm a bride.'

She picked up the rich damask folds of her skirt and swept me a deep curtsey.

'Your grace,' she murmured, peeping up through her eyelashes.

'You plan on meeting Margaret of Anjou?' I was astonished because I'd heard nothing of the Stanleys being close to the king and queen.

'I plan on having my husband rise high in royal favour.'

'Well, don't forget me when you reach your lofty perch.'

Alianore giggled. 'If father hasn't found you a husband by the time I'm the queen's favourite lady, I'll see what I can do.'

A chill fluttered through my belly at the thought of having no husband. What would I do? I couldn't remain forever at Alice's beck and call and the thought of a life of prayer and self-denial behind the walls of a convent was too horrible to contemplate.

My sister placed her hand on my cheek. 'Don't worry, Kat. There will be a husband for you one day and he will be utterly perfect.'

I gave a small smile although I wasn't convinced.

'Did you hear about Lady Cromwell? Wasn't it dreadful? Do you think Lord Cromwell will remarry?'

Alianore put her hands up to her mouth to stifle her giggle so that no-one should hear. 'What if a new wife were to give him a son?' she whispered. 'What hope would there be then for Maud's inheritance? Can you imagine how angry Tom would be?'

'Ali?'

'Yes.'

'This is the last time we shall be together like this, just you and me. Always before when you've gone away you've come back but this time it will be forever. After today you won't be a Nevill any more, you'll be a Stanley. You will write, won't you?'

She put her arms around me and, ignoring her wonderful wedding clothes and the risk of crushing the precious fabrics, she held me close.

'I cannot imagine how it will be but I shan't forget you, Kat. And yes, I *will* write.'

I had promised myself I wouldn't cry so I blinked away my tears.

'You have been the best of sisters.'

'And you will always be my little Katkin. But the years of servitude to our mother and Aunt Stafford are ended and it's time for the taming of Thomas Stanley.'

Once the wedding celebrations were over and Thomas Stanley had proudly assumed his ownership of Alianore, I had only Margaret to keep me company and, truth to tell, she was no company at all. So I was not sad to leave Middleham. We were to travel to London for the Nativity celebrations. Alice would remain at Ravensworth, unwilling to leave her youngest child who was ailing and Maud had already gone to Tuxford. The unexpected news of her mother's death meant abandoning her plans to travel with us and she hurried south with only half her chests, leaving the others unpacked. She was accompanied by Tom who was anxious to secure his wife's inheritance before it was stolen by anyone else. The manor of Tuxford was not rich and Maud's mother held only a third share in the estate but Maud had confided to me that her half of the small income would be very welcome.

Maud called Margaret my mother's little ewe lamb but I doubted there had ever been such a troublesome lamb in any flock and if there had, its mother would have abandoned it long since on some lonely fellside.

'Why is Maud not with us?' said Margaret, staring at our mother's women. who were riding in front of us.

'I told you why.'

'I've forgotten.'

I sighed. 'Lady Stanhope has died.'

'Why did Maud leave her chests behind?'

I leaned over and whispered,' If you don't stop asking questions I shall push you into the next river.'

After that we rode in silence.

Waiting to meet us at The Erber was our brother Richard and his wife who had come from their lodgings at Greyfriars.

Countess Anne smiled sweetly and greeted my mother in the way a daughter-in-law should, with deference. She was, I thought, under no illusions as to her value to our family and yet she was the kindest of creatures.

'Now that Alianore is wed you must hope to marry soon,' she said that evening when we found ourselves seated together waiting to be called for supper.

'I have hopes but I am nervous,' I replied, for once telling no more than the truth.

'Of what? Marriage is every young woman's destiny.'

'My husband will probably be someone I don't know. Maybe he will dislike me.'

'I doubt that. Of course Richard and I married when we were children so we had plenty of time to grow accustomed to one another. We thought to spend our life together in Yorkshire but my niece died, I became an heiress and everything changed.'

'Two years ago I longed to be an heiress,' I admitted, giving a rueful smile. ' I wanted to be like Maud and have hopes of inheriting great wealth. You'd have thought me very young and very foolish.'

Anne shook her head. 'To be an heiress is a mixed blessing. I never thought to inherit but my good fortune has set my sisters against me.'

'You have sisters?' I was surprised. Nobody had spoken of any Beauchamp sisters.

'Three. They are much older than me. Their mother was my father's first wife. It has been nearly five years and they are still squabbling, saying that what I have should be theirs.'

'It is the way with sisters,' I sighed. 'I think mine would squabble if I inherited a fortune.'

A week later we were joined at The Erber by Tom and Maud who had completed their business at Tuxford.

'I am not weeping for my mother,' explained Maud as she wiped the tears from her cheeks. 'She is safe in God's care.'

'Then why?' asked Anne.

'It is my uncle. He has . I cannot tell you it is too demeaning. I feel a fool.'

'We are your sisters now,' said Anne kindly. 'You can tell us.'

'Yes,' I agreed. 'We know you are far from being a fool.'

'Tom is furious. He says my uncle has behaved outrageously.'

'What has he done?' I asked, wondering what great iniquity Lord Cromwell could possibly have committed.

'He has rendered an account for the year I spent in his household.'

I gasped. Maud was his niece. Lord Cromwell owed her his care. To make her pay for her bread and board was outrageous.

'Every item of expenditure: candles, food, repairs for my shoes, even the cost of cloth for my maid's winter clothes. He expects me to pay for the privilege of being forced to shelter under his roof. It is shameful.'

Anne hissed with horror. 'And Lady Cromwell so lately in her grave.'

Maud sniffed miserably. 'My aunt would have been shocked to the core. She could not have imagined my uncle would behave in such an unchristian way.'

'What will you do?' I asked, wondering how much Lord Cromwell had asked for.

'Pay. What else can we do.'

'You could refuse.'

'I fear he might sue me through the courts. And besides, I am one of his heirs. I dare not anger him lest it prejudices my hopes of inheritance.'

That winter the duke of York in his role as protector of the realm played host to two great feasts. Everyone came to Castle Baynard, men of importance and those who wished to be important. My uncles were invited as were my brothers and dozens of my cousins. The duke of Norfolk, who was my father's nephew and known to hate the duke of Somerset, came with his wife and his two

Bourchier brothers-in-law. My mother said she had never seen Aunt Cecily look so grand: a different gown for every occasion, each one made of the richest of fabrics. Maud and I thought her robes owed their fullness and elegant fall of the sleeves to linings of silk and pured miniver but my mother swore it was lettice from the snow weasel.

'I'm surprised she doesn't use sable,' remarked Anne. 'The queen is said to favour the black variety and it has become very fashionable.'

'I think by using fur of the purest white Cecily is emphasising her allegiance to her husband's device of the white rose,' said my mother.

'Must we women now wear our husbands' liveries next to our skin?' laughed Maud.

'And with our fur trims?' said Anne. 'I have miniver for the trimming at the neckline and hem of my new gown. I must ask Richard if it meets with his approval.'

'Fur trims will be noticed by all,' said my mother, smiling, 'but it is only a husband who sees what warms your skin.'

There were plays and dancing and special Christmastide games but throughout the festivities Edward barely acknowledged me. It was as if I no longer existed. Edmund smiled when our eyes met across the hall but he remained stuck to Edward's side and neither of them came to pay their respects.

'What have I done?' I wailed.

'Nothing,' said Maud.

'But how do I get him to notice me?'

'Are you sure you want him to?'

I blushed. 'Yes. I like him.'

'Does he not like you?'

'I thought he did.'

I was sure that Maud, who had flirted with Uncle Fauconberg when she was young, must know how to attract a man. She took my hands in hers and made me sit beside her.

'There *are* ways to catch a man if that is your aim,' she said, 'but you must be clever; a certain amount of deception is required.'

'Deception?'

'You must let him think you do not care for him.'

'But I do.'

'That is why it is called a deception.'

She then explained exactly what I should do but warned me to be careful.

'Remember, you are not stalking a mouse but a young lion, and lions have sharp claws.'

I cared nothing for claws, all I cared about was Edward.

For two panic-stricken days I watched as Edward smiled and danced with a young woman. I thought my chance was lost but on the third day an opportunity presented itself. Edward and Edmund were standing with a group of young men by the hearth in the great hall where the yule log was still burning brightly.

I could hear Edward's voice from my position in the gallery where I was hidden from view. He was laughing at somebody's joke and boasting that he could do better. Taking a deep breath, and using every ounce of my courage, I picked up my skirts and began to go down the stairway. I didn't look to my left or to my right and I didn't look at the young men. I kept my chin up, my shoulders back and assumed an air of absolute indifference. I took small dainty steps, one delicately shod foot stepping in front of the other.

Once in the hall I walked very slowly and very deliberately past the little group without glancing at anyone. I wanted to turn to see if Edward had noticed me but willed myself to keep facing forwards. Behind me, the young men's voices became hushed and my heart began to beat faster but I didn't turn round.

'What now?' I asked Maud as I collapsed onto a chair in the safety of her room.

'Wait a while and then do it again.'

'Again?'

'Yes, but this time, just after you've walked past, glance over your shoulder and catch Edward's eye.'

'What if he's not looking?'

'Then you must do it for a third time. Sooner or later he will look. But remember, just a quick catching of his eye, nothing more. No smiling, no pausing, merely carry on as before.'

It took four attempts before Edward noticed me and on the last occasion, as we gathered for supper that evening, I felt his eyes follow me as I walked to my seat at the table.

'What shall I do?' I asked, catching up with Maud next morning as she walked to mass. 'He looked at me. He must care, mustn't he?'

'Keep away. Don't go near him, don't look at him and whatever you do, don't smile or speak to him.'

But…'

'Let him come to you.'

'What if he doesn't?'

'He will. Trust me. Just remember, this is a game and like all games there are rules. No meeting alone. Whatever is said or done must be in full view of others. No secret assignations. You have a reputation to protect.'

I was barely listening so intent was I on thinking about Edward.

'Did you hear what I said?' demanded Maud.

'Yes, yes, of course I did. You said there are rules.'

But in truth I didn't care about rules. What young woman does when she thinks herself in love?

Maud's plan might have worked if it had not been for the Twelfth Night festivities. She forgot the rowdy dancing and games and the forfeits demanded by the Lord of Misrule, the newly chosen lord for the day who could order us as he pleased. This was a family affair, just the Nevills and the Yorks and their closest friends. I had a sprig of holly in my hair and had already been swung into a carol by John Conyers. Everyone was laughing as the Lord of Misrule, masked so that no-one knew his identity and with a paper crown balanced precariously on his head, assumed his throne at the head of the hall.

'A forfeit for the duke!' shouted a voice from the back.

Uncle York frowned, misliking the thought of looking a fool.

'For Lord Salisbury!' announced the make-shift king in a shrill voice. 'To kiss his wife.'

'No hardship,' called my father, laughing as he walked over to my mother, raised her from her seat and kissed her firmly on her mouth. It was no formal peck but a lingering kiss from a man who loved his wife.

My mother blushed and smiled at my father as the cheering in the hall rose to the rafters.

'Another!' someone shouted and my father put his arms round my mother's waist and pulled her into an embrace and kissed her soundly.

'Is that what you wish for?' whispered Maud. 'A marriage like theirs.'

'Yes,' I breathed. 'Oh yes.'

I had never thought of my parents as people who had once been young like me but seeing them at that Twelfth Night celebration I knew I'd failed to notice them properly. Had my mother once felt for my father the way I felt for Edward? Had she too wanted to be noticed and loved and cherished? It barely seemed possible but here was the evidence right in front of my eyes.

The minstrels took up their instruments and once more I was in a dancing circle with other young people, leaping, tossing our heads and singing loudly. The music became faster and wilder until I was shouting with laughter like the others and my hair had come loose.

'Forfeit for all young men who are as yet unwed. Kiss the girl you like best!' shouted the voice from the top of the hall. Before I knew what was happening, someone had grabbed my sleeve, pushed me into the shadows behind one of the pillars and a young man's lips were pressed onto mine. I thought for a moment it was Edward but it was only Edmund. The kiss, if you could call it that, was only a boy's kiss. I knew the difference because Alianore had told me how grown men kiss and it was not like this. Edmund kissed with his lips closed.

'Stop it, Edmund!' I said, pushing him hard.

A tall figure stepped between us.

'My turn, I think,' said Edward, elbowing his brother out of the way. 'Make yourself scarce little brother. Kat's mine.'

Kat's mine! How I had longed to hear those words. I stood perfectly still, my heart thumping, my every sense tingling with anticipation, waiting for Edward's kiss. I felt his arms encircle my waist, his fingers press firmly on the fabric of my gown. Slowly he lowered his head. I trembled as his lips touched mine.

I had dreamed of this moment. Night after night in the darkness I had dreamed of him smiling at me, touching me, kissing me.

But like all dreams, the moment ended before it had even begun and I would never know if he would have kissed me like a man with his mouth open and his tongue teasing mine,

At the moment our lips touched and I began to melt, a loud voice rang out.

'The king is recovered! The king is recovered! He has regained his wits.'

A man was running down the hall shouting the news – 'The king is recovered!'

Immediately the entire hall was in uproar with people cheering and laughing and asking was this a Twelfth Night jest. Was it true? Could it possibly be true?

'No jest!' shouted the man. 'I'm come from Windsor. Bishop Waynflete's seen the king. His grace is alive and well and talking with his servants. He is recovered.'

'A likely tale,' shouted a voice from the far side of the hall. 'Tell us another one.'

'Is Somerset joining us?' laughed my brother Richard with an edge to his voice as sharp as a sword.

'Harry Holland's riding his Nativity nag all the way from Pontefract! He'll be with us before dawn!' said one of the serving men to his friend.

'Nay, 'tis true, 'tis true!' shouted our bringer of glad tidings. 'The queen showed him the little prince and the king is well pleased.'

I glanced over to where Uncle York sat. His face was impassive but my father was scowling.

The crowd moved aside and Edward and I stood there in full view of everyone, his arms round my waist and my blushing face a testament to what we'd been doing. Then he removed his arms and turned away without a word, like a man who'd seized a stray maidservant for a quick kiss and passed on without a second thought.

'I shall not ask what you were doing,' said Countess Anne, appearing suddenly at my side. 'I shall merely say this is not the time to indulge your fancy for a young man you must know can never be yours. Come with me. Your mother will need you.'

I wiped my mouth with the back of my hand and meekly followed her up the hall. My mother and Aunt Cecily sat surrounded by a flock of worried ladies twittering in concern. All pretence of continuing with the festivities had been abandoned as the enormity of the king's return to health and what it meant for every person present became apparent.

'It is a miracle,' bleated an elderly dowager.

'It be a disaster for York,' murmured her thin-nosed companion.

'What shall we do?' said her hovering daughter, looking around as if the answer could be found nearby.

As usual Aunt Cecily knew exactly what to do. She also knew it must be done directly to dispel any doubt in the matter of her husband's loyalty.

'We shall go to the chapel and give thanks to God for the king's recovery. What better news can there be at this festive time. It is truly a blessing.'

She spoke loyal words but the look in her eyes was one of blank fear.

'Is the king truly recovered?' whispered Margaret, clutching my hand.

'It would seem so.'

She bit her lip. 'Will he be angry with Uncle York for ruling in his stead?'

'No,' I said gently. 'Uncle York obeyed the council. It was their wish that he should be the protector. The king will understand.'

Margaret looked doubtful, perhaps remembering past conversations about the duke of York and his closeness in blood to the throne.

'What of the queen? Will she understand?'

I realised I had underestimated my sister. Margaret was not as stupid as she looked. She knew the queen had wanted the reins of power for herself and had resented the council's decision to allow the duke of York to become protector.

'The queen will remember that it is not she but the king who rules the kingdom.'

'And the duke of Somerset?'

He bright little face looked up at me as if I had all the answers.

'The duke of Somerset must answer for his crimes. The king will decide what is to be done with him.'

'The queen will want him set free.'

Mother of God! Where did this child hear such things? Who had told her about the queen's friendship with the duke of Somerset?

'If I were Uncle York,' she said with all the wisdom of someone three times her age, 'I would ride as fast as I could to one of my northern castles and pull up the drawbridge before the duke of Somerset came for me.'

I knelt down so that my eyes were level with hers. 'The king will keep order. It is his duty. He will not permit his nobles to squabble.'

She looked at me as if I was the one who was stupid. 'Alice said that if Somerset were set free it would be more than a squabble, it would be a fight to the death.'

I gave her arm a good pinch. 'Do *not* repeat that.'

'Ouch! You hurt me.'

'I'll do more than hurt you if you don't keep your mouth shut.'

Of course she was right in every aspect but I hoped she remained unaware that it would not only be Uncle York involved in the duke of Somerset's fight to the death, it would be our father and our brother Richard.

7

ST ALBANS 1455

A pall of gloom, thicker and more stifling than the worst London fog, wrapped itself round The Erber like a shroud. The women in my mother's service took to creeping around her chamber like frightened mice, murmuring prayers under their breath and crossing themselves devoutly at regular intervals. Our own maid, usually quiet and competent, was so scared she managed to snag some of Margaret's hair while dragging the comb through her tangles.

Our father had just announced that the duke of Somerset was about to be released from the Tower and there would likely be trouble.

'Why let him go?' said my mother, her voice higher in pitch than usual. 'It was the council who agreed to incarcerate him, why not keep him there?'

My father shrugged. 'They know his faults but say there are no grounds for imprisoning him further as he has not been convicted of a crime.'

'Have they forgotten his misdeeds so quickly?' cried my mother.

'I doubt it, but Somerset is a man close in blood to the king and that makes the council uneasy. They fear it is only a matter of time before the king asks why they have his kinsman imprisoned.'

I watched in dawning horror as my mother began to crumble. She turned away and covered her face with her hands to stop my father seeing her eyes fill with tears. For him she wanted to be strong.

'Take heart, my dear,' he said quietly. 'Somerset will not have complete freedom. The council have ordered that he is not to approach the king or involve himself in matters of politics, not until he replies to the accusations against him. My brother-in-law, Stafford, is to stand surety for him as will the earl of Wiltshire and Lord Roos.'

My mother turned back and cried out, 'What of Cecily's husband? What will become of him?'

My father sighed. 'He will have to tender his resignation. With the king returned to health there can be no further need of a protector.'

'And you?' She laid her hand on my father's arm as if she could shield him from whatever horrors he might face in those cold January days.

He smiled sadly. 'I am the king's chancellor. I must stay until he dismisses me or until I find my situation untenable.'

I'd never seen my mother so distressed or my father so worried. I was unsure what awfulness would make his position untenable but thought it unlikely he'd keep his post much longer. A chancellor requires his king's confidence and we all knew the king was ruled by the queen and the queen was in thrall to the duke of Somerset and the duke of Somerset hated my father. For some reason he hated him even more than he hated the duke of York.

'What would you have us do?' said my mother, dabbing her eyes.

119

'I would have you take our daughters to Middleham. Keep them safe. Tom will accompany you.'

'And our son, Richard?'

'Richard stays with me. He is sending his wife to Warwick Castle.'

'Not to Caversham?'

'Warwick is better defended.'

I knew that if Richard was concerned for the defences of his houses he must fear another descent into violence. I began to shiver, surprisingly glad to be returning to Middleham where the walls were high, the access difficult and where my father's men would defend d us to the death against an attack by the duke of Somerset.

Despite travelling as fast as we could it took our party two weeks to reach Middleham. Snow clouds could be seen gathering in the far north but mercifully the roads to York remained dry though the night skies were clear and we woke each morning to a hard frost. The last few miles were difficult as the tracks were heavily rutted but the thought of home kept our spirits high and we were still singing as we passed through the gates of Middleham.

Three days after our arrival a man in Nevill livery rode in with a message from my father. The duke of Somerset had been taken secretly from his prison room in the Tower by Uncle Stafford and the earl of Wiltshire and Lord Roos.

'They have released him,' said my mother flatly. 'Never was a man so able to avoid punishment for his evil deeds as Edmund Beaufort. I should know for he is my cousin and I was acquainted with him when we were young.'

'Will the king take him back?' I asked, wondering who on the council had ordered the duke's release.

'I would imagine the queen has had the duke of Somerset's chamber made ready for him with hangings of silk and cushions of the finest velvet. The royal cooks will have roasted a fatted calf and the grooms laid fresh rushes on the floor. It will be as if the duke's imprisonment was only a momentary interruption, an error by others who must now pay the price for their presumption.'

'I'm scared,' whispered Margaret, creeping close to my skirts and clutching my hand.

I said nothing, because I too was afraid.

My father's next letter said the king had ordered him to release the duke of Exeter from Pontefract but that, in all conscience, to obey such an order was something my father could not do.

'Surely he must obey the king,' I said. 'He cannot refuse.'

My mother shook her head. 'You are right, as chancellor your father cannot refuse. Instead he will resign.'

By the end of the second week of March it was as if the world had turned itself upside down, as if Fortune's Wheel had spun on its axle: my father was no longer chancellor and my Uncle York had surrendered the king's sword. At a ceremony in the chapel at Greenwich the great seal of silver in its black leather bag, which had been in my father's keeping for less than a year, was returned by him to the king who handed it to Archbishop Bourchier. At the king's behest the archbishop ordered the release of the duke of Exeter from Pontefract and there was nothing my father or anyone else could do.

All charges against the duke of Somerset were withdrawn and once more the duke sat comfortably at the king's side, whispering policy in his ear. The earl of Wiltshire was appointed treasurer and with the council packed by partisans of the duke of Somerset nothing of any worth to the Nevills or the Yorks could be accomplished. My father, my uncle and my brother, Richard, said they would withdraw to their estates, with or without the king's permission.

'The king says he is in charity with the world but I see precious little sign of charity towards myself,' growled my father that first evening at Middleham as we sat listening to his woes. 'I have been relieved of certain of my offices and the king has sent no less a personage than my brother-in-law Stafford's heir to escort the duke of Exeter, back to court. If that is not an insult to me, I do not know what is.'

'Are you in danger?' asked my mother.

'Not yet,' said my father. 'But Somerset is more dangerous than ever. He will strike back, but how or when I do not know.

'What of Richard?'

'Safe at Warwick for the moment but seething with fury. He hates Somerset even more than we do.'

'Because of Anne.'

'Yes. Somerset still claims some of the Warwick inheritance should have come to his wife.'

'Why would that be? ' I asked, unsure what the duke of Somerset's wife had to do with Anne.

'Somerset's wife is a Beauchamp,' explained my father. 'Old Warwick had four daughters from his two wives.

Edmund Beaufort says they should have inherited equally.'

'We have been through this before,' said my mother. 'Five years ago. It was settled in Anne's favour. She received the bulk of the Warwick inheritance and the title.'

'Doesn't make it go away,' said my father gloomily.

'But it's not right to drag it up again, not when the matter has already been settled.'

My father stared into the dregs of his cup. 'The king might decide it *is* right – with a little persuasion.'

I sat quietly beside my mother remembering the horror of Heworth Moor and the night Maud and I had spent at Tuxford. Alice had once said the world beyond Middleham was one teeming with wolves which prowled and snarled, ready to tear a man apart. I'd thought it was only the Percys who wanted to destroy our family but now we had another yet more dangerous enemy: the wolf with the sharpest teeth of all, Edmund Beaufort, Duke of Somerset.

Instead of the glorious sounds and scents of springtime, the castle precincts at Middleham echoed with the noise of hammering and reeked with the acrid smell of hot iron. The armoury forge was lit from early morning and wagonloads of supplies were coming in from miles around. It was like preparing for a siege. From dawn to dusk our tenants came in their droves to offer support and every day messengers rode in with letters from my brother Richard at Warwick or from Uncle York at Sandal Castle. When my father was not talking with his head armourer he was shut in his rooms having lengthy meetings with his council.

'What is happening?' I asked Alice. 'Has Lord Fitzhugh told you anything?'

'Trouble,' she said shortly.

'Bad trouble?'

'What other kind is there? The king's great council is to meet at Leicester in two weeks time.'

'Leicester! Why not Westminster?'

'Lord Fitzhugh says London is a powder keg, ready to explode at any moment. The king wishes for somewhere peaceful to meet and talk with his great men.'

'Will our father have to attend?'

Alice placed both her hands on my shoulders and looked straight into my eyes. 'He must. If he and Uncle York are not there, the duke of Somerset will have them put in the Tower.'

'He cannot do that. Father has done nothing wrong.'

'Don't be stupid, Kat. You know how a family can be brought down. Look what happened to the Percys when they opposed the king's grandfather. They lost everything.'

'But our father is not opposing the king, He is loyal.'

Alice smiled uncertainly. 'Let us hope the king believes that.'

'Why would he not?'

'If a man tells lies, particularly if that man is persuasive, those lies become truths in the ears of a listener. Our mother says the duke of Somerset can be very persuasive. He is a man whose tongue was forked from the day he first drew breath.'

I felt my eyes widen at the thought of a babe with a forked tongue: a devil child. Perhaps such a child might have dealings with night demons, even though my grown-up self no longer believed in such apparitions.

'What shall we do?'

'Pray the king is merciful.'

The king might be merciful but what of the dark and handsome queen, her body warmed by the fur of five hundred dead and bleeding sables, the woman who listened, not to her pious husband but to the vengeful duke of Somerset? I imagined the king not knowing our father wanted to swear loyalty, while Somerset hissed untruths into his ear. And I imagined Margaret of Anjou smiling as she ordered her scaly son to sharpen his little white teeth on the tender flesh of my father's neck.

The next day Maud and I watched from the walls as my father's men rode south down the road which led to Pontefract. The sunlight gleamed on their swords and spurs, the wagons rumbling behind them piled high with harness and weaponry. They were going to meet my Uncle York at Sandal Castle then ride to join with my brother Richard and his men close to Leicester.

'John says the duke of York will bring his bombard,' I remarked. 'The one he calls "Terror".'

Maud snorted in disbelief. 'Does he imagine the duke is planning to lay siege to a castle?'

'He says our uncle has a supply of sulphur and saltpetre.'

Maud twitched her lips.

'For gunpowder,' I added in case Maud didn't know.

'And what does John think your uncle is going to do with his bombard and his sacks of sulphur and saltpetre once they are dragged down the roads to Leicester? Threaten the king's council?'

'He didn't say.'

'No, because your uncle is not so foolish as to make war on the king's friends. He and your father are going to swear loyalty and plead for the king to dismiss their enemies from his side. That is all.'

I had never seen a bombard fired but I knew my Montagu grandfather had been killed by one while fighting in France. My mother said they were creatures from a hell of man's own devising, monsters which belched fire and smoke and gunstones.

I had an uneasy felling in my belly that something was not as it should be but I knew Alice was right and all we could do now was pray. Our father would go to Leicester and seek an audience with the king. He would tell him that he was a loyal subject and the king should not listen to the lies of others who were my father's enemies. The king would welcome him with open arms and kiss him on both cheeks.

Or would he.

The days crawled by with unrelenting slowness. My mother did her best to keep us amused, to stop us worrying about what might be happening at Leicester. We paid a visit to some friends near Jervaulx Abbey and made a hawking expedition up Coverdale, but as the days lengthened and the warmth spread a mantle of green across the fells, we kept close to the castle, anxious for news.

When I could escape my mother's watchful eye I would loiter in the stable-yard. I wandered up to the old man who saddled my horse and idly stroked the velvety nose of my mare.

'Do you know where Sir Thomas has gone?'

It was unwise to appear too curious as it was none of my business where my brother went or what he did. Every morning for the past week he had ridden under the gatehouse and down the track towards the river. He returned before dusk but nobody knew where he'd been. Maud said he was angry at being left behind like a nursemaid to a pack of women.

The old man sucked on a length of straw. 'He didna say, m'lady.'

'But you would know.'

'Would I?'

He smiled slyly. We'd often played this game before and I knew eventually he would tell me what I wanted to know.

'We-eell!' he drew the word out to its full length. 'Seems to me and seeing as how Sir Thomas took no-one but the one lad, he'd not be going much past Masham.'

Masham was a little place a few miles to the east along the river. There was nothing there but weavers and sheep.

'Why would he go to Masham?'

'Ahh, happen that be a question.'

'It's not a woman, is it?' I asked anxiously.

The old man chuckled. 'Sir Thomas warms hisself at home these days, m'lady; no need of slippy women.'

'Is he meeting with someone?'

'Came home lonesome, yesserday. Didna have the look of a man who spent his day yacketing.'

'So what was he doing?'

127

'Waiting, I guess.'

'For what?'

'News, m'lady. Messengers come up through Masham. Sir Thomas reckons on being the first to know what's happened to our lord.'

'In that case I shall take my mare and ride down to the gate to wait for him.'

'No riding off on your own like.'

I smiled. 'I promise I'll not go outside the park.'

'I'll get a thrashing if you do. I ain't forgot the time you and that Lady Maud did go a-careering off on your own.'

'I thought it was I who got the beating.'

'Nay. Six of the lads had a thrashing from your father that day. Said they should'a taken better care of you.'

He shuffled off to prepare my horse leaving me to wonder once more at my youthful stupidity.

I trotted slowly down the track and was almost at the high wall which surrounded our park when I spied a great cloud of dust and a man riding fast along the road. I watched and as he came nearer, the boy who lived by the gatehouse scrambled to lift the bar and drag open one of the heavy wooden gates.

It was Tom. He sped past, yelling at me to get out of his way.

'It's Kat!' I shouted.

He turned in the saddle at the sound of my voice.

'Somerset's dead!'

I saw the triumphant grin and before I realised what he'd said, he put his spurs to his horse and was off up the track. I wasted no time but went after him, galloping as fast as I could, clods of earth flying in all directions, my heart thudding. As I neared the bridge I slowed to a gentle walk and allowed my mare to pick her way slowly across the echoing boards to the safety of the inner gatehouse. Once in the yard I slid from the saddle, threw the reins to a groom and ran up the steps. I made straight for my mother's room arriving only moments after Tom.

'Edmund Beaufort?' my mother was saying as I came in, her eyes wide in disbelief.

'Cut down by one of Richard's men in the streets of St Albans.'

Alice had her hand to her mouth. 'Merciful Mother of God! I thought they'd gone to Leicester. What were they doing at St Albans?'

'Seems they planned to intercept the king, petition him before the great council was poisoned by Somerset.'

'Did you say Henry Percy?' said Maud.

'Yes, and Lord Clifford. Both dead.'

'Sweet Holy Mary!' said my mother. 'Somerset, Northumberland and Clifford. What a bloody affair. But your father is safe; and Richard?'

Tom nodded. 'Both safe.'

'What of the king?' asked Maud. 'Where was he while your brother was slaughtering the king's nobles?'

Tom grinned. 'Someone overturned his banner.'

Alice clutched her chair. 'You mean the king was in the battle?'

'Hardly a battle,' said Tom. 'More a skirmish.'

'But the king?'

'He wasn't hurt, Alice. Nothing but a flesh wound in the neck from an arrow.'

Alice looked as if she might faint. 'Who fired the arrow?'

Tom shook his head. 'It was a stray one.'

'To attack the king is treason,' she whispered.

'Where is the king now?' said my mother.

'Uncle York escorted him to the abbey and asked that the fighting should cease. By then he and Richard had those they wanted dead. The king agreed the truce and our father and Richard and Uncle York knelt and swore allegiance. It is finished and we are the victors.'

Amidst the cheering, the shouting and the cups of wine in celebration, only Alice was quiet.

'This will not end well,' she muttered.

'Alice, it *has* ended well,' I said. 'Our enemies are dead and the king knows that we Nevills are loyal.'

'I do not like it. Whatever Tom says, it was treason.'

'He said there was hardly any of the royal army there. They were mostly Somerset's men and Northumberland's and a few of Clifford's.'

'The king was there. His banner was unfurled.'

'The king understands the fighting was necessary. He has forgiven everyone. He has been merciful just as we prayed he would be.'

'No matter. It was cousin against cousin. The king is right. His nobles should live in amity, not scrap like dogs on a dunghill.'

From what we heard later there had been very little scrapping. After the order was given to stop fighting the remaining enemies of the Nevills and Yorks were stripped of their jewels and their horses and left to flee on foot.

Alianore wrote that her father-in-law, Lord Stanley, was disappointed to arrive too late to participate in the battle and furious when our brother accused him of deliberate evasion. She said perhaps Richard should mend his manners before he alienated every one of his friends.

The day following the battle the king was taken from the abbey and escorted to London with my father riding on one side of him and my uncle on the other. My brother Richard, whose decision it had been to climb through the gardens and into the streets of St Albans and whose men were credited with the actual killing of Somerset and Northumberland and Clifford, rode before them carrying the king's sword.

Within a week Uncle York was appointed Constable of England and my brother Richard was made Captain of Calais. It was decided that Archbishop Bourchier, being sympathetic to Uncle York, should continue as chancellor but my father wrote that the city was restless. His men still wore their harness and so fearful were they of an attack, they stuffed his barge with weapons each time he made the journey to Westminster. The son of the dead duke of Somerset had been given into Richard's care while the young man recovered from his wounds but my father doubted he'd be reconciled.

'The young of the serpent will strike again,' Alice said gloomily.

But no-one was listening to Alice. We were awaiting the summons to join my father in London where there would surely be glorious celebrations. Somerset was dead; Northumberland was dead and two of his sons were imprisoned in Newgate Gaol; and Lord Clifford, who had foolishly allied himself with Northumberland, was also dead. The Percys as a family had been crushed by my brothers, and Edmund Beaufort was no more. The feud, which had poisoned our lives for as long as I could remember, the great rivalry between Nevill and Percy, had vanished at St Albans and nothing was left but a legacy of stories we would tell to our children.

Tom said it was all very satisfactory.

When the summons finally came Margaret and I were in the garden playing a game of touch with two of the little Fitzhugh girls.

'Your father has found you a husband,' announced Maud, coming down the steps with a smile on her face. 'I thought you'd want to know.'

'Are you certain?' I said, pausing to push my hair out of my eyes.

'He has asked your mother to bring you to London and ensure you are beautifully gowned as befits a daughter of the earl of Salisbury.'

'Beautifully gowned!' I gasped.

'That's what the letter says.'

'Do you know who it is?'

'No, but I'll wager your mother does.'

I wrapped my arms round my waist trying to contain my excitement. A husband!

'I shall go and ask her,' I said, picking up my skirts.

'She won't tell you,' Maud called after me.

I stopped at the foot of the steps. 'Why not?'

Maud insisted I came and sat beside her on one of the stone benches.

'Listen! The beautiful gown is so that when his family

sees you they will think you worth having. That's how it works. First, the lawyers devise a marriage contract so tight it satisfies everyone. Then his family inspect you.'

'But why?"

Maud smiled. 'To ensure you are as your father has described: young, obedient, well-educated and with a pleasing countenance. They know your mother has given your father many children so you are likely to be fertile but never forget what they really want is the connection. You are a Nevill. And since St Albans your father is more powerful than he was before.'

'And my husband-to-be? What does my father expect of him?'

Maud shrugged. 'It may be your father already knows him.'

'Oh!'

My father's friends were mostly elderly men from his years of fighting on the northern march. I could not imagine being married to any of them.

'Will you come with me to London?' I pleaded, nervous of what lay ahead and feeling the need of Maud's hand in mine.

'Of course I'll come. I rather think we shall all be going to London.'

'Even Alice,' said Margaret who had left the young Fitzhughs to their nursemaid and come to sit at Maud's other side.

'Even Alice.'

'She won't like that,' said Margaret firmly. 'She says the men in London are wolves and the women are serpents.'

I looked at Maud and we both burst out laughing.

8

BISHAM 1455

It was late summer by the time we arrived in London and my mother's rooms at The Erber smelled musty. I would have liked to open the great oriel window which overlooked the river but a breeze was blowing up from the quays at Billingsgate and my mother disliked the stench of dead fish. So we sat and endured stale air and our bodies sweating gently in the heat.

'Will they come today?' I whispered to Alice who had come from Lord Fitzhugh's house near St Paul's Wharf.

'If you keep hopping up and down, nobody will come. Sit still.'

Alice was infuriatingly calm, stitching away at an intricate strip of embroidery.

'What are you making?' I asked.

'A trim for one of my kirtles.'

Alice was the best needlewoman in the family. She would create beautiful images by couching gold threads and coloured silks and never pricked her fingers like I did. She said if I concentrated a bit more I would do better.

The first visitors came in the early afternoon: two men who were acquainted with the widowed duchess of Suffolk. I was duly presented and after some pleasantries and enquiries as to whether the almshouses at Ewelme were finished and how much m'lady Suffolk was pleased with them, my mother asked for a message to be taken to her stepmother.

More people came: a fat old cleric from Bisham who had known my mother as a young woman and wished to reacquaint himself with her; and a man from the city who had news of a silk woman my mother had been hoping to find. By late afternoon I was tired but obligingly rose once more, this time to greet an elderly lord who had come in with my father. As I came up from my curtsey I was surprised to find him still looking at me.

He had a full beard and bushy eyebrows which swept out to the side. His face was weather-worn and wrinkled around a pair of piercing black eyes, and the hair beneath his hat was nearly white. His clothes were unfashionable but grand, blood-red vermillion and green, trimmed with grey fur, and heavy brown boots with sturdy straps and laces.

I held my breath. I was being examined carefully by this old man, much too carefully for a common acquaintance.

'A pleasure,' he said to my mother, casting his glance wide to encompass us all.

His voice had an accent I couldn't place, something unusual. I knew my father might choose an older man for my husband and that such marriages could be beneficial. I thought of Edward and the feel of his smooth bronzed skin and the flash of his perfect white teeth, of his abundant dark golden hair and his supple limbs. I truly did not want an old husband.

'Lord Bonville,' said my mother at her most gracious. 'My husband has told me a great deal about you.'

The name was familiar but I couldn't recall why. Nobody had told me I'd be required to speak but twice my mother cunningly brought me into the conversation. I was asked had I seen the queen and replied that I had but fumbled over my words when asked what I thought of the wonders of London.

'I'd like to travel by barge again,' I said, hesitantly. 'Under the arches of the bridge but my lady mother says it is too dangerous.'

'Aye, the tides can rip a man to pieces should he fall out. Many a lad's been lost that way; 'twould be a shame to lose a young woman such as yourself.'

I blushed and looked down at my slippers hoping the interrogation would soon be over.

Eventually my mother said to Alice, 'I think it is past time you went back to Lord Fitzhugh, daughter. Kathryn will go down with you to say farewell.'

I curtsied to Lord Bonville and to my parents and followed Alice out of the room and down the stairs.

'Is that him?' I whispered, clutching her sleeve.

'Oh I doubt it,' she said, maddeningly calm. 'I would imagine he's just seeing if you meet his expectations.'

'Did this happen to you?'

She laughed. 'No. Lord Fitzhugh and I knew each other long before we were married. His father lived at Ravensworth and our two families were acquainted. It was like marrying a cousin.'

'I wish I was marrying a cousin,' I muttered.

Alice placed her finger on my nose. 'Well you're not. Wait and see what comes of this. I wager you'll be pleasantly surprised.'

'And if I'm not?'

'You will make the best of it because it is what our father has chosen for you. Now kiss me.'

I kissed Alice and watched her swing easily into the saddle and wait while her Fitzhugh escort fell in behind. I climbed back up the steps and went through into the great hall where two men were carefully unfolding napery to spread on the high table and two more were checking that cushions had been correctly placed on my parents' chairs. Clearly we were not going to sup *en famille* this evening but would eat with the rest of the household.

My father had a private chamber to one side of the hall. It was where he conducted his business and there was a little ante-chamber adjoining where people could wait. As I walked past I saw a man perched uncomfortably on one of the petitioners' benches. The ante-chamber's walls had recently been painted with my father's devices and was usually full of people wanting to beg favours but it was late in the day and everyone had gone home except for this one man. He wasn't young, probably as old as my father, and was dressed in a robe of plain black cloth with a black velvet cap on his head. There was no sign of our steward so, as a kindness, I thought to tell the man that my father would likely be a while.

He looked up at my approach and marking me as someone of importance in the household rose stiffly and gave me a small bow.

I dipped a polite curtsey and said, 'If you are waiting to see the earl, my father, he is otherwise occupied and may be some time.'

'Thank you kindly, young lady, but nonetheless I must wait. This bench has, I think, seen many a man sit out his hours in patience and solitude.'

He had a beautiful voice, low and melodious, the kind which sounds well in harmony when accompanied by a lute.

'Is it not tedious to sit in silence?'

'A man can always contemplate.'

'True. Are you a cleric?' The clerics I knew spent hours in silent prayer but he didn't look like a priest.

He smiled. 'No, forgive me, my name is Nicholas Radford and I am a man of law, a simple attorney.'

I returned his smile. 'A man who makes contracts.'

'Amongst other things,' he agreed. 'And with whom do I have the pleasure of conversing?'

'Oh! How rude of me! I am my father, the earl of Salisbury's daughter, Kathryn,' and added in case he should be in any doubt, 'I am a Nevill.'

'A Nevill far from home, I think?'

How odd. I had said nothing about Middleham.

'How do you know?' I asked.

'It is the way you speak, not the words but the hint of an accent. Yorkshire, if I'm not mistaken.'

'Yes. I live a day's ride from York. But you are not from Yorkshire?'

He laughed. 'You do not recognize my speech? Yet my clients tell me I have picked up none of the London lawyers' jargon.'

'You talk like the lord who is with my parents.'

'Lord Bonville?'

'Yes. Do you know him?'

'I do. We are Devonshire men, Lord Bonville and I.'

'I do not know Devonshire. Is it far?'

'It is but when you get there you will not want to leave. It is a place of incomparable beauty and riches. But perhaps every man thinks that of his home.'

'Will you be returning to Devonshire soon?'

'When Lord Bonville is ready. At the moment I work for him.'

'Writing contracts.'

He laughed. 'What else!'

I laughed with him. He was easy to talk to unlike most of my father's acquaintances.

'Is the work difficult?'

'Sometimes, when the parties cannot agree. If one man wants a particular thing and the other man is unwilling to concede, then I must use my skills of diplomacy to bring about a solution.'

I imagined my father on one side of a table and my future husband on the other, shouting loudly, with Master Radford, his arms outstretched, keeping them apart.

'My grandfather was a diplomat, that is when he wasn't being one of the king's captains,' I explained.

'Your Montagu grandfather?'

I stared at him. 'How do you know?'

He leaned a little closer and smiled. 'We lawyers know everything.'

I wondered what else he knew about me and what he was doing in my father's house waiting for Lord Bonville, a man who asked too many questions and must surely be far too old to be thinking of taking a young wife.

'I should go back upstairs,' I said uncertainly, making another little dip. 'My mother will wonder where I am.'

He bowed most politely. 'Till we meet again, Lady Kathryn.'

As I hurried up the stairs I wondered how he knew we'd meet again. My mother had said nothing about a journey into Devonshire.

At the top I felt a tug on my arm. It was Maud

'There's no need to run, he's gone.'

I leant against the wall and took a deep breath.

'I thought...'

'I know you did,' she said, smiling.

'Will it be him?'

'Possibly.'

'And if not?'

She shrugged. 'Maybe he has a son.'

My mother was sitting where I'd left her, talking to one of her women but if I'd hoped for a sign of some kind to put my mind at ease I was to be sadly disappointed. When she looked at me her gaze was one of bland indifference. She knew but she wasn't going to tell me, not until everything was agreed and approval had been given.

It happened so suddenly. One moment I was talking to Master Radford, the lawyer, wondering who would be my husband and the next I was standing in the solar in our house at Bisham while my sisters and sisters-in-law pinched and pulled at my wedding clothes telling the seamstresses to pin this and snip that and stitch the seams tighter so that the bodice fitted more snugly.

'Hair loose and falling to the waist,' ordered Alice.

'We should perhaps twist it under a small henin,' suggested Maud. 'A wide-set veil would be fashionable.'

'She is not trying to impress the queen,' remarked Anne.

'Kathryn should make the most of her youth,' said my sister Joan who had arrived that morning from Arundel and was already wielding her seniority. 'Pluck the hairline, pull the hair back and catch with a bridal crown of flowers – carnations and roses.'

'And let it flow down her back,' agreed Alice.

'What about her gown?' said Margaret, determined to be heard. 'It's terribly dull.'

Alice gave her a pinch. 'It is the essence of simplicity and youthful elegance. There is nothing dull about it, you foolish child.'

I stroked the skirts of my over-gown: a luxurious blue samite which swirled round my feet and was held beneath my breasts by a belt of red and gold links.

'Will he like it?' I asked when I was really asking – will he like me?

Alice kissed my cheek. 'He'll be a fool if he doesn't. But remember what I told you.'

'I know,' I sighed. 'He's only a boy and won't be fourteen until next year.'

'And nor will you.'

Maud laughed. 'The pair of you can look but you may not touch.'

Alice sniffed the way she often did when Maud spoke like that. 'The church does not permit a young man to lie with his wife until he is fourteen years of age and the Bonville boy lacks six months.'

'If we cannot live together why am I getting married now?'

'Because Lord Bonville is anxious to return home and needs the matter of a wife for his grandson settled,' Alice explained.

'Unnecessary haste,' Joan said.

But Maud's opinion was different. 'If you will forgive me, you are wrong, Lady Arundel. With only one son and a single grandson it is a matter of urgency to get the boy married.'

At that moment the sound of footsteps clattered on the floor outside and as the door swung open, a sudden influx of women appeared and in came Alianore accompanied by two maids.

'I thought I was going to be late,' she said, breathless, kissing me on both cheeks. She held me away from her and examined me from top to toe. 'My, but you do look delicious, little Katkin. I shall have to keep you away from Thomas Stanley.'

I giggled. 'I thought you had him on a leash?'

'I do, but he likes to imagine he's a free man.'

She gave me a hug and then set me aside.

'So who have they got for you?'

'The Bonville boy,' said Alice. 'His mother's a Harington and the boy will inherit.'

Alianore's eyes gleamed at the news. 'And the father?'

'Only son, mother a Grey of Ruthin, grandmother was the Fitzroger heiress.'

I smiled at my sister, wanting her to know that mine was no hole-in-the-corner marriage arranged by my parents as a last resort to get a younger daughter off their hands. One day I would not only be Lady Bonville but also Lady Harrington just as one day she would be Lady Stanley. Alianore might think that being two years older than me made her infinitely more important but my marriage showed her that she was wrong. We were equals.

'Well, this is very pleasant,' said Alianore, looking at the dozens of gowns and kirtles and fine linen chemises strewn about making my room resemble the cloth hall at York. 'I'm glad you're here, my sisters, because I wanted to share my news.'

With a flourish she swept open her cloak to show us a smart green riding gown with a broad crimson belt tied securely under her breasts, and a decidedly rounded belly.

'Another Stanley,' she said, unable to keep the note of triumph from her voice.

I placed my hand gently on the smooth green cloth but could feel nothing.

'Are you sure?'

'Has the baby moved?' said Joan who, as the mother of two small boys, knew about these things.

Alianore nodded. 'A week ago. I have promised Thomas Stanley a son wrapped in swaddling bands for the New Year gift-giving.'

'You cannot possibly know it's a boy,' said Alice. 'Only God knows that.'

'Alice, you told me if I was good, God would bless me. And I have been wonderfully good,' smirked Alianore. 'You can ask my husband.'

'If I was your husband, I'd whip you,' remarked Alice. 'You're wilful, just like you were as a child.'

The day before my wedding I met my husband-to-be. I have to admit he was a disappointment. I'd been dreaming of the golden splendour of Edward, the lightly tanned skin and long supple limbs but Will Bonville had straight brown hair, olive-tinged skin and what looked like a new doublet, red brocade with white embroidered stars. He was neither short nor tall, in truth he looked remarkably ordinary. If he reminded me of anyone it was Edmund.

We were given a little privacy to sit together unobserved other than by Alice who sat on the opposite side of the room pretending to sew.

'Can you fight?' he said, staring at my slippers.

'Fight?'

He raised his head with a jerk. 'You know, with a stave. I doubt you're allowed a sword.'

'No,' I said feebly. 'I'm not.'

'I suppose being a girl, it would be impossible.'

'I am a young woman,' I said, correcting his assumption that I was still in the schoolroom.

'You don't look it,' he said rudely. 'Grandfather has stories of young women who carry swords and ride into battle, yet you say you cannot handle a sword.'

'No more I can. In my family women do not fight,' I said firmly, wondering if once we were wed he'd want me out in the tilt yard before sun-up.

'Grandfather says everyone should fight: men, women, children, horses, dogs. If he had his way he'd have the beasts in the fields armed and ready. Our villagers practise at the bowmark every week even when there's snow on the ground. Grandfather fines anyone who lies abed claiming they're sick.'

'Who does he plan to fight?' I enquired.

'The pig.'

'Pig?'

'Courtenay. Earl of Devon.'

'And this earl of Devon is your grandfather's enemy?'

'Yes. Did they not tell you?'

'They told me nothing.'

I wondered what else I'd not been told. Had I escaped my family's feud with the Percys and the duke of Somerset only to be pitchforked into another bloody conflict, this time with the Courtenay earl of Devon.

He looked at me pityingly. 'Are you afraid?'

'No, why should I be?'

His eyes gleamed.

'Grandfather says girls are scared of close combat and that I must remember to be careful.'

'I'm not sure I want…'

'Yes you do,' he said and I noticed how when his eyes narrowed he looked much older than his thirteen years. 'When Grandfather allows, I'll give you a lesson.'

'Thank you,' I said politely, noting it was the grandfather who ruled young Will Bonville, not the father. I wondered what else he had in mind for me to learn – garrotting perhaps.

'Grandfather says it's a pity we can't get down to business at once but your father insisted we wait.'

'What business would that be?'

'You know – marriage business. What husbands do to their wives.'

He lowered his gaze to where the neckline of my kirtle skimmed the top of my breasts and smiled. I could feel a warmth creeping up my neck and into my face and wished I'd not asked.

That night, my last as a spinster woman, I curled up next to Alianore, the way we had a hundred times before.

'Don't be nervous,' she whispered across the pillow.

'I'm not,' I lied

She gave me a gentle push.

'A little maybe,' I admitted. 'The grandfather is pleasant enough, for a man, but you should see the step-grandmother.'

Three weeks earlier, I'd undergone an inquisition from an elderly Lady Bonville. She had settled down in my mother's chamber one afternoon intent on questioning me as if I was a maidservant.

'Books?'

'I am fond of reading, my lady.'

'Romances no doubt. They're what my husband's daughter-in-law reads,' she said with a distinct sniff of disapproval.

'I enjoy romances, my lady, but I also like the writings of Catherine of Sienna which I read with my mother. On occasion we study the works of Christine de Pizan. She is very forthright in her opinions and my mother is not sure all her ideas are acceptable.'

Lady Bonville nodded approvingly. 'Can you sing?'

'Yes but to be truthful, my lady, I am not certain how tuneful I am.'

'Dance?'

'When it is permitted.'

'And can you manage a household?'

'I have been taught. Lady Fitzhugh, my sister, has instructed me and I spent some years with the countess of Shrewbury, Lady Talbot, learning how to manage a noble lady's household.'

'So an unmannerly steward would not frighten you?'

'I hope my husband would not appoint an unmannerly steward, my lady.'

She snorted. 'Are you afeared of anything?'

'Lord Egremont, my lady. But he's in prison so I've no need to be frightened of him any more.'

'It's never the husbands,' confided Alianore. 'It's always the mothers-in-law.'

'I've not yet met mine. Lady Bonville says she keeps to her bed.'

'Is she sick?'

'I believe so.'

'Then you have only to contend with the chief dragon.'

I smiled ruefully. 'Yes but she's a fire-breathing dragon like the one in the Corpus Christi plays.'

'And him?'

'Who?'

'The boy you're marrying, stupid.'

'The same age as me which is something.'

Alianore smiled. 'Easier to train. Like dogs – catch them young and make of them what you will.'

I giggled. 'That's what he's called – Will.'

'Will, grandson of Lord Bonville of where?'

'Chewton Mendip.'

Alianore collapsed into giggles. 'Truly? I have missed you Katkin. What funny things you do say.'

I was nearly ready. My sisters were supervising the last of my dressing and, as Joan said, if anyone could improve on God's handiwork, it was Alice. I was now as perfect as I could be. I peeked in my mother's tiny looking glass and a different Kathryn Nevill looked back – lips delicately coloured, a slight dusting of pink on my cheeks and my hairline plucked to accentuate a broad white brow. The bridal crown which restrained my shining brown hair was contrived of pink carnations and white dog roses, interwoven with tiny blue speedwells. I looked almost beautiful.

All of a sudden our peace was disturbed by a commotion at the door. From what I could hear, my maid, Christine, was trying to prevent someone from entering.

'No, my lord. It is not possible. My mistress is in her wedding clothes.'

From outside came a familiar, wheedling voice.

'No men permitted,' Alice said loudly,' poking a last rosebud into my bridal crown.

'Lady Fitzhugh says you may not, my lord. Oh, my lord!'

'Who is it?' said Joan, fastening a narrow gold chain round my neck.

'An intruder intent on abducting the bride,' said Uncle Fauconberg, trying his hardest not to laugh as he advanced softly across the floor in his doeskin boots.

All four of us stopped what we were doing and gave him the shallowest of curtsies while he in turn honoured us with an exaggerated bow.

'Fairest mistress mine,' he said looking straight at me, 'will you come with me into the greenwood?'

'Lord Uncle, you know I cannot. I am about to be married.'

He swore an oath under his breath which made Alice utter a shocked, 'My lord!'

He was dressed in his wedding finery, a doublet of pale grey with silver buttons, and looked magnificent as only Uncle Fauconberg could.

'I know, my little Yorkshire rose, but surely, a few moments, a tryst amongst the greenery, just you and I?'

'Impossible!' said Alice firmly.

'Uncle, you will create an unnecessary scandal,' said Joan. 'Kathryn must remain here until she goes to her wedding.'

Uncle Fauconberg looked at my sisters ranged against him like an enemy defending their citadel and smiled beguilingly.

'How I love you, my nieces but, as I said, this is not a matter for debate, it is an abduction. Come Kathryn!'

He offered me his arm and I placed my hand lightly on his damask sleeve. As we swept out of the room I looked back over my shoulder and smiled at the shocked faces of my sisters and a voice calling vainly, 'Kathryn! Your maid!'

The air was early morning cool and the inner courtyard still in shadow. Two men were laying a blue carpet along the short approach to the chapel door while another was placing a basket of rose petals by the steps. I moved closer to my uncle, wanting to savour this moment because today I was leaving my family behind and I was aware of how fond I was of Uncle Fauconberg.

'You behaved badly, Lord Uncle. Alice is cross with you.'

'I know, dear Kathryn, but I am about to lose you.'

'Is marriage a matter of loss?'

'Assuredly, for the Bonvilles will keep you for themselves. You forget, I have suffered imprisonment at the hands of an enemy and have endured many dark nights of the soul when I feared I would not see my loved ones again, when I would willingly have given my right arm for a single hour in the arms of the woman I loved.'

'You can visit.'

'I shall be too busy keeping your brother and the king's friends apart. And Devonshire is a great distance away.'

'Perhaps my new husband will bring me to London.'

'If I were him I'd keep you in a tower and bar the door.'

'If you were him, Lord Uncle, the Holy Father would declare you an excommunicate for marrying your niece.'

Uncle Fauconberg pushed open the tiny gate to the Lady's Garden, named for a long-dead Montagu wife, and led me to a turf bench where a servant had thoughtfully placed several cushions.

We sat down and my uncle, not a man usually lost for words, stared in silence at the rose bushes smothered in blooms.

'Why are we here, Lord Uncle?' I asked when the silence deepened to an uncomfortable degree.

He turned to look at me. 'Why? Oh yes, of course, you imagine I plan to make off with you?'

'I think not. A man bent on abduction would have a horse at the ready or would climb out of a window. He wouldn't sit quietly in a garden.'

'True.'

'So why are we here?'

'Because I have no skill at writing. If I did I would pen you a pretty verse on how it pains me to part with you to another who will not treasure you as I do. Captivity draws a man inwards, makes for introspection and leads him to know what is of value in his life.'

'Am I of value?'

'Do you need to ask?'

'No, you have always been kind to me.'

'And today I wish to be kinder. I wish to give you something.'

'A wedding day gift?'

'No, something else. Hold out your hand.'

I did as he asked and was surprised when he placed something small and hard in the palm of my hand. It was a ring, a gold band with what looked like a sapphire held by a cluster of tiny diamonds.

'Oh but it is beautiful.'

'Sweetest Kathryn, it is a mere trinket, but it was made for me by a man in France and I wish you to have it.'

'Surely this should go to one of your daughters?'

He held up his hand. 'Stop! My daughters have no need of more jewels. Also they have husbands to care for them.'

'After today, I too shall have a husband to care for me.'

'Will Bonville is a boy.'

'But he will be my husband.'

'Give him five years to grow into a man but until then I'd be happier if you had someone to call on if you found yourself in danger.'

I laughed. 'But my lord uncle, there is no danger any more.'

'There is always danger.'

I smiled at him. 'I'm going into Devonshire. What harm can come to me there?'

He patted my hand. 'Take the ring, Kathryn, and if you need me, send it back and I'll come.'

'And what if the king should need you?'

'The king has other men he can call upon, you may have no-one.'

The hairs on the back of neck began to prickle the way they had that day on the road to Tattershall.

I had a father, I had brothers. I had cousins. There was always someone to call on. Why should Uncle Fauconberg think there might be no-one?

'And Kathryn, I have another gift.'

This time he held out a small dagger in a leather sheath.

'Is that for me to use on my husband?' I said, laughing.

'Keep it somewhere safe. There will come a time when you may need a weapon.'

An hour later after enduring a stern rebuke from Alice, my father came to bring me to my wedding. He escorted me to the door of the chapel where Lord Bonville and four other men were waiting. They wore extravagant robes of dark blue, green and a tawny brown, wide sleeves hanging almost to the ground and fur collars which gleamed sleek and dark. For a panic-stricken moment I thought one of them was to be my husband as there was no sign of Will Bonville. But then they moved aside and I saw Will clearly. He glanced at me and then looked away at the open door and the crowds of people inside the chapel. He was clearly no keener for this marriage than I was.

I had imagined the ceremony itself would be lengthy and solemn but it was finished so quickly I could barely believe I was actually married. I was waiting for something else, some momentous happening, when I felt a nudge on my back telling me to follow the bishop into the chapel for the nuptial mass. My new husband walked at my side and together we knelt at the altar rail. I stole a sideways glance and found myself surprisingly close to his face, so close I could smell his breath and the faint aroma of lavender from his linen.

I remembered Alice's words as she'd made last-minute adjustments to my hair. 'It won't be tonight. You and he are to live apart for six months. So there is no need to look as if you're on your way to your execution.'

'I'm not,' I'd protested, feeling a huge wave of relief. It wasn't that I didn't want to or that I was afraid, because Alianore said it was quite enjoyable once you got used to it, but I would have preferred our first night together to be away from my sisters and their intrusive questioning.

'I insist you tell me everything,' Alianore had said.

And from Alice. 'You understand that on your first night Lady Bonville will require an examination of your sheets.'

'Yes,' I muttered. 'I know.'

They were behaving as if it was their wedding, not mine.

As there was no bedding ceremony, instead we had entertainments and a jousting tournament which was won by my brother, Richard.

'Lord Stanley says Lord Bonville is a bear of a fighter.' remarked Alianore as we sat in the ladies' stand watching Richard collect his purse. 'Our brother should have been diplomatic and let your husband's grandfather take the honour.'

At the mention of diplomacy I looked for Master Nicholas Radford. I wanted to ask him if lessons in the art of combat had been mentioned in the marriage contract. As if in answer to my wish, he appeared in front of me.

'Lady Kathryn,' he said, pulling off his hat and making a gracious bow. 'May I offer my felicitations on this happy day. And Lady Alianore, greetings.'

Alianore inclined her head. 'Must brides be happy?' she asked. 'Can you enforce it with a clause in a contract?'

Master Radford smiled. 'We lawyers do our best. We provide the foundations and the necessary building materials. We hire masons and roofers and engage an artist to paint the arms of the husband on any surface he desires. But the creation of a warm and godly household is beyond the scope of my profession. That responsibility lies with the man and his wife.'

'One more than the other?' said Alianore.

Nicholas Radford smiled. 'I would say equally, but I warrant that most of my clients pay no heed to the happiness of a bride; their sole interest lies in what she brings to the marriage.'

'You would be a poor lawyer indeed if you failed to satisfy your client's requirements,' said Uncle Fauconberg coming to join us. 'For when matters go awry with her husband who can a woman turn to?'

'None other than God, my lord,' said Master Radford. 'In the eyes of the law a woman is as much a man's chattel as his dog or his horse. That is why a man should urge his daughters to treat their husbands kindly.'

'I see you have not yet taken the coif, Radford. Do you not wish to be a Justice of the King's Bench?'

'I am content where I am, my lord.'

'And make more money, I'll wager.'

Master Radford smiled as if Uncle Fauconberg's words were congratulatory, then made his usual muted farewells, bowing more extravagantly than usual.

'I shall doubtless see you on our journey, Lady Kathryn, that is if you deign to speak to a humble apprentice-at-law such as myself.'

'Be off with you, Radford. Nothing humble about you, you crafty old devil,' said Uncle Fauconberg, swatting the lawyer on the shoulder.

We watched as Master Raford picked his way carefully across the field and was lost amidst the striped pavilions.

'Rich as Croesus,' Uncle Fauconberg said. 'I'll wager his house is as fine as those of his clients if not finer.'

At the last I almost disgraced myself by weeping. The sight of my mother and father, my uncle, my sisters, my brothers and their wives, my father's friends who were like friends to me, my mother's women, the maids and the family servants I'd known all my life, everyone standing on the steps at Bisham – it was too much of a loss. My chests had been loaded onto the bridal wagon and I was mounted on my favourite mare whose tail and mane were plaited with blue ribbons for the occasion. Beside me sat Will Bonville, not looking at me but watching his grandfather who rode his great black horse. Lord Bonville was accompanied by his steward, his chaplain and his lawyer, Master Radford. Two Nevill minstrels were to travel with us to make our journey merry and there was a small contingent of Lord Bonville's men to provide an escort. Lady Bonville sat in a litter behind thick red curtains and gold tassels with four not-quite-matching greys to carry her to Devonshire. Her own horse, a sturdy roan, was led behind by a groom. The only piece of home I would carry with me was my maid, given to me by my mother. Christine was happy to accompany me. She said she longed for an adventure.

9

CHEWTON MENDIP 1455

The journey to the West Country was less alarming than I feared. The first day was easy riding. We passed through farmland and occasional stretches of woodland with the Nevill minstrels capering in front of us, singing and banging their tabors. Men appeared silently from amongst the trees to watch us go by and at every village, women and children threw kisses or sprigs of blossom. A couple of girls darted out to touch the hem of my gown for luck and one asked, laughing, which man was my bonny husband. I was cheered by their kindness and wished I had pennies for the children but had nothing in my purse.

The first night we rested at Reading where friends of my father made us welcome with a fine supper and platters of tiny bridal cakes. Next day we set off towards the town of Newbury along what townsfolk called the King's Road. The town nestled in a shallow valley and a little way to the north lay the castle of Donnington where my mother's one-time stepmother resided.

I had no idea if the dowager duchess of Suffolk approved of my father's choice of husband for me but she was very gracious. She welcomed us and was particularly kind to Lady Bonville who was in discomfort from the jolting of her litter on the uneven surface of the road. Next morning we left with a wedding gift of a silver cup, a recognition of the dowager duchess's kinship with my mother.

On the third day we passed through Savernake Forest, trying not to draw attention to ourselves. I'd heard stories of women abducted when riding through dense woodland and had not forgotten the horrors of Heworth Moor two years ago.

'You've no need to be afeared, Lady Kathryn,' said Master Radford, riding up beside me. 'We are no target for outlaws today, not with Lord Bonville's banner and our armed escort.'

'I wish I was like you and could carry a weapon,' I said, scouring the darkness amongst the trees for any sign of danger.

Master Radford laughed. 'I carry only a dagger.'

We rested at Marlborough and after two more days travelling turned off the road and headed south along a broad track. Ominous clouds were gathering on the horizon but Master Radford said the heavens would not permit rain to fall on a bride so I should not worry.

We saw a creature, black, half-naked and terrifying, but Master Radford said it was only a man fresh from digging coal. 'See!' he said pointing at a wagon piled high with rough black stones.

'Is it for building?'

'For burning. The fumes are noxious but it burns for many hours. Longer than wood.'

'Does Lord Bonville have men who dig coal?'

'Oh aye. And lead. We are busy folk down this way, Lady Kathryn. It's not just fine living.'

We spent our last night at a little place called Radstock and in the morning Lady Bonville announced she would forgo her comforts. One day's ride would take us to Lord Bonville's manor of Chewton Mendip and the terrain was unsuited to travelling by litter. I also suspected she wanted to arrive in style, perched high on her horse.

It was an early autumn dusk of the palest grey when we came to the manor of Chewton Mendip. The house sat overlooking a cluster of small cottages which straggled along a well-used track. A group of men, women and children, about thirty in all, had gathered outside the cottages and at the sight of the Bonville banner they raised a great cheer.

We guided our horses wearily up the track towards a high stone wall which stretched for more than a hundred paces in either direction. About halfway along the wall was the gatehouse where someone had thought to have torches lit to guide our approach. The gatehouse itself was a formidable affair, two storeys high and decorated with carved devices. The porter, doubtless forewarned of our imminent arrival, had flung open the heavy wooden gates and was standing to one side as we passed slowly beneath the arch and into the inner courtyard.

Immediately a servant was at my side with cupped hands ready to help me dismount. Bone-weary after seven days in the saddle, I allowed him to assist me down. Once on the ground I had no time to take notice of my surroundings before I was hustled inside by Lady Bonville. Our small group of women passed rapidly through the great hall and slipped silently through a side door on the dais into a little chamber and then through an archway and up a winding stone stairway. At the top were a succession of rooms, the second clearly being the main solar where Lady Bonville's bed had been made ready.

While the maids attended to Lady Bonville, removing her travel-stained clothing and providing a bowl of warm water so that she could wash her face, I waited to be told where I was to sleep. I hoped it would not be with Lady Bonville who snored.

'Is it you?' The whisper came from behind me.

I turned. A middle-aged woman with pale wispy hair and worried eyes was staring at me from within one of the window embrasures. She must have been sitting there quietly all the time, yet I'd not noticed her.

'Shhh!' She put one finger to her lips and then beckoned me forward.

I glanced at the others but they were busy with Lady Bonville, Nobody was paying attention to me. I walked towards the woman uncertain who she was but her clothes were fine and her jewelled buttons and embroidered sleeves spoke of someone with time on their hands, and hence servants, so I dropped a respectful curtsey.

She smiled and I noticed she was missing a tooth which spoiled what looks she had. She put out her hand and stroked my face.

'Are you the bride?'

'Yes,' I said. 'I am the bride.'

'I prayed to Our Lady you'd be coming. I was on my knees day and night and see, my prayers have been answered. What is your name sweet child?'

'Kathryn, my lady. Kathryn Nevill.'

Her hand went up to her mouth. 'A Nevill,' she breathed. 'Truly?'

'Yes. My father is Richard Nevill, Earl of Salisbury.'

Her eyes widened and she uttered a little gasp. 'The Nevill earl of Salisbury!' She put a hand on my sleeve and made to draw me closer into the embrasure away from the other women. 'She swore she'd outdo me but I never thought it would be a Nevill. And what a pretty one they've found for my boy! I was afeared you'd be plain and pock-marked and they'd keep you from me.'

So this was my mother-in-law, a fey little creature with a soft voice and a gentle smile.

'Dame Elizabeth! what are you doing here? Why are you not at Shute?' Lady Bonville's voice disturbed our conversation. It was clear she was not pleased.

My mother-in-law rose from her seat and holding onto my arm moved out into the room.

'Is it not expected that a woman should greet her son's bride?' she said artlessly. 'Your husband certainly thinks so. He sent for me.'

My mother-in-law's pale green eyes widened as she gazed at Lady Bonville. There was no sound of triumph in her voice but I detected a faint smile hovering about her lips as if she knew herself the victor in this little encounter. We were all subject to Lord Bonville's orders, even his wife.

The maids shrank back against the walls, keeping their heads lowered, while Lady Bonville and my mother-in-law faced each other. I had no idea why there was bad feeling between them although Alianore said a mother-in-law could be a difficult woman to deal with. I tried to move back into the embrasure but my arm was too tightly held and I had to remain where I was.

161

'You look weary,' said my mother-in-law to Lady Bonville. 'Of course you are no longer young and travel can be so very tiring for the old. Perhaps you will allow me to mix you a potion of chamomile to soothe your frayed nerves and help you sleep.'

'There is nothing wrong with my nerves,' snapped Lady Bonville. 'And I do not need to sleep. And I do not require help from you, Dame Elizabeth. Rather you should look to your own concerns.'

'Indeed I should,' laughed my mother-in-law. 'So my daughter-in-law and I shall leave you. We shall see you at supper unless you wish to partake of a dish of bread and milk here by the fire.'

'Lady Kathryn will stay with me,' announced Lady Bonville, choking over the last two words.

'Oh I think not. Lord Bonville left instructions that she should sleep with me. He does not wish your slumber disturbed. And I know how greatly he cares for your comfort.'

Not waiting for a reply, she dropped the shallowest of curtseys and slipped out of the room towing me behind her.

'Fear not,' she laughed. 'She will blame me, not you. For the moment she does not wish you upset. You are precious cargo.'

Was I indeed precious cargo? I supposed I was. Maud had said the Bonville's needed another heir and the only way they could get one was from me – with Will's help of course. I'd barely seen my husband since our wedding day. He'd ridden alongside his grandfather on our long journey to Chewton Mendip and apart from a polite acknowledgement of my presence each morning, I had been ignored.

Once we were out of the room, my mother-in-law let go of my hand.

'You wish to come with me, sweet child?' she cooed.

'Yes, my lady, I do.'

She flashed me another of her gentle smiles and lifted up her skirts with one hand and held onto the rail with the other as she began to go down the steps. They were steep and I followed her carefully, down the stairway and through the maze of tiny rooms which lay behind the hall. We passed through an archway and climbed another set of steps which wound round a central pillar. It reminded me of Tattershall and Maud's wedding day when she and I had climbed the tower together.

At the top of Lord Bonville's stairway I found myself in a small room which from its curved shape must have been part of the original tower of the house.

'This is somewhere we can hide,' my mother-in-law laughed gaily. 'She won't find us here. Her old legs cannot climb this far.'

'Perhaps I should go and make my apologies for leaving so abruptly, ' I said uncertainly.

Dame Elizabeth grabbed hold of my arm in a grip that was remarkably strong for one so frail-looking. 'No, no, you must stay with me. If you go back she will try to steal you the way she stole my boy.'

She looked sane enough but I began to wonder if my mother-in-law was slightly deranged. The way she giggled and the odd remarks she made, reminded me of Uncle Fauconberg's wife.

I looked round the room. There was a bed hung with red damask, a couple of small chests and a stool. Underneath the bed was a mattress on a small pallet for my mother-in-law's maid.

'You will sleep with me,' she said. 'You will be mine.'

'What about my maid?'

'We shall have them bring another pallet.'

'Will Lord Bonville not mind?'

She smiled. 'He will refuse me nothing.'

'You are fortunate to be so favoured.'

She giggled again. 'He loves my boy. I gave him the boy. It is more than she did, That's why she stole my child. I thought it was the fairies took him but my husband said it was her. A bad mother is what she called me but 'twas a lie. I loved my boy.'

'Now come!' She pulled the stool over to below the only window which was high up on the wall. 'You must climb up,' she ordered.

I hesitated, wondering why, then nervously reached above my head and, placing one foot on the stool, grasped the rough edge of the sill. I heaved myself up with no difficulty and found I could just see through the gap. But this was no oriel window with a vista of the fells of Middleham, merely an opening not much wider than an arrow slit. There was nothing to see but the glow of a distant lantern and the occasional silky moth attracted by our candle flame.

'Do you see them?'

'See what?'

'The ghostly ones. 'Tis near time for them to come.'

I nearly fell from my perch on the stool. Ghostly ones! What did she mean?

'I c-can see nothing,' I stammered.

I was about to say I had no wish to see ghosts when over to my left, in whatever lay beyond the back wall of the house, I saw a flicker of light. First one then another and then another. My belly twisted with fear as out of the darkness came six figures clothed in spectral white. They had no faces and glided like creatures conjured up by the devil. They had no hands and no feet, like the dead man I'd once seen wrapped in a shroud, Whatever they were they passed slowly by and then disappeared, merging into a deeper darkness.

'What are they?' I whispered.

'I told you. The ghostly ones. They keep watch over us.'

'Are they malevolent?'

She gave a little girl's giggle 'Only to those who cross them. I leave offerings so they do me no harm.'

Merciful Mother of God, I thought. What place have you brought me to? A mad woman and a procession of phantoms risen from the dead.

Next morning I was weary from a poor night's sleep. I had lain awake for hours worrying about the ghostly figures and about the ill-feeling between my mother-in-law and Lady Bonville. I owed a duty to them both but as this was Lord Bonville's manor, his wife, Will's step-grandmother, must surely be given precedence.

After we had broken our fast I excused myself and found a servant. I asked where I might find Master Radford. He was the only person I could count as a friend and might know what I'd seen.

'In the courtyard, young mistress,' said the old man giving me a deferential nod of his head. 'Making ready to leave.'

I should have stayed with Lady Bonville but hoped I could return to her rooms before she would notice I was missing. I ran quickly through the hall, remembering the way we'd come in last evening. Master Radford was indeed in the courtyard, talking to one of the grooms. When he saw me he raised his hand in a salute and made a small bow.

'You have caught me, Lady Kathryn. I was just coming to make my farewells to the ladies.'

I seized his arm which was not what I should have done but I was past caring.

'Master Radford, have *you* seen them?'

'Seen who?'

'The phantoms, the ghostly ones. My mother-in-law showed me them last night.'

He looked startled. 'What phantoms would those be? Lord Bonville has said nothing to me of such matters.'

'Six of them. White ghostly figures, behind the house. And lights which moved. They came out of nowhere and then they disappeared into the darkness.'

'Six you say?'

'Yes. All in white with no faces and no hands.'

'About the size as a man?'

'Yes.'

Master Radford smiled. 'Not phantoms, Lady Kathryn. Those are the brothers from the priory.'

'They cannot be. They were white, a truly ghostly colour.'

'Be assured they are not phantoms. They are men as surely as I am a man. They are Carthusians and their rule insists they wear white. That is all you saw, just a procession of monks making their way to the church.'

I gasped with relief. I'd not heard of the Carthusian order – Dominicans and Franciscans, yes but not Carthusians.

'They are not a military order, they do not fight?'

Master Radford smiled. 'No, they are peaceful. You are perfectly safe here.'

'My uncle, Lord Fauconberg says nowhere is safe. He says there is always danger, wherever you are.'

Master Radford rubbed his nose. 'Lord Fauconberg is a wise man and he is right. There is always danger, especially in these uncertain times, but not from the Carthusians. They are a devout order who spend their time in solitary prayer.'

'And they will not trouble us?'

'I doubt they will talk to you. They prefer to keep separate from the world and not speak to others.'

I smiled at him. 'Thank you, Master Radford. You have put my mind at rest as you always do. I am truly sorry you are leaving, I have enjoyed our conversations.'

'I too. One day I hope my wife and I will have the pleasure of entertaining you and young Will at our house at Upcott.'

I beamed with pleasure. 'I should like that very much. I should like to meet your wife and see your house.'

'My poor wife fell from her horse two years ago, Lady Kathryn. She can no longer walk and keeps to her bed. As you can imagine she values company so I know she will enjoy meeting you.'

I murmured how sorry I was about his wife's accident and thought what a cruel tragedy to be unable to walk. God tested us in so many ways. And Master Radford was such a kind man.

'Master Radford, there is one other thing. It is probably none of my business but I have no-one to ask other than you.'

'What is it you wish to know?'

'Why my mother-in-law and Lady Bonville are on such bad terms.'

He smiled. 'You need not concern yourself, Lady Kathryn. Their quarrel has nothing to do with you. As so often with women it is a matter of jealousy. Ask your husband, he will explain. Now I must go and make my farewells to Lady Bonville.'

In the days that followed I discovered a little more about the Bonville family. Lady Bonville had been born a Courtenay and was a widow when she married Lord Bonville. Her first husband was the Harington heir but died before he could inherit and there were no children. What angered Lady Bonville was that my mother-in-law then became the new Harington heir. I was a little unsure how this came about but it was clear the Harington inheritance was at the root of the bad feeling between these two women

'Old wife's jealous, m'lady' said Christine, lacing me into my gown. 'She'd dearly like to have given her husband a son, but the servants reckon she be barren. She were spitting fire when the young lady gave Lord B a grandson.'

Normally I would have discouraged Christine from gossiping but had to admit I found the insights she'd gleaned from the Bonville servants highly instructive.

'Dotes on the boy, he does, m'lady.'

'What about my husband's father?'

'Not seen much. Mostly lives at some place called Shute.'

'Shute?'

'Aye. Strange names they have in this godforsaken place.'

'Christine, it is not godforsaken, merely different. This is the West Country not Yorkshire and we must get used to it.'

However there was no time to get used to Chewton Mendip with its beautiful church and Carthusian priory, because after a week Lord Bonville announced we were to remove ourselves to another of his manors at a place called Lympstone. Having business in Devon, he and his grandson would first make a detour to visit tenants in the area and thought Lady Bonville might care to renew her acquaintance with Dame Thomasina.

'Take Lady Kathryn with you, show her off.'

'And your daughter-in-law?' enquired Lady Bonville, coldly. 'Where is she to go?'

'Shute. Best place for her.'

Lady Bonville relaxed her shoulders and gave an almost audible sigh of relief. To be rid of Dame Elizabeth was what she'd been hoping for.

I had no idea who the mysterious Dame Thomasina was but doubtless I would find out.

10

The tracks became narrower and twistier the further we ventured into Devonshire. The hills were steep, all ups and downs with rounded stones underfoot which my horse, unused to this kind of terrain, found difficult to manage. Stunted trees, windblown and bent, clung to the grassy slopes and once in the valley bottoms, streams impeded our path. I thought only a mule could tread easily on tracks like those in Devonshire. There was no even ground and I understood why Lady Bonville had left her litter at Chewton Mendip. Our chests were strapped onto frames on the backs of small sturdy horses and the rest of our belongings crammed into baskets hanging over their sides.

At last we stopped on the summit of a hill where Lady Bonville pointed out what she said was once a castle built in the time of our ancestors when giants roamed this part of England. All I could see was a grassy tor crowned with trees but it was not difficult to envisage great stone walls, gatehouses, towers, and men of unimaginable size and strength striding over these hills.

'Below is the earl of Devon's manor of Bickleigh,' she said. 'There is a fine crossing of the river by his house but it would be unwise to go that way, not with matters between my brother and Lord Bonville being so unsettled.'

'I thought my uncle of York had made peace between them,' I said shyly, not being privy to the exact details of the trouble between Will's grandfather and the earl of Devon and not wishing to offend Lady Bonville.

She gave a joyless laugh. 'Is that what they told you?'

She stared out at the surrounding hills and then said, 'This is where I spent my childhood. I was a Courtenay and would not have believed that one day I would find myself married to my brother's enemy.' She shrugged. 'But that is the way for a woman and now I espouse my husband's cause.'

'Naturally,' I murmured, remembering lessons I'd been taught about a wife's duty.

'And my brother is in the wrong – always.'

As the horses moved off again I cast one last look at the site of the ancient castle and then followed the others down a track which became more and more precipitous the closer we got to the bottom. After a brief halt we set off again up the other side of the slope. But this time it wasn't long until we reached our destination. We descended yet another steep track and on the far side of a small stream came upon a huddle of dwellings grouped near a church. The track wound past the dwellings but the village was deserted. The forge was empty, the fire cold with not even a lad inside to work the bellows. An urchin of about three years old was playing on the step of the church but at the sight of our horses he was snatched away by a girl not much older, both disappearing into a nearby hovel. Despite Lady Bonville's warnings I was not frightened. I'd seen plenty of villages like this in Yorkshire.

Our horses plodded on past a muddy pond where someone had carelessly left an upturned bucket in the shallows, then along by the edge of a high wall. At the end of the wall we turned up a hill. Ahead of us the road curved to the left. We heard the noise before we rounded the corner. It began as a distant hum and gradually grew louder and louder the closer we got until it filled the air. There were men shouting and a woman screaming. At the sound of the scream I began at last to be afraid. The captain of our escort raised his hand to halt our party.

'I'll send one of the men ahead to find out if it's safe for ye, m'lady,' he said.

Lady Bonville shook her head. 'A village rabble. Nothing more. We shall proceed.'

The captain looked doubtful but obeyed. He waved the escort on but ordered them to close up so that Lady Bonville and I were almost completely surrounded by armed men and I could see very little.

We rounded the corner but I was still unable to see what was happening. There appeared to be some kind of altercation. In the gaps between the bodies of our escort I caught glimpses of a stone gatehouse and people, pushing and shoving. A woman had her hands over her ears and was wailing, two others were clutching each other and a little girl had her face buried in her mother's apron. Perhaps there'd been a fight. I tried to see if there was an overturned cart or some other cause for the trouble but could only see legs and arms and occasional faces. Then two of our escort spurred their horses forward and the crowd of people fell back.

At first I was unable to understand what I was looking at. The grass at the side of the track was muddy with footprints and hoof marks and signs of a mighty scuffle.

In the middle of the track lay a heap of old clothing and beside it what looked like a discarded black boot. The bundle was surrounded by a slow-spreading pool of oily dark liquid. At first I thought someone had spilled a keg of wine from a cart, a common enough occurrence. Then I realised what this was.

Oh Merciful Mother of God! The liquid was blood! The heap of clothing was a human being. A man! One of his legs stuck out at an awkward angle and I thought perhaps it was broken and that was the cause of the blood. But there was far too much blood for a simple leg wound. This was something far worse. I'd seen ne'er-do-wells huddled in the streets of York, drunk or sometimes asleep in a doorway or in a dirty corner by the walls. And once I'd seen a man who'd been mangled by the wheels of a passing wagon. He'd been lying flat on his back staring up at a patch of sky between the overhanging roofs and at first I'd not realised he was dead.

A man in servant's livery was kneeling beside the body. He was weeping noisily. Two other men were vainly pulling at the man's clothing trying to turn him over. As they moved first a shoulder and then an arm, I saw his robe. Black cloth. The finest kind money could buy. A furred collar. This man was someone of importance and this had been no village brawl. Yet still my mind refused to believe what I was seeing.

The crowd fell silent. At my side Lady Bonville sat immobile on her horse. She did not move and seemed beyond speech. She must surely have recognised him before I did? Of course she knew exactly where we were and whose house it was that lay beyond the gate.

Behind the men a small knot of women, ashen faced and frightened, stood by the entrance to an imposing manor house. The gatehouse was fire-blackened as if someone had recently set a fire against the wall. Two great oak doors lay on the ground, splintered beyond repair, their hinges hanging, useless. They'd been attacked with an axe and partially burned. All around were hundreds of smashed tiles and broken shards of pottery and inside, beyond the arch of the gatehouse, I could see a trail of destruction leading all the way across the garden.

In front of his gatehouse, dressed in the black robes I'd come to know so well, lay the dead body of Master Nicholas Radford.

I put my hands to my mouth to stifle my cry. He couldn't be dead. He couldn't. I'd known him such a short time and yet felt I'd known him all my life. I counted him as a friend.

Tears seeped from the corners of my eyes and trickled down my face. I wanted to howl. How could this happen? Who could have killed such a dear kind man?

'We must go in and see Mistress Radford,' said Lady Bonville, her voice shaking with emotion.

I grabbed the reins of her horse. 'No, my lady. You cannot go inside. We do not know if it is safe. What if the men who did this are still inside the house?'

She nodded and then turned to the captain. 'Send men to search the house. And the outbuildings. Quick!'

He issued orders and two of our men rode at once through the ruins of the gatehouse.

I got down from my horse and walked over to where the body of my friend lay on the ground. I could not see his face, just the back of his head. The villagers had mostly drawn back at my approach leaving just three men who from the look of them and the respectability of their clothing, must be Master Radford's senior household servants.

'Are you certain he's dead?' I asked the older man who I thought might be the steward.

'Aye, mistress. There were nigh on a hundred of them. He didn't stand a chance,' he said, tipping his hat.

The man kneeling, looked up at me. 'He were duped, mistress. Said they'd not harm him. Just wanted a bit of a chat.'

The other man who'd been trying to turn the body over, scrambled to his feet and pulled his cap from his head. 'He told 'em he'd no be able to walk, mistress. Said he'd need his horse. But those whoresons had took 'em all.'

'Aye, took his big silver bowl too. Used it for a piss pot. Beggin' your pardon, mistress, but that's God's truth.'

I walked unsteadily back to my horse and allowed one of our men to help me into the saddle. I closed my eyes. I felt nauseous and hoped I would not disgrace Lady Bonville in front of everyone. Remember you're a Nevill, I whispered to myself. You are someone of importance. I swallowed hard, opened my eyes and raised my chin. I was the daughter of the earl of Salisbury and I would show these people I knew how to behave.

One of our men came hurrying out through the arch of the gatehouse.

'Place is a right mess, sir,' he said to the captain. 'Ripped apart.'

'Any sign of the culprits?'

'Nah! Long gone if you ask me. They'd not hang around. Took what they wanted and scarpered.'

Lady Bonville signalled to the captain. 'Ask him about Mistress Radford. Is she safe?'

In a quiet voice she said to me, 'You know she's bedridden?'

'Yes, my lady. Master Radford told me.'

'Dame Thomasina is a good woman, a strong woman. But this?' She looked about her in bewilderment. 'No woman could survive an attack like this.'

I could hear the man who'd been in the house talking to the captain. 'She's upstairs, sir. With the maid. Can't get no sense out of neither of them. Seems they tipped the old crone out of bed. Took the sheets from under her. Took the covers and the curtains and all. Lucky for us they didn't take her nightshift. Bag of old bones she is and that'd not be a pretty sight.'

The captain cuffed him to remind him of our presence.

'Forgive me, m'lady,' the man mumbled. 'No disrespect.'

Lady Bonville frowned.

'Where is his chaplain?' she asked.

There was a muttering amongst the servants and eventually one stepped forward clutching his cap. 'Beggin your pardon, m'lady, he be hiding in tha' store room along with the carcasses. Reckoned he'd be safe there.'

'Fetch him!' said Lady Bonville. 'And why is the body of your master lying out here in the road? Carry him inside this instant. And if you cannot find the chaplain, fetch the priest. Unless he's run away too.'

She turned to me. 'Feckless lot some of these so-called men of God. Ah!'

Hurrying up the track from the village came a little old man wearing what passed for clerical garb. He was obviously the village priest. His gown was none too clean but in the present circumstances that was of no matter. Someone must have run for him because in his hands he held what was necessary for administering the last rites to the dying.

'Too late,' said the kneeling servant.

The priest knelt down and began to mumble some Latin words.

I sat with my head bowed listening to the familiar words of comfort. I refused to think that even though it had already flown from his body, Nicholas Radford's soul would not be accepted by God. A man as good and kind as he was must surely be received into Heaven.

'Come,' said Lady Bonville once the priest was finished. 'The servant's will bring him in. We will go and attend to Mistress Radford. I know that girl of hers – simple as a newborn babe.'

Even though we'd been forewarned, I was ill-prepared for the scene of utter devastation that met us when we stepped inside the door of Upcott Manor. The walls were completely bare. On the floor lay huge lumps of plaster, fallen when the hangings were ripped down. A great oak chest, too heavy to move, sat with its lid open, all the contents removed except for one torn piece of moth-eaten cloth.

There were no sconces or pricket candlesticks anywhere, only a couple of wax stubs left lying in a corner. The boards were gone, the benches taken. The rope which held the circular candelabra had been severed with a single slash of a sword and was hanging loose, the candelabra disappeared with the rest of the booty. There must once have been a fine display of silverware in the armoire but that too had been taken.

In the parlour behind the hall, the glass in the windows had been smashed and even the handsome surround of the hearth had been attacked with a hammer. Here there would have been rugs and cushions and books, perhaps a musical instrument or two, all the evidence of fine living. But everything had been taken and someone had put an axe through the long wooden settle which they'd tried unsuccessfully to pull out through the doorway.

Lady Bonville, who must have been here before because she knew the way, led me across to the stairway in the corner, once hidden by a heavy curtain which would have hung from the rail.

She held out her hand. 'Come here!'

I moved to her side and she leaned heavily on my arm as we made our way awkwardly up the steps. At the top, the same signs of devastation met our eyes. The bed curtains were gone, only two hooks hanging forlornly where the thieves had been hasty. All that remained of what once must have been a handsome bed was a bed-frame and a mattress that had been slashed with a dagger so that duck feathers and bedstraw spilled out and had come to rest underfoot.

A woman lay on the floor, moaning. She was wearing a thin woollen nightgown and had a nightcap tied under her chin. What could be seen of her hair was brown, tinged with grey streaks, but her feet, which were bare, were those of an old woman: bony, twisted and yellowish. Sitting beside her, ineffectually stroking her forehead, was a young woman not much older than me. Every so often she patted her mistress's head and murmured, 'Amen to that.'

At our appearance she looked up but failed to rise, as she should have, merely looked at us blank-faced.

Lady Bonville took in the situation with one sweeping glance. She marched forward and then turned to me.

'Help me down, grand-daughter.'

It was the first time she'd referred to our supposed kinship but in front of the maidservant she could hardly call me anything else. I supported her as she knelt down beside the woman on the floor.

'Dame Thomasina! Can you hear me?'

The woman's eyelids fluttered open and she stared up at Lady Bonville.

'I prayed you would come,' she whispered in a thin little voice.

The horror of being attacked by armed men in her own bed must have been shocking. With her infirmity she could not defend herself and the maidservant probably hid under the bed.

'What happened, old friend?' said Lady Bonville. 'Who did this to you?'

The woman shook her head and groaned as the movement clearly pained her. 'Nicholas said 'twere the earl of Devon's men outside. He went downstairs.'

Master Radford said he had sometimes worked for the earl of Devon. But why would the earl send men to rob and kill his man of business? It didn't make sense.

Dame Thomasina began to weep. 'I heard their boots on the stairs. I cried out that I was naught but an old woman but they gave me no mercy. They took everything, all my lovely clothes, my books, even the embroidered cover from my bed. Then one said, "What about the sheets? The old hag has no need of they". So they tipped me onto the floor and when I recovered my wits they were gone and so were my sheets.'

Speaking had exhausted her and she closed her eyes.

Lady Bonville leant on my arm as she struggled to her feet. She looked round the room once more, then turned her attention to the maidservant.

'Fetch your mistress a cover of some sort. It is not right she lies half-naked for all the world to gawp at. And a pillow for her head. And send two strong men to fetch a pallet mattress and help lift her onto the bed.'

The maid looked sideways and muttered. 'There be no covers.'

'I can see that you impudent girl. Go and find some.'

It was obvious the girl was incapable of obeying even the simplest of instructions.

'Shall I go?' I said.

'Yes, yes. You go. There must be something somewhere. Not everything can have been taken.'

I hurried down the stairs wondering where to start looking but to my relief found Christine and Lady Bonville's maid hovering at the door, too scared to come in. I dispatched the two of them in search of a pallet mattress, a clean one, preferably feather not straw and certainly not bracken. Then I peered into a room which must at one time have been where Nicholas Radford carried on his business. The desk was overturned. Everywhere was liberally splattered with ink and littered with pages torn from his books. Most books must have been taken but a few remained, lying where they'd been tossed, trampled on by the earl of Devon's men. There was nothing here to use as a covering for Dame Thomasina.

To one side of the hall were two shallow steps leading into a small chapel. I was surprised by the beauty of the window, hundreds of tiny panes of coloured glass depicting a kneeling man in front of two winged angels with a surround of devices I didn't recognise. The autumn sunlight shone through the window making splashes of colour on the floor tiles. In its emptiness the chapel looked peaceful. Whatever carved chests and ornamental cloths Nicholas Radford had purchased for his chapel had been taken but the pillagers had stopped short of breaking the windows for which I felt ridiculously pleased. After all what was the joy of a beautiful window compared to the loss of a friend.

On the altar there would have been a cross and perhaps a pair of candlesticks but they were gone. I remembered Alice's story of the Percy brothers dancing on the altar at Garston. This altar looked as if the earl of Devon's men had done more than just dance; there were clods of mud, traces of red wine and pools of a pale yellow liquid which didn't bear thinking about.

I made my way out of the chapel and through to the offices which served the house. The first must have been the ewery. It was empty apart from two broken ewers, a wooden mazer and a dripping keg of ale. I ventured further. The kitchen looked as if an army of horsemen had ridden through. The floor was strewn with unbaked dough trodden into crevices, green leaves and onions and shards of twisted metal and broken pottery. A great cauldron lay on its side, a hole gaping in its base.

On the wooden table which dominated the room a few battered pewter bowls lay where they'd been thrown, discarded as not being worth the taking, and lying underneath were three large ladles of the sort found in most kitchens. From the smears of blood on the floor I guessed they'd dragged carcasses of meat from the store room out through the door to the yard along with any other foodstuffs they could manage to carry. Perhaps they'd also dragged out Master Radford's chaplain.

Near the hearth was a huddle of frightened servants. They stopped talking the moment I entered. I squared my shoulders, pulled myself up to my full height and tried to remember the lessons Alice had taught me on the ordering of servants.

'Your mistress is in need of a cover for her bed,' I said loudly.

No-one moved and no-one spoke.

I took a deep breath and tried again. 'Which of you is in charge here?'

There was some shuffling of feet and one or two glanced at an older man, thick-set with massive shoulders and a square flushed face. Eventually he took a step forward.

'I be master's cook, mistress, if that be your question.'

'And your name?'

'Sim be what I be named.'

'Very well, Sim. Your mistress is lying upstairs without a shred of covering. Send one of your lads to find some cloth – bedcovers or curtains, any kind of cloth, something to keep her warm. Then tell me what has happened here.'

'They took my roasting irons,' the man whined. 'Said they'd slit my throat with my knife if I made a fuss.'

'The cloth,' I persisted.

'There be none, mistress.'

A flaxen-headed lad with a dirty face sidled forward.

'Beggin pardon, mistress.'

The cook turned and gave the boy a clout which sent him flying. 'Open yer gob again and I'll slit yer tongue, ye ugly little shit,' he hissed.

'Stop that!' I sounded braver than I felt. 'Leave the boy alone. What is it you wish to say, lad?'

The boy scrambled to his feet, rubbing his ear and keeping a wary eye on the cook.

'Tha be a roll of cloth in a box at back of old store room. They durst take nuffin' from tha.'

I rewarded the boy with a smile. 'Well said! Fetch it for me.'

He scampered off, dodging a mangy dog licking blood from the floor. I thought the boy's feet might slip on the slimy leaves but he was nimble footed and obviously well used to detritus.

I fixed the cook with what I hoped was an icy stare. 'What else have you got hidden away?'

'Nothing, mistress. It be only cloth for the cheese. I durst not think it right for the mistress.'

'Your mistress is cold, next to freezing and at a time like this unless you can conjure up some thick woollen cloth, this will have to do. You're certain there are no chests of old curtains stowed away anywhere?' I addressed this last to all the servants.

They consulted with each other and then shook their heads.

The boy returned lugging a huge bolt of unbleached linen in his arms. It was the cheapest sort you could buy and was not what I would have chosen as a bed covering but it would have to do.

'Have you milk?' I asked the cook, hoping there might be a cow or a goat still giving milk this late in the year. Devonshire was warmer than Yorkshire and I'd seen beasts in the fields that morning down near the river crossing.

'There be nothing.'

I raised my eyes heavenwards. This oaf was going to be no help.

'Nothing indeed! Your mistress needs sustenance and something to drink. Send two lads to the village to get ale, a jug of milk and some bread. Make up a basin of bread and milk. I shall send Mistress Radford's maid; she can carry it upstairs.'

The cook looked pained. 'What if they ask for payment? Knowing the master's gone and all.'

'Merciful Christ! Use your wits. They know they'll get paid, and if they make trouble tell them Lady Bonville will see they get a whipping.'

I turned to leave. 'And get this mess cleaned up. The place is a disgrace.'

As I walked away I felt amazingly powerful. Behind me I heard mutterings but saw two lads heading off towards the gatehouse. Hopefully they would soon return with food and drink. I went back into the main hall and looked around, vainly hoping a miracle would occur to deliver some thick warm cloth for the poor benighted woman upstairs.

A young man of about twenty with a pale narrow face and a shock of black hair peered out from behind the archway to Master Radford's room. He had his cap in his hand.

'Beggin' pardon, mistress.' He looked almost too frightened to speak.

'Yes.'

'I know where master keeps his best robes, the ones he wears when visiting great men. He did show me once and bid me mind where he hid the key.'

'I fear they will have been taken,' I said sadly.

'Nay, they still be there. I seed them.'

'Where? Are you certain? Show me.'

This man was clearly a cut above the other servants, Nicholas Radford's valet, or possibly his clerk.

'They took the silver candlesticks from the chapel. 'Twas a shame. They were master's pride and joy they were that fine. And they took the jewelled cross.'

'The robes,' I reminded him. 'You said you knew where they were.'

He led me to the back of the room where he'd been hiding and showed me where a cunningly concealed closet had been built into a narrow recess. There were some small tattered shreds of cloth attached to the wall above and I thought a painted hanging must once have kept the closet hidden from view.

The man took out a small iron key and inserted it into the lock. He turned the key and the door swung open.

Inside was a deep chest and to one side a perch from which hung a lawyer's black gown and a black hood. On a small table lay a chaperon with a feather in it. In the chest was a deeply furred black robe, another of dark green worsted and a blue doublet with black buttons. Underneath was a red velvet cushion embroidered with silver thread. I ordered the man to carry the clothing up the stairs to his mistress's room while I followed clutching the cushion.

The kitchen boy was loitering at the foot of the stairs doubtless afraid to go somewhere he'd never been before. The cook would have threatened his kitchen lads with a beating if they ever so much as set one foot in the master's private rooms. I told him to follow me and all the way up I could hear his little bare feet pattering behind me. At the top I told him he should set down the cloth and then return to his duties. He honoured me with a flash of surprisingly white teeth before disappearing back down the stairs.

It took us an hour or more to organise some comfort for Dame Thomasina but not long after noon we had her back in her bed lying on a pallet mattress stuffed with duck feathers and covered with her husband's furred robe. She was being fed a basinful of bread and milk by the maidservant.

'My lady?' I said quietly to Lady Bonville.

'What is it?' she said sharply.

'We cannot stay here tonight. There is nowhere for you to sleep and little enough food. Until the place is set to rights the servants will find it hard enough to cope with Dame Thomasina.'

For myself I had no objection to a night on the floor but my bones were young and supple not old and creaking like Will's step-grandmother.

She gave me a tired smile. 'You are right. I have sent for the sheriff and the coroner though with Master Radford's standing in the county I fancy this will be far beyond them. Luckily the steward had wit enough to send for the son.'

'Master Radford has a son?'

'A promising young man, not yet twenty-one.'

I felt a wash of relief at knowing there'd be someone to care for this poor woman. A son would bring order to chaos and see to the burial of his father.

Dame Thomasina, having eaten, was already half asleep so we left the bedchamber and went in search of the steward.

He was waiting for us in the hall, outwardly calm but his eyes red-rimmed from weeping. He told us exactly what had happened.

'It was the earl of Devon's men, God curse them. Roused the master and told him to open the gate. Master was reluctant but the earl's son gave his word as a knight and a gentleman that the master would not be harmed.'

'And he believed him? In the middle of the night?'

'He were cozened, m'lady. The earl's son were a sweet talker, speaking with a forked tongue like they Cornish. Master put on his robe and offered him wine and he were kept talking while those whoresons ransacked the house. They even took the horses to carry away their ill gotten gains.'

'Why did your master go with them? He must have known it was dangerous.'

'Yon Courtenay said his father wanted to speak with the master. Enticed him out beyond the gate. Then rode away. He had told his men to use a glave on my poor master. It were a heathen act, near sliced his brains in two.'

I put my hand over my mouth as I felt bile rise in my throat at the thought of what had been done.

The steward wished us to see the body, to absolve him of any charge of not caring for his master in death. With no boards and no candles there was nothing dignified about the way Master Radford was laid out in the chapel. I had ordered a strip of the cheesecloth to cover his body and in a vain attempt to bring some grandeur to the proceedings had placed his hat with the feather on the floor by his head. I knelt by his body and murmured the familiar words I'd so often heard during candlelit vigils for the dead,

'This one night,
This one night,
Every night and all
Fire an' fleet an' candlelight
- And Christ receive thy soul.'

Yes I thought, may Christ receive thy soul. I told him I would never forget, then leaned over and gently kissed his forehead.

11

LYMPSTONE 1455

With nothing to detain us further we left Dame Thomasina and Upcott Manor, a sorry, silent party, plodding back the way we'd come.

'You did well, grand-daughter,' said Lady Bonville. 'There's some would have screamed or fainted away but not you. You dealt with what needed to be done, showed you had more in your pretty head than romances and ribbons.'

I coloured, surprised at the praise.

'Lady Grandmother, why did it happen? Master Radford was no great man to have enemies. He told me he was naught but a humble lawyer.'

'You saw the house, hardly the home of a humble lawyer. Nicholas Radford may not have coveted high office but he was exceeding wealthy. I'll wager they were after his money.'

'But to kill a man in that way.'

'Petty revenge. Dame Thomasina said her husband had entrusted a large portion of his treasure to another. Perhaps my nephew expected more from his thievery. Or perhaps he was sending a warning.'

'A warning to whom?'

'To those who choose to do business with the Bonvilles. Master Radford was once held in great esteem

189

by the Courtenays, godfather to my brother's son. But the Courtenays do not trust those who offer their services elsewhere. I fear the duke of York underestimated the enmity between our families. My brother and his sons will not rest until they have rid Devonshire of every single Bonville.'

Merciful Mother of God! What danger had my father sent me into. Uncle Fauconberg had known and tried to warn me but I'd not believed him. Ever since Heworth Moor I'd known what could happen. I'd ridden countless times across the moor to my father's castle of Sheriff Hutton but on that August day, danger appeared where I'd least expected to find it. Now nowhere was safe.

'Shall we return to the safety of Chewton Mendip?' I asked remembering the comforting high walls and sheltering hills and the large number of Lord Bonville's nearby tenants who owed him service.

'Certainly not. We shall go as planned to Lympstone.'

'I've not heard of Lympstone. Is it far?'

'A half day's ride beyond Exeter. We shall stay tonight with the nuns at Saint Katherine's. You will like Saint Katherine's, it is a pretty little priory, but I think you will like Lympstone better. We have neighbours there I know you will enjoy.'

The nuns of Saint Katherine's had a small house with a parlour and store room below and rooms above for their visitors. There was a tiny cloistered courtyard round which were the priory buildings built of a yellowish stone. The floors were covered with decorated tiles but the food was scant and unspiced. Lady Bonville said the pleasingness of our surroundings was deceptive, the priory was poor.

'The sisters collect tithes but do not have enough to support themselves so in charity we offer money in return for their hospitality.'

The sisters were friendly, praising Lady Bonville's generosity and asking me where was my young husband, and was not Our Lady gracious to grant them such bounty. They knew nothing of Master Nicholas Radford's death but willingly said prayers for his soul at Lady Bonville's request.

Next morning with nothing to delay us we set off early. A fine mist hovered over the stream running past the priory buildings and I shivered in the autumn chill. Our meagre breakfast of a slice of bread and a small piece of cheese had done little to improve my spirits or warm my belly. Once the mist lifted I had sight of Exeter's massive cathedral. It had a long pointed roof and two huge towers and from a distance looked even larger than the Minster at York. I didn't like to ask if we might stop so that I could admire its beauty so had to content myself with twisting round in the saddle as we passed along the ridge.

The track descended to a salmon pool on the River Exe and before long the glories of Exeter were lost to view behind a belt of trees. Lady Bonville said once we reached Topsham she would send one of our escort ahead to forewarn the servants at Lympstone of our arrival.

'We shall call first at Nutwell. Lady Dynham keeps a good table and is sure to welcome us – you in particular.'

We rode down the track to Nutwell with a gentle breeze blowing in our faces. On either side the track was thick with trees, most still carrying their leaves, and beyond the trees were the wide grey waters of a river flecked with choppy little waves.

'Which river is this?' I asked the captain of our escort.

He laughed. 'That be no river, young mistress. That be where the Exe moils with the sea. There be shingle and mud when the tide be low.'

I recalled when I was a child, Alice telling me how sea serpents slid into rivers on the incoming tides and how frightened I'd been. I was no longer frightened of sea serpents. I knew now there were far worse horrors than creatures which came out of the sea. Any night when you least expected it, men could come out of the darkness, men with torches and glaves and swords; men with murder in mind.

'Fine harbour at Lympstone,' commented the captain. 'There be good trade. Brings the ladies fancy goods from the Frenchies.'

'Is that France?' I said pointing at the distant shore.

He laughed. 'Lord bless you, no, young mistress, that be Powderham.' He chuckled to himself, 'France eh!'

I said nothing else, afraid of sounding even more ignorant. I had no idea what Powderham was. Later I would ask Lady Bonville who was sure to know.

Just then the trees thinned and the home of the Dynhams came into view. To my surprise Nutwell Castle was built right by the water's edge. Although it was much smaller it reminded me of my Aunt Cecily's house in London where the outer walls of Castle Baynard sat in the river even when the tide was low.

At the sound of our horses entering the yard a half dozen lads tumbled out of the stables to help us down and lead away our weary mounts. Three servants came down the steps to carry our belongings but Lady Bonville waved them away.

'We are for Lympstone once we have eaten. I have sent our chests there.'

'Greeting, greetings! Will you not stay the night?' A woman's voice with a clear ringing tone came from the top of the steps. This must be Lady Dynham herself.

Jane, Lady Dynham was tall and well-built, not overly plump but most certainly not spare. She was dressed plainly with a large apron over her grey skirts.

'Forgive me, dear friend. I was showing my cook how to make cheese from the damsons and was up to my elbows in fruit when I heard you arrive.' She took one look at me. 'And is this your surprise?'

Lady Bonville honoured me with a smile. 'Lady Dynam, may I present Will's bride, Lady Kathryn. Kathryn is the earl of Salisbury's daughter, a Nevill from Yorkshire.'

'Yorkshire? My, you have come far, Lady Kathryn, but you are twice as welcome for being a bride. My girls will be that envious.'

'Thank you,' I said, thinking how kind she was. 'You have daughters?'

'Daughters!' She roared with laughter. 'Lady Kathryn I have five of them. All at home; all to be clothed and fed and educated and all of them needing husbands. But come, my manners are awry. We were about to dine until the damson cheese got in the way. You will stay and eat?'

'With pleasure,' said Lady Bonville.

'Then let me introduce your Will's bride to my girls.'

Lady Dynham's five daughters looked very alike: round faces, unruly dark hair and rosy cheeks. None of them were what Alice would have called pretty, more pleasant-looking.

Margery, the eldest spoke for the others. 'Lady Kathryn, we should like to take you to our room where we keep all kinds of secrets our mother knows nothing of.'

Lady Dynham laughed. 'Be gone, daughters. Take good care of Lady Kathryn, she is unused to your rough ways.'

One of the younger ones, Lizzie, whispered. 'We are not so very rough, Lady Kathryn, but our mother despairs of us. She says no man will marry us if we do not improve.'

The youngest, Kitty, surely only just out of the nursery, said, 'Is that boy not to wed Margery?'

One her sisters cuffed her gently. 'That boy is called Nicholas Carew, you dolt.'

Margery smiled at me. 'Do not mind my sisters, they like to pretend they know everything whereas in truth they know nothing.'

I was hustled up the stairs to a room with three large beds set in a row against one wall and a window with a fine view of the grounds. While we waited for the maid to bring water for me to wash, Margery explained their situation.

'My poor mother has eight of us here at Nutwell: our three little brothers and the five of us. Our father and our eldest brother are often away from home – in order to escape the noise they say – so my mother has to manage everything.'

'She is soon to lose you to the Carews, Margery,' said a girl of about my own age with a sprinkling of freckles over her nose. 'How will she manage then?'

'I wish we might lose you, Edith,' said Lizzie.

'Hush! There must be no squabbling in front of our guest.'

Margery reminded me somewhat of Alice, ordering her sisters and keeping the peace. It was comforting after the horrors of the last few days to be somewhere which felt like home with young women and girls of my own age.

It was not long before a maid arrived with a jug of hot water followed by another younger servant with a basin which she set on the chest. Once I had washed my face and hands I was given a small napkin to dry myself with. While I was doing this the Dynham girls watched with great interest.

'Is something wrong?' I asked, uncertain if I'd offended them in some way.

'Oh no,' said Edith. 'We want to see if you do things differently. Our mother says you are an earl's daughter from Yorkshire and we thought perhaps there are different ways of doing things there.'

I smiled. 'Not washing. I think that is the same everywhere.'

'Oh no,' said Kitty earnestly. 'Lizzie says there are some women who choose to bathe in fountains.'

The others laughed.

'Have you seen London?' asked Edith.

I admitted that yes, I had been three times to London.

'Is it far?'

'I think it would take you more than a week.'

'I should love to go to London,' sighed Edith. 'I've been nowhere.'

'Neither have I,' said Margery, 'and I'm older than you.'

'Did you see the king?' breathed little Kitty.

'No, not the king, but I saw the queen.'

There were five identical gasps.

'The queen!'

'What is she like?'

'Is she beautiful?'

I tried to recall what I remembered of Margaret of Anjou. 'She was smaller than I expected, dainty with dark hair and delicate features. She is very beautiful although my sister Alice says any woman who dresses in silks and satins with jewels on her clothes will look beautiful.'

Edith sighed. 'I'd love to see her.'

'Perhaps your husband will take you there one day,' said Margery. 'That is if father manages to find you a husband.'

'That will never happen,' smirked Lizzie. 'Girls who scrabble about in the dirt and get mud on their clothes are unmarriageable. No man would want a wife like that.'

I smiled at Edith. 'My sister-in-law, Lady Maud, says if your father does not find you a husband you can always go hunting for one yourself.'

Lizzie giggled. 'What fun that would be.'

'And you?' said Margery. ' Our mother says you are wed to Will Bonville.'

I nodded. 'Since more than a month ago but he stays close to his grandfather. We have barely spoken two words. Do you know him?'

'Do we know him, sisters?' said Lizzie, her eyes dancing.

'I'm not sure. Do we?' said Edith.

Little Joan jumped down from the bed. 'Stop teasing. It's not kind.'

Margery agreed. 'No more it is. Of course we know Will. We've known him since he was in baby gowns.'

'Edith kissed him once,' said Lizzie.

'I did not,' retorted Edith.

'Yes you did. I saw you.'

'Lizzie listens to too many stories,' said Margery. 'She imagines every young man is a handsome knight intent on whisking one of us away to his castle over the hill.'

'Whereas in truth they are all as dreary as Nicholas Carew,' grinned Edith.

Eventually the three younger ones became tired of our conversation and ran off to play leaving me with Margery and Edith. They were curious about my family.

'Do you have sisters?' said Edith

'Yes, I have four; and four brothers.'

'Are all your sisters married?'

When I explained that Joan was a countess their eyes widened.

'You must live very grand,' said Edith.

'No, not really and none of my other sisters has made such a good marriage as Joan.'

'Who did they marry? Do we know their husbands?'

I hesitated, unsure whether Lady Dynam's daughters would know anyone of importance.

'My sister Alice is married to Lord Fitzhugh and my sister Alianore to Lord Stanley's heir. But they are men from the north. I do not think they visit Devonshire.'

Margery said. 'We do not know them but no matter,

they must be grand if they are married to the daughters of an earl. And now you have married Will. Has Lady Bonville shown you his inheritance?'

My eyes suddenly filled with tears as I remembered where Lady Bonville had taken me.

'What's the matter?' said Margery.

'Have we upset you?' added Edith.

I told them what had happened, how the earl of Devon's men had robbed and butchered Master Radford and how I'd seen my friend lying dead in the middle of a muddy track.

'I didn't know such horrors could happen here,' I sobbed. 'I thought I'd be safe. I know it's foolish and most unbecoming in a married woman but I wish I was home with my mother and my sisters. Instead I'm all alone here in Devonshire.'

Edith put her arm around my shoulders. 'You're not alone. You've got us. We will look after you.'

Margery looked doubtful. 'Our brother said the trouble between Lord Bonville and the earl of Devon was finished. This shows he was wrong.'

I wiped my tears away with my hand and sniffed. 'Lady Bonville says the earl will not rest until every Bonville is dead. But I don't know why there is such ill feeling between them.'

Margery tried to explain from the little she knew. 'It is a matter of the king's favour. Lord Bonville has the stewardship of the duchy of Cornwall which the earl says should be his. My brother says it is a very lucrative office and the earl is angry. He sees his power waning as Lord Bonville's power grows.'

'I didn't know that,' said Edith.

'That is because you never talk to John.'

'Our brother is twenty-one and has his own household,' explained Edith. 'He lives at our father's manor of Hartland but sometimes comes to visit.'

'Is Hartland nearby?'

'No, it is more than two days ride away across the moor on the other side of Devonshire, by the coast.'

Now I knew the full extent of the Dynham family: a mother and father with one full-grown son living away and five daughters and three little boys in the nursery here at Nutwell. I gathered from their conversation that the Dynhams were one of Devonshire's most respected families. Their father had many estates and their mother was an heiress when he'd married her.

'The abbot of Hartland accuses our father of stealing his cattle and sheep but our brother says the abbot is so old he can no longer count how many he has,' laughed Edith. 'Imagine that!'

We stayed for dinner, then Lady Bonville insisted we must ride on to Lympstone. The day was growing late, the wind was already rising, there was moaning in the trees and splatters of rain on the windows.

Lady Dynham came to the top of the steps to see us leave. 'My daughters tell me they wish to keep you here, Lady Kathryn, so you must come again. Tomorrow maybe?'

I felt a wash of warmth at her welcoming words. Edith was right. Here I was among friends.

'I shall have to ask Lady Bonville. It may be she has duties for me. And I do not know how long we shall stay at Lympstone.'

Lady Dynham regarded me fondly as if I was a new-found daughter, one she'd somehow mislaid. She laughed and gave me a quick peck on my cheek.

'Oh you will stay at Lympstone until Lord Bonville comes. My servants tell me he is not yet arrived in Exeter. I warrant it will be many more days until he returns.'

Indeed it was nearly a week before Lord Bonville clattered into the yard at Lympstone. He swept in like the autumn gale which had just battered the coast, bellowing with fury, making the windows rattle and causing Lady Bonville's maids to cower in the buttery. He had with him a large contingent of men but was without his son and his grandson. I was beginning to wonder if I had imagined my wedding day. A wife with no husband seemed barely a wife at all, an odd creature poised in between two estates, neither spinster nor married woman.

At supper Lord Bonville sat glowering at his household where they sat on benches in the lower part of the hall waiting for the dishes to be brought in. He took a great gulp of wine then set his cup down on the table with a crash.

'A travesty of an inquest!' he growled to those of us sitting with him on the dais. 'Young Courtenay had no right to hold one, no right at all.' He lifted his cup again and this time downed the rest of the contents. 'Mouthing away, daring to pretend Radford died by his own hand.'

'Oh no!' I whispered.

'Ordered the servants to take their master's body down to the church. Didn't even wait for his robes, just threw an old sheet over him.'

'What a mercy Dame Thomasina was not there to see her husband treated so ill,' murmured Lady Bonville.

'Oh that was not the last of it, madam. They tipped his body into an open grave with no more compassion than if he'd been a Jew or a Saracen. No ceremony, no mass, nothing!'

I gasped. Indignity already heaped on my poor friend had been doubled.

'Took the stones Radford had bought to build his tomb and cast them on top of his body. The man who brought the news was weeping. Said his master's bones were broken and his body crushed. Not even his mother would have recognised him.'

I put my hand up to my mouth and bit my finger hard to stop myself from crying out. Poor Master Radford! Butchered like an animal in front of his own house and now his corpse treated as if he were a traitor to his king. I wanted to run away and curl up in a corner but of course could do no such thing. I reminded myself once more that I was a Nevill and Nevills were taught to endure.

Three days later, when Lady Dynham and her elder daughters were visiting, a man burst into the hall. We had just risen from the meal and were about to go up to the solar. Lady Bonville hesitated at the back of the dais, waiting to see if the matter was of importance.

Lord Bonville ran his eyes over the message he'd been given. 'Thomas Courtenay's men are running amok in Exeter,' he growled. 'They've seized the keys. God's teeth! Do they think they are the lawful garrison? I tell you, they are not. The king has put the castle under *my* command.'

'This is the second time this year there has been trouble,' murmured Lady Dynham as we ascended the steps to the solar.

Edith ran ahead of us. 'Look! There are men in the yard.'

'Come and sit down,' said her mother. 'It is not polite to stare out of Lady Bonville's window.'

Edith climbed down from her perch and resumed her seat.

Lord Bonville's manor was built high up near the church with an excellent view of the water. From the solar we could see everything that went on, not only in the yard but in the street going down to the harbour. Like everywhere in Devonshire, the lanes around Lympstone were narrow and closed in on both sides by trees or quickset hedges so that it was hard to see anyone riding along them. But the street leading down to the water's edge where the ships came in was bordered by nothing but a multitude of tiny stone hovels.

Lady Bonville looked calm but her fingers were restless in her lap. She leaned towards her friend. 'My husband is massing his men. If my brother's ruffians are despoiling Exeter it is possible they will come here next. You must see to your defences at Nutwell.'

I swallowed hard and tried not to feel afraid. My legs were trembling and I found I was murmuring prayers under my breath. Please God they wouldn't come here. Please God this would not be like Heworth Moor.

'I doubt they will bother with us but they may take this opportunity to settle their scores at Powderham,' said Lady Dynham carefully.

'Forgive me, but what is Powderham?' I asked.

'Powderham Castle is the home of Sir Philip Courtenay with whom we have a marriage connection,' explained Lady Bonville. 'Nay, do not look alarmed. Not all Courtenays are our enemies. Sir Philip is a distant cousin. He and my brother are far from being friends. Sir Philip supports Lord Bonville which enrages my brother. He would take Powderham if he could and pitch Sir Philip into the sea. It may be that is his plan.'

'To pitch Sir Philip into the sea?' said a smiling Edith who clearly had no great liking for the lord of Powderham Castle.

'Or worse,' said her mother darkly.

During the next five days, hundreds of men came and went and I seldom saw Lord Bonville other than in the yard giving orders. On the sixth day Edith visited again with her mother and she and I walked down to the quay while Lady Bonville and Lady Dynham sat with their heads together worrying over what was going to happen.

'Did you hear what happened in Exeter?' said Edith once we were away from the house.

'No, I've been told nothing. Lady Bonville believes I should be kept in ignorance.'

'The earl of Devon's men ransacked the houses of Lord Bonville's friends and then looted the cathedral.' Edith's eyes grew wider in the telling. 'The treasurer was made to hand over Master Radford's valuables.'

'Why was Master Radford's treasure in the cathedral?'

Edith shrugged. 'Maybe to keep it safe.'

'So the earl of Devon's son got what he wanted in the end,' I said bitterly, remembering the carnage at Upcott.

'He did and our mother says there were men arrested who had to buy their freedom.'

'The earl has no right to do that. His men are savages.'

'Indeed they are but there is no one to stop them. Are you afeared?'

I was horribly afraid. I knew what men could do and the thought of them coming to Lympstone made my belly quake.

'Yes, I am afraid. Are you?'

Edith considered the question. 'I don't know. Our mother has always kept us safe.'

'My mother kept me safe but danger came when it was not expected. We were returning from a wedding on a sunny summer's day.'

Edith took my hand in hers. 'Don't think about it. It is in the past and there's nothing you can do.'

It was impossible not to remember what had happened on Heworth Moor but Edith was right. It was in the past.

We took a shortcut through a tiny alleyway and found ourselves at the stone quay where two large ships were tied to sturdy wooden stakes. Several smaller boats lay on their sides, pulled up onto the shingle out of reach of the tide. The water today was calm with only a few little waves breaking against the bulky outcrop of reddish rock which sheltered the harbour to the north. Men carried barrels up from the quay to the waiting packhorses while others sat by the shingle mending sails. Several of them sang while they worked. I wondered how it was they sang so contentedly when the earl of Devon's men might descend on us at any moment. But of course I had seen what his men could do and perhaps these people had not.

In the middle of the wide expanse of water between Lympstone and the opposite shore a small boat with a single sail was heading our way. I watched as it tacked from one side to the other coming closer and closer. There were two men on board.

'Look! Over there!' said Edith suddenly, pointing in the direction of Powderham. Her eyes were sharper than mine because I could make out nothing unusual. All I could see was the now familiar shape of Powderham Castle down near the water's edge.

'What's happening?'

'Men! Look! There, beyond the marshland. On the higher ground. Hundreds of them.'

I strained my eyes and could just make out a multitude of dark figures gathering on the slopes above the castle.

'Are they?'

'Yes, they must be the earl of Devon's men. Quick we must hurry back and tell Lord Bonville what we've seen.'

At that moment the little boat which had been coming our way reached the shore. The men leapt out calling to others to pull their boat up onto the shingle.

'Powderham be under attack!' they yelled as they ran.

I grasped Edith's hand.

By the time we reached the house the men were already in the yard talking excitedly to Lord Bonville. We paused nearby but could only hear the occasional word – 'great cannon', 'serpentines', 'powder and fire'.

'What are serpentines?' asked Edith.

'Sea serpents?' I said doubtfully.

'A serpentine is a cannon,' said a man's voice from behind us.

I turned and saw a man I didn't recognise. But Edith did. The man bowed and she gave a modest curtsey.

'Master Bonville,' Forgive me, I did not see you.'

The man peered at me. 'And who is you friend. Miss Edith?'

Edith giggled. 'Oh Master Bonville, surely you recognise your son's wife.'

So this was my father-in-law, the man who allowed his father to steal his son and who had failed to attend our wedding. He was of medium height with fairish hair and the kind of face it was easy to forget, a nothing sort of face with a weak soft mouth. To hide my confusion I dropped a curtsey far lower than was necessary.

'Daughter-in-law, greetings,' he said in a disinterested voice as if I was nobody in particular. 'I suggest you return to the other women. Your place is not here with the men.'

With that he bowed and strode off to join his father.

Edith and I ran up the stairs to the solar. At the top we almost bumped into my husband. He had grown taller since I'd last seen him but his manners had not improved. He gave me an appalled look, mumbled a greeting and fled down the stairs.

'See how he runs! I think he's afeared of you,' giggled Edith.

'Nonsense. He is just a boy. My York cousins were the same when they were younger.'

'You have boy cousins?'

'Yes, four.'

Is their father also an earl?'

'No, their father is the duke of York.'

Edith's mouth dropped open. 'The duke of York?'

'Yes. He is married to my Aunt Cecily, my father's sister.'

'But the duke of York is a very great man; he knows the king.'

I smiled. 'Yes, I suppose he does. They are close kin.'

'Did your father not wish to marry you to one of these York cousins whose father is close kin to the king?'

I knew I was blushing at the thought of the kiss I had shared last Christmas with Edward and how, for an instant, he held me in his arms.

I sighed. 'Maybe he did but we are not grand enough for the Yorks.'

'What could be grander than an earl's daughter?'

'A duke's daughter or a foreign princess perhaps.' I tried a little smile to hide my embarrassment.

'You are joking.'

'No, truly. That is what my aunt Cecily wants for Edward.'

'Edward?'

'He is the eldest son.'

'The one who will inherit his father's title?'

'Yes.'

'The one you fancy?'

'I do not fancy Edward.'

Edith gave me the sort of look Alice sometimes did when she knew I was lying.

'Of course it doesn't matter if you do or if you don't because now you are married to Will Bonville and that's an end to it.'

'Yes,' I said, feeling utterly deflated. 'Now I am married to Will Bonville and that is an end to everything.'

Next morning Lady Bonville told me she was sending me to stay with Lady Dynham. It was for my own safety, she said, but I believe she found me yet one more problem when she was already overburdened. I offered to help but she was one of those women unwilling to cede one inch of responsibility. It was as if she had already forgotten how well I had acquitted myself at Upcott.

I was unsure how much safer we were at Nutwell. We could hear muffled booms from across the water as the earl of Devon's great cannon pounded the walls of Powderham Castle and from the upper rooms could see smoke and occasional flashes of fire. Tom had told me how once the powder was set alight, the cannon would send huge lead balls crashing into the stone. Shards of rock and splinters of wood would be thrown skyward and men would die. I wondered if my Montagu grandfather had been scared on the day he'd been killed by one of the French king's cannon.

'Lord Bonville is taking ships across to Powderham,' Lady Dynham said at dinner.

'Is he going to rescue Sir Philip Courtenay?' said Lizzie.

'He's going to steal their great cannon,' said Kitty firmly. 'That's what I would do.'

'You'd hide under the bed,' said Joan.

Their mother ordered them to be silent or they could join their little brothers in the nursery for their meal.

'Is what Lord Bonville doing, dangerous?' I asked.

Unlike Will's step-grandmother, Lady Dynham saw no need to protect me from the reality of what was happening.

'Naturally it is dangerous but Lord Bonville and his men are armed. However I hear the earl's men number more than a thousand.'

After dinner, instead of going up to the solar as we were supposed to do, we stood on the steps and watched Lord Bonville's ships making their way across the water.

'I cannot bear to watch,' said Joan. 'What if their ships should be hit by a ball from one of the great cannon."

'Cover your eyes, you baby,' said Lizzie.

Kitty already had her face buried in Margery's skirt and was refusing to look.'

'Watch if you wish,' said their mother. 'But you would do better to offer up your prayers. Lord Bonville's plan is reckless and he will need all the prayers he can get.' She clicked her tongue in disapproval and disappeared in the direction of the chapel taking Margery and the younger girls with her.

Edith and I retreated to the room she shared with her sisters and sat on the floor so that we were not tempted to look out of the window.

'What will you do when all this is over and we are at peace again?' asked Edith.

'Set up a household with Will Bonville, I suppose.'

'Think what fun it will be to have your own servants.'

I shrugged. 'I suppose so.'

'And to have a husband.'

'Do you want a husband?' I asked. 'Like Margery.'

Edith pulled a face. 'Ugh! Who would want to marry Nicholas Carew.'

'Your mother says it is a good marriage.'

'Maybe it is for Margery. But I don't want to get married yet. I want to travel to London. I want to see the wonderful places you've told us about and I want to see the queen. Perhaps I can be one of her women. She must have women.'

'Yes, she does. All great ladies have women to keep them company. My Aunt Cecily has half a dozen.'

'Then that is what I shall do. I shall come with you when you go to London and you will beg a place for me with one of these great ladies you know.'

'I doubt I shall see London again,' I said miserably. 'Or my family. I think I am fated to remain here in Devonshire as Will Bonville's wife.'

Edith came and put her arm round me. 'You and I shall have wonderful adventures together, like Josiane and Bevis in the stories you've told us. And if he behaves himself we shall allow Will Bonville to come with us.'

I gave a weak smile. 'What a comfort you are, dear Edith. You are a like a sister.'

She gave a look of utter disgust. 'Thank you but I have quite enough sisters. You are my friend, my most special friend.'

Lord Bonville's expedition force to rescue Powderham returned to Lympstone in tatters. They had been intercepted at sea by Henry Courtenay, the earl of Devon's second son and two of our men were killed by Henry Courtenay himself. Lord Bonville wisely retreated before his ship was captured and he and the remainder of his party butchered. He now planned to make the journey to Powderham by road, bypassing Exeter. It would be dangerous riding straight into the teeth of the enemy but Will's grandfather was a brave man, determined not to accept defeat. He said if the earl of Devon and his sons behaved as if Powderham was in enemy country then he would declare war on them as if they were the enemy.

'I am sending you to Shute,' said a worried Lady Bonville.

'Why?' I blurted out, forgetting it was impolite to question her decision.

'Because you of all young women must be kept safe. Dame Elizabeth is at Shute with her household so you will be cared for. And I have spoken to Lady Dynham. She has graciously offered one of her daughters as a companion for you. Margery is soon to be wed but Edith is eager to make herself useful.' She twisted her mouth into what might in other circumstances have passed for a smile. 'I doubt you would enjoy a month of undiluted witterings by Dame Elizabeth. She is a most tedious woman.'

'That is very kind of you, Lady Grandmother, but...'

'There is no but to be said. You will leave early tomorrow. I shall order the escort myself and your father-in-law will accompany you. But remember, it is a hard ride at this time of year with the days short so you must not delay. Haste is essential.'

12

SHUTE 1455

When we left next morning the lanes were still drenched in darkness but a greyness the colour of a dusty pearl was slowly colouring the sky beyond Lympstone. With torches to guide us we rode swiftly up the hill, leaving the houses behind. As the sky grew lighter we passed several small villages where the people came out of their dwellings to stare curiously at our party. My father-in-law ignored them, making no greetings. He was a taciturn companion and I was glad of Edith's presence or I would have felt very alone. We crossed a small stone bridge over a river but the track was still rough and once or twice my horse stumbled. By the time we reached the Honiton road the surface had become flat and the going easier for which I delivered a silent prayer of thanks.

The ride was arduous and it was dusk before we reached Gittisham where I was told we were to spend the night. The Beaumonts, who owned the manor, were kin of the Dynhams through marriage and they greeted our party with obvious pleasure.

'Welcome, welcome,' boomed Sir Philip Beaumont. 'You are that fortunate to find us at home. We should have returned to Shirwell by now but we have been delayed.'

'Greetings, my dears,' said Lady Blanche, a tall willowy woman who topped her young husband by an inch. She was, Edith told me in a hushed aside, born a Bourchier and the marriage had been a coup for Sir Philip.

I was slowly beginning to understand the webs of kinship which bound these great Devonshire families together: the Courtenays, the Bonvilles, the Carews, the Dynhams and now the Beaumonts. It was like the Nevills, the Percys and the Cliffords in Yorkshire, intermarrying time and time again down the years.

'We hear the king is sick,' remarked our host at supper, dabbing his mouth with his napkin. 'York's to be protector once more.'

My father-in-law nodded in agreement. 'Is that so? Yes, I see that it would be.'

It was clear that my father-in-law had no opinions of his own merely echoed what was said to him by others. He was a perfectly pleasant man but I understood why Lord Bonville had taken Will into his own household to rear. He was determined that his grandson would shape up to be the kind of Bonville heir the old man wanted.

'Such unsettled times,' murmured Lady Blanche to me. 'I gather there is trouble again in Exeter.'

'Yes, my lady. I believe there is.'

'And you are bound for Shute.'

'Yes, my lady.'

She sucked at her teeth. 'Let us pray the duke of York will come and bring order as he did before.'

I nodded agreement, hoping that if he came, he would also bring Edward. Though my mother's letter had said Edward was still with my brother, Richard.

'Did you hear that harlot of a sister-in-law of mine

has married Bodrugun,' growled Sir Philip. 'The man's a scoundrel and she should be horsewhipped.'

This sounded like gossip of the highest order and I sensed Edith pricking up her ears.

'She is a Courtenay,' whispered Lady Blanche. 'Married to my husband's poor brother. It is the most terrible scandal and such a worry.'

'Why for?' I asked.

'Oh my dear, she preferred Sir Henry Bodrugun's company to that of her husband – if you understand me. Then my husband's brother died most conveniently for her and now there is a child, a boy. Nobody knows which man is the father and the wife is not saying. It is utterly shameful.'

I made sympathetic noises but I knew none of these people despite now knowing their most intimate secrets.

Lady Blanche glanced at Edith and whispered to me, 'Edith is unwed, but you, my dear, as a married woman, will understand how these things can happen.'

I murmured that, yes, I did understand, although in truth I knew nothing of matters between husbands and wives having not passed more than a handful of moments in the company of my husband.

Sir Philip cleared his throat. 'Colcombe was attacked day before yesterday, so my steward tells me. Ruffians got away with a fair bit of loot. That your father's doing?'

'I wouldn't know, Sir Philip,' said my father-in-law staring miserably at his fish.

'Probably was. Mind you what else can young Courtenay expect, killing a man like Radford. You know about that, I presume.'

214

'Yes indeed. Very sad.'

'Sad! It was monstrous. Gave Radford a commission myself last year, nothing of great importance, y'know, just a small matter. Clever man though. Great loss to us. Yes, a great loss.'

'I told Sir Philip to double the guard on the outside gates,' whispered Lady Blanche. 'One cannot be too careful when there are armed cut-throats riding around murdering innocent persons in their beds.'

'No indeed,' I agreed.

'And will you be alone at Shute,'

'No, my lady. We are to join my mother-in-law.'

'Ah yes, Dame Elizabeth. A Harington if I remember aright.'

'Yes, my lady.'

She sucked at her teeth again. 'And your husband is to inherit? What a fortunate young woman you are.'

I agreed with her that yes, I was a most fortunate young woman. I would have what every one of my sisters had assured me was desirable in marriage: a title and a wealthy young husband. Love, as Alice had told me a hundred times, had nothing to do with marriage. And yet Sir Philip's sister-in-law had risked everything for love of Sir Henry Bodrugan.

I would have liked to stay longer at Gittisham and listen to more Devonshire gossip and the indiscretions of Sir Philip's family but my father-in-law insisted we leave early in the morning.

'Come and visit us at Shirwell,' called Lady Blanche from the steps as we mounted our horses and made ready to leave.

215

'Yes. yes!' called Sir Philip. 'Perhaps the duke would care to accompany you, Lady Kathryn,' he laughed. 'Fine hunting on the moor, y'know.'

'He imagines you intimate with the duke of York,' murmured Edith as we waved farewell to the Beaumonts and trotted up the track towards the road. 'Whereas, if the truth were to be known, it is the son with whom you are intimate.'

I was tempted to reach over and give her a push but instead chose to ignore her remark.

The sky was overcast but there was no sign of rain and it wasn't long before we reached the town of Honiton. Here we turned off the road onto a muddy track which led up a steep hill and thence onto a series of narrow lanes, stony and dirty and all up and down, like the ones I'd become used to in Devonshire. We crossed a meandering brook and entered thickly wooded country, the kind which provides perfect cover for an ambush. I thought longingly of the flat open marshlands of Lincolnshire and how foolish I'd been to believe them threatening. This terrain where you could see no further than the nearest tree, was far more dangerous.

After another hour's travelling we began descending a slope, Ahead of us, in amongst a dark tangle of bare trees, I saw the top of a stone building, and beyond, a valley stretching away to the south.

'Shute,' said my father-in-law with no great enthusiasm.

The house at Shute was solidly built of a greyish stone, not large but tall with narrow lancet windows and a little tower to one side. There were outbuildings, stables and the like, and a church nearby, much smaller than the one at Chewton Mendip. We rode to the side of the house and round into a small courtyard where an old man and a boy stood waiting. My father-in-law helped me down while the captain of our escort, having taken one despairing look at the old man, offered his hand to Edith.

'Where is your mistress?' my father-in-law enquired.

'A-praying,' shrugged the old man. 'She'em usually a-praying.'

My father-in-law ignored the man's rudeness and led the way through the door.

Inside, the house was dark with very few windows yet no-one had thought fit to light candles. The hall was unkempt with yesterday's ashes cold in the hearth and a ripe odour rising from the rushes at our feet. I wrinkled my nose in disgust and noticed Edith doing the same. We were both used to cleanliness and she must have wondered, as I did, why the servants had not laid fresh rushes for our arrival. We were about to ascend the narrow stairway at the back of the hall when my mother-in-law appeared. She came tripping down the steps like a young girl, her skirts trailing behind her, disturbing a fine layer of dust. To my surprise she was dressed in pale yellow silk as if for a grand occasion rather than in a sober gown which is what most women wore in the daytime. Her hair, instead of being confined in a coif, was loose and flowing like a bride's.

I curtsied. 'Forgive me, Dame Elizabeth. We have disturbed you. Please pay us no heed.'

To my even greater surprise she ignored me completely. She ran towards her husband and flung her arms around his neck, nestling into his riding cloak in the way of a motherless chick seeking warmth.

'You have come!' she breathed.

Showing not the least bit of emotion her husband detached her arms from his neck and set her away from him. He gave her the slightest of bows.

'Greetings, madam. I have brought your daughter-in-law and her companion, Lady Dynham's daughter, Miss Edith.' He pulled a letter from his purse. 'I have here instructions from my father's wife. She prays you keep well and asks for your prayers in return. Please read the letter and see that her wishes are carried out.'

Without another word he gave a small bow and walked away. He treated her as if he was another man's messenger. He hadn't kissed her or shown any pleasure at her presence. It was a cold homecoming.

His wife stretched out her hands and gave a plaintive mew of distress. 'Husband! See! I am clothed to please you. Husband! I will do whatever you wish but please come back. Do not leave me again.'

A distant door slammed as my father-in-law went out into the yard.

'He's gone,' she said in the bleakest of voices.

'He has to hurry back to Lympstone,' I said gently. 'The earl of Devon's men are laying siege to Powderham. Lord Bonville has need of him.'

'And my boy?' she asked.

'I believe he is with his grandfather.'

She nodded. 'Of course. Where else would he be. It has been so long I have forgot what he looks like. Have you seen him, pretty bride?'

'Yes, but just the once.'

'He was a handsome boy,' she said wistfully.

'He is good-looking, still,' I lied, remembering the truculent youth of our wedding day and the way he had scowled at me.

''I must instruct the cook. My husband will want dinner.' She gave me another sad smile. 'I shall have the kitchen make those little spiced cakes he enjoys so much. And then there is the matter of wine. My husband will want his favourite but I have forgot what it is.' She looked at me, her eyes brimming with tears. 'I have forgot.'

'Your husband does not intend to dine, my lady. He said he did not have the time.'

She gave another mew and covered her face with her hands.

I put my hand on her arm. 'Do not distress yourself, Dame Elizabeth. It is a matter of urgency, you understand. I am certain he would take dinner with you if Lord Bonville had not ordered his immediate return.'

Now I understood why the hall was dirty and the candles unlit. Dame Elizabeth was a careless mistress who had not the wit to take interest in her surroundings. Her husband ignored her and she had allowed her servants to become lazy. Perhaps my first appraisal was correct and she was like Uncle Fauconberg's wife, a woman without a sensible thought in her head, unable to keep order or converse with anyone other than the furry creatures she kept for company.

I spent the next few days investigating the household at Shute, poking my head into dark and cobwebby storerooms, exploring a warren of little outbuildings and observing the servants as they worked. As expected, I saw waste and idleness everywhere. Ale was allowed to go sour in the barrel, boys failed to scrub out pots as they should, and the steward, who should have been setting an example to others, was removing candle ends for his own purposes.

Alice had warned me how petty thievery could become rife in the best of households if a woman was not vigilant. A piece of green silk, one you had almost forgotten in the bottom of your sewing box, might go missing; a shortage in the delivery of wine would be blamed on the carter from Hull; and there would be the surreptitious selling of victuals at the kitchen door. I was told to pay close attention to my accounts.

After a week I asked Dame Elizabeth if I might suggest some ideas to our cook.

'Perhaps you might care to try a dish my mother enjoys at Middleham.'

She looked at me out of her vacant blue eyes. 'Pretty girl, do as you wish. You are the bride now and this is a house for a bride. My husband said those words to me on our wedding day. He said this would be our home and our children would be born here.'

Her mouth curved into an odd little smile as her mind wandered into the past where once she had been happy. Then like a candle snuffed out before sleep her mouth turned down and her eyes filled with tears. 'But there was only Will and they took him away.'

'I'm sure he will come back,' I said.

She brightened visibly. 'Yes, he will come back.' Then her face crumpled again. 'But I am no longer a bride. I am fifteen years wed and they will send me away. They have bought you for Will, to be rid of me. I knew that one day you would come. But I am not ready. I shall give you this house and I shall give you my life and I shall pray you have more joy of it than me.'

Edith looked embarrassed and, to hide my discomfort, I became brisk and businesslike.

'You do not mind if I make some suggestions to the cook and perhaps to the other servants?'

'I do not mind. Why would I.' she whispered.

'Is she mad?' said Edith, as Dame Elizabeth drifted away towards her seat by the hearth.

I smiled sadly. 'Not in the way you mean. I think she is sunk in a profound melancholy. There was a woman like her at Middleham. Her children were all dead and when her husband drowned she lay on her bed and would speak to no-one.'

'What happened to her?'

'She died.'

I left Edith tending to Dame Elizabeth and went down to the hall to start a reorganisation of our household. 'Begin at the top,' Alice had told me. So I summoned the steward. He was a lean fellow of about thirty with lank dark hair and a shifty look in his eyes. His tunic was none too clean but I noticed his boots were new and costly.

I looked him straight in the eye until he lowered his gaze. The first rule, Alice had said, was never look away. Your servants must respect you and they must fear you, otherwise you will have trouble. This man, I sensed, might well be trouble. I had met his sort before. They whined and wheedled and protested their innocence at every turn, and would sell their grandmother for sixpence if it suited their purpose.

I spoke firmly. 'As you know I am Mistress Bonville, and before he left, my father-in-law asked me to take charge of Dame Elizabeth's household duties. She is unwell and requires special care. I shall interview all the men of the household but knowing your senior position I thought to begin with you. First I should like to see the accounts.'

I saw panic flare in his eyes and knew my suspicions were correct. He had been involved in some kind of thievery. I doubted it was vast but it might take a while to uncover exactly what he'd been doing. Absent master and careless mistress was a recipe for disaster, that much I did know.

If the next week was uncomfortable for me it was many times more uncomfortable for the servants. They could no longer idle their way through their work as I expected each task completed to my satisfaction and would accept no excuses. The man charged with bringing in the logs complained bitterly of his aching back and his boy, who had previously slept in the hearth at night, was forced to find other accommodation much to his disappointment.

'The fire in the hall must be kept alight at all times as must the one in Dame Elizabeth's chamber,' I ordered. 'Lord Bonville would not want his daughter-in-law to take a chill from your idleness and neglect.'

I had discovered that mention of Will's grandfather struck terror into the servants, especially those in the yard where I'd found the stables unswept and the horses ungroomed. The lads had failed to clean the leathers properly and the hayracks were near-empty. The old man received his orders in a state of sullen silence but my sharp words reduced to tears the small boy whose task was to collect up any horse droppings.

The red-faced cook who served dinner whenever it suited him and supper too early in the day, was surprisingly amenable to change. Perhaps he had longed for order and direction. Certainly his kitchen boys worked faster and more willingly once I had explained what was required. Despite our meatless Advent days, inviting smells soon wafted through to the hall where three house servants were occupied scrubbing boards of months of accumulated grime.

I put on my cloak and walked to the tiny church where I'd been several times to hear mass. The air was chill, a light frost powdering the ground. With no sun, branches which only yesterday wove a delicate tracery of different hues were now painted in unrelieved black. I shivered, more from an indefinable fear than from cold. I opened the chapel door and discovered Sir Robert, the old priest, peering at a piece of intricate stonework on a pillar.

He was a strange man, surprisingly unlettered for a priest and yet knowledgeable in many other ways. Who else would take interest in a master mason's old carvings. He was cared for by a slatternly young woman who, according to Dame Elizabeth's maid, was most certainly more than just a housekeeper. The priest's cottage was small and there was rumoured to be only one mattress.

'Sir Robert, you know who I am.'

'Aye mistress, I know.'

'I have to tell you that Dame Elizabeth lacks spiritual care. You do not visit her as you ought.'

He rubbed his hands on his sleeves and seemed to shrink inside his clothes, the white bristles on his stubbly chin wobbling slightly. 'It be not my fault, mistress. I said she'm were mazed and he told me to stay away. Said I were naught but a God-spouting prattler.'

'Who told you to stay away?'

'Master, him who be her husband. Raised his fist to me.'

'And do you still think Dame Elizabeth mazed?'

He eyed me suspiciously. 'The devil sups in the halls of the rich as easy as in the cots of the poor, that much we do know. I'd drive him out but the master would have none of it. Called me a meddler, said he'd hang me from the bell rope if I laid so much as a finger on her. But it bain't her, 'tis the work of Satan.'

I'd already heard him preach hell-fire and damnation to the people of Shute and feared he might do more harm than good to Dame Elizabeth by interfering. If I wanted help I would have to seek it elsewhere.

I looked at him severely. 'I think maybe it is better if you attend to your flock, Sir Robert and I shall mind Dame Elizabeth.'

With my chin held high I left the old man muttering away about the devil and all his works and walked back to the house, wishing there was someone to share my burdens. Edith was a pleasant companion and I loved her dearly but I couldn't load my problems on to her shoulders, that would not be right.

Once the house was cleaned and meals served on time, I turned my attention to devising entertainment for Dame

Elizabeth. I thought an amusement of some kind might rouse her from her melancholy. The season of Advent was nearly done and it was time to start thinking of Christmas festivities.

'What does your Aunt Cecily do?' asked Edith, ever curious as to the goings-on in the York household.

I smiled. 'I do not think we can have grand celebrations like my aunt does at Castle Baynard but we might entertain our neighbours to a feast.'

Edith looked doubtful. 'We've been here four weeks and I've yet to see anyone who doesn't belong to the manor. Perhaps there is no-one. Perhaps we are all alone out here in the wildness of Devonshire.'

Perhaps we were. Certainly no-one had visited since we'd arrived at Shute and knowing how curious people were who lived in country places, I found that odd.

When I broached the subject with my mother-in-law, Dame Elizabeth was vague. 'I used to dance in my satin slippers. Do you like to dance, pretty girl?'

'I do. But have we no neighbours we might invite if we had a musical entertainment?'

There were no minstrels at Shute but I reckoned I could hire some. There were always bands of players wanting employment especially nowadays with men back from France. Even if it meant sending to Honiton or Exeter we would surely find someone.

Dame Elizabeth stared into the flames. 'My husband stood beneath my window one May morning. He sang for me. 'Twas the year my Will was born. The hall was decked with spring flowers and he said I was his treasure.'

She was lost again in another of her reveries. This was getting me nowhere so I went downstairs and sought out the steward. He would know who were our neighbours and since I'd exerted my authority over the household he had become less hostile.

He shuffled his feet and looked evasive. 'Colcombe be the nearest, mistress. Two mile down the valley.'

The name was familiar. Someone had mentioned Colcombe recently but I wasn't sure when.

'Who lives there?'

'Ye don't want to have no truck with the folks at Colcombe, mistress. That'd be most unwise. Yes, most unwise.'

'My father-in-law must have dealings with them.'

'Aye. They do send their swine up when it be mast time. Reeve do say they beasts be away soon for the killing.'

'Mast time?'

Mast was a word I'd not heard before but Devonshire was full of strange new words.

'Ground in they woods be covered with mast in a good year. Swine have a rare fancy for they.'

Now I understood. The hill behind the house was thick with beech trees and our neighbours at Colcombe sent their pigs to clear our beech nuts. A not uncommon practice. I wondered what we asked for in return.

'If we do business with them then we must be acquainted. Whose manor is it?'

He glanced at me and then looked away. 'Earl of Devon, mistress.'

I gave an involuntary gasp and raised my hands to cover my mouth.

The steward grinned at my discomfort. 'Sir Thomas Courtenay do live there when it do please him.'

Merciful Mother of God! Two miles away! The man who had ordered the killing of Nicholas Radford and the sack of his house could be quartered two miles down the valley at this very moment. We'd heard nothing of events at Powderham since we'd arrived at Shute and by now this eldest son of the earl of Devon might have ridden back to his home at Colcombe. Then I recalled who had mentioned the name.

'The castle was attacked a few weeks back, was it not?'

'Aye, mistress, it were.'

'By Lord Bonville's men?'

'Aye, praise be.'

'And what will Sir Thomas Courtenay do when he returns and finds his house in ruins.'

The steward shrugged. 'Like as not send his men to Shute to settle the score. But we be ready for 'em.'

From nowhere the words which Maud had spoken on Heworth Moor jumped into my mind. "Do not let them see you are afraid".

But I was afraid. I was afraid of what Sir Thomas Courtenay's men would do to me, to Edith and to my mother-in-law and what they would do to our home and our servants. I'd seen the results of their savagery at Upcott. Here there was no-one to turn to for protection and it was too late to summon Uncle Fauconberg. Perhaps neither of us had imagined the urgency of a situation like this but it was clear my safety and that of my household depended on me. The servants would look to me to make decisions. Merciful Mother of God! What was I going to do?

'How many men-at-arms do we have?' I asked, trying to ignore the knot of terror in my stomach.

The steward scratched his head. For a man so clever at covering up his thievery he was remarkably slow with numbers.

'There do be two old muttonheads live in the guardhouse down by the gate. They'm used to be handy with a pike, years back.' He thought some more. 'And there do be a dozen young scrappers round and about. And cook's good with an axe. Have ye seen him cleave a beast in twain, mistress? Fair makes a man jump, that great chopper of his.'

'You think that will be enough? Have we no-one else?'

'Used to have plenty, but they went with master t'other day. Said he needed they for hisself.'

How could I tell my mother-in-law that her husband had taken her men-at-arms and left her unprotected. My father-in-law must have known the danger we could be in with the earl of Devon's castle a mile or more down the valley, yet he had removed our guard.

I ran back up the stairs, my heart pounding, all thoughts of entertainment and festivities banished. Edith was playing a game of fox and geese with Dame Elizabeth. They looked so happy and at ease I did not have the heart to tell them what I'd discovered. I walked over to the narrow window and stood staring out over the valley. It was nearly dusk and apart from an occasional glimmer of light from one of the dwellings by the gate, there was nothing else to be seen. I prayed they would not come yet.

I lay awake most of the night making plans and when I finally fell asleep I dreamed of dark pools of blood and Lord Egremont waving an axe in my face, snarling how he'd split me in twain. I woke, sweating with fear, my throat dry and my body trembling. After that I was too scared to sleep. If demons were lying in wait I'd rather be awake with my wits alert than struggling to escape through the mire in a dreamlike state.

As soon as the house began to stir, I slipped out of bed and crossed the floor to my chest. I opened the lid and rummaged around through carefully layered piles of clothing. Uncle Fauconberg's gift lay at the bottom. I lifted it out and withdrew the dagger from its leather sheath. I stared at the blade. Even in the dim light from my single candle it gleamed wickedly. As I turned my wrist the metal flashed and I recalled my uncle's words – "There is danger everywhere." I returned the dagger to its sheath and laid it under my pillow.

I woke Christine and had her help me dress, then, in the half-light I walked down to the gatehouse to have words with the two old soldiers in the guardroom. I found them taking their ease with a cup of ale, their rusty pikes stacked neatly in the corner. Having given them instructions and made certain they understood the importance of what they had to do, I returned to the yard. There I sought out the old man who was supposed to be in charge. I ordered him to find me two boys. They would need to be strong as well as sensible as the task I had in mind would be difficult. They were to take a message to Lympstone, a ride of two days, and they must have wit enough not to get lost or allow their horses to be stolen. I could not afford to send one of the men, I needed every able-bodied man we had here at Shute.

The steward was difficult but I'd expected nothing less.

'It b'aint be my province, mistress, not ordering them outside men.'

'Well it is most certainly not mine,' I snapped.

He wriggled his shoulders and fiddled with the ends of his sleeves, trying to look put-upon but succeeded only in resembling a recalcitrant schoolboy.

'Do you wish me to tell Lord Bonville you left Dame Elizabeth to be attacked in her bed?' I said.

'Nay, mistress.'

'Then you will do as you're bid. Remember, it is to be *every* man. And tell the reeve to have men sharpen the scythes and the billhooks.'

I went next to the kitchen and had words with the cook. He had a fine display of knives at his disposal. The cleavers hanging from hooks on the walls resembled vast axe heads of the kind men carried slung from their saddles; the great two-handled one used for splitting beasts looked particularly dangerous. In truth, any of the cook's metal implements could be used as a weapon if we were attacked. A blow on the head from his great cauldron would knock the brains out of a man as effectively as a war hammer. I eyed the spit uneasily, imagining a man skewered by its long central spike.

There was an air of simmering excitement amongst the kitchen boys who doubtless were looking forward to what they hoped would be a great brawl, giving no thought to losing limbs or friends dying. They talked of boiling oil and flame-tipped arrows, and their eagerness to disembowel a Colcombe man I found quite disturbing. But the cook was sanguine. 'Innards be what they learn about, mistress. They do wish to see if a man have chitterlings in his belly same as they beasts. 'Tis only natural.'

It might be natural but it was not pleasant.

13

SHUTE WOODS 1455

That night I was lying awake in the near silent house when I thought I heard a noise. Edith's body was warm against mine, her breathing peaceful. I sat up and twitched open the bed curtains. Outside in the yard were men's voices and from the stairway, footsteps. I leapt out of bed. I was fully dressed.

'You cannot wear your outer garments and your boots!' Edith had said as we'd prepared for bed.

I'd taken her by her shoulders. 'My mother said that when her great-grandmother's husband came home from his soldiering he would leap into bed with his wife without even removing his boots. If he did it, so can I. I shall feel safer.'

Edith had fussed as she changed into her warmest and plainest gown and thick stockings but insisted on wearing her nightcap. Dame Elizabeth had made no complaints at all, treating my insistence on boots in bed as part of the strange new order I was bringing to Shute.

I was fastening my cloak when Christine, opened the door to the steward.

'Torches, mistress. Hundreds of them. Coming up the valley. They be men from Colcombe. Ye'd best hide.' He took one look at our boots and warm clothes and nodded approvingly. 'The church, that be the best place. They'll not harm ye there.'

I had no intention of going to the church. I'd seen what the earl of Devon's men had done at Upcott and I remembered how the Percy brothers had danced on the altar at Garston. Men fired up in a frenzy of savagery forgot they were Christians and behaved like infidels. And everyone knew what infidels did to women.

I grabbed the dagger from under my pillow and attached it to my belt. Using a taper I lit the lantern I'd placed on the chest the night before and, picking it up, urged the others to follow me down the stairs. Instead of crossing the hall, I led them to a side door which gave out onto a rough patch of grass. The door was locked and bolted but I had obtained the key and with Edith's help pulled back the bolts and pushed open the door.

We were protected by a high wall to one side and by the house on the other. Holding the lantern up high I hurried along the path. I had explored this route the day before and knew exactly where I was going. I could hear our men shouting to one another, the low growl of older men and the excited voices of boys urging the earl of Devon's men to "come and get 'em if they dare."

We passed through a small gate onto another path which led between a screen of bushes to the church. A single candle flame flickered in the darkness behind one of the narrow windows. Suddenly there came a great clanging as someone began ringing the bell. The warning would bring people running from the outlying hovels and I was glad we'd gone before chaos overtook the house. Already I could hear women screaming and children crying. I led the others through the burying ground. We climbed over the low wall at the far end, helping Dame Elizabeth and trying not to snag our skirts on any protruding stones. Once over we set off up the slope towards the woods.

'Mistress, where be we going?' cried Dame Elizabeth's maid.

'Into the trees.'

The stupid girl stopped. 'There be demons in they woods.'

'There are demons coming up from Colcombe, you foolish girl,' I hissed.

'But I be afeared, mistress.'

She was about seventeen years old, slow and stupid. I gave her a sharp slap across her face. 'Be quiet! The men who are coming are no respecters of women. Do you want to be raped? Or murdered? Because that's all they know. Now, stop complaining and follow me.'

She snivelled and trailed unwillingly after her mistress but by the time we reached the trees she was nowhere to be seen.

'Where has she gone?' I said, looking around.

'She'm went back, mistress,' said Christine, looking as if she too would like to run back to what she perceived as safety.

'She'll have gone to the church,' said Edith.

I hesitated. Inwardly I cursed the girl. Our situation was dangerous enough without having a stupid young women hindering our escape.

'Perhaps we should go and find her?' Edith sounded hopeful.

'Leave her be,' I ordered. 'She's made her choice and we've not got time to go back.'

With a hand that shook I reached inside the lantern to extinguish the candle, burning my fingers in the process. We were plunged into immediate darkness. I was afraid to show a light up here in case it was seen. Above the house a sliver of moon shed a pale wash over the rooftops but as I watched it disappeared and the darkness became absolute.

'Should we not have stayed?' whispered Edith looking longingly in the direction of the buildings.

'No. The men have their orders and besides, think what the earl of Devon's men might do to us.'

I'd told Edith of the narrow escape I'd had on Heworth Moor and how Lord Egremont had wanted Maud for his own evil purposes. She nodded uncertainly but loyally followed me into the trees. There was no path. I had no idea where to go but reckoned if we kept climbing we'd get further and further away from danger. When the earl of Devon's men came searching the woods they'd not know where to look and I'd told the others to make sure there were no snagged pieces of cloth or other signs of our passing.

As we threaded our way through the trees, climbing higher and higher, Dame Elizabeth held onto the back of my cloak while Edith and Christine brought up the rear. It was hard going. The ground was covered with treacherous tree roots and dead branches which snapped under our feet, making our progress slow. Before long we heard the dull crackle and roar of a great fire accompanied by distant shouts and piercing screams. As we struggled on, the sounds pursued us relentlessly through the trees.

We continued to climb until the only noise was our laboured breathing, all other sounds had faded into the distance. Still we pressed onwards.

'What's that?' whispered Edith, stopping suddenly.

I peered into the darkness but could see little. Then Edith screamed. Just once before I grabbed her and put my hand over her mouth. Mutely she pointed. Now I too could hear what she'd heard: a grunting, snoring sound. At first I thought Dame Elizabeth's maid was not mistaken and these were the sounds of demons but as I peered into the darkness I could just make out several large humped shapes lying in a deep hollow.

'What are they?' whispered Edith, shivering with fear.

I squashed the desire to laugh. 'The Colcombe swine taking their ease.'

Dame Elizabeth sank to the ground and began crooning a song under her breath.

'Can we not stop? We are weary to the bone,' said Edith.

'Very well but first we must find somewhere to hide. We cannot stay here in the open, we need shelter.'

I was growing accustomed to the darkness and it didn't take long to find where a tangle of undergrowth had spilled over a bank and the ditch below was dry, making a natural space where we could secrete ourselves.

'Are we not too close to the pigs?' worried Edith.

'They are our protectors. If men come searching, the noise from the swine will be so great they'll not hear us.'

It was very cold but we snuggled up close together, covered almost completely by our thick hooded cloaks, whispering to each other. I said prayers which gave the others some comfort because from their voices I knew how scared they were. After that the whispers became fewer. First Dame Elizabeth fell silent and then Edith and

Christine and finally, worn out by the climb, I too drifted into an exhausted dreamless sleep.

I woke to the sound of grunting, I opened my eyes. The darkness was not as deep as it had been during the night. I didn't move but lay watching what I thought was a branch. Gradually the branch developed a clear outline and soon I could make out other branches and the trunk of a tree. The ground was covered in husks and twigs and dead leaves but, tucked into the ditch, we were invisible to all but the most diligent searcher. Then I remembered the hounds at Middleham. What if they brought hounds into the woods to find us!

As quietly as I could, without disturbing the others, I wriggled out of our hiding place. By now there was light in the sky above the branches and I could see the Colcombe pigs moving quietly in amongst the trees, rooting for something to eat. I crawled on my hands and knees until I was well clear of the undergrowth, then I stood up. There was no sound other than our night-time companions grunting to each other so I ventured a little further and then a little further still. I listened carefully but could hear nothing. By now I was in a small clearing out of sight of the others but feared to go further in case I got lost. I turned and, as I did so there came a single high-pitched scream. I was unable to make out where it had come from but it was a young woman's scream. For a moment I was too frightened to move. Then, remembering Uncle Fauconberg's advice, I withdrew the dagger from the sheath on my belt and quietly retraced my steps.

It was as if he had dropped from the trees because I'd not heard him come. He was a bulky man in a brown quilted gambeson, his hood pulled low over his face. I thought I saw the flash of a badge as he turned but was not certain – dull gold, crimson roundels, the arms of the earl of Devon. There was no sign of a sword or other weapon but he must have a blade somewhere on his person. No man would venture into the woods without carrying a knife. He had broad shoulders and wore no shirt, his arms were bare, muscles bulging, the veins on his lower arm corded like ropes.

He had Edith by her hair, his other hand clamped hard over her mouth. She was struggling, trying to kick his legs and bite his hand. Leaning back he dealt her a savage blow across her face. She went limp and dropped to the ground in a crumpled heap. The brute prodded her with his boot then looked around to make certain he was unobserved. I was in the darkness amongst the trees and knew how to remain unseen. As children, my sisters and I had practised tracking deer in our father's woods at Middleham and I remembered the hunt-master's advice: move slowly, watch where you put your feet and, above all, learn to stay still.

Dame Elizabeth and Christine cowered in the undergrowth, too terrified to come to Edith's aid. I could see their white shocked faces but only because I knew where to look. I gripped the handle of my dagger more tightly and crept closer. The man knelt down and began pulling roughly at Edith's skirts. He was too intent on what he was doing to notice me approach from behind. He hoisted himself astride Edith's body, grunting like one of the Colcombe pigs and began fiddling with the front of his breeches.

I knew where to strike. I'd seen boys at Middleham practise this move a hundred times. But there would be only one chance. If I missed, he'd have me on the ground like Edith and I was no match for a grown man. I thought of Will promising to teach me the skill of close combat; of Tom saying how a man should be ever alert to danger; and I thought of Maud. Maud who was brave, Maud who was fearless, Maud who believed a woman could do anything. Maud who would not have hesitated.

I didn't hesitate. I grabbed his hair, jerked his head back and slashed at his throat with my blade. He shrieked and clutched his neck. I jumped back out of reach before he could grab me. I had done the job well because blood was gushing out of the wound. As he lay threshing on the ground he cursed me and called me every foul name known to man. He grappled at his belt, wanting to pull out his own knife but was unable to twist himself round sufficiently to reach it. He attempted to raise himself up on one knee but quickly collapsed, screaming in pain. An unwise movement as he tried crawling towards my feet made him cry out in a fury of agony. Any thought of retaliation was futile It was much too late, the damage had already been done.

He moaned and writhed, trying in vain to staunch the wound with his hands. As blood-stained bubbles appeared at his mouth his movements became weaker. He could barely lift his head and his mouth opened but no words came out, only a strangulated gurgle. His fingers twitched convulsively. Then he stopped moving, exhaled once and lay still.

I was terrified of him suddenly rising up, crazed with fury and wanting revenge so I waited but I knew in my heart that he was dead. He was not just badly injured or weak from loss of blood. I had actually killed him.

I sank to the ground feeling as cold as ice and found I could not even form the words of a prayer. Killing was a mortal sin and I had killed a man. In my mind I could hear the priest at Middleham thundering, "Thot shalt not kill."

After a few moments I wiped my blade on the ground to get rid of his blood and then thrust the dagger back into its sheath. I felt sick and weak and wanted to sit and weep but there were things which had to be done. There might be other men in the woods, men who had heard the screams. The dead man might have been one of a group searching the woods for a party of women known to have escaped from Shute.

I got to my feet. I was shaking with fright but with my last ounce of strength managed to drag a half-conscious Edith across to our hiding place. Dame Elizabeth and Christine, wide-eyed and speechless, clutched each other and made no attempt to help me. I tucked Edith's skirts over her legs and wondered if she was dead. Her lips were pale and her eyes closed but when I placed my face next to hers she appeared to be breathing. I crawled out and looked at the body of the man I'd killed. He would have to be hidden, I couldn't leave him lying on the ground for anyone to find.

'Christine!' I hissed. 'Come over here.'

Reluctantly she removed herself from my mother-in-law's side and crawled out after me. She stared at the body and began to whimper.

'Stop that!' I said roughly. 'Help me pull him into the ditch.'

'But we be in it.'

'There's nowhere else to hide him and we can't leave him here. Come on!'

She shook her head and began to weep. This time I slapped her hard across her face. 'You fool! There's no time for that. We've got to get rid of the body. Now do as I do – take his legs.'

Together we pulled and shoved the body until it was poised over a part of the ditch a little way from where the others were hiding. I stopped to let us both recover and then with a final heave we rolled it down into a tangle of leafless brambles. The body was not well concealed but it would have to do. A man walking by wouldn't notice unless he clambered down into the ditch.

We returned to our hiding place where to my profound relief Edith had opened her eyes. Dame Elizabeth was gently stroking her face as if she was a small child, humming a tune under her breath. We lay there, huddled together, for an hour or more, too frightened to move.

I knew the others were as scared as I was at having the dead man's body only a few yards away. Perhaps he had been sent to make sure no-one was hiding in the woods or perhaps he'd left his comrades ransacking our house and climbed in amongst the trees to see what he could find. There was a chance he was one of a larger search party so we had to lie still in case someone else came looking for him or for us. But no-one came. There had been only the one man.

Eventually we crawled out. By now we were weak with hunger and thirst. I was worried about Edith. Her face was far too pale and she was shivering. She needed something to drink even if there was nothing to eat. I cursed myself for failing to tell Christine to bring bread and a goatskin of wine with her when we fled from the house. There had to be water somewhere in the woods. I knew water flowed downhill so if we crossed the woods rather than climb higher we would surely find a stream. I remembered a man at Middleham saying animals would always find a drink for themselves because they had no servants to bring them ale. My brothers had laughed at the joke.

The sky through gaps in the tracery of branches above our heads seemed lighter now, I guessed the sun had risen and there might well be people about. I told the others to be very quiet. We must have searched for a full hour before I found a little path worn by animal tracks. The furrow through the undergrowth flattened by some small creature was far too narrow for a person to have made but by holding our skirts close to our legs and watching the ground carefully we were able to follow it through the trees. After a mile or so the undergrowth gave way to more open ground with only occasional bushes but the path still showed clearly, a little trail of trodden down earth leading us towards a bank of moss-covered rocks.

The path ended abruptly where a spring trickled out from beneath a huge boulder, creating a tiny pool. We knelt down on the ground, cupped our hands and drank. Two days earlier I would not have done such a thing but, like the others, I was too thirsty to care about my dignity. All of us were filthy, covered in dust and mud, our faces scratched raw by branches and brambles. Edith looked worse than the others, she had a red mark on one side of her face where she'd been struck. I sat back on my heels noticing how my hands were still shaking. There were splashes of blood on my sleeves and on the front of my gown and I idly wondered, the way one does even at moments of danger, if the laundress would get it clean by scrubbing.

Once we had drunk our fill everyone looked happier and even Edith gave a tentative smile.

'We cannot stay here,' I said.

'Why not, mistress?' said Christine.

'There may be wild creatures, wolves or suchlike, living in the woods and this is where they will come. See! There are paw prints over there.'

Christine squealed in fright.

'Do you think it safe to go back?' said Edith, a slight flush now colouring her cheeks.

Dame Elizabeth spoke for the first time since we'd left our hiding place. 'Has my Will returned?'

I touched her hand. 'Not yet, dear lady. But he'll come soon.'

'Then I must go to my chamber. I am tired of walking in the woods. I cannot think why you brought me here. I want my bed and I want my maid. Where is she?'

I sighed. It had been easier when my mother-in-law was lost in some silent reverie. I did not relish dealing with a petulant woman who had no notion of the danger we were in.

'She has gone to make things ready for you, my lady,' I lied. 'We shall return to your chamber very soon.'

'How shall we find our way out of the woods?' asked Edith.

I said nothing because I had no idea how far we'd come. I thought if we clambered down through the trees we would eventually come out to where we would see open country. With luck we might find a dwelling and ask the way to Shute.

In the end it was remarkably easy. It could not have been an hour before we found ourselves standing at the edge of the wood gazing down at the walls of Shute church far below. The others were eager to hurry down the slope but I advised caution.

'Wait! The men from Colcombe may still be there.'

Dame Elizabeth gave an annoyed sigh and sat down on the ground like an obedient child. Christine crouched beside her.

'How shall we know if they've gone?' Edith said.

'One of us must go and find out.' I touched her bruised face. 'Don't worry. I shan't ask you to go, not after everything. I shall go. You stay here with Dame Elizabeth.'

'What if you don't come back?'

I took her ice-cold fingers in mine and kissed her gently, wondering how she'd managed to lose her gloves. 'Don't be afraid, Edith. I promise I shall take the greatest of care.'

She was grateful I'd not suggested she should be the one to venture forth and settled down beside the others, placing one arm around Dame Elizabeth's shoulder.

I waited a little while, hearing nothing but an occasional rustle in the trees behind me. A thin chill mist hovered over the buildings of Shute but there was no sign of people and no shouting. I watched as the mist crept up towards the trees. It wasn't thick but would serve to hide me from anyone glancing up the hill. I slipped along the edge of the wood and then ran quickly down to the wall which surrounded the burying ground. Part of the wall had crumbled where a yew tree grew hard against the stones pushing them out of place. I waited in the dark beneath the overhanging branches, then, hearing no sound, scrambled over the wall and dropped lightly onto the grass on the other side.

I stayed crouched where I was, still in the shadow of the yew but there was no sign of the Colcombe men. I crept forward to the shelter of a large gravestone. Still no sound except for my breathing. I glanced towards the church. The high arched windows were dark, no wavering yellow candlelight and no sound of bells. I waited a moment and then ran to the shelter of the next gravestone. In that way I moved across the burying ground until I came to the back wall of the church. I edged along until I came to the end, grasped one of the quoins and peered cautiously round the corner. My heart leapt and I almost screamed. Where the path ended, dead leaves had blown into a narrow arched doorway, and beside the steps leading down to the door, was a woman's body.

She lay flat on her back, her coif ripped off, her skirts bundled up round her waist, her bloodstained legs spread wide apart and the eyes in her battered face staring sightlessly at the sky. I didn't need a second look to know who she was. She was Dame Elizabeth's maid, the young woman who had refused to venture into the woods last night because she feared it was too dangerous.

I fell to my knees beside her.

'You foolish, foolish woman,' I whispered. 'Why did you not listen to me?'

Even with my limited experience of York's narrow dark streets and unsavoury taverns I knew what had happened. 'How many were there?' I whispered. 'How could they do this to you here on holy ground?' I put out my hand and gently closed her eyes the way I'd seen the wise woman do to the dead in the cottages at Middleham. Then I pulled down her skirts to give her some decency in death.

'*This one night,*' I murmured, remembering how the ritual was done.

'*This one night,*
Every night and all
Fire an' fleet an' candlelight
- And Christ receive thy soul.'

The words came as easily as the tears which trickled down my cheeks. She was undeserving of so hideous an end, such a cruel, senseless death. And it was all my doing. I should have insisted she came with us. I should not have allowed her to turn back.

I have no idea how long I sat there, my fingers plucking idly at the cold grass, damp seeping slowly into my skirts. I cared nothing for the danger I might be in or thought of Edith and the others waiting anxiously in the woods above the church. I was lost in a darkness of my own making.

The sound of a man's footsteps roused me and I looked up. It was Sir Robert.

'Mistress Bonville!'

He sounded surprised.

He spoke words but I didn't hear him. I was too sunk in misery. Then there were other men, other voices: the old man from the stables, the kitchen boys, the men from the gatehouse, the steward, Everyone was speaking.

'Mistress, come away inside. There's naught ye can do for the lass. Leave it to us.'

'Where be the others, mistress? Be ye alone?'

'Come away, mistress. They Colcombe men be gone now. Ye've no reason to be afeared. Come with us.'

But I couldn't move. Since the day of my wedding, Devonshire had delivered one horror after another: Master Radford lying dead in a pool of blood, his brains spilling out onto the track; Lord Bonville's ship off Powderahm under attack from the earl of Devon's son, the sound of the great cannon on the shore; leering faces in the torchlight as the Colcombe men marched towards Shute, clubs and staves and knives at the ready; Edith lying unconscious and helpless on the ground in the woods; and the body of Dame Elizabeth's maid, here beside me, dead.

Shute Manor was not a place I could ever sleep easy and these were not my people. I didn't want the Bonvilles or the Dynhams, the Shute servants or those at Lympstone. I didn't want Lady Bonville or Dame Elizabeth or even Edith. I wanted my sisters. I wanted my mother and my father and my brothers. Above all, I wanted to go home to Middleham.

14

CANTERBURY 1457

I lay propped up on an enormous pillow, my eyes closed and my arms outstretched in the way I'd been instructed. It was not easy because I was immensely curious but somehow I resisted the temptation to peep. There were rustlings and whispers and a surreptitious giggle from the direction of the doorway. Then something hard and scratchy was placed on top of the sleeves of my nightgown.

'You may look now,' said Will.

I opened my eyes and smiled. In my arms was a sheaf of willow shoots tied together with a length of green satin ribbon. I touched one of the fluffy grey catkins. It felt soft and slightly damp. He'd gone out onto the river bank behind the inn that morning while I was still asleep and, with his own hands, cut the flowering shoots of the pussy willow.

'They are beautiful,' I said.

'Like you, my Lady Harington.'

I lifted the bundle to my face and pressed the catkins against my cheek, breathing in the familiar scent of springtime.

'I have nothing for you,' I said apologetically. It was fifteen weeks since we'd spent our first night together and today, like every day, we regarded as a celebration of our marriage.

Will climbed onto the bed and removed the pussy willow from my arms. 'Untrue,' he said, starting to undo the ties at the neck of my nightgown.

'Will! You are wearing your boots.'

'I am?' He didn't pause in his attempt to expose whatever he could of my night-time nakedness.

'Yes, you are.'

'Do you object?'

In my belly a familiar sensation began to uncurl as he succeeded in sliding the nightgown off one shoulder. I offered him my mouth. 'Very much and we shall be late.'

'The innkeeper says Canterbury's a scant hour's ride,' he said in between kissing my lips and my neck and what he could reach of one of my breasts. 'Your brother will understand if we are a little late.'

I arched my body against his, wondering at the half-life I had lived before this. 'I doubt my mother will,' I whispered into his hair.

Within moments we were lost in a tangle of silk and furs and the fine white linen of Will's best shirt, gasping, crying and, when it was all over, laughing.

He lay beside me stroking my nose with a blade of grass he'd found in amongst the bedcovers. 'I cannot believe I had no liking for you on our wedding day.'

'I'd no liking for you, either,' I said, smiling at the memory of my scowling husband. 'But you were not Lord Harington then.'

'How foolish we were.'

'We were young.'

'Are we old now?'

'Ancient. Yet there are years and years ahead of us. We shall live together, have at least a dozen children and we shall be happy.'

'Eleven sons and a daughter.'

'Six sons and five daughters.'

He laughed. 'Come along, Lady Harington, mother-to-be of a brood of handsome children. Time to make yourself presentable for your family.' He put his head on one side and regarded me lying in the debris of our lovemaking. 'Although I do prefer you like this.'

It was a year after Lady Bonville's men rescued me from Shute and brought me to Chewton Mendip that Will's grandfather decided Will and I should live together. His battles with the earl of Devon and the subsequent dismissal of my Uncle York as protector of the realm had made him uneasy about the future of his family and anxious for another heir.

Will had grown a foot since I'd last seen him at Lympstone and was almost unrecognisable as the truculent boy I'd married that September day at Bisham. In truth we had both changed and not just in appearance. My experiences at Shute had made me more sober, more wary and infinitely more ready to accept my young husband as he was and not as my foolish girlish heart had once wanted him to be.

I'd told no-one other than my confessor at Chewton Mendip what I'd done that night in the woods at Shute, how I'd slit a man's throat with my dagger and let him bleed to death in front of my eyes. Edith must have guessed the truth but she'd said nothing. We didn't talk about her ordeal or about the death of Dame Elizabeth's maid. I longed to confide in someone but couldn't, not even to Will to whom I'd given my heart. I had discovered there were secrets a woman will tell and some she hugs close, unable to breathe a word to anyone.

Dame Elizabeth had refused to come to Chewton Mendip, preferring to stay where she was. Despite the damage to the house, the burning of the outbuildings and the looting of so many of her comforts, Shute was where she felt at home. She said nothing but I suspected she was waiting for her menfolk to return. It was a sad warning of what could happen to a woman who failed to please her husband or her husband's family but though I felt sorry for her, nothing would have induced me to remain in a house two miles away from the men who had caused me so much pain.

The summer before Will and I began living together as husband and wife, Dame Elizabeth fell ill with a wasting sickness. My father-in-law arranged for the best physician he knew to attend her but she died in the darkest time of the year. We wore mourning clothes for three months and pretended Dame Elizabeth was greatly missed, a vital link in the family gone, but in truth she was quickly forgotten. Then a month ago Will's Harington grandfather died. He was a man I had never met but his death marked a great change in our circumstances. Now it was Lord and Lady Haringtom who lived at Shute Manor and Edith insisted on curtseying deeply to me every time she came into the room.

Today was not a day to think about death because today, we were travelling to Canterbury for a wedding.

My brother John was to marry the earl of Worcester's niece, fourteen-year-old Isobel Ingoldisthorpe. She was sole heir to her father's fortune and this was an excellent match for my brother. I would see my mother and my sisters though sadly, not Alianore. I supposed her too busy attending to her infant son and the continued taming of Thomas Stanley. And Lancashire was a great distance from Canterbury as Lord Bonville had remarked to me last month after the invitation had arrived.

As we neared Canterbury the road was not only dusty but crowded with people. It was like fair day at York. The travellers were a motley collection, a few on horseback, others walking, some barefoot. But all were in festive mood: singing, dancing, banging tabors, blowing whistles and making a tremendous cacophony.

'Pilgrims!' exclaimed Edith excitedly.

We had first seen the cathedral from a great distance, towering high above the city walls, dominating the countryside in all directions. The closer we got the more impressive it became.

'It's enormous,' said Edith. 'Look how small the houses are, like toys; and the people are like tiny scurrying ants.'

My brother Richard had taken a house some way outside the city where the Nevills were to gather before the wedding. As a stranger to this part of Kent, Will had to stop a passer-by to ask the way. The man scratched his head, had a lengthy conversation with his companion, and then directed us along a lane where the trees were already in bud. A froth of white cloaked the hedgerows and as we rode further along the lane I noticed clumps of primroses and violets hiding in crevices on the banks.

251

The house was large, stone-built, two storeys high with turrets and a row of oriel windows just below the roofline. The gardens were delightful, low box hedges surrounding wide beds, the whole enclosed by a maze of paths and a trellis of leafless fruit trees.

'No pussy willow,' whispered Will as he helped me dismount.

I blushed and turned to see my mother smiling at me.

Poor Edith had been sadly disappointed the wedding was not to be in London and said Canterbury would be a poor substitute. But when we arrived not only was she overawed by the magnificence of the cathedral but also by the Nevill men in their wedding finery.

'So tall and so handsome! What a shame you have no more brothers, Lady Harington.'

I grinned. 'I shall introduce you to my uncle, Lord Fauconberg. He is neither tall nor handsome but he is highly entertaining and particularly partial to young women. So beware!'

The wedding was joyous as all weddings are meant to be though I doubted I found much joy at my own. When I recalled my thoughts of Will as a husband I wanted to blush but in those days I was young and foolish and knew no better. Isobel Ingoldisthorpe was young but clearly not foolish, a clever, charming and self-confident young lady who would suit my brother, John, very well.

The following day there was a joust and some merry-making. Then Richard called the men of Canterbury and Sandwich before him and thanked them for their goodness in the victualling of Calais. It was two years since his appointment as captain of Calais but Uncle Fauconberg said problems with the garrison and the company of staplers had delayed Richard taking possession.

'Money,' he whispered in my ear that morning. 'The bane of a man's life. As vexing as a disobliging woman.'

'Whose money, my lord uncle?' I laughed, thinking how Uncle Fauconberg never changed.

'A sensible question, my little Yorkshire rose. Who indeed is to sustain our outpost of Calais. The garrison need wages and the merchants must have their loans repaid.' He sighed. 'Too costly to keep, too valuable to let go. That is the conundrum of Calais.'

'Surely the king will pay.'

'Richard relies on it but if he is to win friends over there he will also have to dig deep into his own coffers.'

Watching my eldest brother, I wondered who had paid the good folk of Kent for their provender – the king or his captain.

'Richard needs their goodwill,' whispered my sister-in-law, Anne, who was seated beside me. 'I worry for him and for my daughters.' Her face softened as she spoke of her two little girls in the nursery.

The previous year my brother had been blessed with another daughter. Alice had written a letter oozing disapproval from every line. She was in no doubt that lack of a Warwick son and heir was Anne's fault. In her opinion, two girls in thirteen years of sharing a bed with your husband was a poor return on our brother's investment.

'Will you go to Calais with Richard?' I asked.

'Yes, and he has agreed we shall take the children.'

Anne looked nervous as well she might. Calais was known to be a cold rough place with endless quarrels between traders and the garrison. There would be very few women and even less entertainment, but the making of a Warwick son and heir was of greater importance than Anne's comfort. I most certainly did not envy her.

'I suppose you have heard the news about Sir Thomas Courtenay,' she said, anxious to talk about something other than the prospect of her imminent departure.

The name Courtenay sent ice slithering through my veins as it always did. I chose my words with care. 'There is bad blood between the Bonvilles and the Courtenays. We hear nothing of the family.'

'He has married the queen's kinswoman, a daughter of the count of Maine. I hear Margaret of Anjou herself promoted the marriage.'

'So the Courtenays have made their choice at last,' said Maud who was seated on my other side. 'Once Sir Thomas Courtenay inherits his father's earldom he will support Margaret of Anjou and the duke of York will have lost another supporter, not that the Courtenays were anything other than fair-weather friends.' She inclined her head towards me. 'An opportunity for your new family, Kathryn.'

Anne excused herself, wishing to oversee the packing of the children's clothes. 'The maids cannot be trusted,' she apologised.

Maud and I watched her go, her slender figure, beautifully erect with the bearing she had learned in childhood, but her steps were uncertain,

'She seems nervous,' I said.

Maud spread her fingers in her lap, idly examining her rings. 'She lives in a state of fear. The queen is openly hostile. She supports young Somerset who has sworn vengeance on your brother. Now Anne hears Somerset is aided by our friends Exeter and Egremont.'

'That is impossible. Lord Egremont is in prison,' I said, recalling the leering faces of the Tuxford conspirators and the horrors of Heworth Moor.

'Apparently he has engineered his escape.'

I wrapped my arms around my waist as if to keep myself safe, half-wishing I too could escape to Calais, anywhere out of reach of Lord Egremont.

'If Richard is in danger, cannot my father petition the king to intervene?'

Maud gave an unladylike snort. 'The king is helpless. Everyone knows he is a godly man who prays for peace but it is the queen who rules. And Margaret of Anjou believes enemies should be destroyed.'

She had seemed such a sweet creature at her *élevée* four years ago, flushed with triumph at having given her husband an heir. Now my family believed her worse than one of Alice's shiny-coiled serpents; more a sharp-clawed, yellow-eyed she-wolf prowling the royal chambers by night relentlessly seeking her prey. And it was my brother Richard who was to be the main dish at the feast.

All too soon it was time to leave Canterbury but first I went to say farewell to my mother. I had seen little of her in the past few days. There were a great many people at the wedding celebrations and, as countess of Salisbury, she was required to converse with every guest. Today she looked weary and worried.

'Come, sit with me.' she said, patting the bench where she sat in the pale afternoon sunshine. Her seat was in a corner of the garden sheltered from the breeze and hidden from curious passers-by. Two of her women sat a little way off where they could watch guests stroll along the path to the pavilion yet not disturb my mother with their gossiping.

'We are leaving tomorrow and I do not know when I shall see you again,' I said, feeling the familiar panic at parting from my mother, a fluttering in my belly, a fear that one day she would be gone beyond my reach and I would be alone.

'We shall write to each other.'

'I know, but letters are...'

'...a poor substitute.'

'They are not the same.'

She smiled and leaned forward to give me a kiss. 'Nothing remains the same, Kathryn. We follow the path God has ordained for us and trust He will keep us safe.'

'Are we safe?'

'Your father and I made good marriages for you and your sisters. We chose men who have the means to keep you away from danger.'

'And my brothers?'

I thought I saw a flash of fear in her eyes but I might have been mistaken. My mother was afraid of nothing, not even death.

'Naturally I am concerned for my sons. Richard has chosen to set himself against the queen.'

'And you think that ill-advised.'

My mother gazed at the peaceful surroundings and sighed. 'I might have wished it otherwise but Richard does what he believes he must. It is a mercy he and Anne sail for Calais tomorrow because, as your father and your Uncle Fauconberg will tell you, Margaret of Anjou should not be underestimated.

We talked for a while of Middleham, of the people I knew there: the marriages, the births, the inevitable deaths, the small doings which make up a person's life and are of interest only to those who know them.

'Tom is not taking much enjoyment from John's marriage,' I remarked. 'Does he disapprove of my father's choice?'

'No, not at all. It is not John's marriage that is making him angry. Doubtless Maud will tell you herself but perhaps it is better you are forewarned.'

'Not if it distresses you.'

'At my age I have learned acceptance and am beyond being distressed. It is the matter of Maud's inheritance.'

'Her Cromwell inheritance.'

'That is the problem. The Cromwell inheritance is not hers. Tom swears he's been cheated, which of course he has. It appears there was another document, one he and your father knew nothing about, one hidden from everyone. I do not know what Maud and her sister did to deserve such treatment but they have been disinherited. It seems Lord Cromwell was a rogue.'

I gave a gasp. It was hard to believe such a thing could happen. It was more than a year since Maud's uncle had died and I assumed Tom and Maud had received Maud's portion. But apparently it was not so. Lord Cromwell had changed his mind.

'Did no-one know?'

'Only the bishop of Chester and a trusted servant. The document was in a locked casket with the key kept on Lord Cromwell's person. The servant had orders to retrieve it when Lord Cromwell died, before the executors were informed.'

'What treachery!' I said.

'Indeed. Tom says that when her uncle sent Maud an account for her stay at Tattershall, she should have been suspicious, she should have realised he had turned against her.'

'She was not to know.'

Lord Cromwell had performed a clever and cunning deceit, perfectly legal but despicable nonetheless. The defrauding of your heirs was even more heinous when the inheritance they'd been promised was an accepted part of marriage negotiations. No wonder Tom was incensed.

How hard for Maud to suffer the transformation from desirable heiress to the niece of a cheat and a swindler. Tom doubtless blamed her for Lord Cromwell's perfidy. I felt desperately sorry for her.

'Now, let us talk of something else, something pleasant. Tell me about Devonshire. Is it all you hoped for?'

I hesitated, wondering how much I should tell my mother of my terrors and the things I had done.

'Devonshire is not like Yorkshire,' I said, filled with a sudden longing for my childhood home.

'No, it is not, but Lady Bonville tells me you have done well. She praises your courage.'

'I do not think I have been courageous.'

My mother reached out and took my hand in hers. 'There were times when you were afraid, were there not?'

'Yes.'

'Yet you did your duty.'

I thought of the ordering of Master Radford's household at Upcott and of the terrible night at Shute when I feared we might all be killed. At the time, none of it had felt like courage.

'When I was frightened and didn't know what to do, I would think of Middleham and the lessons I'd been taught as a girl. That guided my actions.'

'Courage is the word Lady Bonville used and I am certain she is right. She also believes you and your husband are well suited. Do you agree?' Her eyes were bright with amusement as I blushed. 'Shall I tell you a secret? When I married your father I was frightened of him.'

That made me smile. My parents were comfortable together. I could not imagine my mother in awe of my father.

'I did not like Will at first but now...'

'You need say no more. Your feelings are written on your face when you look at him. You have tender feelings?'

I nodded. 'Yes, I do.'

'Is it love?'

I blushed. 'I think it might be.'

It was, but I was not ready to share that information with anyone other than Will, not even my mother, the woman to whom a daughter was supposed to tell all her secrets.

'I'm glad. To love one's husband is indeed a blessing. But remember, love is the least part of any marriage.

Steadfastness, loyalty and obedience: these are the virtues you must cultivate. Love only carries you so far.'

I nodded in agreement thinking how, despite her words, my mother knew very little about love, not the all-consuming kind of love that Will and I shared.

'Lady Bonville has been immensely kind and I have Edith. She is a daughter of Sir John and Lady Dynham of Nutwell, and the best of companions.'

'I do not think I know the Dynhams.'

'They are close neighbours of Lord and Lady Bonville at their manor of Lympstone. Their eldest daughter is to marry Nicholas Carew.'

My mother looked wistful. 'How easily you talk of people and places I do not know. I think you are well-settled in Devonshire with your new household and a husband who, I suspect, is as enamoured with you as you are with him. I believe you do not miss us at all.'

'I do miss you but not like I did at the beginning. Then I was drowning in misery whereas now I feel like a wife, a proper wife, a young woman who has found her place in the world.'

'As the wife of young Lord Harington.'

I smiled. 'Yes.'

'Then perhaps we shall meet again when your husband receives his royal summons.'

'Or when you find a husband for Margaret. But that will not be easy for she is a most aggravating girl.'

My mother laughed. 'Be off with you, daughter, and may Our Lady take good care of you.'

15

THE ERBER 1458

Today was the Feast of the Epiphany, a celebration of the day when the three kings brought their gifts to the Christ Child. In the kitchen at Shute our cook was inventing a new dish of stewed eels and the smell was not appetising. Yesterday during our Twelfth Night revels we had dined on a fine haunch of venison, a gift from Sir Philip Beaumont, sent over with one of his servants. I had suggested a sauce of pickled damsons but something had gone awry. The cook swore he'd followed my instructions to the letter yet the resulting mess tasted most peculiar. I made a note to ask Lady Dynham, who had given me the recipe, what he had done wrong.

The dancing and foolery of last evening had exhausted us, so today Edith and I were sitting quietly beside the fire in the solar, wrapped in our shawls, reading extracts from a book lent to me by Lady Blanche.

'It is very improper,' Edith said. 'Look! See what he writes here. It is obvious he is saying one thing but meaning another.'

She showed me the offending page and I giggled at the innuendo. 'Lady Blanche has a library of such books. Do you think her husband knows?'

'Does yours?'

Despite the outside chill, here in our private quarters I felt warm and deliciously lazy. A moment later my contentment was disturbed when the sound of hooves clattering into the courtyard announced the arrival of a messenger. I shivered. Since last summer's attack on Sandwich by the French I lived in constant fear of an invasion. Will said we were perfectly safe at Shute, it was not like Lympstone where French ships could sail up the estuary to the very gate. Not that they would choose Lympstone, he had explained patiently, Dartmouth would be a far more tempting proposition. Besides, his grandfather said the aim of the French attack on Sandwich was to frustrate the earl of Warwick's efforts from Calais. The French had no interest in Devonshire.

But Will did not have memories of the Colcombe men marching up the valley to Shute that night two years ago, not like Edith and I did. I told him that if the French could attack Sandwich with impunity they could attack anywhere but like all men he thought women knew nothing of warfare and ignored what I said.

There were voices in the hall below. Perhaps this was a message from Lord Bonville. In November Will's grandfather had gone to London at the king's command, to attend a great council meeting and Will was eager for news. All we knew was that the king was concerned his lords were not living in amity. My brother Richard's recent appointment as Keeper of the Seas had displeased the duke of Exeter who, unsurprisingly, had raised a complaint. A letter from Alice at Christmas said the noble duke was a lazy good-for-nothing and did little when he held the post. Now our energetic and capable brother was in charge he would keep the seas safe for English trading vessels and ensure there'd be no further attacks. Men could sleep easy in their beds at night, safe from French pirates burning their houses and stealing their women and children.

I left Edith with the book and went down the winding stairway to the hall. Will stood with his back to the hearth, a letter in his hand.

'Is that the royal seal?'

'No, it is from Grandfather. He commands me to join him in London when the great council reconvenes at Westminster at the end of this month.'

'You are to sit on the great council?' I was unable to hide the awe in my voice. My husband on the great council!

Will shrugged. 'Alas, no, I am considered too young. But Grandfather says it is never too soon to remind men that I am now Lord Harington so he wants me with him.'

He grinned with such obvious pleasure that I wanted to cover him with kisses. Sixteen-year-old Lord Harington was going to Westminster, even if he was not allowed to take his rightful seat beside men like my father and my brother, Richard.

'Oh Will, how wonderful! May I come with you?'

I thought he would refuse, say London was too far, the journey too difficult at this time of year and he needed me to stay at Shute to take care of his interests. But Will had not yet fallen out of love with me despite Alianore saying all men did after a year of marriage.

'Men were not bred for fidelity,' she had pronounced on my wedding day.

'What of Joan's husband?' I had replied.

'An aberration.'

'Our father?'

She had looked at me sideways. 'Do you really want to know?'

'Uncle Fauconberg?'

At that we had collapsed into giggles until Margaret sidled up, wanting to know what was the joke.

The journey to London was uneventful apart from an inconvenient detour of several miles upstream to a ford because a bridge had been washed away in the autumn rains. Will's grandfather met our small party some way outside the city and advised us to be careful.

'There may well be trouble. The mayor has done his best. He's got the duke of York and his supporters lodged within the walls but he won't have the young hot-heads in the city. Exeter and Somerset have been quartered out beyond Temple bar.'

'Are we in danger?' I asked timidly, as always somewhat in awe of Will's grandfather.

He seemed surprised by the question. 'No, my lady, you are not. No lord with a care for his head would allow a quarrel to get out of hand at the moment, not with the king due any day. But it is best to be careful.'

'Where is the king?' whispered Edith.

'Coventry,' I whispered back.

Edith looked bemused. She had no idea where Coventry was. It was odd how little she knew about places outside Devonshire but as she had told me, she was unused to travelling.

While we talked in low voices, Will was receiving instructions from his grandfather.

'The guards on the gates are expecting you. I have left orders for you to be let through.'

'Are you not coming with us, my lord?' I asked politely.

'Nay, that I am not. I have lodgings out at Holborn. But they're not fit for a fine young lady like yourself. I've talked to the earl, your father, and it's decided you and my grandson will lodge at The Erber. Keep you safe.'

'Is my mother there?' I asked eagerly.

'Aye, and a gaggle of young women to keep you company while my grandson is about the king's business.'

I was touched by his kindness and tried to thank him but he was busy with Will.

'Now remember, boy – keep your men under control. I doubt Somerset's men will harry you on your way through but take care, don't get drawn into any arguments. And once inside the city make sure none of you are carrying weapons. The mayor don't want trouble.'

There must have been close on two thousand camped out in fields north of Whitefriars Priory. Gangs of men lounging by the roadside shouted and jeered and questioned our allegiance but beyond name-calling and obscenities, which I pretended not to hear, we were not harmed in any way. I caught glimpses of Percy livery amongst a group of jostling, shoving men, and the red, blue and gold of the duke of Exeter's followers. A crowd had gathered around a couple of brawny lads stripped to the waist, locked in each other's arms, wrestling. As I watched, the taller threw the other heavily to the ground and stamped on his face.

'Ye're no match for 'im, Codface!' shouted an onlooker.

Instinctively I moved my horse closer to Will's.

The place was a morass of mud, each wagonload of supplies making further gouges into the field. Captains had men marching up and down in ragged formation, berating them loudly for their stupidity. Young women wandered amongst the tents, one, younger and bolder than the rest, hauled up her skirts to show off her bare legs.

I felt a wave of relief as we passed through into the city. The inns outside the city where the London lawyers did their work were undefended yet offered an illusion of safety, but thick stone walls, twenty feet high were better protection. The porter on the gate created no difficulties, merely tipped his hat to Will and smiled at Edith. The guards, huge swarthy men with hard faces and cudgels at the ready, stepped aside to let us pass.

London was crowded and even noisier than the fields outside. Hundreds of my brother Richard's followers were heading towards Greyfriars, all wearing red jackets carrying Richard's device of the white ragged staff front and back. A contingent of my father's men sporting the familiar golden griffin clawing the air with wings upraised, marched with them. As we passed Baynard's Castle I saw archers with the York device of a white rose, eyeing the mayor's patrolling men-at-arms advancing along Thames Street towards the Tower. If I had held out my hand I could have touched the threat of danger. The air was thick with it.

Edith was bouncing up and down in her saddle with excitement.

'What's that building up there?'

'St Pauls.'

'And those?' she said pointing towards the river.

'Cranes.'

'No, those huge tree-like things.'

I laughed. 'I told you – cranes: machines for lifting goods from the barges onto the wharves.

She shrugged. 'Cranes? How odd! And the boats? There must be hundreds. Where are they going?'

'Southwark perhaps – that's Southwark over there on the far bank, or perhaps the king's palace at Westminster. That one with the canopy might be some great man's barge travelling upstream as far as Windsor or to Bisham, which is my father's manor where I married Will.'

'Oh look! That boat came through one of those arches under the bridge.'

'It's the apprentice boys showing off. They dare each other to shoot through the arches when the tide is running. It's very dangerous.'

'What's beyond the bridge. I can't see? There are too many chimneys,' she cried, trying to rise up in her saddle.

'Sea-going ships. And of course the Tower.'

'You talk like a Londoner,' complained Will from my other side.

'And you, sir, talk like a newly arrived country yokel.'

The Erber. I touched the wall with the flat of my fingers, feeling a warp in the panelling close to the hearth. Despite familiar furnishings I'd known since childhood, this place no longer felt like home. I thought returning here would fill me with gladness but it didn't. I had forgotten the luxury yet found myself missing our single winding stairway and cramped rooms at Shute. Every room here was spacious, hung with the finest of tapestries or, like this one, panelled with layers of thin wood. Warmth enveloped me as I mounted the wide stairway, soft-footed servants at my shoulder waiting to satisfy my every wish. Yet I was homesick for our oily-tongued steward and the stammering boy who brought in the basket of logs.

As soon as we entered the great hall, Will was passed into the capable hands of John Conyers to be taken to my father while I was wafted upstairs to my rooms. Christine, who was laying my blue woollen gown and green kirtle carefully on the bed, said how wonderful it was to be back and didn't I think London was the very best place for a young woman to be. I wasn't sure I agreed with her.

As soon as I was clean and wearing a fresh gown, I hurried to my mother's rooms.

'I could have wished the situation better for you,' she said, a slight furrowing of her brow the only sign of how worried she was.

'Is there trouble?'

'Somerset and Exeter tried to kill your brother.' Her voice was flat but her hands trembled.

'Merciful Mother of God! I didn't know. What happened?'

'Your father refuses to tell me, just said that the attempt was unsuccessful and Richard unharmed.'

'Has the king been told?'

My mother looked up, her eyes full of anger. 'The king has recruited thirteen thousand archers. Of course it is not the king's doing. The queen is behind it.'

'Thirteen thousand?'

'Yes.' She gave a mirthless little laugh. 'They are for the king's service. He used them last autumn to overawe the

Londoners but we all know what the queen will do with them.'

I felt as if I had walked onto a smooth stretch of grass only to discover that I was teetering on the edge of a cliff which was crumbling under my feet.

'What will she do?' my mouth was dry and I could barely form the words.

'Support her friends, the sons of those killed at St Albans: Northumberland, Somerset and Clifford.'

I had thought danger in all its forms was behind us but I was wrong. It wasn't. It was here in front of me, waiting to happen. If our enemies had once tried to kill my brother, they would try again. The future would be full of fighting and bloodshed and tears.

As always we women were powerless, there was nothing we could do but wait.

One afternoon in the middle of March Aunt Cecily marched into my mother's room at The Erber, her face red with fury. She barely managed to carry out the necessary civilities of greeting before she burst out, 'Insolent puppies! How dare they demand so much! It's a disgrace! It's an insult!' She looked at our blank faces. 'Of course, you've not yet heard.'

My mother was calm. Over the years she'd had plenty of practice in dealing with Aunt Cecily's storms and knew to wait until the gale passed before venturing to speak.

'The last I heard you were at Ludlow, Cecily. Since you are here in my chamber and I have not conjured you up from my imagination, I presume you are currently installed at Baynard's Castle.'

Aunt Cecily sat down. 'Naturally I was at Ludlow. I refused to go to Ireland: horrible, wet, barbarous place, full of uncivilised people. The appointment was designed for my husband, not for his family.'

'You let him go alone?'

My mother was showing Aunt Cecily that her behaviour was not always that of the loving, supportive wife she claimed to be.

'I knew he would not stay long and I was right. If the queen thought to be rid of him by sending him to Ireland, she was mistaken.'

'Hmm! And what is it you have come to tell me? I presume it is important.'

'It is outrageous. The king has been persuaded to award vast sums to those who lost a father in the fighting at St Albans three years ago. Of course we all know who did the persuading. This has Margaret of Anjou's fingerprints all over it. My husband has been ordered to pay five thousand marks to young Somerset and his mother.'

My mother let out a gasp. 'Five thousand marks! That is a vast sum.'

'It is an insult. Naturally he will not pay.'

'Cecily, he must. He cannot refuse. That would play right into the queen's hands.'

Aunt Cecily laughed. 'He is already owed ten times that amount by the Crown. He will make over his tallies to young Somerset and much good it may do the churl when he tries to squeeze money out of Henry's exchequer.'

'And we Nevills? I presume it is not just your husband who is expected to make reparations.'

'Your son, Richard, is to pay one thousand marks to young Clifford.'

'It could be worse,' murmured my mother.

'Considering it was your son who was responsible for the slaughter and considering it was he who cut down Edmund Beaufort, I fail to see why my husband has been singled out to pay the most.'

My mother sighed. 'Be sensible, Cecily. If your husband receives the harsher fine it is because he is viewed as the more dangerous. Margaret of Anjou is no fool. She is fully aware that your husband's royal lineage threatens not only her husband but her son. Richard may make trouble but he is not such a fool as to have designs on the throne. He knows he could never be king. Your husband not only could be king but was once touted as such by the rebels in Kent.'

'That was a long time ago,' sniffed Aunt Cecily. 'And it was not my husband's doing. It has all been forgotten.'

'Margaret of Anjou forgets nothing.'

I considered the slightly built, dark-haired man who was Edward's father and the tall, swaggering figure of my brother, Richard. I reckoned Richard would be the more dangerous enemy. But what did I know. I was only a young woman.

'There is more,' said a hard-voiced Aunt Cecily, clearly not liking the truths my mother was telling her. 'Your husband does not escape lightly. He is to compensate our dear sister, Henry Percy's widow, for the death of her husband. And your husband and your son are to forgo the fines imposed on Lord Egremont and his brother.'

My mother said nothing, merely lifted an eyebrow and glanced at me. I knew my encounters with Lord

Egremont had not been to her liking. Maud had told me she was relieved to have the noble lord in prison and me dispatched to Devonshire where it was unlikely he would ever set eyes on me again, even if he were free.

'And there is to be a chantry to pray for the souls of those who died. Forty-five pounds each year in perpetuity! My husband, your husband and your son. Outrageous! Of course everyone knows it is the queen's doing, the king would never be so vindictive.'

'And what of your "insolent puppies"? What is to happen to them and the others who fought against our men at St Albans?'

'Nothing.'

'Nothing! Are you sure?'

'I believe Lord Egremont is to be bound over to keep the peace.'

My mother sighed again. 'Foolish, foolish man. Can he not see? No I suppose not.'

'The king sees nothing, The queen has closed his eyes while her voice whispers untruths in his ear.'

When Will came back to The Erber that night he confirmed Aunt Cecily's story. His grandfather said the meetings of the great council were exceedingly bad-tempered. There were a few who urged compromise for the sake of peace, and implored all present to rally behind Henry as their anointed king, but battle lines had been clearly drawn: supporters of the duke of York on one side and those opposed to him on the other. The peacemakers' voices were drowned out in a clamour for revenge. And now that a settlement had been reached the king foolishly believed his lords were at peace once more. On Lady Day there was to be a solemn procession to St Pauls to thank God all were in accord.

Even I knew that very few were in accord.

The love-day procession was headed by the king. He was followed by the queen and the duke of York walking hand-in-hand, unsmiling, their shoulders rigid with dislike, and behind them other lords, each holding the hand of his enemy. My mother said it was the greatest number of people she had ever seen crowded into St Pauls and an amazing spectacle which the king believed would usher in a new era of harmony and peace.

On my return to The Erber, I met Aunt Cecily on the stairs. 'My lady aunt,' I said, bobbing an awkward curtsey.

She made as if to pass then changed her mind, barring my way. 'Let me give you a word of advice, Kathryn. Have your husband take you home. I am leaving for Ludlow and have urged your mother to return to Middleham.'

I blinked in surprise. 'But Aunt Cecily, there are to be festivities, feasts, jousting. My lady mother says the queen is to have a great celebration at Greenwich. Surely you will stay for that?'

'Take heed of the words of the wise women: if you sup with the devil you should use a long spoon. I prefer not to feast with Margaret of Anjou. Go home, Kathryn. Go home now.'

'Are we in danger?' I enquired, noting how pale my aunt looked.

'If you are a Nevill there is always danger but you already know that. Your mother has told me what happened to you. I am not often wrong but it may be I have misjudged you.'

I wondered what my mother had said. Admissions of failure rarely passed Aunt Cecily's lips, she was far too proud to admit to mistakes, yet this sounded suspiciously like an apology.

'I trust I have done nothing to offend you, my lady aunt,' I said politely.

'You have not. I admire courage in a woman, Kathryn. It seems you possess that virtue in abundance.'

'Thank you,' I murmured.

'Your sisters are good women but I doubt any of them would have acted as you did. So heed what I say: this peace accord will not last and when the storm breaks you should be as far away as possible.'

'My lady mother says...'

Aunt Cecily raised her hand for me to be silent. 'Your lady mother has not seen what you have seen. Sometimes it takes real danger to open a woman's eyes. Remember this: Margaret of Anjou intends to destroy our families and she will use every means at her disposal to achieve her avowed aim.'

Her words sent terror running down my spine and caused my belly to clench in fear. I looked to left and right as if an assassin might be lurking somewhere within the walls of The Erber.

'But the king desires peace. He would not allow the queen to harm us.'

Aunt Cecily pursed her lips 'Have you seen our king?'

I'd seen the king at the love-day procession: a man slightly stooped, clad in simple robes, innocence shining from his face. If I'd not known who he was, I'd not have thought him a king or indeed any great man.

'I have seen him at a distance.'

'I have seen him close. He is weak. He is a holy fool, a simpleton. He is like a child and yet old before his time. He does as he is bid, as he has done since he was a babe. He follows what his councillors advise and those councillors are loyal and obedient servants of the queen. There was a time when Henry had wise councillors, men like the old earl of Warwick and Archbishop Bourchier. Now it is Exeter and young Somerset who whisper in his ear.'

'My husband says the duke of Norfolk and my Uncle Stafford are men of moderation. Do they not advise the king?'

'Norfolk says he will leave on a pilgrimage overseas. So too will the earl of Worcester. They know what is coming and wish to play no part.'

'And my Uncle Stafford?'

'He will stay loyal to the king. I doubt he likes what is being done to our families but since his heir died he will cleave to Henry no matter what.'

My mother had told me young Humphrey Stafford had died of his injuries, a sword thrust from one of Richard's men at St Albans. In the circumstances I doubted Uncle Stafford would lift a finger to protect my brother.

'What will the queen do?'

'She is doing it already; stripping our men of their power, little bit by little bit. Every day she nibbles away at the positions they hold and what should be theirs by right. I doubt she'll dislodge your brother from Calais. Richard already understands the danger. He has rid himself of Lord

Rivers and put my brother, Lord Fauconberg, in charge.' She laughed. 'I hear they have turned to piracy.'

I was shocked. Piracy was against the king's law. 'Why would they do such a thing?'

'Money. What else? Margaret of Anjou thinks to starve Richard of funds. If he wishes to survive he must look elsewhere to fill his coffers. He knows there will be trouble if the garrison is not paid.'

I remembered Uncle Fauconberg's words at John's wedding, how Calais was too costly to keep and too valuable to lose. It seemed my brother had found his own solution to the conundrum. Attacking foreign ships might be risky but would be lucrative and keep the men of Calais loyal to their captain.

Aunt Cecily gripped my arm. 'Heed what I say, Kathryn. Go back to Devonshire before it is too late.'

16

EDWARD 1459

I slipped back into the life I'd lived before going to London, the pleasurable daily routine of ordering our little household at Shute and the joy of long nights spent wrapped in my husband's arms. That first winter we visited the Dynhams at Nutwell for a family celebration and went hunting twice with the Beaumonts at Gittisham. Mindful of our responsibilities, we celebrated the Nativity in fine style with our tenants at Shute, entertained by a band of travelling players from Exeter and feasting on a fallow buck brought down by Will himself.

As the year unfolded there were letters from my mother and my sisters telling me their news but in many ways I would rather they'd not written. Disasters came tumbling one over the other, less a nibbling away at my family's wealth and positions of influence, more the taking of deadly voracious bites.

At a meeting of the council held at Coventry, those closest to the queen accused the duke of York of treasonous activities and he was only saved by a merciful gesture from the king. Then Uncle Fauconberg lost his position as Constable of Windsor and my brother Richard was recalled from Calais to answer charges relating to his piracy. But worse was to come. On his return to Westminster, Richard was attacked by a group of royal servants and only narrowly avoided being killed. My mother said my father had written letters to the queen expressing his family's loyalty to the Crown but the future was beginning to look very bleak indeed for the Nevills.

Already preparations for conflict were being made: five hundred pikes and five hundred leaden clubs gathered for the protection of the royal household; great serpentines brought for attacks on the castles of rebellious lords; and letters of array sent out by the queen to every town and village. This last act caused my father to summon his sons to Middleham.

'Can you not sleep?' whispered Will into the darkness.

It was the middle of October, more than a year since we'd returned to Shute, and I'd not heard from my mother for twelve weeks.

'I am too frightened to close my eyes,' I admitted.

He gave a little chuckle. 'I shall protect you.'

'Will, I am not afraid for myself but for my family.'

'Am I not your family now?'

I felt for his hand under the covers and squeezed his fingers. 'Of course you are but you are here and you are safe, my father and my brothers are not.'

'Sweetheart, you must not worry. Grandfather received a summons to parliament five weeks ago. If anything was amiss he would have written.'

'That's what I tell myself.'

His hand slid over my belly, pausing briefly then reaching for the hem of my nightgown.

'Shall I divert you?'

'What if news has reached Chewton Mendip?'

Will sighed. 'One of my men went to Honiton yesterday. He heard nothing of any significance.'

'Perhaps Sir Philip has returned. He might know more than the Honiton townsfolk.'

At that moment we heard the noise of a horseman in the yard: a challenge, a response, a clanging and grating as the great door was unbarred and the sound of footsteps running up the stairs. Will was out of bed, a dagger in his hand before his squire was in the doorway with a candle.

'A messenger, my lord.'

'From?'

'Leominster.'

'Where?'

'Leominster, my lord. He's on his knees, my lord. Says he's not stopped for near two days.'

Wearing only his nightgown Will disappeared down the stairway in the wake of his squire. As soon as he was gone I slipped out of bed and threw a robe over my shoulders. Deep inside I felt a cold, certain terror. For a man to ride through the night across tracks where a horse might easily stumble and break its leg, whatever message he brought must be vitally important. I ran quickly down the steps. Our servants were sleepily moving themselves out of their lord's way, dragging themselves and their mattresses off to the furthest reaches of the hall. Will was by the hearth holding a letter in his hand. The man, filthy and bedraggled, his garments soaked from last night's rain, finished speaking just as my foot left the last step.

A servant took the man's arm and led him away to where a jug of ale and a platter of food had been placed on a hastily erected table. I moved to Will's side.

'Is it news?'

'From my grandfather.'

'What does he say? What's happened? My lord, for pity's sake, tell me?'

By now the whole household was out of bed, anxious to know what was amiss. Will ordered one of the servants to bring a jug of wine and two cups up to my Lady Harington's room. Then he took me by my arm and led me back up the stairs. I was trembling. While the servant poured the wine Will sat me down on a chair by the hearth.

'Drink this,' he said.

I took the cup but my hands shook so much, liquid slopped over the rim, splashing my nightgown. Will took the cup and held it to my lips. The wine tasted strong and slightly tart. I could feel a rush of warmth spread down my throat and into my stomach.

Will sat beside me and took my hands in his. 'There was a battle. Your father's men met the royal army under Lord Audley at a place called Blore Heath, somewhere near Drayton. Audley was killed and your brother Tom and your brother John were captured. Grandfather says they have been taken to the castle at Chester.'

'My father broke the king's peace?'

I could not believe that my honourable peace-loving father would do such a thing. Will's grandfather must be mistaken. Perhaps my father had been attacked and was merely defending himself.

'There is worse.'

'What can be worse than a man forced to fight against his king?'

But I knew what could be worse – far, far worse.

'It is not good.'

I swallowed hard and told myself – I am a Nevill. I can bear this. Whatever it is, I can bear it.

'Tell me please. I am ready.'

'After the battle, your father joined with your brother Richard and the duke of York. Together they swore an oath to protect themselves and to uphold the king's high estate. They swore the truth of this to the Garter King of Arms. He was to take their assurances of loyalty to King Henry.'

'And the king did not listen.'

'It is possible the message was not delivered. Maybe someone deliberately kept it from the king.'

'It has to be the queen or her friends. If Henry was told he'd be inclined to mercy. But the queen would not want my family's assurances of loyalty to reach the king's ears.'

'It is not certain what happened. All my grandfather knows is that Exeter, Somerset and the Percys are determined to make an end of their enemies.'

I closed my eyes, seeing once more the leering face of Lord Egremont on Heworth Moor and the bruised arms of my York cousin, Nan, that winter night at Tuxford.

Please tell me. Are they dead?

'As good as.'

'What do you mean?' I screamed. 'How can a man be as good as dead? Either he is dead or he is not.'

I was half on my feet, ready to run downstairs and ask Lord Bonville's man if he'd seen my father but Will pulled me back onto my chair.

'Listen, dearest. I'll try to explain. The duke and your father knew a huge royal army was marching towards them so they retreated with their men towards Ludlow. They dug themselves in by the bridge The duke began firing his cannon but the men could see the royal standard flying and realised the king was with the royal army. One of your brother Richard's so-called loyal followers from the Calais garrison, Sir Andrew Trollope, could not stomach a fight against his king and crept away with his men to join the royal army. Grandfather says the duke knew morning would bring disaster so he advised his men not to fight but to submit to the king. Then he and your father together with your brother Richard, your cousins Edward and Edmund and a few trusted followers quit the camp and fled into the night.'

'They ran away? Like cowards?'

'What else could they do. To fight would mean certain defeat.'

'They could have thrown themselves on the king's mercy. Henry would not have had them killed.'

'Dearest, be sensible. You know Somerset and the others would not have allowed that to happen. Somerset was outmanoeuvred last year at Coventry when Henry went soft on them. This time he would have made sure the king remained resolute.'

'My father and my brother didn't fight. They escaped. They're not dead.'

'No, they are not dead. But what they have done will be viewed as treason. Somerset will see they are attainted. And you know that is as good as a death sentence. Your family will lose everything.'

'That is impossible. The Nevills are powerful, they are the lords of the north. Not even the queen can destroy my family. Oh Will! What of my mother?'

He shook his head. 'Grandfather doesn't know where she is.'

'Perhaps my father left her at Middleham with Margaret. He would know they'd be safe there.'

Will was very gentle with me.

'If there is an attainder, Middleham will be taken by the king.'

'No!'

Middleham could not be taken. I'd been born there, I'd lived there as a child, No-one could take Middleham from us. But despite my protests I knew they could. The Percys had once been lords of the north until they were destroyed by a king. So why not the Nevills.

'My brother, George, will help. He is bishop of Exeter. That must count for something.'

It was a miserable hope, I knew that, but I needed to grasp at any straw, no matter how weak.

'One man's raised voice is not enough. If he has any sense your brother will keep quiet.'

'But where will my mother go? How will she live?'

He shrugged. 'It is possible the king will be generous.'

'The queen will not allow any generosity. She will have my mother wander the lanes in her kirtle,' I cried.

'Sweetheart, it will not come to that.'

But it would. Margaret of Anjou would force my mother to beg for her bread. and anyone bearing the name Nevill would be ground into the dust under the queen's small elegant heel.

'I cannot bear it,' I cried. 'I truly cannot.'

Will tried to put his arm around my shoulder but I pushed him away.

'What of Tom and John? Are they to be killed too?'

'It may be your sister Alianore's husband can see they are treated well.'

'Did Thomas Stanley stand with my father?'

'Grandfather does not say.'

'Oh, why do we not know more?'

'There is nothing we can do.'

Will was blunt with the truth and I hated him for it.

I refused to go back to bed but instead sat huddled like an old woman by the hearth with Edith holding my hand. I was beyond tears. There was a coldness inside which no heat from the fire could dispel.

'Where is Will?' I said, eventually lifting my gaze from the glowing embers.

'He has gone to see Lord Bonville's man in case he knows more.'

But the man had no further information and we were left to wait and to worry.

Those were the longest two weeks of my life. Will travelled to Honiton and to Axminster for news but no-one knew anything about events which didn't concern the price of wheat or the cost of repairing the town's bridge. The Beaumonts were the length of the county away at Shirwell and a visit to Exeter yielded nothing. The days grew shorter, the early autumn gales blew leaves round the walls and the last of the animals were brought into the byre. One night there was a howling in the trees and rain hurled itself against our shutters. By morning, water streamed through the yards and down the paths. Puddles formed against the banks and Sir Robert came to inform Will that the church roof was leaking.

'I cannot bear this any longer,' I wept. 'I have to know if they are alive or if they are dead. It is the waiting I cannot endure.'

Edith glanced at Will who was chewing his lips in an agony of indecision.

'I shall go to Chewton Mendip. Maybe they will have news.'

'I shall come with you.'

Edith shook her head and Will said, 'No, dearest. The roads are dreadful, knee deep in mud and I shall be faster alone. I'll take a couple of men and be back before you know I've gone.'

I tried pleading, I even got down on my knees, but it was no good. Will was adamant. I must remain at Shute.

He kissed my forehead. 'You are the most precious of my belongings. I need you to be safe. Stay here. You have Edith for company and I shall be back very soon.'

It was almost the Eve of All Hallows. Each night I told myself he would return and each day I was disappointed. I was unable to sleep, unable to eat. I could barely form the words to pray. At night, protected by the bed curtains, there was nothing to hear but Edith's breathing. I lay there, sleepless, images flitting across my closed lids: my mother, abandoned, starving, somewhere alone in the rain and the cold; my father cut down, his body dishonoured by a jeering group of the queen's friends; and my brothers, led one after the other to the block, an executioner with a rope, an axe and a sharp knife, smiling in anticipation.

I thought I heard a noise. Carefully, I sat up and pulled one of the curtains aside. The room was dark but I was right, someone *was* outside in the yard. I slipped out of bed and padded over to the narrow window. A light wavered to and fro. A man with a lantern. I listened. No sound of horses but a man talking, not loudly, but urgently. I threw a robe over my shoulders and opened the door, disturbing the boy who slept across the threshold in Will's absence. A glow from a single candle was coming up the stairway.

'My lady!' It was our steward. He was frowning, annoyed at having his sleep disturbed.

'I heard someone in the yard. Is Lord Harington returned?'

'Nay. A young man. Won't give his name. Friend of my lady's husband, he says. Got a message for her.'

He sounded disbelieving. I almost pushed him aside but remembered just in time who I was. 'Wait while I get a light,' I said.

With a candle in one hand and the other gripping the rail I followed him down the stairway and into the hall. Our visitor was standing with his back to me, warming himself by the hearth. The rain must have been heavy as a small puddle of water had gathered on the floor around his boots. He was tall, taller than Will, dressed in a dark cloak, mud-spattered, sodden, the hood pushed up over his head. I gave my candle to the steward and took three uncertain steps forward.

The man turned and his hood fell back.

I gasped. 'Edward!'

My first thought was how grown-up he was: broad shoulders, long legs, a man's careless arrogance; my second, utter terror that he'd come to tell me my father was dead. Doubtless I looked foolish floundering around, trying to remember his titles and how he should be addressed. I unclasped my hands, swallowed twice, then lowered myself into an obedient curtsey.

'My lord, you are welcome to Shute.'

'Lady Harington.' His voice was deep, more of a man's than the boy's treble I remembered. But It was five years since that Twelfth Night feast at Baynard's Castle and of course he had changed. 'I apologise for the late hour, my lady. I see I have roused you and your household from your beds.' He was looking at my bare feet.

I hastily withdrew them under the folds of my nightgown. 'It is of no consequence, my lord. You must have come far. Would you care for something to eat and some wine?'

'I would.'

I looked round, panic-stricken, for a servant. 'Refreshment for the earl of March and be quick.'

'God's truth, it's dreadful roads you have here in Devonshire. Almost broke my neck coming down that hill. Is your husband not at home?' Edward's smile broadened as he noticed my obvious discomfort.

'No, my lord. He has gone to Chewton Mendip for news.'

I wanted to scream, tell me, tell me, tell me what has happened, but I was a lady and ladies were not mannerless.

'Oh yes, news.'

'You are unharmed, my lord?'

'I am. You can rest easy. We are all unharmed.'

He was looking around our undeniably small hall.

'You live here?'

'For most of the year. My husband has other manors but he prefers Shute.'

He raised his eyebrows and grimaced, saying with his expression what he was far too polite to say out loud – who on God's earth would prefer to live here?

The servants managed to produce a slice of cold mutton pie, cheese and some of yesterday's bread. And for our noble visitor, wine served from our best enamelled ewer poured into a silver gilt cup, a gift to Will from his Harington grandfather. I gestured in the direction of the top table where a clean cloth had been hastily laid over the scored and worm-pocked surface. 'Please, my lord, sit and eat.'

'You will sit with me?'

I lowered my head demurely. 'If that is your wish.'

Edward handed his filthy cloak to a man at his elbow and waited for water to wash his hands. I prayed the boy would not bring it freezing cold as he had when Sir Philip and Lady Blanche had once paid an unexpected visit. But the steward, overawed by the presence of an earl in our hall, supervised every move made by the servants under his command. The water was warm and the napkin clean and neatly folded.

Edward sat and I watched with pleasure as his fingers, cleaned of the grime of travel, picked up a morsel of cheese. 'When you've eaten as we have these past weeks you have no idea how good it is to enjoy a meal in pleasant company in a warm, dry hall,' he said.

He ate fastidiously which surprised me being used to Will's rougher manners and when Edward tasted the wine he complimented me on its quality. While he was eating I had to contain my impatience but once he had emptied the plates and refused more, I asked him to tell me what had happened.

He glanced at the servants busy removing the last of the dishes and said, 'Is there somewhere we can be private? I need to talk to you alone.'

'My husband is from home. I cannot be alone with you. It is impossible. People would talk.'

He grinned. 'We've been alone together before or have you forgotten?'

Of course I'd not forgotten. A girl's first kiss is a precious moment, one to be treasured all her life.

'No, I have not forgotten but I am a married woman, my lord, and you must know I cannot do what you ask.'

He shrugged his shoulders. 'Very well. If we must have an audience then let us at least be comfortable. He rose from his chair and threw his cushion onto the floor against the wall, then picked up three more and threw them to join the first. He held out his hand. 'Come, my lady. Pray join me in my private pavilion.'

He regarded me, his dark lashes half-closed over his bright blue eyes, a secretive smile hovering round his mouth, challenging me to refuse. I looked at the red and blue velvet mound lying invitingly against the stitched hem of the tapestry on the back wall. Suddenly I didn't care. My family were not dead. They were alive and anything was possible. Even sprawling on the floor with my unmarried cousin was possible.

I lowered myself gingerly onto the cushions, tucking my bare feet well out of sight. Before I could say anything, Edward dropped down beside me, taking up most of the cushioned space and sitting far too close for propriety. I glanced round but need not have worried. We were completely hidden behind a wall of snowy white napery, the folds giving an illusion of privacy and the remaining chairs on the dais hiding us from servants passing through to the stairway.

He grinned at me. 'I said this was a good idea.'

Now that the servants could no longer see or, hopefully, hear us I was able to treat him like a cousin and not like an earl.

'Edward, tell me, please. Where are the others?'

'I left them at Nutwell.'

'Nutwell? Near Lympstone?'

'Yes, with Lady Dynham.'

'You know the Dynhams?'

'John Dynham is an old friend of mine. But we're not staying. It's only for a few days.'

'So why have you come to Shute?'

It must have taken him half a day and half a night in the saddle to travel from Nutwell to Shute. And all that time he'd been in danger of being recognised.

'I came to see *you*.'

I smiled. 'No truly, why?'

'I told you, to see *you*.' He glanced left and right to make sure there were no eavesdropping servants, then leaned closer until our heads were almost touching. 'How much do you know?' He spoke in a low voice.

I told him everything Will's grandfather had said.

'Christ knows but we were terrified that first night riding away from Ludlow. We thought they'd be at our heels but I guess Trollope didn't think we'd run, otherwise Somerset's men would've been out looking for us.'

'Where did you go?'

'The wilds of Wales. There are caves in the mountains. It's a good place to hide from your enemies. But my father reckoned it was safer to split up, said he'd sail to Ireland where he'd got friends, take Edmund with him and raise men. Told me to go with your brother and your father to Calais. I wanted to go to Ireland with my father but he insisted Edmund and I should not stay together.

Why not?'

'Ah Kat, can you not see? Edmund and I are the future of the Yorks. Think what might happen if we were both to fall into the queen's hands.'

'But you're not full grown. The king would not allow her to harm you?'

'Because I'm not a man?' He leaned across and placed his mouth gently on mine. 'I am very much a man, my lovely Kat.'

I remained absolutely still, wondering why his lips felt so warm, so sweet, so utterly familiar when they were not my husband's lips. His arms remained at his side and we stayed like that, mouth against mouth, breathing in each other's warmth, for what seemed like an eternity, my heart beating uncomfortably fast. At last he withdrew and gave a sigh.

'Je te désire,' he whispered.

I pretended I'd not heard. He should not be saying these words to me and I should not be savouring them in the way I was.

'What will you do now?' I hoped my voice was steady, wondering why after all this time he still had the ability to unsettle me. I was no longer that girl of five years ago, blinded by what I thought was love. I was a happily married woman and I loved my husband.

Edward sighed like a man disappointed then grinned and said, 'We sail for Calais as soon as we can. John

Dynham is getting a ship, He's gone to Exmouth where he says he'll find one and the magnificent Lady Dynham is rustling up a crew.'

I smiled at the thought of a magnificent Lady Dynham. She would appreciate that description.

'How did you know to make for Nutwell?'

'We didn't. We'd hired a small boat to take us from the Welsh coast and fate and the tides brought us to Hartland. I remembered Dynham's place and sent one of our men to find him. Lucky for us he had his feet up counting cattle in the byre, or so he said.'

'And he brought you to Nutwell.'

'I doubt we'd have found our way without him. Devonshire's worse than Yorkshire: endless moors and rocks and streams in spate, and every river crossing controlled by Courtenay's men.'

'Edward, do you have news of my mother?'

He shook his head. 'Your father sent word. telling her to flee Middleham but we don't know if she got the message. That's why I've come to you, Kat. You'll be the only one to know where we've gone. Guard the knowledge with your life and be careful who you tell. Not all your kin are loyal supporters of my father.'

My Nevill grandfather's first family had battled for years against my father. They hated him and would never take the same path. And what of my sisters' husbands? Joan's husband had stood with my father at Blore Heath but Lord Fitzhugh was loyal to the king. And Alianore's husband, Thomas Stanley was known as a man who sat on the sidelines, unwilling to commit himself. He could not be counted on. And my sisters-in-law? Ties of family were hard to break as I knew. My mother had told me to cleave to my husband but never forget I was a Nevill.

'Has my father had word of my brothers? Lord Bonville said Tom and John were taken to Chester but knew nothing else.'

'Your father reckons they're safe for the moment. They are merely minnows and Somerset and the queen have bigger fish in their sights.'

'If you make it to Calais, will you stay there?'

'He smiled. 'Perhaps it is better you do not know our plans.' He put his head back and closed his eyes. 'I am so weary, Kat, I could stay here just where I am on these cushions for a week at least.'

'Shall I ask the servants to make you a bed? We have a guest chamber.'

'No, dear Kat, the temptation is great, in more ways than one, but I must get back to Nutwell. Your father wanted to send a messenger and was not amused when I said I'd go myself.' He laughed. 'I'll not be forgiven if our sailing is delayed by my dallying with his daughter.'

I stood in the shelter of the doorway, the candlelit hall behind me, watching as he swung himself easily into the saddle. I'd insisted he took one of our horses as his own poor beast had barely time to be rubbed down, fed and watered before being expected to plod wearily back to Nutwell through the rain.

Edward raised his gloved hand. 'Farewell, my lady,' he called. 'Until next time.'

Three days later Will came home. He sat down and gestured for me to sit beside him.

'Grandfather took the oath of loyalty as the duke of York advised. He has been welcomed back into the king's peace but it is as we feared; a bill of attainder has been read naming the commanders who took the field at Blore Heath against the royal forces led by Lord Audley. Not just your father and your brothers, but others: John Conyers and Tom Stanley's brother. They have also named your mother.'

'But my mother did not take the field.'

'It is said that while at Middleham she planned the death and final destruction of the king.'

I clutched at his sleeve. 'But she is my mother!'

'My love, you must prepare yourself. You know what they'll do If they catch her.'

I shook my head.

'They will burn her.'

'They can't!' I sobbed. 'They can't!'

'It is the law. A woman found guilty of treason suffers death by burning.'

'No! The king will not permit my mother to be burned. He knew her when he was a child.'

I wanted someone to tell me all would be well, that this was no worse than the other horrors I'd endured. Have courage, my mother had said. But what good would courage do me now.

'What of my uncle of York?' I whispered.

'The duke and his eldest son have both been found guilty and will suffer attainder.'

I thought of Edward's careless laughter and how he had shrugged off the possibility of imminent disaster. He'd been enjoying himself. He knew what the king's parliament would do but, like my brother, Richard, he was a man who relished the excitement, the challenge, the danger and was not afraid.

I felt sick with fright.

Next morning when I awoke, terror rushed back and I vomited. Fear and sickness churned round in my belly and I was unable to lift my head from the pillow until it was time for dinner when I suddenly felt hungry. But when the sickness settled into a regular pattern of vomiting each morning I knew it was not only fear but another reason. Will and I were going to have our longed-for first child.

For more than a month there was no news. My family, once so solid and secure, was in disarray: two brothers imprisoned in Chester Castle, another brother and my father fled in fear of their lives to Calais and my fourth bother, George, silenced by the weight of the Church. I had no knowledge of where my mother was or my sisters-in-law. Will said Maud would have been turned out of Eresby as Tom's property would now be in the king's hands. Had she perhaps gone to her sister? And what about Isobel Ingoldisthorpe, barely seventeen, thrown out of John's house. Was Anne with her two small girls safe in Calais where Somerset's men could be hammering at the gates any day?

Will rode twice to Chewton Mendip to discuss at length with his father and grandfather as to what they should do. Orders had come from the royal council for Lord Bonville to act with the new earl of Devon, Sir Thomas Courtenay, to raise the men of Devonshire and Cornwall for the king.

There were to be musters of archers and men-at-arms. Watches and beacons were to be appointed in the usual places and various persons of interest to be arrested and committed to prison.

After the feast of the Nativity rumours began spreading like wildfire along the coast. The duke of Somerset, newly created captain of Calais, had been denied entry to the port by the garrison and been forced to make for Guisnes, one of the outlying forts which protected the town from the French. Disaffected Englishmen were fleeing daily from Kent and its neighbouring shires to join the earl of Warwick in Calais, supplying him with arms and provisions. And there were reports of Lord Fauconberg, seen in Kent.

The Bonville men, whatever their sympathies for the duke of York and the Nevills, hesitated to put themselves and their families in further danger but when a letter brought by a ship's captain to Lady Dynham, arrived, there was no further reason to delay. Their course of action was clear. They would declare for the duke of York.

In the middle of January the king's new fleet, intended to aid the duke of Somerset in Guisnes, had been commandeered by Sir John Wenlock and Edith's brother in a daring raid on Sandwich. Together with seven hundred men from Calais they had captured not only the ships but also Lord Rivers and his son who were supposed to be on guard but who'd been found asleep in their beds. "Low-born scum" was what my brother called Lord Rivers, when he was brought before him at Calais; though how that particular piece of gossip found its way back to England I had no idea.

A month later news came from Dartmouth. The earl of Warwick's fleet had routed the duke of Exeter in the king's great ship *Grace Dieu*. The earl was returning to Calais in triumph from Ireland, bringing his mother, the countess, with him and had threatened to attack the duke's fleet. The duke, knowing he was no match for my brother, had declined to fight and ran for a safe harbour. At last I had news of my mother. She was safe and would by now be reunited with my father in Calais.

It was early summer when we heard that Edith's brother and his men had taken the town of Sandwich and executed its captain, a man appointed by the king's council, Will was jubilant.

'See! Now it has begun. At last your brother has his bridgehead. I told Grandfather he was being too cautious. We should have left for London a month ago.'

My brother had support, not only from the men of Sussex and Kent, but also from the garrison and the merchants of the staple in Calais. Now we all knew Richard would return to England with my father and with Edward and we also knew that when they did, the king, the queen and the royal army would be waiting for them.

Will put his arms around me as best he could considering the size of my belly and told me he wished he could stay but I knew he was eager for whatever lay ahead. Like all young men he thirsted for glory and honour and excitement, not a life of quiet, peaceful domesticity. He had told me as much on our wedding day.

'Surely they do intend to kill the king?' I said, profoundly nervous at the thought of what might happen.

'No-one intends to kill the king, my love, merely those who've given him bad advice.

'You mean Somerset and Exeter.'

'Yes.'

'What of the queen?'

'Put back in her proper place where a woman belongs,' said Will firmly. 'She is not the ruler of England and she must learn that lesson.'

'Where does a woman belong?' I asked, curious as to what he would say.

Will smiled. 'Under her husband's roof, in his bed and bearing his sons.'

'You think God will bless us with a son?'

'I do. But if by any mischance it is a girl, I shall return and together we shall make another child and this time it will be a son, Lady Harington. Remember what we said: eleven children.'

I smiled at the memory of that day three years ago on our way to Canterbury: the damp shoots of pussy willow, the length of green satin ribbon and my husband too impatient to take off his boots.

Will left with his men in mid June, when Shute was at its most glorious, trees in full leaf, the scent of honeysuckle filling the air and I, a week or more away from giving birth to a new Bonville heir.

Next day I was luxuriating in my idleness as I sat in the solar with a half-finished baby gown spread on my knees and my sewing bag on the table nearby. It must have been an hour since I'd picked up my needle and Edith had made a sharp remark about the virtue of work in the furtherance of God's holy plan. I was about to bestir myself when the slight ache at the base of my spine which I'd noticed earlier, turned into a gnawing somewhere deep inside my body.

I gave a gasp and bent over as if to squeeze out what was causing the pain. Edith took one look at me and summoned the midwife from her corner. Before I could tell her I was alright and not to make a fuss, I was bundled into bed as another wave of pain began. The old woman told me to rest, saying birthing was a lengthy affair and I would need all my strength. First babies were known to take their time. I vaguely remember both maids hurrying to and fro with basins while the midwife sat down to enjoy yet another pot of ale.

Before evening they had me out of bed walking the floor and then the screaming began. I had never known such pain, a relentless grinding agony as if as if the hounds of Hell were tearing my body apart. I tried to pray but as the pain threatened to engulf me I found myself calling out for Alice and for my mother.

Mercifully my daughter came quickly. Cecily, the most beautiful baby in the world and her father's child in every way.

'She is asleep so you can wipe that anxious look off your face, Lady Harington,' said Edith who had elected herself in charge now that I was not allowed out of bed 'Ceci may be perfect but she will not wake to order just because you'd rather whisper baby talk than listen to me'

I smiled at her apologetically. It was true that whatever was happening far away was of less interest to me here in my chamber than watching my baby change day by day, trying to make her smile, examining her perfect, tiny body, counting her fingers and her toes, stroking the fuzz of golden hair on the top of her head and gazing with wonder into her deep, dark eyes.

Edith, sitting beside me, had her mother's letter in her lap and was tapping her foot impatiently on the floor. 'Don't you want to know what your husband is doing or have you forgotten him now you have a baby to play with?'

'No, please Edith. Tell me what your mother says.'

Edith peered at the letter. 'This writing is very small. I swear that new clerk of hers is trying to make me squint. How am I meant to read what he has written?' She held the offending letter close to her eyes. 'She has received another note from my brother. He says your father, your uncle, your brother and the young earl of March have arrived from Calais with two thousand men. Tomorrow they set out for London. Everywhere men are flocking to their banners and in London the king's men have shut themselves in the Tower.'

'Mercy! Does your mother say if the royal army will march on London?'

Edith peered at the letter again. 'She says the king and queen are in Coventry. But ballads in praise of the duke of York and his Nevill kin are being sung everywhere. And your brother has penned another manifesto.'

'More blame heaped on the shoulders of the king's advisers for the loss of Normandy and Gascony and for the despoliation of the kingdom?'

'The earl of Warwick has a fine way with words: greed, violence, tyranny, malice and spite. It makes ones blood run hot. If his ire was aimed at me I'd be quaking in my shoes.'

I laughed uneasily. 'I hope Will is safe.'

'No man of honour wishes to be kept safe. Danger is his meat and drink.'

'I know but he is my husband and I cannot imagine a life without him.'

'Then you'd better pray because this is not over yet.'

The brightest of leaves were already fading when I walked to the church one late summer morning for the short service of purification. The hay meadows had been cut and the calves weaned from their mothers and the apples were colouring nicely in the orchard. But the wheat yield had been poor again this year, spoiled by too much rain and not enough sun, or so the reeve said. In the house we had celebrated the news from Northampton: the royal army defeated, King Henry captured and the queen fled. And a letter had come from Will saying he would be coming home.

'It is over,' I said to Edith. 'The fighting is finished. No more worrying, no more nightmares. The Yorks and the Nevills have won.'

It was hard to believe how much had changed in the outside world when here at Shute the seasons passed in the same way as they had always done: autumn, winter, spring and summer, God's plan working out day by day.

I stood on the step, waiting as Will and his men rode into the courtyard. He swung himself out of the saddle and dropped to the ground. He grinned at me but I knew he must first see to his men. Inside the hall, the tables were set with our best pewter plates and cups, the elaborate silver salt cellar given to us by Will's grandfather placed carefully in the centre of the cloth on the top table. Jugs of our best wine stood on the shelf in the ewery, the tiny room newly built next to the buttery, and great pitchers of ale had been made ready for those at the lower tables. In the kitchen, last minute touches were being put to the feast, the venison from Sir Philip Beaumont roasted to perfection.

Will and I, Lord Harington and his lady, sat side by side on the dais, Will's companions ranged on either side of us. I wore my most costly robes, my forehead plucked, my hair hidden beneath a smart crimson henin with a silver ribbon tied under my chin but to my dismay all the men talked about was the battle.

'You see, my lady, the enemy couldn't fire their cannon,' said the man next to me, trying to explain the more bewildering of their tactics.

'Why not?' I asked politely.

'It had been raining since daybreak,' interposed Will.

'Ay, my lord, that's the trouble with firepower. Fair enough in a siege but in the field a good longbowman is worth a dozen of them cannon.'

'Especially when it's pissing down,' laughed the fat man on Will's other side. 'Beggin your pardon, m'lady, but it's true'

I inclined my head and wondered when we might talk of something else. I'd listened to praise for the inspired leadership of the earl of Warwick, the retelling of numerous deeds of valour performed by Lord Fauconberg, and the story of the fortuitous defection of Lord Grey of Ruthin. My neighbour had given me a blow by blow account of how Lord Egremont and my Aunt Stafford's husband, the duke of Buckingham, had been slain outside the king's tent and I'd been told three times how the young earl of March had inspired them with his courage and his leadership. But of the king they were dismissive.

'Never saw a king so humble,' said my dining companion. 'Thought he'd be a big, powerful man like Lord Bonville, but he weren't. The poor wight was more like one of they penitents you see crawling on their hands and knees. Simple he were.'

'I have only seen him once.'

'Not much to look at and no commander of men. Not like the earl of Warwick. Now there's a bonny fighter.'

It was strange to hear my brother universally praised when not so long ago he had been an attainted traitor.

Eventually the last jug of wine was emptied, the last dish removed and the last song sung in celebration of a battle which could not have been won but for the brilliance of Lord Harington's men. Our guests, slightly tipsy but still on their feet, were seen to their guest quarters and at last I was alone with Will.

'Come and see her,' I said taking his hand and leading him to the little room I'd made into a nursery. The young nursemaid rose from the chair next to the cradle where she'd been dozing and gave a deep curtsey.

Ceci lay fast asleep, her hair covered by an embroidered cap. Will peered at his daughter.

'Sweet, but not as sweet as her mother.'

At that moment our voices disturbed the baby and she gave a little whimper.

'Is she in pain?' asked Will anxiously.

I smiled. 'Perhaps she is dreaming of her father's great victory. Shall I wake her?'

He shook his head. 'Leave her be. I am going to take her mother to bed.'

17

THE END OF DAYS 1461

That autumn Will took me to London. If there were to be celebrations for the duke of York's triumphant arrival he said we should be there. I wanted to take Ceci with us but decided, reluctantly, that she was too young and should remain at Shute in the care of her wet nurse and the nursemaid. Will employed the respectable widow of one of his father's friends to oversee our daughter's little household in our absence. I wept when I left her but Will promised me we would return soon.

When we reached London I realised that my family, far from being attainted traitors, were now riding high on the crest of a wave. My father held the title of Great Chamberlain of England and our brother George had been extracted from his bishop's palace at Exeter to become Chancellor. Richard, as well as his original posts of Captain of Calais and Keeper of the Seas, was Warden of the Cinq Ports and, more importantly, King Henry's acknowledged chief councillor. Tom and John had received lucrative positions within the royal household in recognition of their unjust imprisonment in Chester Castle. The Nevills were unassailable.

Naturally not everyone was pleased. The queen was reported to have fled to Wales to the castle of Jasper Tudor, her husband's half-brother. The duke of Exeter had slithered away to join her, and young Somerset, who'd been forced to swear an oath not to take up arms against my brother Richard before he was allowed back from Guisnes, was sulking at Corfe. According to my mother, Somerset was the worst kind of snake: good-looking, silver-tongued and highly dangerous, just like his father.

'It is a shame the duke of York arrived late for the parliament,' remarked my sister-in-law Anne as we sat in my mother's chamber at The Erber.

'Did you see Duchess Cecily?' said my brother John's new wife, Isabel, all wide eyes and breathless. 'Is she not magnificent. I have never seen a blue velvet in that particular shade before.'

Aunt Cecily had certainly looked imposing: lavish amounts of fur-trimmed brocade, a silver and crimson cap with gold bands, and a pair of shoes with high heels to disguise her lack of inches.

'Too gaudy for my taste,' replied Anne.

'Did you hear what her husband did?' said Alianore.

'No,' said Isabel, agog with curiosity. She was like me seven years ago on my first visit to London, all wide-eyed and breathless.

My mother leaned towards this new daughter-in-law who was so young, so sweet-tempered and so highly prized.

'The duke of York sat in the king's place. Claimed it was his by right and by inheritance and said he would keep it, live or die.'

Isabel gasped, shocked to the core of her innocent young soul by the actions of Aunt Cecily's husband.

'Unwise, considering what is being said in the city,' I remarked.

Alianore raised her eyebrows. 'Listening to gossip again, Kat?'

I ignored her. 'Londoners are not pleased. They've no love for Henry but he's their anointed king. They do not want him set aside.'

'Unlike what's being said about the queen's little bastard.'

'Alianore!' said my mother sharply. 'Keep a civil tongue while you are in your father's house.'

'Forgive me, lady mother.' Alianore smiled blandly at our mother then turned and whispered to me. 'They say the child is not Henry's son.'

I'd heard the rumour from the wife of an aldermen in Gracechurch Street. She'd said Edmund Beaufort, the dead duke of Somerset, had taken the king's place not only in the queen's affections but in the queen's bed to get her with child. Everyone knew. The taverns off the Cheap were alive with tittle-tattle and vulgar songs about what the hated foreign queen had done.

'The duke has taken the king's chambers at Westminster,' ventured Anne. 'Richard says he broke down the doors and the king has been forced to lodge elsewhere.'

'Most unwise,' remarked my mother. 'It shows arrogance.'

'Is Aunt Cecily preparing for her coronation?' piped up Margaret.

Alianore delivered a sharp slap. 'Ignorant child!'

'I am not ignorant!' howled Margaret.

'Yes you are. Even if you think such a thing you're a fool to say it.'

My mother called for peace.

'What will happen now?' I asked.

My mother regarded the six of us. 'Your father says Archbishop Bourchier has refused to crown the duke and without the archbishop there can be no coronation. So I fear someone is going to have to tell your Aunt Cecily's husband he cannot be king.'

There was silence while we all looked at each other.

'I hope they do not expect John to do it,' said Isabel.

Maud shook her head. 'It would be nigh impossible for many to see King Henry set aside. I cannot believe it will happen.'

'Our husbands won the battle for the duke of York,' replied Anne. 'It is only right for the duke to be crowned king.'

'Do you think it sensible for a man to claim the crown by right of conquest?' My mother remarked, sounding exasperated as if her daughter-in-law had said something incredibly foolish.

'The duke has as much right to the crown as Henry. He has royal blood flowing in his veins,' replied Anne stubbornly.

'And would the duke sit easy on his throne knowing someone might come along with a larger army or with greater firepower? You clearly do not know the story of the king's grandfather, the fourth Henry.'

'Our men will not accept the king as long as he is under the queen's influence, not after all that has happened,' muttered Anne.

'If the duke cannot be king and our men will not accept Henry, what will parliament do?' I asked my mother.

'We shall have to wait and see. And now I think you should go back to your lodgings and prepare for supper at

Castle Baynard. It will not do to be late. And remember – mind what you say.'

I followed Alianore out of the room and down the stairs. 'What does Thomas Stanley think?' I asked.

Alianore smiled. 'On my advice he pursues the same policy as our mother – wait and see. He believes parliament bends one way and then the other so unless a man knows how to harness the winds he may find himself blown onto the rocks. It is better to bide ones time.'

'Sound advice from a sail-trimmer,' I retorted. 'Will stands with the Nevills as does his grandfather. The Bonvilles are loyal to the Yorkist cause.'

We had reached the yard and while we waited for our horses to be brought, Alianore said, 'Then I pray the Yorkist cause is the right one for I should not like to see you mourning your husband and your son like poor Aunt Stafford.'

'Don't say that. Besides, my child is not a son, she is a daughter.'

'Then let us both pray your Will comes home safe to make another child with you and this time you manage to give him a son.'

It took a long time and much arguing but by the eve of All Hallows the lords and the commons had reached an agreement. The duke of York's right to the throne was upheld but Henry was not to be deposed or asked to resign the throne. Instead Margaret of Anjou's son was set aside from the succession and the duke named as Henry's heir. It was called the Act of Accord and was, so Alianore said, a neat piece of card shuffling.

Will came home late that night and crept into my bed.

'It was odd seeing the king taken away in the darkness, like a mourner in a funeral procession with no corpse. Grandfather says the duke of York went by torchlight to the bishop of London's palace and told the king that *he*, the duke was the rightful king, not Henry. It was not exactly a threat but there was menace in the way the words were spoken.'

'It is the same with Aunt Cecily. She behaves as if any moment a summons will come to move to the Tower where she'll be arrayed in her coronation robes. There will be a procession to Westminster Palace through the streets of London and dancing and singing and trumpets blowing.'

My mother had once told me about Queen Katherine's coronation feast where she'd watched my father perform his duties as carver. She had described hundreds of dishes, the intricate subtleties created by the royal confectioners and the sight of my Grandmother Nevill conversing with the king of the Scots.

But I remembered the *élevée* of Margaret of Anjou: lords dressed in satin doublets, claws sheathed in velvet sleeves, sharp white teeth hidden behind false smiles and treachery disguised as friendship. And leading the way, the queen, seemingly meek and mild but who had proved the most dangerous enemy of them all.

'If I were Margaret of Anjou I would not accept the disinheritance of my son. No mother would.'

He wound a sleepy arm around my waist and pulled me closer. 'Margaret of Anjou can do nothing. Without the king she *is* nothing.'

'But what if she were to raise an army?'

'She does not have the support.'

I thought he was wrong but nobody wanted to hear the worries of a young woman like me.

'Will, I should like to go home. I do not enjoy what is being done here. I would rather be with our daughter at Shute.'

He said nothing. He was already asleep.

We parted in the courtyard of a small inn near the Holy Trinity priory where the great road from London diverges, one way leading to Bath, the other to Salisbury. We spent our last night together entwined in each others arms, whispering inconsequential nothings until sleep overcame us and we slept. When the sound of bells woke us, he made love to me one last time, lying cocooned in a great fur cover he'd brought to keep me warm on my journey back to Shute. He kissed me tenderly and told me how much he loved me and promised he would be home for Christmas.

I watched him ride away up the road back towards London and then set my face resolutely towards the South West and home. It was only six weeks till Christmas.

The man wore my brother's livery of the white ragged staff which was odd in itself because Richard never bothered with me. I was his little sister, born when he was almost a man, ignored as all small sisters doubtless are. Yet here in my hall was his messenger, removing a sealed package from his pouch. The man's cloak was damp and his boots covered in mud but it was the look in his eyes which intrigued me most. He had pale eyes with lashes so fair as to be almost invisible and the message I read there was fear. But he had no cause to be frightened of me. I was only the lady of Shute, wife of young Lord Harington. I had no power. So why was he frightened? But when I looked again I realised I was mistaken. It was not fear, it was pity.

He offered me the package and I noticed his hands tremble slightly. The red wax seal was clearly that of the earl of Warwick, unmistakably Richard's. All movement ceased. Everyone was looking at me. The servants stood still, piles of white napery held in their arms; a boy halted, a basket of kindling at his feet, unsure whether to proceed; even the steward was standing, silent, waiting.

I broke the seal but found myself unable to unfold the letter. I did not want to read what my brother had written because something told me that once I'd read the words there would be no going back, no pretending, no believing in personal happiness any more. I could hear Edith's breathing and the expectant hush in the hall and remembered my mother's words – love only carries you so far. She had praised me for my courage. If courage was what was required of me then that is what I must have. I unfolded the letter and noticed my brother's scrawled signature at the bottom, and above it, the words "Fear not, all will end well". I read the letter once barely taking in what he'd written, then read it again.

They say that when a man is stabbed and the blade pierces his heart, he feels no pain. For several moments there is nothing but the sight of his lifeblood oozing from a mortal wound. I felt no pain. None at all. I turned and walked back through the hall and under the archway to the little door we'd used as an escape the night the earl of Devon's men came up the valley from Colcombe. It was unlocked.

I went out into the cold January air, oblivious to the clammy mist, the damp seeping into my shoes and the unsuitability of my clothing. I had no cloak, no gloves, no boots yet I felt nothing, not the damp or the cold. I walked along the path and through the small gate set in the wall. Unthinking, I walked past the church, half-aware of a muted glow behind one of the windows. I walked on up the slope to where the trees began.

'I am frightened of the trees,' I had told Will, trying to explain my reluctance to go with him into the woods. 'Why? They are only trees,' he'd said, taking my hand and making me face my fears.

'Only trees,' I whispered. 'Only trees. Nothing to be afraid of.'

The old tree stump where I'd sat on Will's knee the year we'd first lived together at Shute, looked unwelcoming: streaks of green on the bark, dead leaves congealing in a soggy mess at its base. I looked down over the rooftops of Shute, dark shadows almost lost in the shifting lighter grey of the morning mist.

I have no idea how long I stood there or what I was waiting for. There was no dagger, no blood and yet the wound was fatal. I knew that much. I wondered when the pain would begin.

In my head was a muddle of images: the sight of Lord Cromwell's tower rising like a finger of flame into a clear blue afternoon sky; Tom laughing at the roadside as he hoisted me into the saddle; my father kissing my mother at the merry Twelfth Night feast at Baynards Castle; and Will – always Will. Always, always Will. His strong fingers reaching for mine beneath the folds of napery as we sat side by side in his grandfather's hall; his laughter the day he triumphed in Sir Philip's hunt at Gittisham; and the look in his eyes when he'd surprised me with a morning gift of willow shoots tied up with a length of green ribbon. And that last time, in the early dawn when I'd clung to him in the yard of the inn near the priory. Each memory painted on the illuminated pages of a book, each one a moment held forever, unchanging, immutable.

I looked down. A drop of blood on the back of my hand, bright red. I recalled a sharp thorn bush near the gate. I gasped. I couldn't breathe. Blood! There would have been blood. Blood everywhere, Gushing from gaping wounds, from severed limbs, from mouths shrieking uselessly for mercy. I'd seen a man die at my feet. I knew what happened when men died. There would have been so much blood, more than I could imagine. My ears were deafened by the noise of thundering hooves, screaming, shouts of terror as the Percy men with their battleaxes streamed across Heworth Moor towards me. My eyes were blinded. I was drowning in a sea of blood and Will was not there to save me. I doubled up in pain and sank to my knees.

I took great gulps of air and tried to breathe. I was beyond the ability for prayer but from somewhere, a long ago time when I was a child, came the well-remembered words:

'This one night,' I whispered. 'This one night,
Every night and all
Fire an' fleet an' candlelight
- And Christ receive thy soul.'

314

I sensed rather than heard Edith's approach. She stood behind me and when I didn't move she squatted down beside me.

'I have brought your cloak,' she whispered. 'You should put it on or you will take a chill. See, I shall place it over your shoulders.'

Her face was devoid of tears as was mine. When death comes it is too late for tears, too late for everything.

'*And Christ receive thy soul*,' I whispered.

'*And Christ receive thy soul*,' she murmured in return.

'He was only eighteen.'

'We know not the hour,' Edith replied, repeating the empty words given to all petitioners who seek answers for a death which cannot be explained, a death so untimely as to be cruel.

If I'd known, I would not have left him. I would have stayed until the last moment, waited, watching, waving farewell as they'd quit London, riding north to put down some minor local uprising which turned out to be so much more than that. As they approached Pontefract they'd ridden into the path of the queen's army. I was right to fear Margaret of Anjou because it was her friends who killed him. They had killed not only my husband, but his father, my father and my brother Tom. And in the slaughter near Sandal Castle they claimed the greatest prize of all: the heads of the duke of York and his second son, Edmund.

Alice had warned me on that distant day when I'd set out with my family for Tattershall. "Serpents," she'd said. "Snarl you up in their shiny coils, they will." Margaret of Anjou's glittering coils had ensnared many men and had proved far more dangerous than even Alice could have imagined.

The Yorkist cause was dead. Like Will. Like my father. Like Tom. And to ensure everyone knew this was true, the queen ordered the heads of the duke of York, his son, my father and my brother Tom, pinned on the Micklegate bar at York. Nobody said anything about Will and I didn't want to know what they'd done to him. I wanted to remember him just as he was: young and whole and perfect.

18

THE EARL OF WARWICK'S HOUSE 1461

Beyond the walls of Shute time passed as it must for saints and sinners alike. Offices were sung for the dead, the season turned and people dried their tears. Under louring skies and accompanied by peals of demonic laughter, Dame Fortune's wheel spun faster than anyone imagined was possible and three months after Will's death, our defeated army of the winter became the victorious army of the spring.

On Palm Sunday, half a day's ride north of Pontefract, with snow blowing cold in their faces, thousands of men died fighting for Margaret of Anjou and her poor benighted Henry against an army led by Edward and my brother, Richard. By the time darkness fell, rivers and streams near the village of Towton ran red with blood and amongst the dead lay the Percy earl of Northumberland and Sir Anthony Trollope, the man who'd deserted my father at Ludlow. The day before the battle, Lord Clifford and my father's treacherous Nevill kinsman, who'd betrayed him at Sandal Castle, were killed at the crossing of the River Aire. And justice was finally done when Thomas Courtenay, earl of Devon, the same Thomas Courtenay who had ordered his men to Shute that night five years before, was executed at York.

'Richard was right,' said my sister-in-law Anne, smiling. 'All did end well. Don't you agree?'

Ended well for you, I thought bitterly, biting back the words. *You* didn't lose your husband, your father and your brother. The only suffering you endured was a few uncertain weeks in Calais not knowing where your husband was.

'I hear the Woodvilles have bent their knee.' Anne laughed. 'Poor Lord Rivers! Humiliated twice. Of course the Woodvilles are low born and marrying the duke of Bedford's widow has not made Lord Rivers a duke, although he pretends he is. Even your sister Alice's husband, Lord Fitzhugh, has seen sense and submitted to Edward.'

Of course Lord Fitzhugh had seen sense. What future was there for a man in supporting a king who had run away out of his realm. How much wiser to bend your knee and submit.

Anne continued. 'Naturally there is sadness but we are taught, are we not, that sacrifice is noble. Our Lord Christ sacrificed himself for us upon the cross so what can be more honourable for a man than to sacrifice himself for a noble cause.'

I glanced up at her flushed face and thought, yes, you have everything a woman could want: a husband lauded wherever he goes, two healthy daughters and a multitude of beautiful homes. From where you sit the cause is indeed noble. But change places with me and you might wonder if it was all worth it.

'You must be pleased Richard had you brought to London in time for Edward's coronation,' she said with half an eye watching ten-year-old Isabel at her sewing. The girl had a neat hand with a needle and had been taught well, sitting upright, a small smile on her lips.

'Yes,' I replied. 'It was kind of him to think of me.'

Anne patted my knee. 'You are his sister. Naturally he thinks of you. And there is your daughter to consider.' She paused as if waiting for me to say something but changed her mind and hurried on. 'Ceci is growing fast.'

I gazed at my daughter, sixteen months old, a pretty child with her father's dark hair and eyes. Isabel's younger sister was trying to interest her cousin in a woollen ball which she rolled along the floor but Ceci wanted Isabel's sewing. Staggering forwards on her fat little legs she made a grab for the piece of cloth but was foiled by her nursemaid who scooped her up and, with a nod from me, carried her out of the room to an accompaniment of frustrated howls.

Anne murmured something to her elder daughter and Isabel dutifully put away her sewing, took her sister by the hand and, after curtseying prettily to both her mother and me, walked out of the room.

Anne sighed. 'Daughters are such a worry.'

I said nothing. Ceci was not a worry, she was my salvation. Without her I would be nothing.

Anne regarded me with a critical eye. 'You look better now you've laid aside your mourning gowns, That blue brings colour into your cheeks. I'm glad I thought of it.'

The order from my brother had come delicately couched in a suggestion from my sister-in-law but I had taken note of what was not said as well as the actual words: it was time to stop mourning my loss and begin facing my future.

'You are very kind,' I murmured.

She smiled, this time showing her even white teeth. 'Richard tells me you are to have a visitor today.'

My heart began hammering and I felt nauseous. The company of other people caused panic because they expected me to be someone I was not, to be happy when I was sad, to have forgotten when I had not.

'You are a Neviil,' my brother Richard had snapped when I'd begun weeping on the morning of the coronation. 'Behave like one.'

'I do not wish to see anyone, Anne; you know how I am. I wish to be quiet. You say contemplation is good for the soul; well, I wish to contemplate.'

Anne pursed her lips, giving me one of her more disapproving looks, the one she used when wishing to demonstrate her superiority over me. She was, after all, the wife of the king's cousin, the kingmaker, the man who'd put Edward on his throne, his senior councillor.

'My dear Kathryn,' she said smoothly. 'There are some duties a woman cannot avoid and this is one of them.'

I bent my head, knowing when to admit defeat. 'Who wishes to see me?'

'The king.'

For a moment I thought Henry would shuffle in wearing a simple penitent's robe, then realised my mistake. It would be Edward, our golden Yorkist king.

It was not long before I heard noise in the ante-chamber, footsteps, laughter, and then in swept a group of richly clad men and in the middle, half a head taller than everyone else, Edward.

I rose and lowered myself to the ground aware of Anne beside me. The royal hand bade us both rise and there he was, smiling. The conversation was smooth and polite but after a little while, Edward leaned forward.

'Countess Anne, you are most kind to offer your hospitality this afternoon but I know your duties keep you fully occupied so I shall not detain you. Do you perhaps have a room where I may talk to my cousin in private?'

Anne, a little flustered at this unexpected request for privacy, gestured towards an inner chamber, a room she described as small but which was larger than my hall at Shute. There were mumbled apologies for the paucity of her welcome, a conversation back and forth, the gentlemen followers given the task of filling the outer room with their presence, entertaining the countess's women, then, with a firm hand under my arm, I was ushered into the room and the door firmly closed.

'There! That's got rid of them.' Edward gave a quick glance round the room as if to make sure there were no eavesdroppers.

'You wished to see me, your grace?' I said quietly, wondering what he wanted to say that could not be said in front of others.

He smiled broadly. 'Are we to be formal? I thought perhaps we might forgo our titles and simply be cousins again – Edward and Kat.'

I'd been warned by Anne how affable Edward was, yet how in an instant he could slice a man to pieces with his tongue. The cloak of kingship had slipped easily onto his shoulders and he clearly enjoyed the weight of royal purple. 'It is not wise to offend him,' she had said. 'He may be your cousin but never forget he is also your sovereign.'

I stumbled over my words. 'I-I thought perhaps you would prefer formality now that you are an anointed king.'

He took my hand in his and pulled me down onto one of the cushioned settles. 'It is a bore to have everyone bow and scrape all the time and you and I have lost too much in this to bother with conventions. You cannot know how sorry I am you had to endure such suffering.'

Tears began to prick the back of my eyes. It felt strange to receive care from someone like Edward. So few people bothered to comfort me. Everyone was too busy forging their place in this brave new world of Yorkist rule to bother with me. No time for looking back, they said.

'You lost your father and you lost a brother,' I said awkwardly.

'True, but you lost a husband as well.'

I thought of Canterbury and the damp shoots of willow.

He began stroking the back of my hand with his fingers, gently as one would a small frightened animal. 'I think you are still lost in your sorrow.'

'I feel very alone.'

He put his arm around me and pulled me close until my head rested on his shoulder. 'Ah Kat, you are not alone.'

The velvet of his doublet was soft and warm, his voice low and familiar, the feel of his arm reminiscent of so much that had gone before. He spoke quietly. 'Tell me about your husband. We met once but he was not a man I knew.'

To talk of Will was a pleasure. Anne said it was best to forget, not talk about the past, but she didn't understand how grief eats away at you when it is confined. Edward was a good listener. He let me speak of the small doings of my life with Will, the everyday moments we had shared, until eventually I ran out of words. Then with his fingers he turned my face up to his and placed his lips on mine as he had once before at Shute: a gentle kiss, a sad kiss, a kiss between cousins who shared the same loss.

I half heard his words, my cheek pressed hard against his chest. '*Je te désire.*'

Gently I pulled myself out of his embrace.

I said nothing.

'Will you lie with me, Kat? For comfort. For pleasure.'

I shivered, remembering how with capitulation would come sweetness and this was a man I had once loved. But no-one can recreate the past. It was gone, lost, disappeared beyond reach.

I bent my head so that he could not read my thoughts and spoke in a low voice. 'Edward, you know I cannot.'

'No-one need know. We could put cushions on the floor as we did once before.'

My head jerked up. I was truly shocked. 'You would have me here? In my brother's house?'

'Tonight then. I shall send a servant for you.' His voice was eager, his eyes bright with lust.

Was that all this was – lust. Did he truly imagine I had so little care for my honour.

'No.'

The word was barely out when I felt myself forced back, his mouth hard on mine, hands pulling at my clothing, a soldier's body, fierce and determined, pressing me against the back of the settle. I struggled, trying to extricate myself from this unexpected onslaught but he was ten times stronger than me and far more experienced in close combat. This was no agreeable surrender of a woman to a would-be lover. This was rape.

'No!' I gasped. 'Please, Edward, no!'

He pulled back, his hands still grasping my shoulders so that I couldn't move. His voice was thick with unconsummated desire. 'Please let me Kat, I want you so very badly.'

I stared back at him. 'Not like this.'

'Do you not love me?'

'Oh Edward, you know I do.'

'Then lie with me.'

'Edward, you have been my dearest, dearest cousin since I was a little girl, but this would be wrong.'

He adopted the sulky expression he had used as a boy when he couldn't get his own way, mouth turned down, eyes veiled and there was resentment in the way he spoke. 'I suppose like all women you hold out for marriage.'

'I hold out for nothing.'

I thought better of you, Kat. I thought you cared for me.'

'I *do* care but you know I cannot do as you ask.'

He sat back, still holding me and regarded me carefully.

'I am your king. I could command you.'

I stared back at him, shocked he would say such a thing. 'And exactly what would be your command, your grace?'

He grinned boyishly. 'A betrothal if you wish.'

For a moment I caught my breath – a betrothal! To the king! He was offering to make me his queen. But his words were too glib, they slid too easily off his tongue.

'My brother would not be pleased. He plans to marry you to a French princess.'

'Your brother does not own my heart.'

I smiled sadly.

'Edward, you know it is impossible. You must marry to strengthen your position as king. You and I cannot marry.'

'We could do it tomorrow, keep it secret, tell no-one. Say yes, darling Kat, and I shall arrange matters.' He grinned. 'You'd be amazed at what a king can do. And once our union is blessed we can be together.'

I shook my head in disbelief.

He seized both my hands. 'Kat, I want you any way I can and if marriage is what you want then marriage it must be.'

'And if I don't agree?'

He gave a sideways smile. 'There is always the matter of your daughter.'

I blinked in surprise. 'My daughter?'

'If you came to my bed I would let you keep her.'

'My daughter is mine.'

'No, darling Kat, your daughter is mine. You know the law. A fatherless child is a ward of the king. I am the king and can dispose of your daughter's wardship as I please. I could let her live with you or I could sell her wardship to someone else. It is your decision.' He lifted my hand to his mouth for a soft, persuasive kiss. 'She is a valuable commodity.'

He wanted me, I knew that, but I didn't trust him. I didn't trust his so-called secret marriage and I didn't trust his offer to let me keep Ceci.

'You propose to prove your love for me by stealing my daughter and tricking me into your bed.'

'No trick, Kat. Like any would-be lover I am simply

laying out my terms. Whether you accept them or not is up to you. Think about it.'

'I do not need to think. The answer is still no.'

He shrugged. 'Very well. I shall not ask again. Kings do not beg for favours.'

I blanched in dismay at the coldness in his voice. In an instant the unknowable Yorkist king had reappeared, replacing my one-time beloved cousin.

He rose, looked at me with distaste and walked to the door. 'Farewell, my lady. If you change your mind, send me a note. I shall consider it.'

I had disappointed my cousin and offended my king which was unwise but I valued my honour more than anything. Except Ceci. Maybe if he swore an oath to let me keep my daughter I would give him what he wanted. Maybe I should run after him and tell him I'd changed my mind. Or perhaps it was already too late.

Two days later I had another visitor.

'Lord Hastings,' announced the Warwick usher in his sonorous tones.

I knew the name, the face was vaguely familiar, seen at various York gatherings over the years. To be honest he was not a handsome man: brown hair, brown eyes, not as tall as my brother but with a surprisingly easy manner. When he smiled I forgot the plainness of his face and the requirements of my widowed state and nearly smiled back. He looked as if at the slightest opportunity he would seize my wrists and swing me into a dance. Slowly I removed my hands from my lap and lowered them, gripping the sides of my chair to steady myself.

There followed an awkward interlude where Anne, the perfect chatelaine, spoke politely of inconsequential matters while Lord Hastings, equally polite, made pleasant conversation and I said nothing at all.

Eventually Anne rose. 'I know you wish to speak with my sister-in-law in private, Lord Hastings, so if you will forgive me, I have letters to write. Please stay as long as you wish, there is no need to hurry away.'

She walked out of the room followed by a small train of rustling ladies, leaving just two elderly women to protect my reputation; they were seated at the far end of the room, sewing.

Lord Hastings' gaze followed the exiting ladies then turned back to me.

'The countess is, as ever, most hospitable. Now, my lady, shall we to business?'

I glanced at the two women hoping they could not hear what he was about to say.

He noticed and smiled but made no attempt to lower his voice. 'I believe in a situation such as this it is for the man to introduce himself. My name is William Hastings.'

Now I knew exactly who he was. Edward's friend, doubtless come to exert pressure on me to accept Edward's proposal. I said nothing but my silence seemed of no consequence to Lord Hastings who carried on blithely.

'I should explain that although I have titles bestowed on me by the king's generosity I was born a gentleman. I would not want you to imagine I was nobly born when I was not. I am not like you, Lady Kathryn, born into a powerful family. My father was a humble knight. He fought at Agincourt. He was not an earl like your father.

My mother was the daughter of Thomas, Lord Camoys, so there is a touch of nobility there if you care to look hard enough. But she was not the same as your mother who is a very great lady indeed.'

'Lord Hastings…'

'Please! I am as yet unaccustomed to my title and should feel easier if you would call me Sir William.' He smiled ruefully as if to apologise for his humble origins.

'Sir William. I know why you are here and who sent you.'

This time he laughed. 'Forgive me. I know this is not a matter for hilarity.'

'You come from the king.'

'The king certainly approves of my visit.'

'He has given you orders.'

He demurred. 'I would not put it like that.'

'How would you put it?'

'Lady Kathryn, I find myself in a somewhat awkward situation. My father, may God preserve him, was an able man who served the duke of York for many years so it was natural for me, when I came of age, to offer my services to the duke. I thought my duties would be somewhat dull but the duke discovered in me certain talents which he found useful and I made rapid progress, far more rapid than I would have believed possible. But a man should not appear too boastful so I shall say nothing more.'

He smiled that pleasant easy-going smile, encouraging me to agree with him but I decided Lord Hastings was a man who needed no encouragement.

'When it comes to combat I leave it to others to rate my courage and competence in the joust although I have to say I am yet to be unhorsed. However, in warfare no man is aware of how he acquits himself, he is too busy with the matter in hand, trying to stay alive. By God's grace I survived when I am aware that others did not. You, Lady Kathryn, have suffered grievously.'

Somehow his unexpected words crept under the protective shell I wore, poking unerringly at my wounds. I had thought I was able to do this, converse politely with a stranger, but suddenly tears threatened to engulf me, the realisation of everything I had lost, the memories of Will, my father, my brother Tom.

I could not weep in front of someone I didn't know. I stood up.

'You must excuse me Sir William,' I gulped. 'You have nothing to say to me that I wish to hear.'

I picked up my skirts and fled from the room.

Next day he came back. I didn't want to see him but Anne insisted. She said it was a matter of not offending Edward as we both owed our obedience, not only to her husband, my brother, but also to the king. I should be careful, she said, but was not prepared to say exactly of what and why.

I was dispatched to the room with the green hangings where three days earlier I had met with Edward. This time I noted that my honour was sufficiently protected by the presence of just one old woman whom I knew to be totally deaf.

Lord Hastings was ushered in. He was formally dressed, as before, in a tawny coloured doublet cleverly embroidered with dark thread which showed slightly more of his black hose than the previous day. He gave a deep bow, took my hand and brought it to his lips. His mouth touched my fingers and I swiftly withdrew my hand. If Edward thought Lord Hastings was going to change my mind with a display of chivalric good manners, he was mistaken. I thought it was time to make myself plain.

'Lord Hastings, Sir William, I am fully aware of your purpose in coming here today.'

He looked surprised. 'But I have not said.'

'You do not need to.'

'Lady Kathryn, it seems to me you have the advantage in our conversations. I have told you about myself whereas you have told me nothing.'

'I am not obliged to tell you anything, Sir William.'

'True, but if we are to get along together it would be easier.'

'Are we supposed to get along? I was not aware it was a requirement.'

My voice was sharper than I intended but I thought him the kind of man unlikely to take offence.

'I like to be friends with the women with whom I do business.'

I felt the colour rise into my cheeks at the explicitness of his words. This was a business deal: my virtue in exchange for my daughter. And like any business deal the king had left it to his trusted lieutenant, Sir William Hastings, to sort out the details. But I was no fool and would not be cheated.

'What is it you wish to know, Sir William?'

He smiled, well aware he had won the first round in our battle. 'I should like to know if you were content in your marriage.'

'I was.'

'So you regard marriage as an institution likely to bring happiness to those involved?'

'Sir William, I had a friend once, a man of law, who advised me that in matters of business one should always lay out the indisputable facts before attempting to negotiate, it saves misunderstandings. So let me begin by saying that when the king visited me the other day he made his wishes perfectly plain.'

'He did?'

'Yes. He wishes to marry me?'

There was an extremely lengthy silence where neither of us spoke. Tiny dust motes danced in a shaft of sunlight from the window opposite the hearth and all I could hear was the unsteady beat of my heart and a slight hiss from the fire. William Hastings gazed at me speculatively.

'Forgive me, Lady Kathryn, I am unused to a woman speaking her mind. Most women I know, dissemble. They would not dream of letting a man know their innermost thoughts.'

'I can assure you this marriage was not my idea, Sir William, and it was not one of my innermost thoughts. It was the king's suggestion.'

'Lady Kathryn, if you will forgive the indelicacy, I rather think the king wished to lie with you, not marry you.'

A wave of heat rushed into my face and I knew I was blushing. I should have said nothing. William Hastings had just made me look a complete and utter fool.

'Not that I am surprised,' he said, ignoring my flaming cheeks. 'You are, if you will forgive me for saying so, a remarkably attractive young woman. I think any man given half a chance would want you. But that is not why I have come.'

'Why *have* you come?' I knew my words sounded abrupt, hostile even, but I was trying to cover my embarrassment.

'Can you not guess?'

I swallowed hard. 'No, Sir William. I do not possess the gift of foreseeing.'

He grinned. 'An unpardonable oversight, but since God has seen fit to grant you many other pleasing attributes, it is understandable.'

Damn the man! He was trying to flirt with me. The impudence! He clearly considered me fair game for anything. I wanted to throw him out but remembered Anne's words to have a care.

'Sir William, what is it you want?'

'If you do not know, Lady Kathryn, then I have not explained myself properly. Perhaps if you bear with me a little longer, all will become clear.'

I sighed. 'Very well.'

'As I said, the king has been generous. He has appointed me his royal chamberlain which, as you are doubtless aware, means I am the man closest to him. It is a position of great privilege. Anyone who wishes to see his grace must first approach me.'

'A gate-keeper, We had one at Middleham when I was a child.'

He smiled at my rudeness. 'Hardly that. You see, not only am I now Lord Hastings with two manors in Sussex and a castle of my own but I am also steward of the honour of Leicester. It will not be long before I shall be master of the king's monies and receiver-general for the duchy of Cornwall.'

'Do you intend to list every one of your offices, Sir William?'

'No, Lady Kathryn, but some of the favours I have received may be of interest to you. Do you know Leicestershire?'

'I believe it is a dull flat county.'

'It has its jewels. I have a pleasant place at Kirby Muxloe which was my father's, and the king has promised me the earl of Wiltshire's manor at Ashby. I plan to build a great house there for my family.'

'You have a wife?'

'Not yet.'

I must have been extremely slow-witted because it was only then that I realised why he had come and what he wanted of me.

I stood up and he scrambled to his feet. 'Lord Hastings, I think you should leave. This conversation is at an end.'

He made no move to go so I inclined my head and walked swiftly out of the door. The rudeness of the man! The insufferable rudeness! How dare he come here. How dare Edward send a minion to sweep up his leavings.

Two days later he returned. This time there was no question of my not receiving him because he came with my brother. Richard was now the second most powerful man in the kingdom and no sister of his was going to thwart a royal decision, no matter her personal inclinations. Anne had told me how in France people were already saying,

"England has two kings, Monsieur de Warwick and... I forget the name of the other one." We were supposed to laugh but I wondered if Edward would appreciate the joke.

Richard clearly had no knowledge of Edward's suggestion that I should share his bed but was fully informed of Lord Hastings' interest in me. There followed a long conversation between the two men during which I was expected to sit and be silent. The matter of my daughter's inheritance was discussed at length, the titles she bore, the vast extent of the Harington and Bonville lands. The death of Will's grandfather, executed on Margaret of Anjou's direct orders a month after I lost Will, had made my daughter the wealthiest heiress in England. Apart from a few of Lord Bonville's properties entailed in the male line, everything had come to Ceci and in the fullness of time she would have my dower and also that of Lady Bonville. As Richard pointed out more than once to Lord Hastings, my daughter was extremely valuable.

As for me? I was merely an adjunct to their plan, a little sweetmeat for Lord Hastings, a wife to decorate his house and a companion to warm his bed. As I sat listening to them I wondered if it would not have been more sensible to agree to Edward's wishes, though looking at my brother I thought perhaps not. Whatever position Edward might have offered me in the throes of passion I doubted it would have been as his queen and Richard would have cursed me for accepting anything less.

Next day Uncle Fauconberg came.

'Marry him.'

'He thinks me a fool,' I wept.

'No, he thinks you do not know what is best for you.'

'And is marriage with William Hastings best for me?'

'Kathryn, listen to me. Edward is newly come to the throne and there are many who doubt his right to the crown. He must make himself secure and to do that he needs all the help we can give him. He needs to draw those with wavering allegiance, closer and bind those who would follow Margaret of Anjou, tight. If he has any sense he will marry your sister Margaret to the earl of Oxford's boy, young John de Vere, because the de Vere's are no friends to the Yorks.'

'Poor Margaret. What a terrible fate.'

'Edward is not consigning you to marriage with a man who hates your family; he is offering you to his closest friend, a man who has risen high and will rise higher still. William Hastings is a fine man, well-liked by everyone. He will make a good husband and if you marry him you will keep your daughter. Hastings already has her wardship. Marry him and she will be yours.'

It all made the most perfect sense except that I had no feelings for him. I still loved Will. But Will was gone, lost forever. My brother said it was time to face the future and my mother had told me love was the least important part of marriage.

'Lord Uncle, I do not love him. I am not sure I even like him.'

Uncle Fauconberg smiled and took my hand in his. 'My little Yorkshire rose, you know we are none of us free to choose love over duty. But I wager if you marry him you will like him within a week and be in love with him before the month is out.'

'And if I am not?'

'Believe me, you will be. William Hastings has a way with everyone. Men swear they have no liking for him but after a day in his company are eating out of his hand like a well-trained hound. As for women!'

'What do the women do?' I asked, curious as to the nature of this man.

'What women always do when a man exerts his charm.'

'Are there many women?'

Uncle Fauconberg grinned. 'Enough to have a wife stay alert to her husband's needs when he comes home.'

I thought of William Hastings, his pleasant smile, his reassuring manner. An easy man to love; a good husband, so my uncle said.

Within an hour of my uncle leaving, Lord Hastings arrived. The two of us sat in silence while Sir William watched me, amused by my reluctance to commit myself.

'I thought it would be pleasant if we spent time alone together,' he said with half an eye on my elderly chaperone dozing in the corner.

'And that is why you are here?'

I'd not meant to sound disagreeable but knew that I had.

'Is your brother's plan not to your liking, Lady Kathryn?'

I tried to look him straight in the eye but found his steady gaze disconcerting.

'Sir William. You already have my daughter. What more can you possibly want?'

He gave a rueful smile. 'My mother, whom I loved

dearly, said her daughters were an especial blessing. I thought it might be the same for you and Cecily.'

His use of her name pierced my heart to its core. Ceci was all that remained of Will and this man was offering me the chance to keep her close.

'Am I that displeasing to you?' he enquired lightly.

'I do not know you, Sir William,' I said, determined not to show any weakness.

'I thought I had laid out my credentials rather well but perhaps I have misunderstood the needs of a woman.'

'I gather you are well informed about the needs of women.'

He leaned back against the cushions and grinned. 'What have you heard about me?'

I shrugged and looked down at my hands where they lay in my lap.

'I am flattered you wanted to know,' he said. 'It shows you are not indifferent to my proposal.'

'I thought it was my brother's proposal.'

'Ah Lady Kathryn, if you want to know the truth, the suggestion came from the king. He said he'd give a fortune to have you for himself but it was not possible. A king's marriage must forge an alliance with a foreign power and he knows you are too virtuous to be anything other than a wife.'

'Do you consider me virtuous, Sir William?'

'I do not know you, Lady Kathryn. You have been careful to keep yourself well hidden so I have yet to find out. But I would imagine you as virtuous as most women.'

'And what do you propose to offer me in exchange for my virtue?'

He smiled as if he thought his battle won, which if I was honest with myself, it was.

'You will find me kind and I promise to treat your daughter as if she were my own child. You understand, I am fond of children and have wanted a family for some time.'

'I suppose the women you approached said no?' I said nastily.

This time he laughed. 'No, Lady Kathryn, the women did not say no but I was not offering them marriage.'

I blushed at the crudeness of his words. He stayed quiet for a moment, allowing me to recover my composure and then said, 'I'm sorry if I offended you, it was not my intention. I have no experience at making offers of marriage.' He put out his hand and curled his fingers round mine. I looked up and what I saw in his eyes caused an unexpected flutter in my belly.

'I know very little of marriage,' I muttered. 'My husband and I were together for such a short time.'

'Long enough to discover love?'

'Yes. Long enough for love.'

'For a man the greatest blessing is to be loved by his wife.'

'My mother says it is the least important part of marriage.'

'And you? What do you think?'

'I no longer know, Sir William. I find that remembering is sweet but increasingly comes with pain.'

'Lady Kathryn, the memories you cherish are those of your springtime, the years when you were growing to womanhood. Your summer is yet to come and it is well known that flowers which bloom in midsummer are no less beautiful because they come late. Think of the treasures you and I might discover amongst the hedgerows.'

I was surprised at the eloquence of his words and wondered had they been gleaned from a book of verse. We sat there, hand in hand, the passing minutes drawing us closer, bridging the gap between what had gone before and what was yet to come.

'Lady Kathryn,' he said in his low beguiling voice. 'What do you want from me?'

I hesitated. What *did* I want from him. What could he possibly give me which would make up for the losses I'd suffered.

Then suddenly, there I was, eleven years old, riding through the gates of Tattershall into Lord Cromwell's domain. Ahead was my magical castle with its flame coloured tower soaring up into a clear blue sky. Within its walls was everyone I loved: my mother, my father, my brothers and my sisters, my friends, all come together to celebrate a wedding. Outside, stretching away as far as the eye could see were fields and woods and hills and rivers, villages, the towns I knew; and somewhere far away in the distance, so small as to be almost imperceptible, a tiny glimpse of happiness.

'A house built of red brick and a tower with more than one hundred and fifty steps,' I said, as the image danced and glittered and shimmered in front of my eyes. Church bells were ringing, people were cheering and there was my father leading my mother up the steps.

William Hastings threw back his head and laughed out loud. 'Lady Kathryn, marry me and I promise it shall be yours.'

And in that moment I knew he was a man who would keep his promise.

Epilogue

FEBRUARY 1463

The six men who carried my mother's coffin into the church, laid it on a hearse draped in black. Together with my sisters and my sister-in-law, Isobel, I knelt in silent prayer. My mother's gold and ruby ring felt heavy on my finger, a constant reminder of the gap left in our lives by her death and by the loss of Uncle Fauconberg who had died before the walls of Alnwick, fighting to keep Edward safe on his throne.

It was more than a year since I had married William Hastings and today my father and my brother Tom, were returning home to Bisham to be reunited with my mother. Richard and John had ridden out earlier to meet the cortège which had journeyed from Pontefract. For the last mile they rode behind our father's banners followed by sixteen knights and squires on foot. My father had been a soldier all his life and was to be buried as a soldier: the banners, heralds and pursuivants all displaying his coat of arms.

We spent a long dark night in silent vigil and when morning came, we laid them to rest. This was no simple burial but a ceremony full of ritual and splendour. My brother, Richard, placed the mass-penny on the altar and afterwards received the offerings: my father's coat of arms, his shield, his sword, his helm and crest. Nobody present that day was left in any doubt that the man being buried here, together with his wife and his son, was a great man, one of the greatest. He was a Nevill.

When the solemnities were over and the feasting, weeping and laughter were finished, it was time to return home, William took me aside and said quietly, 'I must leave you. I have a task to perform.'

'Another supplicant?'

William's closeness to Edward meant a constant stream of requests for him to bring this matter or that matter to the king's attention.

'A neighbour. Lady Grey. A widow.'

'Elderly?'

He smiled. 'Young and very beautiful.'

'Should I be jealous?'

My husband was the most charming of men but wives of charming men will often feel insecure no matter how many times they are told they are loved.

'You know who she is?'

I noticed he had not answered my question.

'Lady Grey, no, I do not.'

'She is Elizabeth Woodville, daughter of Lord Rivers. Married the son of the Greys of Groby. The young man died fighting for Margaret of Anjou. I believe she has two boys.'

'And her request?'

'Oh the usual. The mother-in-law won't release the lands. Dame Elizabeth claims she is impoverished.'

'Will you help her?'

He grinned. 'What shall I ask in return?'

'Not her virtue, I trust.' My voice was light as if making a jest but I was never quite sure about my husband. He was immensely kind to me, just as he had promised and always treated Ceci as his own daughter, but he was often away from home and something told me the beautiful Elizabeth Woodville could prove a threat.

He took my hand and pulled me close. 'Why should I want her virtue when I have an accommodating wife at home.'

'Am I accommodating?'

'Oh I think so,' he said, placing his hand on our, as yet, unborn child in my belly. 'If the lady wants my help she must pay for the privilege and as a Lancastrian widow she must pay doubly. Perhaps we shall have her son and his lands for one of our future daughters.'

'Not Ceci,' I said hurriedly.

'No, not Ceci. She is an heiress and much too valuable to waste on a son of Dame Elizabeth Grey. What d'you say wife? Shall we make a small wager on the outcome?'

I laughed. 'The last time I accepted a wager from an untrustworthy scoundrel I lost my money.'

'Who was the lucky man?'

'My uncle, Lord Fauconberg.'

'What was the wager?'

I smiled. 'That, husband, is *my* secret.'

Author's Note

In 1464, fifteen months after the burial at Bisham, Kathryn's cousin, Edward, secretly married Dame Elizabeth Grey and had her crowned his queen.

Kathryn and William Hastings had four children who survived infancy and appear to have had a happy marriage although William was much occupied with the king's business and seldom at home. In 1480 he began building a fine house of red brick at Kirby Muxloe near Leicester complete with a moat, a vast gatehouse and six enormous towers. Today the house is managed by English Heritage and you can see William Hastings' initials and device of a maunche on either side of the gatehouse.

In 1472 the relentless rise of the Nevill family came to an abrupt end with the deaths at the Battle of Barnet of Richard, Earl of Warwick and John, Marquess of Montagu, and the arrest on a charge of treason of their brother George, Archbishop of York. All three were rebelling against Edward IV, the Yorkist king for whom they'd sacrificed so much to put on his throne.

Maud, Lady Willoughby, married as her third husband, Gervase Clifton, a Lancastrian of low birth. Within two years she left him citing economic abuse and mismanagement. She went to live with her sister, Jane, at Tattershall, her home for the rest of her life.

Acknowledgements

I should like to thank the kind gentleman at St Michael's Church at Shute whose name I do not know but who took time to sit with me and tell me about the manor house and its history. Also the National Trust guide who showed me round the oldest parts of the house.

Thanks to Richard for accompanying me on a wonderful weekend visit to Tattershall where we climbed the tower and enjoyed a display of medieval weaponry in the grounds.

One Saturday we drove to Chewton Mendip and visited the church where we saw the Bonville Tomb, and on another day, to Lympstone where we stood at the sea wall and looked out across the estuary to Powderham Castle, just as Kathryn Nevill did more than 550 years ago.

Thanks also to Ken Cooper for coming with me to Glastonbury for a day's immersion in the world of the Wars of the Roses

As always thanks to the members of the writing group and to my daughters for their support. But most of all a huge thank you to my husband, Richard, without whom none of this would have been possible.

Bibliography

It would take more than a page to list all the books, articles, pamphlets and websites I consulted while researching the story of Kathryn Nevill's life but I would particularly like to mention the three mentioned below which were my faithful companions throughout the writing of this book.

The Nevills of Middleham by K.L. Clark
The Reign of King Henry VI by R.A. Griffiths
The Wars of the Roses by Desmond Seward

Coming Soon

THE WOODVILLE CONSPIRACY

It is 1474 and England is at peace. But beneath the intoxicating glamour of the royal court of Edward IV and his coolly beautiful queen, Elizabeth Woodville, lies a secret with death trailing in its wake.

Into this glorious summer of Yorkist rule comes Cecily, Lady Harington, wealthy heiress and step-daughter of the king's close friend, William, Lord Hastings. Cecily has married Thomas Grey, eldest son of the queen's first marriage – "a nothing" in the words of her mother.

Undeterred by what she sees as her decidedly inferior marriage, Cecily sets about trying to wean her husband away from his mother's influence but she quickly discovers the queen is a powerful and dangerous opponent.

As the mystery surrounding her mother-in-law deepens and people begin dying, Cecily becomes determined to uncover the truth but when tragedy strikes and chaos engulfs her family, she finds herself alone and in danger as those she loves and once trusted, prove false.

The Woodville Conspiracy is a story of love and betrayal with at its heart a secret which will forever lie buried beneath the battlefield at Bosworth.

About the Author

Caroline Newark was born in Northern Ireland and as a child she wanted to be a farmer's wife, have twelve children and live in a cottage with roses round the door. Instead she became a teacher, a lawyer, a dairy farmer and cheesemaker. But other remnants of that early dream survive – she has two daughters, five grandchildren and lives with her husband, Richard, in a house in a village in the West Country with roses growing round the back door.

In 1997 after her mother died, Caroline found a small, red leather-bound book lying in a drawer in a bureau. Inside were details of twenty-one generations of her mother's family starting in 1299 with a marriage between the Royal Houses of England and France. With one book for each generation, Caroline has imagined the lives of these women who lived in our past.

Fire and Fleet and Candlelight is the seventh book in the series.

Website: www.carolinenewark.com
Contact: caroline@carolinenewark.com
Follow: Caroline Newark on Facebook

This book is printed on paper from sustainable sources managed under the Forest Stewardship Council (FSC) scheme.

It has been printed in the UK to reduce transportation miles and their impact upon the environment.

For every new title that Matador publishes, we plant a tree to offset CO_2, partnering with the More Trees scheme.

For more about how Matador offsets its environmental impact, see www.troubador.co.uk/about/